PANSIES' REVENGE

BOOKS BY JEFFREY BUCHANAN

FICTION

The Birds Began to Sing

Harvard's Hatreds

Pansies' Revenge

The Smile of the Dispossessed

Sucking Feijoas

YOUNG ADULT FICTION

The Extraordinary Adventures of Kip Kip and Wendi

Kip Kip, Wendi and the Fabulous History Machine

PANSIES' REVENGE

Jeffrey Buchanan

PANSIES' REVENGE

Copyright © 2025 Jeffrey Buchanan

Published by LGBTQI Press NZ

LGBTQIpressNZ@gmail.com
LGBTQIpressNZ.com

This book is a work of fiction. Any similarities to any person living or deceased to a character in the novel are purely coincidental.

Cover photograph: Audience, Town Hall, Wellington, Dominion Day, 1912. Provided with kind permission by the Wellington City Council Archives (New Zealand).

Typesetting and Cover Design by FormattingExperts.com

This book is dedicated to the memory of all Lesbian, Gay, Bi-sexual, Transgender, Queer and Intersex people who were involved in World War One and the influenza pandemic.

I cannot make you understand. I cannot make anyone understand what is happening inside me. I cannot even explain it to myself.
Franz Kafka, "The Metamorphosis"

All a poet can do today is warn.
Wilfred Owen

1

Alexander Powderham, fortyish, handsome, bohemian, limped his way up Cuba Street. Having been crippled from infantile paralysis, his left leg was supported by a steel brace. He was also dependent on canes, of which he had an impressive collection. On this occasion he was using a cane intricately carved by Aroha Raharuhi, his longtime lover.

The air was unseasonably warm for mid-September Wellington, which heightened the smell rising from the mounds of horse ordure left from the morning's military parade. Outside the Duchess Tea Rooms, Alexander paused and rested on his good leg while he adjusted his tailored jacket, smoothing down the Irish linen, delighting in its texture and colour of golden flax. He adjusted his silk tie, cream coloured with charcoal flecks, loosening the knot at the undone top button to ensure that rakish look of casual elegance. The white cotton shirt had also been crafted for him by the clothiers Munster & Munster who, through four years of war, had survived patriotic vandalism by hanging a sign across their shop windows, WE ARE NOT HUNS. WE SUPPORT KING AND COUNTRY. Alexander's chocolate brown, wide-brimmed hat with a duck's feather poking from the green woven band was also foppishly avant-garde.

With deference he tapped the brim of his hat as Miss Hortensia Rutherford approached. She was obviously rushed but she stopped and said in that cadent voice of the well-educated: "Oh, Alexander, I'm *so* looking forward to our book group. I'm riveted by *Crime and Punishment*. It's so *psychological*. And atonement and redemption! And that brat Raskolnikov! Fyodor Dostoyevsky! Just those names take me to Saint Petersburg." Her eyes looked startled, but it was merely excitement. "My inner mind, Alexander. I feel I'm delving into something…so…*deeply* profound…philosophical, this novel… this novel…"

"Petrograd doesn't have the same *caché*, does it?" said Alexander, smiling. "I can't wait to hear what you have to say at the book group. And what you think about the murder of the two sisters."

"The murders! Oh, I'm so late for class. *Adieu*, Alexander, *adieu*. I don't know how to say it in Russian." She waved as she rushed off in the direction of Wellington Girls' College, her schoolteacher's satchel swinging, her maroon skirts flapping around her red boots.

Standing outside the Duchess Tea Rooms watching Hortensia Rutherford turn the corner, he saw with the usual poignancy that she was the sort of woman he would have married had he been normal. He closed his eyes to the street, to Wellington, to the morning's news of the latest batch of troops being dispatched to the trenches of Europe. Her red boots and maroon skirts swayed behind his lids, but he saw with that familiar stabbing notion that Miss Rutherford was an alien world to him, no matter how eloquent her voice, her social standing, her caring, her desirability. She spun in a galaxy far removed from his and his mind went dark, then darker, as the distance between the two of them expanded into its vast and discordant orbit.

"Imagine, a world with Miss Rutherford as Mrs. Powderham," he thought as he flew through the darkness. But that was an abstraction too great to conjure, too removed at his age, at forty, given his proclivity. All he saw emerging from that void was Hortensia Rutherford unfolding a red sun umbrella in his back garden with the high trees soughing, the sunlight slanting on her as in a painting, her head back, laughing. It was also more a nightmare than a happy vision, the sort where he yelled out, and from which Aroha would wake him saying: "It's only the dreams speaking."

Alexander Powderham opened his eyes. Instead of seeing a laughing Miss Rutherford, he saw his own reflection in the window of the Duchess Tea Rooms and he knew immediately what he was: a Wellington character, a dandy, a cripple in a too fashionable linen outfit with a too fashionable fop's hat. With that same hurtful punch he recalled an acquaintance telling him after an argument: "All the trappings and pretences of a Gothic rake, but without the requisite masculinity."

Throughout his reveries he had been gazing into the tearoom's window, oblivious to those looking out. Coming to, he saw the eyes of three women staring at him, puzzled and fascinated, as if at a spy, one of those creatures that was infiltrating the country sniffing out military secrets and sowing mayhem. Germans, Austrians, Hapsburgs, Red Russians, anarchists, socialists, war shirkers, pacifists; the press was constantly reminding the populace to be vigilant of such unpatriotic malignancy. With a rush of fright, Alexander saw these women assessing him against that list, this creature so very different from their menfolk. Seeing their eyes scouring him, his mind went racing down a dangerous tributary, swift and swollen, in which he was bobbing up and down and close to drowning with all sorts of thoughts during his last moments alive. Arriving from another direction, also bobbing up and down in similarly swift and swollen waters, were the five Finks, the Silesian family who had been hounded out of the premises next door to his bookshop.

"I should have done more for the unfortunate Finks," he thought, turning his back on the staring eyes inside the Duchess Tea Rooms. "I could have saved the Finks. The Ministers know me, I could have pleaded the Finks' innocence." But he hadn't. The dark green river was moving swiftly, taking the five Finks with it. Their boarding house had been shuttered, the façade vandalised. He could see the five Finks standing with a clutch of bags and cases. Little Ursula was crying something in German and in her guttural English Mrs. Fink was yelling: "But we are Jews, Silesians, not Germans!" And all Mr. Fink could do was utter: "We thought we would be safe in Wellington." It was a long list of people Alexander had known and admired and who were now exiled as dangerous aliens to Somes Island in Wellington Harbour. Each of them was reprimanding him for his silence. What had he done to save them? Nothing. His own judgment was swift. The jury in his mind banged down their gavel and shouted: "Alexander

Powderham! Guilty!" The thoughts left him unable to move up Cuba Street. All he could do to look normal was to check the watch on his gold chain and look about as if he were innocently waiting on someone for morning tea in the Duchess Tea Rooms.

"This war. This war. And I'm as mad as that insane Raskolnikov in *Crime and Punishment,*" he thought as he looked about him.

The street was busy with the remnants of well-wishers who had come to cheer as their boys had set off for Europe. Hundreds of reinforcements had marched and waved their way through Wellington, the horses clip-clopping with the hierarchy astride them. He could sense them in the streets, those men at this moment being fed into the hulls of troop ships: farmers, clerks, haberdashers, teachers, fishermen – all sweating after their long march in the sun as they neared the point of embarkation, their vessels with belching funnels waiting to transport them to the trenches in faraway places with names like Somme and Flanders and Ypres and Passchendaele. He leapt forward a few weeks, months, a year, to when these patriots joyfully waving at the doomed file would receive a telegram from over there informing regretfully that so and so was missing in action, had died of sickness or had been killed, buried in Belgium.

"My poor head," he thought. "Poor civilisation. I'm not Raskolnikov yet, surely?" He had deliberately not come into town until the military parade was over, for to witness these men marching off to be sacrificed for a king and country who cared nothing for the person, their sanctity as a human, was too distressing. The smell of horse manure and the thought of those gorgeous men being blown apart was driving him to limp back up the hills to Tinakori Road and the sanctity of his home and be there in case the conscription authorities came again to harass Aroha.

Behind the window of the Duchess Tea Rooms, he witnessed those ladies socialising after waving off the troops and the irony, the hypocrisy, the smugness, sickened him. They were the symbols, in fact the actuality, of everything that was ill about this Dominion at the bottom of the world whose women folk had just cheered away their men for sacrifice to a king seemingly senseless to destruction. He wanted to clutch his head, to throw his hat into the gutter, to scream at them all. Instead, he smiled at the elderly woman whose hunch-backed husband delivered the coal, and she nodded deferentially, the wicker basket over her arm filled with vegetables. A newspaper boy shouted from across the street, his voice alive with excitement as if war were his invention: "Prime Minister's ship leaves Honolulu. In Auckland in two weeks. Russian Revolution chaos!"

Alexander thought the better of going home. His bookshop was just up the street and he knew that Aroha could look after himself if the conscription bureaucrats visited as they had threatened to. He turned and saw that the women in the Duchess Tea Rooms were well into their conversation, their heads close together, their teacups poised. He envisaged them as frozen in time at that exact moment in September 1918 on the day that more men had marched off to fight for something pointless. With none of the beauty with which the poem was usually associated, he saw them as fixed into the eternity of a Wellington tea room as were the ancients trapped in John Keats's *Ode on a Grecian Urn*. He stared at the matriarchs in their frilly outfits, one of whom wore a hat covered in violets. Even the leaves were green and lifelike, so that it appeared as if she had dug a patch from her garden, stuck it on her head, and come to wave at the troops before tea and cakes and gossip. He had to shake his head to clear the visions of Grecian urns and ossified matrons and violet smothered hats. A dog barked, a man shouted, an accordion wheezed and simpered.

"Oh, my God, I'm as mad as Raskolnikov," he thought. As he con-tinued up Cuba Street and approached the corner of Ghuznee Street, he heard cranking up for her crusade the arched and preachy voice of Mrs. Sybil Meatyard, the denizen of the New Zealand Women's Anti-German League.

"Bugger," he thought. "It's the Meatyards." The impulse to take his carved cane and knock Mr. Cecil Meatyard on his head and do the same to his buffoon of a wife, the shrill and odious Sybil, was over-whelming. One knock on her head, one knock on his, and they and their dour Protestant association would be gone forever from the streets of Wellington. It was a fantasy he had often entertained as much to rid the streets of their noisy public stirrings as to eliminate their hatreds.

"Raskolnikov's theory was right," he thought as he leaned on his cane and looked at Sybil Meatyard. "The benefits of killing a nasty and useless human for the betterment of mankind is indeed a justified murder." The thought of having to pass those ardent Protestants on the corner where they had taken up position to voice their tireless tirades against war shirkers, socialists and the godless was almost too much to bear. A gust of wind came rushing off the harbour, right up Cuba Street, as if to purposefully stir the stenches and mix them all up and carry with them the voices of the two proselytisers.

"Bugger, bugger. How much hatred must I carry for these pathetic Meatyards? It's disproportionate, surely?" It was a strain to his thinking to have to acknowledge that his Wellington in which he had always lived, watching it grow from a colonial trifle into a city of considerable standing, one he had tried his best to inculcate with books and culture, was now supporting this demeaning and ideologically driven crusade to harass men like Aroha and him, the so-called misfits and war shirkers.

Alexander looked at the Victorian façade across the street and met the gaze of innumerable gargoyles positioned to support its bulky ledges, their pop-out eyes looking back at him. From an open window, an imposing woman with a high pile of hair stood and gazed down imperiously, her presence reminding him of someone he had seen but could not recall.

Mrs. Sybil Meatyard had a vocabulary of disdain. Some months back, upon seeing Alexander in the crowd, she had shouted: "It's the Oscar Wilde types we must abhor. Effeminates are the biggest war shirkers given their diseased minds!" In her tartan knit hat with its large black pom-poms she had stood on a soapbox outside the Wellington Public Library castigating and taunting him, playing on her fiddle of popularity all the tunes of discord and division. Pointing at him directly, invoking the spectre of Oscar Wilde, she had made the crowd laugh and look around at her victim. Her sarcasm had been infectious. A man in a dowdy bowler hat shouted: "Send Pansies to the Front. Give them a good whipping! Yes to universal conscription, no to war shirkers!"

With the wind had come the dust, which blew around in clouds. From some distance Alexander stood with his handkerchief held against his mouth and nostrils and observed these ideologues as they shouted at the Wellingtonians. Amongst the thirty or forty on-lookers was a tall man in uniform with a row of war medals across his chest. The man's squinty eyes, in an otherwise distinguished face, looked about as if, Alexander surmised, he was a lizard searching for its victim, its long sticky tongue about to dart out. The military man raised his arm with a motion that would have silenced his men, and he shouted: "No special exemptions for coal miners and wharfies. No war shirkers. No exceptions. Equal conscription!"

Sybil Meatyard rewarded him with a wave of her placard depicting a white feather, the symbol of cowardice and raised her arms in a benediction. At the beginning of the War, Alexander had been presented in the street with a real white feather by a young woman with a posh voice. Standing up as straight as he could, he had said: "Should cripples be made to run across minefields too?" There were insignia that men could wear to show that they had legitimate exemptions to conscription, but both he and Aroha had refused to wear them: "My leg and my attitude are my exemption medals," he'd declared.

"There's no compulsory conscription for Māori," had been Aroha's response to the suggestion to wear an exemption medal by their friend Jamey who had volunteered and whose legs had been blown off in the Somme. He had died within minutes, crying, according to his commander, who had written to his parents in Auckland. The thought of Jamey suffering in a French field in winter made Alexander want to weep, for none of this seemed possible. It was as if this war were an invention by some great ugly Gothic monster with the brains of a gargoyle. From history books Alexander understood that war was an alarming lesson from which to learn. However, this real thing was catastrophically empirical and four years of it had swelled his lamentations and neuroses. What had not yet been committed to the history books, was that the majority of New Zealanders supported this conflagration: "Like sheep being herded to the abattoirs," he thought as he stood absorbing the scene before him. "With vicious little Protestant Meatyards yapping at our hooves."

A woman in a black dress and a red hat walked by with a woman in a red dress and a black hat and the latter said to her companion: "I can't understand the price of butter. Or jam. And as for meat, it's ludicrous."

"It's too exhausting to be so human," Alexander thought. "To turn off the brain for a day would be delicious." He sighed, for even in this remote Dominion there were the distractions of war where once there had been the trivia of daily life. That trail of discordant thought disintegrated and assembled into visions of dear Jamey dancing to an opera playing on his gramophone and he thought: "Jamey's parents never replied to my long letter of condolence. They must have known I'm a Pansy."

Another newspaper boy touting for another paper shouted: "Americans push hard at Huns. Forty-seven Kiwi deaths." An elderly man fished in his trouser pockets for change, and with a big smile the paper boy handed him the paper. The same women in the same combination of black and red outfits returned. Pausing in front of Alexander, the one in the red hat said to her companion: "It's all war profiteering. The farmers get subsidies, and the townsfolk suffer." Alexander wondered if he were confused between irony and incredulity, or if there were even a word for what this all represented in a world where millions were dying and people here were simply living in the shadow of its catastrophe and talking about the price rises in butter and meat and shouting about Oscar Wilde.

"This is like the descriptions of Saint Petersburg in *Crime and Punishment* in the eighteen-sixties, and I'm as mad as Raskolnikov," he thought. But he was pulled from his reverie to the shouting at the soapboxes. Cecil Meatyard was gesticulating as if he were someone noble and distinguished. His beard was in the style of King George V. Alexander noticed that Meatyard sported two flashy rings on each hand, an unusual affectation for a man in any position, noble or otherwise.

The female Meatyard was extolling the virtues of equal conscription. She had pounced on the handsome military man's argument and he beamed at his promotion. Alexander noted that despite having a mind of patriotic rubbish, the military man was very handsome and, enviably, had two strong legs.

In the bottom drawer under the socks and underpants in his bedroom, Alexander had hidden an antique silver pistol that his father had bought in Rome when on tour in the 1870s and with which Alexander would shoot Australian parrots that screeched in the back garden. Alexander had a clear vision of that handsome, desperate Russian student and murderer Raskolnikov pointing the pistol at Cecil Meatyard and pulling the trigger. "Just like the Archduke Franz Ferdinand was assassinated in Sarajevo by the Serbian student," he thought. "Shot dead with his wife Sophie, the Duchess of Hohenberg. Oh, nineteen-fourteen seems so long ago. Yes, bullets for Cecil and this faux duchess on her soapbox. Do it for me Raskolnikov, murder them."

A dog barked and growled and a woman in front of Alexander shrieked, the commotion extracting Alexander from his visions of assassinations. The gargoyles stared down at him when he looked up and the woman in the window with the pile of hair shook her head in disbelief and whooshed away phantom-like. He thought: "That was Duchess Sophie Hohenberg. Soon there'll be revolution here too." He shook his head to clear the visions which had elaborated into a Gothic novel with pistols and crazed women. The barking dog slunk off, its tail stiffly between its legs. The woman in front of him was poking into her velvet hat a pin that had been handed out embedded with "Support the War Effort."

"Why more sacrifice?" Alexander asked himself. "I have to do something just as Raskolnikov did. It's as Pavlov said, we respond to repeated messages. Sybil Meatyard is driving me to revenge."

The crowd was getting angry, and spilled into the road so that motorcars could not pass.

"She's a one, isn't she mate?" said a voice next to Alexander. "You got a smoke for me mate?" the voice continued, close to Alexander's ear.

"What?" asked Alexander, looking up, the sun in his eyes.

"She's a one? Who is she, that old bag screaming?" the man said.

"I wouldn't question her out loud," replied Alexander. "You'll get done for sedition."

"Sedition? They wouldn't bloody dare after my sacrifices, the bastards. Can't touch me. Got that smoke mate?"

The man was tall, broad shouldered, sinewy, with dry blonde hair. Given what he had said he was obviously a returned soldier, and his left arm was missing, the jacket sleeve pinned up over where the appendage had been. He stood as if this inspection was to be expected, enjoyed even. Alexander noted that the suit was fashionable and good quality. Despite his working-class voice, he had an oddly polished look, as if he were not quite one thing or the other. Alexander took a cigarette tin from his jacket pocket. On the cover was a cartoon of an Ottoman character wearing a fez.

"You've got Turkish cigarettes, mate. *That's* sedition, isn't it?" His voice had changed from working class to someone higher up the social ladder, a senior clerk, a schoolteacher.

"A tin evidence of sedition?" asked Alexander.

"Nah," the man said. "Just that I smoked them in Turkey. I thought they'd stopped enemy goods." He stared into Alexander's eyes and smiled, the tiny lines crisscrossing around his eyes.

"It's an Ottoman tin from before they were banned," said Alexander. "I place my local cigarettes in it for pretence. Sedition can be fashionable." It was a dangerous thing even to be flippant to a stranger, but he enjoyed it for that, especially to this man with the eyes of a lynx. And a lynx, Alexander knew, wouldn't be a part of the establishment. The military man was a member of the hierarchy, his looks betrayed him. But this man was a one-armed rake, the sort who'd say: "Mate, I'd do anything for a fiver." Alexander shivered and exhaled his smoke through half pursed lips.

Thirty years earlier, Alexander's father had brought back from France a set of postcards which unfolded accordion-like, each card displaying a person with the series encapsulated as: *les Parisiens. Le Parisien* number three in the exotic series was blowing smoke inhaled from a green cigarette in an ivory holder. His slicked back pomaded hair, his tweaked eyebrows, his Gallic nose, the slightly rouged cheeks and haughty air were what Alexander had studied for decades. As he looked at the man with the cropped blonde hair the colour of summer hay, Alexander saw himself as a type, *le homme de Wellington*. He had waited decades to enact the pose of *le Parisien* in front of a rake like this one-armed blonde of dubious background, and the thrill flushed through him.

The man sniggered. "You need to come to your senses, mate," he said. "They don't like sedition, not even little bits. What about that pacifist Parliament bloke they jailed, and those pacifist ones they sent off to the Front and crucified?"

"They *literally crucified* them," uttered Alexander, reverentially, lowering his voice, aware of his surroundings. There would be supporters of the New Zealand Women's Anti-German League around, those hunters of spies and seekers of sedition. The previous week three women enjoying an evening picnic in the Karori hills had been accused of sending signals with their picnic lamps to German military boats in Wellington Harbour, causing official hysteria that even the Minister of Defence had admonished the papers for so much as reporting.

"Where are you from?" asked Alexander, tempted as he said it, to add "mate".

"I'm not from around here, but I keep myself to myself, mate, if you know what I mean?" An inflection in his voice hinted at something.

"Boer?" Alexander wondered, although he had only heard soldiers returned from South Africa mimicking it. He surmised it was not

Australian, for it wasn't harsh enough. With further alarm, he recalled that the press had repeatedly warned the citizenry about this very sort of situation: foreigners with accents infiltrating crowds; Germans posing as Kiwis. He looked into the man's eyes but what he saw was lust, not treachery or sedition.

"Cat got your tongue?" the man asked with an insouciant smile, which showed white, even teeth. "Worried about being crucified?" He hadn't been wearing a hat, which was unusual for a man, but he pulled a cap out of his back pocket as he looked at Alexander, his blue eyes shifty and squinting. With a flick of his one hand he fitted his smart fabric cap to his head and patted it down. In a voice that really might have been Boer, he said softly: "Secrets mate? Secrets? You gonna tell ya Mac?"

"I *do* like your cap. Is it from somewhere exotic?" Alexander said, using the sort of voice *le Parisien* might have used had he spoken English. The man's grin loosened into a smile and creased his tanned, angular face.

"Keen, aren't ya?" he said quietly, his eyes darting about, and giggled at his question. "My name's Mac. For now, anyway, mate."

"There's no one like this man in *Crime and Punishment*," thought Alexander. "Perhaps Svidrigailov." Svidrigailov was the sensualist and murderer, a true lecher, a rapist, the one character Dostoyevsky required his audience to view with repulsion, if not hatred. Alexander again sized up the man, but no, this one-armed man had nothing Russian about him, let alone anything repulsive. He was too much of another type: "More a rogue off a whaling ship," Alexander thought. "More Herman Melville than Fyodor Dostoyevsky." He straightened himself up and shook his gammy leg to get the blood running and prepared to limp off from this stranger who was surely a crook of some sort. "I don't want to get caught in a web with a disreputable whaler or blackmailing sodomite," he thought, with the images of jail doors clanging and a bewigged judge with owl eyes pronouncing sentence upon him for licentious behaviour.

"I haven't read the Russian sounding one, but *Moby Dick* was true to the word, all those whales expertly described, I loved it," said the man.

Alexander was startled at this unexpected literary knowledge. And what popped into his head was that beautiful moment when he had met Aroha in the Botanic Garden when reading *Moby Dick*. His heart beat with the excitement at the symbolic coincidence and everything that this man had just imparted. "*Moby Dick*", he said, "we could drink to that."

"Keen, though, aren't ya mate?" said Mac.

"Keen? Me? My dear, not in the least," said Alexander in a coquette's voice, dropping his cigarette and stubbing it with his good foot before saying: "Good day, sir. I'm off."

The crowd had dissipated and across the road Sybil Meatyard was chatting to the military man and a woman in a blue hat and a green coat.

"But wait, mate," said the man. "I'd genuinely like to talk to you about things." His eyes said that with real meaning. His mouth puckered and spread into an endearing smile. "Don't cast me off, mate, like everyone does. You know what it's like, I can tell that. We're both… different." Alexander was poised to take his first step. His good foot was forward, his lame one behind, but he paused. He looked to his right and saw Sybil Meatyard, the military man and the woman in the blue hat looking at them, their faces all-knowing as they stared at the obvious misfits.

The military man was simply a staring shape, his arms stiff by his sides, his blonde moustache shining. It was as if he were at a military tribunal set up to determine if a man was a genuine pacifist or simply an Oscar Wilde. Or if a man was a disingenuous war shirker claiming an abiding commitment to pacifism through Christianity and who, under questioning, couldn't recall the name of a certain psalm or explain a religious reference. "Jail" was written over each of the three staring tribunal members' faces. And in the eyes of the military man and Mrs. Meatyard particularly was the accusation of "Oscar Wilde". As his eyes met those of the military man, Alexander thought: "His tongue will dart out and get us."

"Don't go that way," Mac said. "Turn around, don't look at them.

Follow me. I know you like books. Talk to me about that Russian one you tried to trick me with, like we're mates discussing about something normal." His voice was polished, as if through elocution.

The man with one arm and the man with a bad leg. It had all the essence of a parable, very Old Testament, and Alexander sniggered at the equation. The unusual heat, the edge of sedition, the enticing stranger; each element combined and rushed through him in a thrilling moment that pulled him from the tedium. He said: "Since you like books so much, you should read the Russians. They're finally being translated. Have you ever heard of *Crime and Punishment*?"

"That's my bloody motto, mate," the man said. "It'd be yours too if you'd been through what I have." He stopped. A scruffy dog came running along, its tail up, and it too stopped, sniffed around a lamppost, lifted its crooked leg and urinated.

"So public, isn't it?" said Alexander, thinking of how Anton Pavlov might interpret this canine action. "So strange that animals have no shame the way we do, as humans."

The man said in a voice that was plain angry, with no pretence at accents: "You didn't get stuck on a beach at Gallipoli being shot at by Mohammedans. You'd know about human shame if you had, mate. Dogs are saints in comparison. My mates got mowed down, shot through the head by bloody Ottomans, so don't talk to me about shame." All that bravado and *bonhomie*, the mateship and innuendo, had evaporated. He was just a man with one arm and no hope, with bombs exploding in his head. The blue eyes had become duller. The dog, a mangy, orangey creature, ran off with a limp, leaving its urine to dribble across the footpath.

The man put his hand on Alexander's shoulder and dug in with his fingers. "Mate, you'll never understand what it is to see a man being cut up, his guts falling out of his stomach."

"My God," Alexander said. "We were the first nation to export frozen carcasses in ships to Europe. Look what that led to, mass exportation of men to slaughter. Sheep, all of us, cows. Their name is Meatyard, they do this."

"Baaaaaa! Baaaaaa!" the man said. "Moooooo!"

"You don't have a home, do you?" said Alexander.

"No mate. I followed you up Cuba, watching you all the while. I knew you were the type I needed."

2

Alexander Powderham's expansive Tinakori Road property was tucked behind a pohutukawa filled gully beyond which stretched the Tinakori hills. Alexander's grandfather, born in Wellington when it was a whaling station, had built the grand house in the 1860s. The wooden structure had wide verandahs, elaborate ornamentation and numerous yellow brick chimneys. Worn and faded, many said deliberately neglected, it was Alexander's and Aroha's haven.

On the afternoon that Alexander had met the one-armed man, Aroha Raharuhi was working in the back garden where he said to himself: "I'm lucky I have two hearts, one here, one in Te Araroa." He wiped the sweat from his chest and smiled at the memory of his mother seeing him as he returned to the village. His father, laughing, hobbling up behind her, had shouted: "Son, you've come back to Te Araroa." In his Tinakori Road garden twenty years later, far from the beaches of Te Araroa, Aroha saw his mother's eyes greeting him at the *marae* on his last visit before she had passed into that other life, just three weeks before his father went off to meet her.

"My mother and father," he thought, "You were in the battles for our lands. Advise me about this war." He looked up into the trees and said in *te reo*: "But I know what you'd tell me, because you taught me how to think." He felt their presence as he watched the trees swaying: "And Alex let me into his world, and you would see what my life is and agree."

For a week Aroha had been digging a pit latrine. Looking into it he thought of digging and burials and, closing his eyes and making the sign of the cross, he prayed for his parents. In those moments he was a boy on his knees in the wooden church in Te Araroa and Father Dominique was praying in *te reo* with his lilting French accent.

When Aroha opened his eyes, he laughed and said: "It's a latrine pit I'm praying into, look up at the trees and pray for your *whanau* because that's where their spirits live."

Three years of studying law and the humanities at the University College of Wellington and living in a house full of books, and on occasion working in the town's most intellectual bookshop, was what had shaped his life since meeting Alexander ten years previously in the Botanic Garden. "*Pākehā*, Māori, Catholic, *Takatāpui, so many situations, philosophies …*" he thought. He had carved a seat under the rimu where he sat thinking about what this mixed-up world of thoughts really meant. He laughed, and thought: "You're right, Alex, I'm an unorthodox Māori, and I know that's why you love me."

Father Dominique's words came to him, the elderly priest saying to the altar boy as they prepared the hosts for Mass: "I see you for what you are, Aroha. *Takatāpui* is within God's vision. Your people accepted this form of love before we came. Listen to the stories, look at the carvings."

A blackbird hopped across the freshly dug vegetable garden. "You're lucky you have wings," Aroha thought, watching the bird as it looked around. "Father Dominique gave me my wings." With a strategic peck, the blackbird extracted a worm from the soil and flew off.

"Poor worm got caught. Like they want to get me in their beaks," he thought. "I'll tell them…" The blackbird returned and was strutting and happy, Aroha surmised, to have this human it was so accustomed to as its guardian against cats and dogs and hawks.

"Don't dig up my radishes and tomato plants, though mate, or I'll get my tui on to you." The blackbird cocked its head and looked about, alerting Aroha.

"I knew," he said. "I knew." He brushed back his long hair, picked up his singlet, and in his shorts and bare feet he followed the path around the vegetable garden and the cottage, which was his hideaway, and went down the side of the main house to the front. When he saw who stood at the gate, he heard his father say gruffly: "Son, prove that your strength means something."

Straight backed, dignified, dressed impeccably in a dark blue suit and black bowler hat, stood Āpirana Ngata. With him was a police constable, the rank obvious from his helmet, and who, like Aroha, was darker than the politician. Aroha approached them, greeted the elder in *te reo*, his head bowed in respect, but thinking: "Be careful, Aroha, danger."

Aroha unlocked the gate, which was very rusted, as was the entire balustrade through which popped the pink heads of naked ladies and the white blooms of snow drops. He stepped aside and the two men walked in, both men's polished boots the features in Aroha's vision, his head being lowered in deference. The gravel path was lined by pāua shells and the sunlight caught the glint of the teal, pearl and indigo within their curves around which violets grew, their purple heads in their green foliage spilling onto the path. Aroha saw his bare feet, their nakedness against those of the well shod men, as he led the visitors to the front verandah. At the bottom of the steps he stood to one side and said in English: "Sir, please," and indicated that they should go up and be seated in the worn wicker chairs. The constable, who was tall, well-built, in a black wool uniform, remained standing.

In *te reo*, Āpirana Ngata said: "This is Constable Muriwai, who assists me on the Māori Contingent Committee. But I'm here to remind you that you still haven't registered for conscription, despite the requirement to do so as a Māori." He smiled, remained poised, his hair was perfectly pomaded and styled, his bowler hat in his hands. Their eyes met. After several seconds, even though by class he was of a higher standing than this man, Aroha lowered his eyes, this being, after all, Āpirana Ngata.

"You can speak," said Ngata in *te reo*.

"I have nothing more to add from last time you came, sir," said Aroha in English, not willing to speak in *te reo* given the unhappy subject. He thought of putting on his singlet to show increased respect.

"That was six weeks ago," the politician said. "We've contacted you several times by letter but now your time has run out. You're my *iwi* and thirty-five years of age and that's the age of a good soldier. I'm here to warn you."

Aroha said: "I did register as I am required to, but I have not been balloted and I have not volunteered. I do not have to." There was silence except for the *clop, clop,* clop* of a horse going up the street, a rattling old cart behind it. "I'm not Tainui-Waikato. My *iwi* is yours, Ngāti Porou, and Ngāti Porou are not included in the conscription orders of the June nineteen-sixteen conscription call up for Māori. Only the Tainui-Waikato are liable for conscription, all other Māori may go as volunteers and I will not volunteer, as you know."

"I know my name. I know my *whānau,* I know my *iwi.* I know my *whakapapa.*" snapped the Minister in English. "I'm the Deputy of the Māori Contingent Committee, boy! I'm the political leader of Ngāti Porou. I was elected."

"Boy" was what Aroha might have been called by an ill-bred *Pākehā* who saw him as nothing more than a brown skinned native. Or with affection his father and mother might have applied that appellation, but as an endearment.

"I voted for you because you have good policies for Māori education and health and tribal land management," said Aroha in English, looking at the Minister. "But that was before the War started, and I do not believe Māori should be fighting a *Pākehā* war, and you do."

"You're the same as your mother and father," said Āpirana Ngata. "And we know where their allegiances lay, don't we? Not with the Crown, which is where Ngāti Porou allegiances have stood since the Treaty of Waitangi. They broke rank, they deserted to rebellion."

Aroha felt the hot air rush at him, but it wasn't blowing up from the harbour. The Minister had come to the house for the first time soon after the requirement for registration for conscription of Māori had been set into law. That law that Āpirana Ngata himself had lobbied for and won despite, paradoxically, as many people commented in the press, there being so many *Pākehā* who objected on account of the dismal demographics for Māori. On that first occasion, Ngata had been accompanied by Nelly Te Atu, the Assistant to the Chairman of the Māori Contingent Committee and a member of their *iwi.*

"Your mother and father were as rebellious as the Tainui-Waikato, even though they were Ngāti Porou elders and nobles," Mrs. Te Atu had said, her eyes dark, angry. She had raised her hands, as large as the Minister's, and splayed them in front of her as if to ward off his rebellion.

"Sir," said Aroha, looking into his eyes, and stung that the Minister would besmudge the names and *mana* of his parents so flagrantly and against all protocol given that they were of higher rank. "My parents were my parents, I respected them, I respect them now, I will die respecting them. They were true Christians and did not believe in killing. They actively supported the Tainui-Waikato because the Tainui lands were stolen by the Crown and their people killed in the land battles."

"Your parents were not alive when the Germans threatened us," said Āpirana Ngata, aware of the seriousness of his rebuke about Aroha's family, but not apologising. "Do you know what will happen if the Germans come here? Would Huns protect Māori with a treaty? Our *iwi* supports the Treaty of Waitangi and what it means to be part of the Crown and as such you have an obligation to defend it."

Ngata was the first Māori university graduate and the first Māori admitted as a lawyer to the Bar and he would not have come to the house of a mere nobody. He tried to modify his voice, to remove the anger. Aroha was important, his connections and his nobility singled him out amongst their *iwi*. He stared at Aroha, smiled, and said: "I'm sorry I called you 'boy'. I should not have. You are of noble lineage and educated. You should be with me in the Young Māori Party, helping your people, as is this young man, Muriwai, who will go far because he is intelligent and willing."

"My parents stood up for the Treaty of Waitangi. *Pākehā* abused it," said Aroha. He had spent three years in law school and had left because of the harassment he had faced there from war bigots castigating him for not volunteering, and he had a deep resentment of bullies, no matter what colour. And, as Alexander had said to him, facetiously: "You'd look ridiculous in a barrister's wig." It was a remark which they had laughed about but one which had undertones of truth, for being a part of the establishment for Aroha was anathema. Like Alexander, he had an abiding interest in European philosophy, and he had studied French for a year with Professor von Zedlitz until the Professor had been dismissed under the Alien Teachers' Act. He pushed his round, gold rimmed glasses up his nose and breathed in deeply. As Alexander had said many times: "You're the only Māori who can tease out the differences between Diderot and Voltaire and with *Pākehā* you should use that logic whenever you can." He looked from the politician to the constable who seemed to be listening intently, his head to one side as if that was the side of his good ear. But the representative of the Māori Contingency Committee had resorted to his other status, that of the patriot, not the *iwi* member. He said, harshly: "And your *mana*? What about the brave Māori fighting for our country?" He moved closer to Aroha, who stepped back because protocol, etiquette, *mana*.

Aroha met the constable's eyes. Turning his eyes to the Minister, he said: "Your mother was of Scottish descent, mine was pure *Ngāti-Porou*. I am from that line that did not think the same as your line when we lost our lands. My line never once agreed to fight on behalf of the Crown against our own people."

Āpirana Ngata took a step back, and then another, and opened his mouth, but no words came out, just dry breath. He said, in English: "What do you think *Pākehā* think of Māori for not contributing fully to the war effort? How will we ever get their respect?"

"I'm not looking for it," said Aroha. "We lost our lands to them, and we got only more kicks in the pants. Who chased and killed those Māori in the Uruwera two years ago for trying to get their lands back? Cullen, the Commissioner of Police himself, and he charged those Māori with sedition."

"I wasted my time coming here, me a Minister, once and now twice. You've shamed our *iwi*. If you won't volunteer, it shows you're a coward."

They were eyeing each other from different sides of the verandah: the sceptic shirtless, in shorts and bare feet. The parliamentarian with status in all things *Pākehā* sweating in his winter suit.

21

"Sir," Aroha said. "Under New Zealand law, only Tainui-Waikato are required to go to this war and that is because they rebelled and are now being punished. Besides, a single son cannot be conscripted. The Conscription Act of June nineteen-sixteen expressly states that a single male child is exempted."

"Well, you're an orphan. And Tainui-Waikato war shirkers are being rounded up," said the Minister, whose pomade was melting. "Queen Te Puea Herangi may be the Queen of Tainui, but this is real war and she'll be arrested for sedition for hiding her men from conscription. Be very careful what you say, you are my *iwi* who is so…" There was a limit to what even he could say given Aroha's place in the *iwi*. He thought how strange it was to be caught like this, where the original hierarchies still reigned despite all of his status and achievements in *Pākehā* lore and structures. He extracted his remaining weapon: "The *Pākehā* you live with is also of the same persuasion. What would your mother and father say about that, this *sickness*?"

"They would say that *Takatāpui* is accepted in our culture." Aroha folded his arms across his chest. "*Takatāpui* is of our culture, and you know that. You shouldn't try and change our knowledge just to suit *Pākehā* who hate *Takatāpui* and call it sodomy and lock us up in jail."

"You were raised a Catholic, you…but then that's another aberration," said the Minister, who was staunchly Protestant. "That's where all this nonsense comes from. French Catholics on our lands. Decadent French. Of course, they believed in that. The French are filthy."

"But you want me to fight in France, for France?"

"For…for…liberty. *Takatāpui* is pre-Christian. I mean, that didn't exist, men did not do that to each other in our culture."

The horse *clip-clopped* back, the same rattling contraption behind it. Āpirana Ngata, an eloquent man and acknowledged orator, was unfamiliar with this sort of dissent from his own people. He looked at his hands, inspecting them as the other two men watched. What Ngata saw was what Aroha had accused him of: his Scottish ancestry; his diluted blood. It was there in the dissipated brown, lighter than the two Māori next to him. A tried and tested thought inched in: What constituted purity when faced with an accusation this noble had thrown at him?

Looking Aroha directly in the eyes, he stated as the official from the Māori Contingent Committee, the Māori strategist intent on his people's survival and wellbeing: "We shall see if it is sedition or perversion that gets you. You may be a noble, but that doesn't count under these circumstances of our nation's survival. The War Regulations Act surmounts everything, culture, class, nobility." He indicated to the constable to follow him down the gravel path where the Minister dislodged a pāua shell which with an elegant pirouette the constable tried to avoid but crushed under his heavy footstep. At the gate, the constable looked back. With a smile, a wink, and a nod, he told Aroha he was on his side. Making sure the irate politician did not see, he signaled by pointing first to himself and then to Aroha, that he would return.

3

The Te Aro Bookshop, which Alexander's father had opened in 1888, was situated in Tonks Grove, a cul-de-sac just off the top end of Cuba Street. The wooden buildings at that end of Cuba Street had not been replaced with fine late Victorian or Edwardian structures as had those closer to the town. Situated next to the bookshop was a tall wooden building that Alexander had leased to the Finks but which had been graffitied by patriots and subsequently shuttered. The graffiti, a nasty slur on certain peoples, he had left to illustrate the result of overheated patriotism. Tucked away as it was in Tonks Grove, the Te Aro Bookshop was the most well-known establishment for those requiring books and specialised journals, and it was commonly referred to as being "highbrow".

Tonks Grove was paved with red bricks salvaged from a kiln destroyed by fire in the late 1890s. As Alexander Powderham limped across the uneven surface, he saw in those bricks a curious but meaningful metaphor of life and what it all meant to be a human. The bricks, charcoal colour where they had been burned, were chipped by wagon wheels and were a dulled, wedged mosaic. For Alexander they were what constituted the history of civilisation, roughened and smoothed by time and circumstances.

"So many wars over time," he thought. "And this one too shall pass but will not be forgotten with so much Kiwi slaughter." He concentrated on a single brick and thought: "Freddy, where are you? I miss you so much. Alive or dead?" That was the big question, but what Alexander saw was Freddy laid out, his helmet still on his head, his arms outstretched: "Freddy in a field in France. My Freddy, so handsome, so bright." Alexander removed his hat as much in respect as to fan himself as he pondered what it all meant to be someone like

Freddy in a filthy trench: well bred, educated, sardonic, wistful, an expert on New Zealand painting, a well-known curator. A Pansy. "Anyway, my dear, darling Freddy boy, your friends all love you. You're doing this for your country." It wasn't cynicism or despair that flushed through Alexander, for those well used ingredients were, for once, out-flavoured by love and respect for Freddy's choice to join up.

"Ah, well," he reflected as he replaced his hat, "perhaps even the Finks will slink in one day, and Freddy, triumphantly of course, as he would. And all will continue until the next conflagration, which will be even grander, with an even bigger Big Bertha." The thought of the big gun trained on Paris stimulated the cynicism, Pavlov-like, to seep back in, and despair followed closely. He was acutely aware of both elements, for he shook his head and said: "Give me some peace! Four years of this is sufficient for a lesson in suffering." He had drunk only two beers with the one-armed man, but their effect, and that of the strangeness and excitement of the conversation, all combined with the unusual heat and the Meatyards and their vigilantes, and he thought: "Surely even Raskolnikov wasn't as tormented as I am today."

A ginger haired boy dressed in knee-length shorts, a red vest and a brown woollen cap, came running over the bricks, his steel hoop making a *clickety-click* sound as it turned. Alexander was revived by the sight of the child enjoying his skill at balancing what he, Alexander, would never have been able to given his leg and his clumsiness. He smiled and thought: "To have two legs like that and to go running about with a hoop is all I want." It was hard to imagine what running might mean, what it would be like to rush down a street or run with excitement across a beach and over the sand. Just to not have to have worn a metal brace all his life was enough. But he had realised many a time, and always with sanguinity, that having a gammy leg had saved him from the trenches.

"Penny for your thoughts, as twisted and tormented as they will be, I give no more than a penny," he heard Elizabeth say behind him. She tapped his head with her finger, took his right arm and whispered into his ear: "Lighten up, dearie. You're not Raskolnikov. Not yet anyway."

"Just some days," he said, turning, looking into her fine brown eyes. "Did you see that cartoon in the press this morning, of the Prime Minister shovelling men into a funnel of a steam engine? Given the censorship I wondered how it got published. The paper even criticised the failure at Gallipoli, albeit obliquely."

"I saw that," she said, brightened by his mood change. "I'm sure the Government knows we're all fed up. They're letting the pressure off the kettle or we might explode, like Russia. The wharfies are agitating again. The farmers are shouting that enough of their men have been sacrificed. Everyone's simply had it."

The boy came back, rolling his metal hoop. He stopped and said: "Hello sir, hello Miss. It's a very hot day isn't it? My grandmother likes your shop. She said brainy people get their books there." He skipped off over the bricks, his metal wheel before him, and disappeared into Cuba Street, where a horse pulling a cart of wooden beer barrels clomped slowly past, its head bent, its yellowish mane artfully plaited. A man appeared then, coming around the corner, and looked up the cul-de-sac as if bemused or confused, or a combination of both. He stared at them, then at the shuttered building, and then up at the sky as if up there he might find what he was looking for.

"He's looking for aeroplanes," Elizabeth said.

"German ones," Alexander replied. "He's a spy for the New Zealand Women's Anti-German League." The mirth stopped for they both realised he was the dreaded telegram man.

"Very Pavlovian, our minds reeling at the sight of him," said Alexander.

"Once upon a time we would miss a heartbeat because it might be an invitation."

"Still Pavlovian conditioning, but a happy one," he noted. "That was drooling, this is the drying-of-the-mouth sensation."

The telegram man approached them, the lenses in his little spectacles catching the sun so that his eyes were obscured. His cap was pushed far back on his head and his grey cotton shirt was sweat-soaked.

"Good afternoon," he said with much cheer. Neither of them replied.

They couldn't. Silence, that dried mouth sort, had become a syndrome and the telegram man was well used to it. "Miss Elizabeth Norris? Know her, do you? Addressed here for the bookshop."

"Yes, that's me…" She pointed at Alexander. "He can vouch…" Her face had whitened: who could it be that had been slaughtered? Her brother Richard? Her cousin Lennox? With a start, she said: "Helen?"

"It's like a plague, isn't it?" Alexander said, referring to the constant news of the war dead.

"Funny you should say that, sir," the telegram man said. "I've noticed a lot of influenza the past three or four days. One lady in Thorndon was so sick she couldn't get to the door to get her telegram." He took from his leather bag a sheet and handed it to Elizabeth to sign, his pen at the ready. "Auckland's a bit down with it too, like the papers say. And telegrams coming in from South Africa say it's rife, actually killing people left, right and centre." He waved the telegram. "It's not bad news. Stop shaking," he said. "Worst job in the world these days, this is. Have to be so…so…I don't know…steeled to it." He nodded goodbye and turned and disappeared into Cuba Street just as a motorcar backfired and set aflutter the pigeons on the verandah awning of the corner shop.

"Odd that he should know what's in this." Her face brightened as she read the telegram. "Helen!" she cried. "Her troop ship has arrived in Adelaide. She should be here within two weeks. Lucky girl! Oh, it must be such a relief after Europe." All of Helen's letters from England, France, Flanders and Palestine from the past three years of her absence were stacked chronologically in an embroidered handkerchief box on the table next to her bed.

"Auckland October twelfth," she read, sniffing the telegram as if it were something Helen had sent scented, as were some of her letters.

"The Prime Minister and Finance Minister arrive the same day on the *Niagara*," said Alexander with much disdain. He imagined the photos of the two men in top hats and dress coats, recently splashed across the newspapers, lined up with fellow dignitaries in London at the Imperial War Conference. But the thing that had most impressed him, other than the enormity of arrogance that constituted that class of human, the warmongers, German or not, was the size of Mrs. Margot Asquith's hat. The wife of the British Prime Minister, that nose so aquiline, her hat at least a foot high, its ornamentation a mass of spikes firing off like lightning bolts. "If only it had been in colour," he'd thought, studying the photo, wondering that even in wartime, one as catastrophic as this, the fashion world pursued its artistic creations.

"Oh, when Helen comes back, we'll learn so much about what it's actually like in the real world. Of course, she couldn't say much in the letters, but I guessed between the lines."

There was an element of truth in what she had said. He pushed his cynicism aside but it bubbled up and he uttered: "The real world? Don't you think the Meatyards and the Women's Anti-German League aren't quite real enough?" Even he knew the real world of Wellington, in this instance, could not be compared to the real world that they all knew pustulated in Europe and the Ottoman Empire. It occurred to him as he watched Elizabeth read the telegram what the term "war effort" might mean for him. His war effort was the suffering of his spirit, of knowing what the world was like, of feeling it, even in Wellington, so removed from that pustulation, but real, hurtful, nevertheless. He realised he felt this pain, and that if he did have anything in common with Raskolnikov then it was just this constant, niggling trauma of overwrought feelings. He said: "Don't you think it's all too mad, like *Crime and Punishment*, as if we too are tormented Russians?"

"Actually," she said, supporting him by the arm into the bookshop, "I was going to mention you might like to take a rest from *Crime and Punishment*. You've read it, what, three times in a row? Don't be obsessed. It's just so…intense. I'm worried about…" She paused to find the right words. "Couldn't you read Walt Whitman or Keats, your old favourites, just to soothe yourself?"

"Four, five times. But it's the most extraordinary novel. I feel I've waited all my life to read it." He looked at her concerned that she might be letting him down. And what he was reminded of was that of course she didn't feel such passion, this daughter of a cleric from Dunedin, an agnostic and modern thinker. She had not an ounce of Russian passion in her.

"Well, I suppose you identified wildly with Madame Bovary. And you didn't turn out to be a French adulteress. So I shouldn't be too worried about you identifying with a brooding, murderous Russian student," she said. "Or should I?"

Elizabeth Norris had been close to Alexander for fifteen years, since they had met at the University College in the School of Modern Languages, where they had studied French and German. But she well knew the loss of his friends and the worry about Aroha being hounded by the authorities had reached inside him. She said: "You're not Raskolnikov and you will not be, will you?" She took off his hat and hung it on the hook behind him. "Don't sink into that, please, Alex."

He didn't answer, but took her hand and kissed it as Monsieur Bovary would have Madame Bovary's in their happier times. In his office, he took out the tin with the fez wearing Turk that the one-armed man had associated with sedition. In slow motion, as if dreaming it, he extracted a cigarette which he lit, barely realizing his action, as he thought about those characters in the streets of Wellington: the two proselytising Meatyards; the military man in medals; the wealthy ladies in hats behind the tea room widows; the working men in the pub downing warm beer and mutton pies that flies had buzzed about as he drank with the one armed man called Mac. He shivered despite the heat. Why would one read Keats in this mess? Reading odes about nightingales was as superficial as Margot Asquith's flamboyant hat when men were being blown to pieces. He drew in on the cigarette, its acrid taste a pleasure, distraction and reward. But his mind was whirring: Whitman could offer up his beautiful words about beautiful men; but why, what beauty was there when those men were being killed in a conflagration that just wouldn't end? What beauty was there in Keats about young lovers frozen in time on Grecian urns when there was just gore and mayhem?

"I have to *do* something," he said. The novel was lying on the table, and he picked it up, tenderly, as he had Elizabeth's hand. It fell open to that well-read passage where Raskolnikov is sneaking up the dark staircase to the old pawnbroker's flat, Alyona, the louse, the rapacious usurer who Raskolnikov had decided would die so that people wouldn't have to suffer under her oppression. In the novel the old woman's eyes made Raskolnikov shiver with loathing; they were staring into his as she grasped his evil intent. As Alexander read yet again the tumultuous lines about righteous murder, he heard Elizabeth's warning: "Don't turn into Raskolnikov."

The world, however, collectively, with all that pain, shouted back: "It's war! Fight. Rid us of oppression." Mr. and Mrs. Meatyard were waving white feathers of cowardice and shouting: "Oscar Wilde!" Freddy and the boys were in the trenches. And for what? He scanned the page to the pivotal passage where Raskolnikov showed his resolve to do something, to make things happen. The axe in his hands, the axe raised above the woman's greasy head, the axe chopping her. Alyona Ivanovna's stepsister Elizaveta unexpectedly coming in, her mouth open in terror and surprise and the axe being flung at her, smashing out her brains.

"Who shall it be?" thought Alexander. "How do I get revenge? Raskolnikov had a plan…"

"Cup of tea," said Elizabeth, pushing open the door with her foot, a tray in her hands. "Oh, I see. Still studying the Bible according to Raskolnikov, are we? The evening paper is in. I shouldn't tell you, given your nerves, but you need to know. Seven hundred New Zealanders killed in action in the last month. Ninety-five of them from Wellington. And by the way, a man with one arm is here to see you. He said he's called Mac, and he has a dubious accent. Should I ask him in here or do you want to see him in the shop?"

Mac entered the room, having followed Elizabeth down the passageway. With his one hand he fidgeted with a coat button while Elizabeth met Alexander's eyes with a look that said everything between "death be upon you" and "praise the Lord." Seeing Alexander's face, ironic, brooding, intelligent, she saw that he was as enigmatically beautiful as Dostoyevsky's description of Raskolnikov. With a wry smile spreading from his lips, Alexander told her with his eyes to get out.

4

The Te Aro Book Group was well established and only classics and contemporary literary novels were chosen for discussion. Rules for the club, which were written in chalk on a blackboard in the ample sitting room at the shop, included: signed legible notes submitted on arrival; questions posed by the chair with responses solicited; no interjections; no proselytising; men to give equal voice to women; two pence donation for each meeting, proceeds to von Z.

Elizabeth Norris was seated in the chintz covered armchair which the deceased Henry Powderham had purchased in the late 1890s from an English family who were returning to the "Old Country", as they put it, on account of being disillusioned with this new one. Seated next to Elizabeth, Alexander Powderham saw his father sitting in that chair on the windy winter night it had been delivered by horse and cart to their house on Tinakori Road.

"I read somewhere," the elder Powderham had said, looking up at his son as he sat in that chair, "that more immigrants return from Argentina to their original country than do people from New Zealand to their respective country of birth. Except for immigrants of a Syrian background. It begs the question as to why, doesn't it?" It was neither a rhetorical nor a whimsical observation, but a serious question. The elder Powderham had been educated at the University College of Otago, the colony's first tertiary institution, and he took very seriously the privilege of a sound, liberal education in which facts were the basis for knowledge. "I need facts," he would insist. "Alexander, never forget the requirement for scientific authority. And don't forget, ever, my old maxim: love literature, worship science."

It had been as windy that night on Tinakori Road as it was this evening in Tonks Grove. The question about Argentinian immigration and emigration, Alexander realised, had never been answered, but the thought of that mysterious country now stimulated his imagination: "Aroha and I should flee to Buenos Aires in the morning," he thought.

From travel books and an exciting encounter with an Uruguayan sailor on the ferry crossing to the South Island, he had learned it was a vast and cultured city with Romance languages spoken while in this windswept outpost, the most southern capital city in the world, one heard only English. Off to Buenos Aires in the morning. Surely a ship would be leaving on the Argentinian run. He could hear its horn blowing as it swept out of Wellington Harbour for Argentina, where there was no commitment to a European war and where they were modelling their capital city on Hausmann's Paris, not provincial England, as was Wellington.

"As rich as an Argentine", the popular aphorism for that romantic country named after its ubiquitous silver held a *caché* of wide-open spaces, rough and tumble cowboys, and the immense and sophisticated city of Buenos Aires. He wanted to worship in *El Teatro Colon*, to savour its grandeur dressed in evening clothes, while at the diminutive Wellington Opera House he would be seen simply as an overdressed dandy posing on the arm of a spinster "lady friend". Hope leapt in him at the thought of Buenos Aires. He saw Aroha and himself on the ship ploughing through the Great Southern Ocean so far removed from Tonks Grove, the Meatyards, and this group of fuddy-duddies who thought Madame Bovary was merely a superficial French bourgeois, or a tart.

He snorted loudly as if he were completely superior to everyone present; but just as sudden as his snort was the crash of his expectations of escaping to Argentina. His mind had been pulled to the realities of this life where men were trapped. All those enticing images of gauchos and elegant theatres were now rushing backwards. He was retreating swiftly from *El Teatro Colon*, his evening clothes being sucked off him as he sped backwards across the Great Southern Ocean to his responsibilities in this cultural backwater to, inevitably, Mr. and Mrs. Meatyard, for he knew utterly, as had Raskolnikov, that such louses needed to be eradicated.

33

The demise of the Meatyards' powerful hold over Wellington became an overwhelming requirement in his rendition of what "the war effort" meant to him. "I do have a mission," he thought. The female Meatyard was hanging upside down like a cow on a rack in an abattoir. Her offensive husband, his straw toupee still glued to his head, was being pulled along next to her, their naked, pinkish and gutted carcasses strung up by the ankles, their entrails ripped out like those from the great beasts hanging alongside them on the same slow-moving death belt being their just reward for producing human sacrifices for the European war debacle.

Elizabeth Norris was addressing the group. Looking at Alexander she said sharply, indicating that her authority as chair overrode his as owner of the bookshop: "If you wouldn't mind, Alexander", and took a defiant puff on her cigarette. She only smoked at these occasions and always a yellow *De Reszke*, the brand favoured by ladies identified with the educated classes who on certain occasions wanted to set aside the conventions. Catching Elizabeth's prissy and authoritarian glance and gritting his teeth at her voice, his mind flicked back Pavlov-like to escape and fantasy: "No, to Hell with thinking about the Meatyards, what do I care? Let them have war. I really should escape. One's soul is destroyed being a Pansy in this place. Oscar should have fled to Paris while he had the chance, just as we should flee to Argentina. In Buenos Aries Aroha can be free of being just a brown boy." He knew that pederast behaviour was not illegal in Argentina due to the civilising effects of Napoleonic Law. That knowledge swelled in him, making him want to jump up and run away for Napoleon *was* extraordinary; Napoleonic Law *meant* freedom. He was walking with Aroha down a marvelous boulevard and all about were Argentinians speaking Spanish and Italian. "I've never read an Argentinian novel," he thought with some alarm, segueing from flight to fiction. "There aren't any in translation. I could go there, learn Spanish, translate their poetry and novels…"

"Is Dostoyevsky a nihilist?" asked Elizabeth. "Doctor Karr," she said, turning her attention to the distinguished professor, "given your voluminous notes, can you please begin tonight's discussions." She waved a sheath of handwritten papers at the twelve people about her, Miss Rutherford's contribution being on top, identifiable by the usual bright green, unlined paper.

"We don't know much about the author, but from my reading I'd say not. He's hammering quite the opposite of nihilism. Rather, it's Russian Orthodoxy he's progressing, that arch conservative ideology which fundamentally supports, albeit they have now been eradicated, the Tsarist regime and its murderous apparatuses, but supported by state religion, nevertheless. Dostoyevsky merely *describes* poverty."

Doctor Karr's pipe was suspended in his hand, his white beard moving up and down as he stated his convictions in his broad Scottish accent. "Dostoyevsky's solution to problems is through Christ's teachings, the Slavonic version. And Raskolnikov must repent and suffer for the murders conventionally, through penitence, that is, in Siberia, in full Christian submission."

"But he doesn't ever repent," said Alexander. "Point out where Raskolnikov says: 'I'm sorry.'"

"These so-called extraordinary men covered in medals don't say they're sorry," interjected Miss Rutherford. "Napoleon didn't, did he? Look at the parallels today and who do we hear say 'sorry'? Churchill? Kaiser Wilhelm? Our Prime Minister?" She was on dangerous territory given the War Regulations Act. Looking around her, she said: "I want apologies for the massacres in Gallipoli and Flanders. Big men, big ideas, murder justified. And if Raskolnikov, that skinny, worn-down, pseudo intellectual thinks he's extraordinary, and can kill as did Napoleon, then, well, I'm mystified about our…our…*raison d'être*."

Elizabeth Norris smiled with satisfaction. At last, there was passion. *Madame Bovary* had elicited nothing like this in the first five minutes. Alexander, however, not waiting for the chair to ask him to speak, opened the novel and fumbled for the page, skimming quickly for his denouement, and read in his most pompous voice: "Read page two hundred and eighty where Raskolnikov rationalises murder simply in accordance with the dictates of one's conscience. So, if we kill for a common good, then we are doing so on our conscience and so, *voila,* it's all justified."

"What an absolute distortion of fact," said Doctor Karr. "You're just agreeing that Raskolnikov can kill two Jewesses as if they're lice, as he himself calls them. We're not here to defend Raskolnikov. No, we're here to *read* Dostoyevsky. Raskolnikov is not a hero, he's a fanatic, like…" He looked around, his mouth open, but he did not finish his thought about Churchill or the Kaiser.

"Pedanticism," said Alexander as he saw Mr. and Mrs. Meatyard reaching the end of the death belt where carcasses are carved up with huge butchers' knives. In a few swift motions the Meatyards were merely big fatty portions to be wrapped in muslin and exported frozen to England. "The lone wolf can act as a Napoleon, he can kill in righteousness for the betterment of mankind."

"Oh, just as that Serbian ratbag shot the Archduke Ferdinand and the Duchess of Hohenberg," said Mr. Oliver Tricklebank, a well-respected, retired banker. "And look where *that* lone wolf silliness got us."

"Oh, Alexander! Is that according to you or Raskolnikov? Or are you one and the same thing now? You seem to be advocating for any man, and I emphasise *man*, to kill anyone he, and I emphasise *he*, and say that would be for the good of humanity," said Edwina Castle, surveying her audience. "But who *defines* righteousness? The Russians didn't think it was extraordinary or right when Napoleon invaded Russia in, when was it, eighteen fourteen?"

"Eighteen hundred and twelve," said Oliver Tricklebank.

"If there is a righteous murder, as Raskolnikov professes, is there no requirement for suffering or repentance, for he feels nothing of the sort, does he?" Elizabeth asked.

"He never repented," said Edwina Castle. "What a self-obsessed narcissist this Raskolnikov is. Is that perhaps Russian? Or must we see him as a forerunner to this catastrophic war? No one's sorry, they all think they're doing this for mankind. For themselves, is more like it. The Huns are the worst. We follow right behind with our ill-informed male patriotism. It's all *men* chopping up each other."

Doctor Karr interjected. "The murder of the two sisters torments him. By 'him' I mean Raskolnikov, not you, Alexander, who appear to condone murder." He stared at Alexander and his eyes narrowed. "He could not endure the consequences of the murders. He collapsed. He was weaker than he thought. It was not the perfect crime. Unlike his hero Napoleon, he is not a great man and therefore not exempt from guilt or punishment, as are the so-called extraordinary men in this treatise, for treatise it is more than novel. Raskolnikov begins to die spiritually. The novel's main point is how Raskolnikov is resurrected, not physically like Lazarus, but spiritually reawakened. Dostoyevsky is challenging people who die spiritually, who are agnostic or atheists."

Silence prevailed. Alexander, sensing he had been outwitted, merely shrugged and retreated to his own narrower version, content with his interpretation, one formed by being different, separated from the herd as a pervert and a free thinker. He saw the Meatyards wrapped in bloodied muslin, as two lumps on a butcher's bench awaiting export, ending up on a table with mint sauce and gravy on the other side of the world.

Elizabeth broke the silence with a question about the role of women in the novel.

"Oh, and who waves the men off to the trenches and blows them kisses on their death march out of Wellington? Who gives out the white feathers in the streets? Who is Sybil Meatyard and who forms the Women's Anti-German League?" said Alexander in anger and piqued that, as had been the case with Madame Bovary, the philistines had turned against his hero, against him.

Elizabeth stubbed out her *De Reszke* and waved the papers as a signal that she was changing the subject. Her glance at Alexander informed him that, like Raskolnikov, he was his own victim, and that was what promoted, in turn, the rise of the lone wolf assassin.

"Abject poverty pervades *Crime and Punishment,*" she said, reading from her prepared list of questions. "Surely that makes for revolution. Did this novel, published in eighteen sixty-six, predict the Russian Revolution?"

Miss Rutherford stood up. She wore an elegant fez-like hat with red stripes. Looking about her, she said: "I can see why there was a communist revolution in Russia. If there was that much social degradation and abuse of power, why would there not have been, *eventually*, given that *The Communist Manifesto* was written by a Russian?"

Alexander imagined her classroom, filled with girls from well-to-do families, and a thrill went through him that Miss Hortensia Rutherford would ask such questions of her impeccably attired and socially advantaged students. He wanted to shout: "Brava! Brava! Pavlov's dogs are all salivating!" Conversely, Mrs. Meatyard came to mind as a lurking, grey spectre, a panopticon watching the carry on, seeing socialists and nihilists and reporting such to the headmistress of the Wellington Girls' College when all that Miss Rutherford stood for was freedom and democracy, the very things that this war was purportedly being fought for.

The door opened and in walked the one-armed man, Mac, which, Alexander had been informed at the time of their hurried but exciting liaison in his office, was short for MacPherson. Alexander flushed, even his neck reddened. MacPherson looked about, caught Elizabeth's eye and, winking at her, he hunched up his shoulders as if to say: "I'm sure you don't mind." He sat down at the back of the room and nimbly lit a cigarette with his one hand, the matchbox between his knees, in order to strike it.

The Te Aro book group had previously dissected *Madame Bovary*, which they had collectively, with only two exceptions, dismissed as being a frivolous French ditty, a bourgeois, sentimental construction. Only Miss Rutherford had really come to its defence when, with some passion, she had said: "And what's wrong with being sentimental in a harsh world of war? And since all of us here are bourgeois, what's wrong with our class? Or is it the fact that the heroine is a woman who commits adultery?" She had looked around, but no one had come to her rescue, not even Elizabeth, who had read it in the French and had thought Madame Bovary was spoilt, shallow and self-indulgent.

On the contrary, Alexander adored Madame Bovary as a character:

her ennui, her attire, her lusts. She had come alive to him, fecund and real, this woman who had supposedly lost her virtue. So much of what she was he saw in himself, someone castigated for wishing for nothing but freedom.

Madame Bovary was the metaphor of being trapped in a metal brace in a country that called men who loved men "Pansies" and spat them out. As he sat listening to the carry on about *Crime and Punishment* with the face of this conformity all about him he smelled that fresh air of the Great Southern Ocean, a wild perfume, pungent with sea salt and kelp and remoteness and he thought: "No wonder the Ancient Mariner was undone by an albatross." He imagined the great bird as it swung and cantered across the swells and deep green ocean and soared above him, up and up and up. And then, when the crossbow downed it, that majesty with the vast wings destroyed by stupidity, it was enough to make Alexander, sitting surrounded by the book club members, want to shriek with grief. "Now the inevitable Christian expiation", he thought. "Now the Ancient Mariner must suffer, like I am. Why is everything crime and punishment? Why is everything so conditioned, so psychological, so Pavlovian?"

Emerging from his reveries about the Ancient Mariner and the rise of modern psychology, Alexander heard Mr. Tricklebank saying: "I think you're talking about the oligarchs behind this war, their rampant justifications of warfare being only for their good. In the same way, Raskolnikov kills the Jewish women for their money. They have the same shoe on the same foot. Simple as that. Forget all his self-promotion about extraordinary men. There is no extraordinary man. Or woman. What if someone were to come in here and kill one of us because we disagree with this war? Would that be justified? Could they call themselves *extraordinary*?"

"Now, now," said Mr. Gerald Hoskins, an elderly beekeeper with an interest in seventeenth century European poetry. "You can't blame the innocent victims in Belgium." Gerald Hoskins rarely spoke, when he did it never quite fitted the moment. However, he wrote the most exacting notes and was in the hope that one day they would be published under the title *A Beekeeper's Literary Manual* as he had repeatedly informed the club members. He mumbled about the Government's abuse of power, then exclaimed: "Our Prime Minister is a drone, a wasp with a sting that inflicts death on the working man and his family!"

"Raskolnikov's justification is simply rational. Kill the pernicious pawnbroker and let others benefit positively from that action," stated Alexander, irritably. "It's social psychology."

"Oh dear," moaned Edwina Castle. "How disillusioning when even the likes of Alex state such rubbish, such anti-Jewish expostulations. Haven't you heard of the pogroms? That's why the Finks left Silesia, and look what's happened to them here." She was a heavy-set woman in her late forties and only wore black. "I'm in perpetual mourning, for everything," she'd told someone who'd asked her why that constant morbidity. The author of educational pamphlets on women's health and wholesome diets for girls, she stood and held up *Crime and Punishment* and declared: "The novel is simply a crime story, a murder mystery. It's neither prophetic nor religious indoctrination but has a lot of rambling philosophy about which we have been getting all twisted up and over, as is my use of prepositions...It's simply a detective story."

Angered, Alexander said above the protestations of the chair: "Let's not dismiss Dostoyevsky with flippancy, Edwina. Can't we be involved in some deep thought for once, immersed in some profundity? Please don't turn into an anti-intellectual, trivialising everything, so very *Wellington*, I beg of you."

"Now, now," said Gerald Hoskins. "The Germans would be down from Samoa in a moment if it weren't for us. Huns are bees, you'll always have a drone and a queen, and they'd be swarming down in their helmets."

The wind rattled the roof and tried to get in the windows and the curtains ballooned out eerily. Otherwise, there was silence except for the *tick, tick, tick* of the clock as the group collected their thoughts, an unease drifting about at the thought of the chaos around the world and the swarms of helmeted Hun bees descending from Samoa on their militaristic path to New Zealand. Trying to break into the circuit of angst, Elizabeth asked: "Given the novel was published in eighteen sixty-six, can we not discuss it as within that time, some fifty years previous to this moment?"

Mrs. Gaynor Massey, who was first cousin to the Prime Minster but was aghast at his conservative shenanigans around supporting better conditions for working women, spoke up: "If we discuss the novel as it was in Dostoyevsky's time, then we can say they were quite primitive because they had barely given serfs their freedom, while twenty years previously in New Zealand the Crown and some five-hundred Māori chiefs had signed the Treaty of Waitangi. We're much more enlightened. Women got the vote before anyone else, and pensions and unions and progressive legislation," she said in her well-educated voice. "And long may modernity continue. We must keep fighting for it. And this revolution in Russia, it's just aiming at equality and egalitarianism, so why is everyone so upset about it?"

"Here, here. Well spoken," said Edwina Castle. "Let's see what happens in Russia. The German revolutionary, Rosa Luxemburg, wants to abolish the family. We might all agree with that on many an occasion."

When the clock struck at nine o'clock Elizabeth declared: "Thank you all for such robust discussion, unlike last time when we dealt with that provincial Frenchwoman." She looked at Alexander and smiled, her lips sticking to her teeth. "By popular agreement, our next read is *The Metamorphosis* by Franz Kafka, and we'll see you all in two weeks."

"Seditious! Seditious! Seditious!"

The eruption at the back of the room came from a tall, pimply man who had sought permission to be an observer, posing as a student of literature. The book group members were all suspended in that moment of processing what had just been accomplished with likeminded people, that intense culmination of reading a great novel with an evening of intellectual stimulation. Everyone had merged into the esoteric world of mid-nineteenth century Saint Petersburg and the hysteria of Dostoyevsky's characters to whom they had been deeply attuned for weeks: the distraught Katerina Marmeladova had run screaming through the streets; Pulcheria Raskolnikov had screeched lamentations about her son's madness; orphans, drunkards, murderers, prostitutes, Poles, Russians, Jews, Germans: the mad panoply of the book produced the same shivering senses of those Hun bees descending from Samoa. When: "Sedition! Sedition! Sedition!" was shouted from the back of the room it was as if in accompaniment to the realities of the novel.

Elizabeth was the first to shout her alarm and outrage: "Who are you? How dare you?"

"I'll be reporting this!" the accuser yelled. "Give me those notes!" He pulled a badge from his pocket. "I've been taking notes. Powderham, you're running a seditious, seditious…institution!"

Alexander stood, but fell awkwardly, hitting his head on the chintz chair and stumbled.

"The Women's Anti-German League is right. The Meatyards know what's going on!" the aggrieved man shouted.

"You're nothing but a vigilante," cried Professor Karr. "You're rabble, not a policeman. He's the one who attacked my wife at the Women's Workers' Union meeting."

Alexander was shaking as he tried to get to the shouting man, lurching from chair to chair, grasping each as support until Elizabeth grabbed him.

"Hold the impertinent monkey," shouted Gerald Hoskins. "No use denouncing the unions."

MacPherson grabbed the vigilante by the scruff of his neck, the strength of his one arm so forceful that the man fell back, choking. He pulled the man to the door, which Edwina Castle had opened, and they pushed him out.

5

It was almost eleven o'clock by the time the book group had turned the event inside out. Elizabeth, Hortensia and Edwina, all of whom resided in Mount Victoria, set off in their hats and scarves and thick coats, their heads bent to the wind, as Alexander bolted the bookshop door and mentally promised the Finks that if they ever came back he would not charge them rent for a year.

The Professor, who always drove Alexander home after the meetings, cranked up the motor and MacPherson slid into the rear seat next to Alexander. No one spoke as they rattled through the deserted streets until, in the cover of the dark vehicle, MacPherson touched Alexander's hand. "This is where we met," he whispered. "Two days ago, mate." He rubbed Alexander's index finger: "I know what you want. Mac will do it."

By the time they reached Tinakori Road and bumped past the big houses, the public lights had terminated. The houses were eerily dark, the exception being dim lamplight in the top windows of the imposing Beauchamp residence where Katherine Mansfield had lived before she had fled abroad, and whom Alexander knew so well from childhood picnics and outings. He had an image of her blowing a kiss to him as she entered her front gate on a summer's afternoon and he thought how alike she and Hortensia were, such beautiful women, clever, educated, and Katherine, he knew even then, destined for fame as a great writer.

"I wouldn't give tonight's events more thought, Alexander," Professor Karr said, as he idled the motor outside the Powderham residence. "There's nothing seditious about discussing a novel. That law is nonsense." The wind didn't seem to think so. It howled and both Alexander and MacPherson held their hats as the grumbling vehicle shuddered off. The gate was swinging back and forth, clanking against the rusted posts. The front door opened when the two men reached the verandah and Aroha stood smiling with a flickering kerosene lantern.

"Thought you'd run off," said Aroha as the wind tussled his long hair.

"Escape to Buenos Aires was on my mind. This is Mac," said Alexander. "A new friend for us, who may or may not be from Australia."

Candles were lit in an antique candelabra In the living room. Alexander tossed *The Metamorphosis* on the table and told Aroha: "Here's your copy, it's about a man who changes into an insect, which might be worth doing given the circumstances." He slumped into the leather sofa next to a good looking man he had never seen before.

"The power went off, the wind…" Aroha said. "And this is Muriwai."

Mac remained standing and observed the surroundings. One wall was entirely covered in oil paintings featuring a mountain. Persian carpets covered the floorboards. On a high inlaid Oriental table stood a bronze deity with multiple arms. "If that's the God of Arms, I'll get down and pray to it," he said, appearing in the candlelight as a supplicant in a temple.

"My great Uncle Percy brought it back from India. It's Kali, the destroyer of evil forces," said Alexander.

"We could do with a bit of her help," said Aroha coming in from the kitchen holding a tray with a plate of sandwiches, a bottle of whisky, a jug of water and four glasses.

"I reckon I can be a bit of a Kali and destroy some evil forces, even with just one arm," said Mac, looking at Alexander. He sat down, his eyes still on Alexander's and stretched his long legs, downed the whisky, and said: "That's much better. Bugger sedition, just get rid of the Meatyards."

"You reckon Kali can get them?" said Alexander, who had tossed back his whisky and had indicated to Aroha to pour again: "We're into the booze this evening, after what's been happening."

"You'd need more than an Indian goddess to get rid of the Meatyards," said Aroha. "And speaking of evil, you have a letter from your sister."

When they each had a new drink, he added: "One, two, three, down the hatch."

"This is good stuff," said Mac. "Must be from Otago?"

"Ah, so you do know New Zealand," said Aroha. "You sounded Aussie."

"I might be," Mac said. "But it's better to have secrets in wartime."

"Go on, you're amongst friends," said Aroha in English. Then in *te reo Māori* he said to Muriwai: "Tell them you're a policeman, but a bad one. He's a good-looking bloke, eh?"

Mac looked from one to the other and said in flawless *te reo*: "And why would you be a bad policeman, mate? And thanks for the compliment."

It was a stage play where everyone had forgotten their respective lines, for no one said a thing. Only the wind sounded as it slapped the shrubs against the windows. In *te reo*, Muriwai said: "You speak with the same accent as my Waikato-Tainui."

Alexander, who spoke reasonable *te reo*, laughed and said in English: "Damn it. This gets better and better."

Mac stood up, leaned down and kissed Muriwai's forehead before rubbing noses in a *hongi*. In *te reo* he said: "Looks like I'm with brothers, so long as you're a bad policeman and not a good one."

"I'm a constable, but sometimes it feels like the Devil's chasing me. My new mate here, he's been telling me not to worry about things. What did you call it? Political…" He looked around and downed his drink, and Aroha got up to pour him another.

"Political philosophy," Aroha said. "Māori used to be pretty good at it."

"That's it. Political philosophy. But you, Aussie mate," said Muriwai addressing Mac in a mix of *te reo* and English. "What you said about needing secrets in wartime, is right."

"Tainui-Waikato, eh? And I might be Aussie, and I might not. Depends, 'coz… 'coz of lots of things," Mac said in an accent that came directly from a New South Wales drover. "Anyway, better off being a Māori than an Aussie Abo, eh?" He stared at each of them before taking a drag on his cigarette. As he stubbed it out, he said in a Scottish accent: "That's what I love about life, it's so bloody complicated, it makes it worth living no matter if you're an Aussie pastoralist or a shopkeeper from Edinburgh." His laughter rolled out of him, and he had an image of buggering a long-haired and deeply sun-darkened man. In the background to that felicitous encounter were hundreds of sheep bleating in the sun. He said: "I've got so many memories, they just come bursting out. I did a bloke in a shearing shed. And one in Auckland who had just got off a ship from Scotland, been here five minutes. When it was done, he bowed and said: 'Thank you, sir, you're an expert at it."

"I reckon you'll be copying how someone in here talks by this time tomorrow," said Aroha. "But which accent, is the question."

"Language changes in me, depending on what man I'm with. The accent just comes out. Sometimes it's wrong, but men like it, the screw, that is."

"Fair enough," Alexander said, scowling, holding up the letter. "Let's see what language I'll be speaking when I read this. But it'll be with a forked tongue, I bet." With the antique letter opener that Aroha handed him, Alexander sliced open the envelope and said: "This'll be drama, being from my sister. Edwina Castle, bless her, said tonight that the Soviets are banning the family. I wish we had that here too."

"Only cold-hearted *Pākehā* could say that. What do you think, Muriwai, Constable Munu?" asked Aroha, looking over his gold rimmed glasses, thinking what a good thing it was to have this family around him. "*Munu.* Lucky you to be named after the moon. Powderham. Can you believe *Pākehā* names? Powder a ham? Mine means Lazarus, Aroha Raharuhi, Love Lazarus." They all laughed, the whisky had set in. Aroha pulled a face and repeated his name as an imperative in English and said: "Munu, you belong with this family now." Looking at MacPherson, he said: "You too, mate."

"I would've shot my old man, if I'd had the chance. Well, I did have the chance and I didn't, but I would have half a dozen times, silly old bastard. That's called patricide, if I remember. I've got two Māori half-brothers up there somewhere," said Mac in an upper-working-class Wellington accent. He pointed to the ceiling and then turned and pointed north. "Waikato, up there in the bush." He gulped his whisky. "Bugger of a place, full of swamps and conmen and landgrabbers. Māori still fighting for it."

"I hope he's a good drunk, not a bad one, because he's going to be drunk very soon," thought Alexander. "But I've got my men here to protect me."

"That was the sort of bloke my father was, so good riddance to him if that's what family is," said Mac. "I reckon us Pansies make our own family." He looked around, studying what this wealthy man had and he didn't. "Bloody dragged me through the bush in the Waikato and Māori brought me up. They did a better job than he did and for that I'm grateful. But look at me. Look at this." He moved what was left of his arm as if to indicate this body, this person, this experience, this world.

"I am looking," said Aroha. "And it's pretty good." He exchanged a look with Alexander as he knelt on both knees to take off Alexander's shoes. As he slipped off Alexander's socks, he turned, caught Mac's eye, and winked. Then, with practiced hands, he gently undid the metal brace and slid it off as he held up Alexander's leg.

"There you go," he said. "Released from prison."

"My Bastille," said Alexander. "My…Muriwai Munu, Water's End Moon, handsome boy, pass me my whisky."

"Ah, don't get me started on bloody prison," said Mac, standing, looking around him. "You got some beautiful things here, Alex, mate. Those oil paintings look right out of a gallery. Must be Europeans painted them, not Kiwis. The strokes are too fine. What's his name, this artist?" he said, pointing to a portrait of a young Māori woman in a feather cape and with a tattooed chin, a child on her back.

"Gottfried Lindauer," said Alexander as Aroha massaged his leg. "He escaped Austrian conscription. Funny how so many of us have to. Our much-missed friend, Freddy, said he'll be a millionaires' artist one day." Alexander watched MacPherson looking at the oil paintings, his body half shadowed, as if in a portrait by Goya or Rembrandt in a painting titled: *The Returned Soldier* or *The Convict.* He laid the unread letter on the sofa and said: "I have to take off my trousers, anyone mind?"

Aroha returned from the kitchen with a wooden tub of warm water and laid it at Alexander's feet. "Help me pull down his trousers, will you," he said to Muriwai. And to Mac: "Get the coal from the kitchen. Ah, mate, if you can."

Mac returned with the coal bucket gripped in his hand and said: "I've done a lot with one hand since its mate got chopped off. Including pulling that bugger out of the bookshop." He squatted and placed coals onto the fire with tongs, while blowing on it, then looked around and said: "Reckon we might not see the last of that, but tomorrow I'll look into it."

Aroha helped Alexander to stand, awkwardly after the whiskies, then he and Muriwai began to undress him as Mac watched, his back to the glowing fire, a cigarette in his mouth, a whisky in his hand. Once Alexander had been undressed to a tight white cotton vest and knee-length underpants, Muriwai said: "Gosh! Good looking man."

"You think all Pansies are pretty, do you? Or just white ones?" said Alexander, looking at Aroha, who smiled with a look that said, "Oh, Alex!"

"I like older white ones much more," Muriwai said. "Brown is good, too, especially ones who ask intelligent questions." With directions from Aroha, he helped Alexander sit down. Squatting in front of him, Aroha gently took Alexander's gammy leg, which he began to massage.

"My story is, and I'm not drunk, much, that I'm a good cop, not a bad one. I'm here tonight for a reason…" said Muriwai looking at Aroha, who nodded, and then at Alexander and Mac. "My reason, I mean, I mean, that I don't want to go to war. I've got *whanau* to support. If I get knocked off, what happens to them in the village?"

"We won't let them get you," Alexander said. "You're too beautiful in every respect for that."

"They won't," said Aroha looking up at Alexander and smiling, seeing why, again, he lived with this *Pākehā.*

"Worry about it later," Mac said. "It's too late at night to think about wars. You're a good mate now, and a good cop, and you've got us to protect you." He downed his whisky, looked at the other's glasses, all of which needed filling, and set to it, stuffing a sandwich down as he did. "Good *kai*," he said. "You got a lady who makes them?"

"I'm the lady today because Orton is sick," Aroha said, pouring the water over Alexander's leg. "Lady Orton, more like it. But we can't have a woman here, they'd see too much." He took a wet towel, rubbed soap into it, and began to scrub Alexander's limb, gently, holding the withered ankle in his left hand. "Orton's a real Fairy, little wings even."

"A good Fairy," said Alexander. "Who keeps her little Fairies in line."

"Good Fairies for our protection," said Mac. "I'll be your good Fairy. I promise you that. I'm a full Pansy and I'm sick of being done in by people like that hag who called my mate here an Oscar Wilde." He asked Muriwai for a light, and when he cupped his hand around the match, he touched Muriwai's fingers, lightly, enough to feel the tips, and Muriwai pressed back. He addressed Alexander, proud of his new position and this job he had acquired: "It's time to act. I know you want that, and I'm here to fulfil it." He drew in on his cigarette and winked at Muriwai, who laughed at him. As Aroha was lifting Alexander's leg out of the tub, Mac knelt beside him and said: "It's my turn now, let me serve you, Alexander Powderham."

6

On the morning after their drunken night filled with intimacies, Alexander woke before the others and made himself a pot of tea. Bleary eyed and dry mouthed, he sat in the living room wearing only his Munster and Munster coat and a pair of his late father's velvet slippers. He opened the letter from his siblings.

"*Dear Alexander,*" the letter stated. Alexander didn't believe the salutation. There was nothing dear about it. The writing, small, turgid, as if spiders had squiggled their way across the paper with inky feet, was inimitably his sister's. He thought: "I should be a specialist in handwriting and catch criminals and divulge their secrets and intentions because this handwriting is an example of such." However Lydia, his sister, had no such need for hidden meanings, for she came right to the point:

Me and our brother Pip have come to the conclusion that you have stolen our rightful property by cheating us out of our inheritance and since you are a criminal of the unnatural nature, we intend to contest this in court. Please be advised that if you do not conform to our request and release the property you stole by deviance from our Father after his death, we will now, finally, get our solicitors to act.

We will be at the house at eleven o'clock on Thursday next, by train from Featherston. We will make our way up from the Wellington Train Station and be there and if you could please make sure that that Māori is not there as I find it offensive as does Pip that you have a Māori ensconced in our sacred family home in which we lived and that we will therefore make an issue of it if he is there and we will not tolerate it any longer desecrating the sanctity of our Father who didn't leave us the bookshop or house either because you held an unnatural hold over him due to your nature of deviance and the ways deviants like you can act with mischievous natures and ways to wriggle our Father around your little finger so that we were disinherited.

You will need to be there at the stipulated hour in order to make sure that we do not lose our tempers as we have suffered quite enough having had to live with our now deceased Mother since the age of fifteen and twelve respectfully when our Father actually did the wrong thing morally and got rid of our Mother with virtually nothing but an annual stipend and cut her out of the will and therefore me and Pip have been left destitute while you got everything and for what, we ask, for what?

We have our theories and Mr. Bernard Shingles our solicitor said it is not legal for a woman to be left with such an unfortunate situation by being expelled from the household and that this is an unfortunate situation because you benefitted unduly with having had an education right up to university level and that we were stuck in the Wairarapa and had no advantages and now at our two ages respectfully we feel that at least there is a need for providing us with some recompense and for expenses that we have endured with no assistance such as you have had in your life and that as you are single and seems you will remain so given your unnatural nature we are bidding our solicitor Mr. Bernard Shingles (Shingles and Sons Solicitors, 166 Sussex Street, Featherston).

Mr. Shingles has a telephone which you can contact him by if you go through a telephone operator but you will know how to do that given your high and mighty status which you have by the very fact that we were not privy to an upbringing such as yours as Mother was not as well educated nor did she do well by remarrying our Step Father who, as a carter, had very few advantages and as you see Pip and I at this age and with the deaths of our Step Father and our Mother we find ourselves in a peculiar situation what with the war and the general state of things without the comforts of life we feel we should be entitled of such. Far be it for me to want to say things about you publicly because of your high position in Wellington society but we have no choice but to bring to your attention that we have been treated illegally and that we will now embark on what Mr. Bernard Shingles calls "redress".

Kindly telephone Mr. Shingles and arrange for the compensation and means of address which he will inform you of. Mother did not also take all of her belongings when she was kicked out and including the jewellery including the pearl necklace she was given by her Grandmother on the occasion of their wedding. There are also her other jewels and necklaces that we believe we should have, Pip and me, and also I would like to know if there are still her dresses as I am sure they were packed up and put with moth balls in cases in the attic as Aunty Betty has informed me and that we would like to see them for sentimental sakes and to have them back as they were hers and she was too upset ever to ask for them once she had been chucked out so unceremoniously. And therefore, when you see us on Thursday, I will expect to have that presented to me, not Pip, for he does not have a wife as he is too poor to marry and we have other situations to engage in when in Wellington so we will be there at eleven promptly and gone by eleven thirty.

Your sister and brother,
Lydia and Pip McCartan

Cupping his head in his hands, Alexander saw the handsome Raskolnikov in his wretched Saint Petersburg tenement, dressed in his equally wretched garments. But with longing he envisaged Raskolnikov's hands, which he knew were those of an aesthete. Held between those long bony fingers, which Alexander wanted desperately to kiss, was the letter from his mother, Pulcheria Alexandrovna Raskolnikov, in which she detailed in exquisite agony in her very long letter the terrible things that had befallen her and her daughter, Dounia. All the Slavic subterfuge and horror that had set in motion the rest of the dense yet moving novel, was laid bare in that anguished mother's tormented letter. Alexander could see so clearly that vast and flattened landscape upon which the two impoverished genteel women had been forced to travel endless miles in a peasant's ramshackle open cart.

In Alexander's mind the ghastly characters, as described in the mother's letter, appeared in the cart as it rattled across the mystical

Steppes towards Saint Petersburg: Svidrigailov the lecher; his wife Marfa Petrovna whom Svidrigailov had murdered; the despicable, grasping, petty bourgeois Lushkin; the gullible, accusatory townspeople.

"Just as Lydia and Pip will come chugging across the mountains in a rattling rail carriage to Wellington," he muttered into his hands. With a feeling of deep presentiment, Alexander squeezed his head between his hands and uttered: "I knew there was a reason for *Crime and Punishment* turning up. Just that title was enough for these times. For me now in my murderous state of frustration and resentment, it's a guide." He carefully folded the letter and, with equal precision, he slid it into the envelope, which he laid on the table, the faces of King George V and Queen Mary of Teck staring back at him. The Queen might have been sucking something sour and He, as He surveyed His staring subject in the cold living room in Wellington, had, in Alexander's mind, the eyes of a witness to the murders of His blood line, Tsar Nicholas and His Tsarina Alexandra and their royal children. Their respective fates had been sensational news in the Wellington newspapers since the Revolution and, some five months later, the world was still shaking at the momentous murders.

"Olga, Tatiana, Maria, Anastasia, Alexei," recited Alexander, in a litany of horror, as he analysed the chances and vagaries of history. "I could have been a Russian Alexander and ended up murdered in a revolution. Here, as an Alexander, I'm merely a crippled Pansy at the mercy of philistines." The images of the royal children shot and dumped in a mine on top of each other with the Bolsheviks celebrating in the name of the Soviet people rushed around Alexander's mind. "What is it about Russians? It's Pavlov again. I get the tremors just looking at these pompous English royals on a stamp and go wild."

There seemed to Alexander to be psychology all over the place, and he saw what it had led to. Everything was about the mind and feelings and was wrapped up in words that these Europeans threw at the world in the name of scientific progress: Dostoyevsky, Pavlov, Freud, Jung, Titchener, Nietzsche; all of whom Alexander had studied. As he finished off the cold tea from his Wedgewood teacup, seeing the Slavic characters rushing across the steppes in a peasant's rickety cart and the Russian oligarchs mutilated, he knew why he had so willingly drunk almost a bottle of whisky and then tumbled around in bed all night with three handsome men.

He shook his head. "Quite enough of this constant analysing, all with psychological thinking," he thought as he tucked the hate filled letter adorned with the British aristocracy into his coat pocket in order that he not have to see either it or them. "Surely the physical pleasures are all we have left." Unsteadily, without his cane, he got to his feet, took off his coat and threw it on the sofa and leaning on the furniture and walls for support, made his way naked to the bathroom.

Mac was up and dressed and smoking when Alexander returned to the living room, still naked.

"Here's that book, *Crime and Punishment*," said Mac looking admiringly at Alexander. "Read me the parts about the Napoleon theory you were all talking about, where the big man has the right to kill for a good reason." He moved the Munster and Munster coat just as Alexander was about to sit on it and, carefully stroking out the wrinkles, he took it to the vestibule and hung it on a hook.

"You should ask the Tsarina's children about the legitimacy of murder for a supposed good reason. Olga, Tatiana, Maria, Anastasia and Alexei. It's poetry, isn't it? Olga, Tatiana, Maria, Anastasia, Alexei. Such beauty. And now all just of the imagination with the horror of what happened to them."

"Cheer up mate. Everyone knows the revolution had to happen. Those Russians were all suffering from their royals. Sit here and read to your boy." He put his arm around Alexander's bare shoulders. "I can be a good little boy when I want to be. Read me about why your good mate Raskolnikov wants to kill old ladies."

Alexander, happy, excited, nestled against Mac, opened the novel and flipped through the sections, worn and dog eared, and read to his willing student.

"I got it," Mac said, finally, downing his cup of tea and stubbing out his cigarette. "I see what it's all about." His eyes had that roughish, shifty look that had beguiled Alexander in the street. "I need a bit of theory behind me before I do a job. It's like the horse races, you need to study a bit. You can't just back one 'coz you like its name. My old man didn't get that. He'd bet on some nag just 'coz it was called Moorish Moonlight or Dainty Delilah." He gently took Alexander's hands and kissed them, first the fingers on his left hand, then those on the right, and he sucked the index finger.

"There might be too much meaning in all of this, and I could be on a slippery slope, but it's exciting, and I love it," thought Alexander. "I'm alive again."

As he maneuvered the lighting of another cigarette, Mac said: "Give me five quid, would ya? And by the way, I'll borrow your hat." He was standing above Alexander, close enough to push his leg against Alexander's withered one, spreading apart Alexander's legs. The hat was on the chair by the sofa, and he picked it up and fitted it to his head as a man would a disguise, a wig or a false beard, tilting it foppishly, in Alexander's style. He smiled, his jaw jutting, his lips a thin crease, and he puckered a kiss. Alexander, seated, naked, his delicate Wedgewood teacup in his hand, the little finger pointed, his heart beating, his mind aflutter, looked up at Mac and thought: "Am I Madame Bovary or Rodion Romanovich Raskolnikov, or a terrible mixture of both?"

"You know," Mac said. "We should have our portrait taken by that photographer who takes photographs of men like us. He's got a whole gallery of them hanging in his studio, all sorts of poses. He's a little Fairy and he loves taking photos of Māori Fairies and *Pākehā* Pansies together, with classical pillars and artificial white roses strewn all around. There's one of a Māori chappie lying in the grass with the sun on him, he's got his best suit on and he's smiling at the camera. I love that photo so much. When I'm rich, I'll buy it."

"Robert Gant was the only Englishman I ever liked," said Alexander, languidly. "He always said: 'Hello, I'm a confirmed bachelor'. I think I should say that by way of introduction. It's so immediately convincing about what we are, we Pansies."

"Just one look would tell us that, mate. But you're not a bachelor, anyway. You're a married man and I reckon Aroha's the lucky one and I know which one is the husband now. I'm jealous." Mac laughed loudly and threw his head back and in that pose Alexander wanted Robert Gant to flash his camera because this man, the enigmatic bad boy in the fop's floppy hat, was so beautiful.

Alexander said: "Don't do anything in that hat that you shouldn't because it's the only one in Wellington like it."

"Mate, I'm a cuckold now, so I wouldn't put you into jeopardy. Not you, mate. Mate, just one other question: Do you think Raskolnikov was a Pansy, too?"

"Elizabeth should have posed that to the book group, don't you think?" said Alexander, feeling content that here was his family, his brother, his friend, talking like this when out there in the world they were castigated for their perverted proclivities. "Raskolnikov was handsome and tormented, so he must have been."

"So, it's for him too, I'll get the Meatyards," said Mac. He blew a kiss and went down the passage to the front door, taking Alexander's coat from the coat hook.

Mac MacPherson shut the front gate and looked up at the house and smiled in satisfaction at the imposing mid-Victorian eaves and decorations, all elegant but in need of a paint. "I'll get to that," he thought. "Cream and white would be nice, with red and grey detailing." It was a house much like the one he'd lived in with another rich Pansy, a fiction writer, on the outskirts of Adelaide. He smiled at the thought of that old geezer fawning over him. And on reflection, as he looked at the garden and thought how the mulberry bushes could go and how roses would be nicer, that old geezer was not unlike the Fairy artist in Melbourne where he'd learned how to assess paintings under such strict tutelage. "All better than a Waikato jail," he thought as he made his way past the naked ladies and snow drops poking through the rusty balustrade.

The stench of the jail cells, however, was what he smelled, not spring flowers, the sordid smells wafting dangerously. He waved his hand across his face to shoo away that powerful reminder of that life he wanted dismissed forever, but what he smelled instead was the happier combination of Muriwai, Aroha and Alexander. Then, in his new hat and Alexander's appropriated Munster and Munster coat, he made his way down an asphalt zig-zag lined with wild fennel and yellow tea roses and went on his mission to see what he could accomplish in the name of his new best mate and that Russian bloke, Raskolnikov.

7

It was ten o'clock in the morning when MacPherson arrived at the narrow wooden house in Kenneth Row, a crooked street of workers' cottages that ended in a tangle of pines and blackberries in the hills at the back of Newtown. A dog that seemed to be smiling rushed to the gate when she saw him.

"Yeah, yeah Eskimo, everyone loves MacPherson," he said, leaning down to pat the dog's head. A row of purple, blue and crimson cineraria mingled with cineraria in the garden, and in the small porch hung a birdcage in which three yellow canaries sang. The front door opened and Rebecca Routledge, a woman in her late twenties, appeared. Her auburn hair was tied up with a red ribbon and she wore a loose fitting, red, silk dressing gown.

"Oh, yes?" she said, smiling. "And what promises of fortune do you bring this morning?" She turned to the yapping dog and said: "Eskimo, darling, he's harmless now, with just the one arm."

"Yeah, it's not my coat, you bugger," he said. "Don't tear it."

"Where did you steal that from? Been in Karori with posh clients, have you?"

"I got a job for you, Rebecca," he said. "Worth a quid."

"Oh, good, just in time. The landlord put up the rent again," she said, looking across the street to the neighbours from where she knew that snoop would be spying out the window, barely disguised behind the net curtain. "You'd think prices would go down in wartime not up, wouldn't you?" She led Mac down a narrow passageway and into a low-ceilinged room furnished with a green sofa, two blue arm chairs and a kitchen table draped with a clean white cloth around which were placed four stools each topped with an embroidered cushion. On the table in a white china vase, was a bright bunch of cineraria.

"How's Jimmy? Any word? They should never have voted in conscription for married men, leaving their wives to cope like you," he said, taking off his hat. "Light me up, Rebecca" he added, handing her the matches and cigarettes. "Bloody hard with only one hand."

"They sent him back to the trenches from a hospital in Sussex. The hospital said he'd recovered from his shellshock, but he said he's got the shakes so badly he couldn't hold a gun. But the letter was two months old, and the censors had blacked out parts of it." She lit his cigarette before lighting her own. "So, who knows what anymore? I haven't heard from him for three months. And how am I supposed to make a living with two children and the rent going up and everything costing a fortune?" She drew on her cigarette and held it aloft as if on further examination she had decided it was poisonous. "These things have increased in price by forty percent. When the Government decided to conscript married men, well, that was the end of it wasn't it? The cost of everything's exploded."

"Why would they send a man back when he's had two years of trenches and gets the wobbles?" he asked as she went into the lean-to kitchen and brought back an ashtray.

"If he gets back, I'll look after him given the sacrifices he's made for us. I admire him." She had the veneer of someone older and worldlier than her age. She pulled her dressing gown closer and smiled as if her mind was far away: "I really miss Jimmy. But I just can't afford to live on pennies. Mac…"

"You always look so pretty. I admire your beauty."

"The one that I have to sell?"

"Well, don't we all? I'm still in the game with one arm, but some blokes fall for it. Don't know why, it just seems to appeal to them. But I want Jimmy back, too."

"I'm sorry, really, about what I've become, but I can't support two kids and his mother on the government handout. Even when I had a job they barely paid me. So much for doing men's work, they don't pay men's wages." She gave a bitter laugh. "I can do accounts. I did my old man's for years at the racetrack and never missed a figure and he said: 'You're better than a bloke at numbers, and self-taught for that,' but when I applied for numbers jobs, the bosses just laughed."

"It's a bastard, eh? The way we have to make a living. Not a lot of men into this game, but it's a living, and what can a man do with only one arm?"

"Oh, go on, Mac. You were doing this long before you went off. You've got charm and good looks, but what will you do when they vanish, I wonder? Better settle down with some good bloke, one with money."

"Birds of a feather, but I reckon Jimmy would understand, if he knew. He was always very open about living. That's why we got on."

"I don't know if he would. But we had a nice little business, now all gone, wasted. That's what happened, just like that, conscripted, and off to fight for what? I admire the sacrifice, but not the cause." She looked about her clean and pretty room and felt a measure of reassurance. There was nothing else she could do but to stay intact somehow: a clean house, homegrown flowers, a vegetable garden, selling her body. She smiled at Mac and said: "When he used to write, he'd say the loveliest things and send me red poppies dried between the pages, but that all stopped when the shakes started. He writes only to his mother who I still support, and her sister who's gone potty." She waved vaguely at the wall, in a direction somewhere to her left, over there, across an eternity of worries, as if to indicate that's where his mother lived, in the streets on the hilly, dark side of Newtown where her children stayed so she could carry on her business.

"You don't need to explain to me, Rebecca, I understand. You're a good wife and mother. It's circumstances, and don't listen to anyone who says otherwise. The ones born with a silver spoon and those ones on about godliness, what do they know about reality? It's just a matter of looking after yourself if you know what I mean?"

"Well," she said. "I've got a few tricks to keep me clean and sane. Never with anyone I suspect of being infected, I have a good look. I can tell you, because…" She laughed and turned away. "Just to find out if they're leaking. Isn't that the secret? You'd know. And I only do military men above the rank of sergeant, and the occasional hobnob. They pay, and they're generally clean."

She left the room and returned with a wooden box which she opened to reveal a stack of letters, all in army envelopes. Her worldliness retreated and Mac saw her as she would be in ten years and something icy went through him. Another woman from long ago with unkempt hair and sad eyes appeared and he wanted to shout: "Mother! Mother!" In his mind she cried: "I never wanted to let you go, but I had to! I have to go!"

He said, with anger, his throat contracting, his hand shaking: "You got a job to do for me, Rebecca. I'll meet you outside the Duchess Tea Rooms in an hour." He stubbed out his cigarette, leaned down and kissed her forehead. But it was his long-departed mother he kissed, not this woman with auburn hair in a red silk gown. He left, quickly, forgetting Alexander's coat and hat. Outside, he kicked the smiling Eskimo and cursed her in a language he should not have used in public. Instead of turning left to catch the tram, he went right, towards the hills but saw in the neighbour's window two men, one old, one young.

"I'll get you for war shirking," Mac thought. "Snoop. Hypocrite." He watched them, the venom rushing about in his mind. His mother was there, so palpably as he stalked up the street, that it might have been all those decades ago when, in German, she had uttered those last words to him.

On entering the bush, he felt the cooler air. The darkness of the pines and flax, thick, shiny, green, and the birds calling he acknowledged for their beauty, but it didn't soothe him. He walked in further, up the damp pathway that led zig-jaggedly all the way to the top of the first hillock and then up and through the trees to the summit that overlooked the ramshackle streets of Newtown, sweating by the time he got there. Swirling in him was the anger, a hard-tough substance. When he looked up at the clouds rushing in the grey skies, he heard his mother uttering in her guttural language those words of abandonment.

The clouds and sky and a strengthening sun glistened, and to the north the green harbour sparkled. He might have been on that ship with that same anger as a boy. But he was on a hill overlooking higgledy-piggledy streets of wooden houses with smoke puffing from chimneys and not on that boat with his mother's mouth moving, her eyes looking down at him. He snarled: "*Ich* this and *ich* that and *weiß* this and *nicht* that. *Du bist. Liebling.* Ugly language. We should cut their fuckin' throats, all of them Huns. Hers too, a so-called mother."

He looked out to the Tinakori hills, at the base of which were the larger houses, from that distance just far away toys. He fidgeted with his cigarettes and matches and lit himself a smoke and thought: "Remember the motto, only the strong survive." On the strength of that, he said: "Get out, all of you," and dismissed the men behind the net curtain; the hurt in Eskimo's eyes; Jimmy shaking in the trenches; the last images of his mother. Drawing deeply on his cigarette, he lay back in the grass in the sun and shut his eyes and relived the night with Aroha and Muriwai and Alexander in that gracious house: the kissing, being told he was beautiful, uttering things he thought he never would have.

Rebecca Routledge arrived at the Duchess Tea Rooms on the hour exactly. She greeted him with a polite handshake as if they were merely acquaintances, tentative and cautious and not, as it were, prostitute and procurer. Her white dress fell to just above her ankles and over it she wore a fashionable grey coat that she had sewn. Her hat, which she had refashioned from one bought second hand, was modern and adorned with white satin roses.

"All set up for a wedding, are we?" he said.

She plucked biddy-bids from his sleeve and said: "Been in the bush, have we? Any crimes up there for you to be involved in?"

"Funny, ha-ha," he said. "I've been looking for the bloke I want you to meet. He's usually about now, that geezer with the toupee wig thing who shouts about God and shirkers."

"That silly one with the New Zealand Women's Anti-German League? With the shrill wife?"

"That's the one. What do you know about him?"

"Nothing much. In Newtown she was shouting how Jesus had called and someone shouted: 'By telephone?' I wish they'd get my shirker neighbour who reckons he's a wharfie." She wanted a cigarette, but couldn't smoke in the street. She saw men smoking and said: "It's all right for some, isn't it?"

"Yeah, what?" he said, looking around.

"Hypocrisies, you know about that, what you've been through."

"Have a cuppa with me, my shout. I've got a few bob from a job this morning."

They went into the tea rooms and a waitress in a stiff linen uniform and equally stiff cap ushered them to a linen covered table by the window.

"I'll have custard cake," said Rebecca. She might have been a wealthy woman given the outfit, but her voice betrayed her. As the waitress' eyes met Rebecca's, they both acknowledged their respective status.

"So, what have you been up to, legally?" asked Rebecca.

"I've been reading this book called *Crime and Punishment*," he said.

"Did you write it?" She laughed and recalled laughing with him and her husband at a picnic at Otaki Beach years earlier. She had an impulse to get up and leave this situation that was leading her towards more degradation.

"Don't be like that. It's a good book all about why you can be a good murderer, when you can justify it, morally."

That warm Sunday on the beach at Otaki, seemingly decades past. A chill ran through her. She saw the man in the toupee with whom she was supposed to liaise and she wanted to run, to bolt. She said: "Really? Morality? Our Mac? But I'm sure you're only involved in nef… nef…" She looked at him for help with eyebrows raised.

"Nefarious. And I keep secrets in wartime." That stock phrase, used most recently on the previous evening, pulled him back to the night of whisky and men. He smiled and thought how much he wanted to be back there for another round of fun and mateship and lovemaking.

The waitress brought the tea and milk and sugar and laid the cups and saucers and looked at Mac with bovine eyes that smiled. Looking at Rebecca's, the cow-like smile disappeared and turned to something nasty. She said: "I'll be back with your…tart."

"Little minx," said Rebecca. "She left school early to work in a laundry but got sacked for being uppity, which she is, but God knows why. She lives in Newtown, for goodness' sake, with her so-called brother, a brute who wiggled out of the military through poor hearing." She saw her own situation, which wasn't much better: a woman in a flash dress and a pretty hat, both of which she had sewn from the rewards of prostitution. She thought: "If Jimmy comes back, we can move to the country and have sheep and fruit trees." It was a vision of a life with no reason to have illegal liaisons with men who sucked her breasts and climbed on top of her. "Jimmy liked you a lot, Mac. He understood your game. Funny enough, he said a real mate would give an arm and a leg for a mate, and you both sort of have." She laughed at the sorrowful irony and glanced out the window. "You're an enigma and a rough diamond and that's why Jimmy liked you. You were a good mate to him."

"And if he knew his mate was finding you work like this?"

The waitress plonked down the plate of cakes and looked at Mac and then at Rebecca and walked away.

"What's the book about?" Rebecca asked. "I'm reading *The Scarlet Plague* by Jack London, about an epidemic that wipes out just about everybody. The thought of plague and turning red and poof you're gone and the world is empty is so scary. The librarian put in restricted reading." As she opened her mouth to bite the custard cake he thought of Muriwai and Aroha opening their mouths and looking up at him.

"I loved it," he said.

"The war?" she asked, her cake poised at her lips.

"No, of course not," he answered, pouring the tea. "Some good things are very powerful. Unexpectedly, when something happens, something…lovely." He met her eyes and lowered his voice: "I want you to get that Meatyard. It's worth a quid."

"Two pounds. I won't ask why, but he's revolting."

"A bit of blackmail can go a long way," he whispered. "Give him a fright, he'll see things differently. In flagrante then squeeze him. There's money in it, I'll split it with you. He's been giving my mate a hard time."

She glanced out the window and exclaimed: "That's him. I can't Mac, not with that. He's ridiculous. Five quid or I won't."

"Blast," he said, signalling the waitress. "I'll get the wife out of your way. You get him for tonight."

8

Elizabeth Norris wore a navy-blue coat inherited from her Aunt Elspeth which she had unravelled and reconstructed in order not to appear as spinsterish as her aunt had after the death of Miriam, her lady companion. As she walked down Marjoribanks Street she wound the woollen scarf Helen had knitted her more tightly about her neck and imagined her aunt dressed in the blue coat before its refashioning, a Victorian handbag over her arm, her hat with black fascinator.

"She was never the same after Miriam died," Elizabeth thought, as she noted a sign in a shop window announcing whalebone corsets: "It's a salutary lesson. Don't get old and spinsterish." She stared with renewed horror at the restrictive garments forced on women. "I mustn't be like Elspeth who let Miriam's death ruin her. Elspeth's decline was just part and parcel of the lives our sort of women have to live. That in itself is seditious."

She continued down Marjoribanks Street following Mr. and Mrs. Bertram Therewold, whom she knew had been married for some forty years. She watched them trotting down the steep street, legitimate, upstanding, secure. "We should have lived in Lesbos," she thought, "where this might all be the opposite, where Helen and I could be the Therewolds. Where Elspeth and Miriam would have been normal as wife and wife."

An old man cowering at the corner held out his hand and said: "Please, Miss," but she was sick of him pleading there every morning when in his jacket pocket was always a bottle of methylated spirits. He wore an old fashioned hat like Raskolnikov's. "It's interesting how Dostoyevsky describes his characters' outfits in such detail," she thought. She imagined Alexander in his fashionable, foppish outfit becoming as filthy and decrepit as the garments worn by Raskolnikov.

As she stood on the corner waiting to cross, a horse neighed and a motorcar rattled. She felt her mind all jumbled up: the women in her life, none of whom were alive or in Wellington; Raskolnikov and Alexander; the previous evening's terrible carry-on with the vigilante.

"Seditious! Seditious!" The refrain had been with her all night, even when she had finally fallen asleep and had stumbled into dreams of judges banging gavels, and clowns juggling batons, and a man with one arm playing a violin and she yelling: "You can't fiddle with one hand." She stood looking at the horse, which lifted its tail and emitted its thick brown droppings in front of her as the coachman whacked its flank and shouted: "Hurry up, Nellie."

"Indeed," she thought, shaking her head to bring her back to reality.

She was about to cross at the corner of Cuba and Manners Street when she saw the one-armed man talking to that vituperous Mrs. Meatyard. A woman dressed in what she thought might be appropriate at a summer's race meeting but not on a cold mid-week morning, was talking to Mr. Meatyard. "This is like my dream filled with chaos and contradictions," she thought.

On reaching the corner of Tonks Grove, she saw with horror that the shop's plate glass windows had been smashed. Standing outside was Alexander and a policeman and, to her added horror, Crawford Denton, the detective associated with her deceased sister, Louisa. She retreated to Cuba Street where she turned and bustled along to the alleyway that led to a patch of ground littered with beer bottles. She opened her bag and pulled out her packet of *De Reszke*: "Really, God, if you exist, then what next?" she said as she lit the yellow cigarette, her hands shaking.

Alexander Powderham was seated in his office, Detective Crawford Denton opposite him. The bookshelves lining the walls and the soft lamp light and the vase of flowers provided a homely, intellectual ambience. He sensed the presence of his father who had spent two decades in the office.

"This is grievous, as we noted," Denton said. "A vandalised bookshop shows the depth of feelings these days what with a drawn-out war."

Elizabeth knocked on the door, pushed it open, and said: "This is disgraceful. Who did it? Alexander, I'm so sorry."

The detective looked at Elizabeth with disdain as he jolted to when she had first appeared in his life, as arrogant and haughty as she now appeared in her finery, barging in as if she owned the place.

"That ruffian did this, and under whose auspices?" said Elizabeth. "I'm going to smoke, despite my usual protocols and adherence to the subjugation of women."

"I want the notes the book group submitted. The police have been informed that things were said that shouldn't be under the War Regulations Act," said Denton. He was middle-aged, grey haired, with a nose that said he drank too much.

"The War Regulations Act enacted for a book group discussing a detective novel?" asked Alexander. He looked at Denton as he would have at the class bully. "I memorised parts of the Act because I knew it would rear its ugly head." He heard his father's enigmatic laugh, and began his recitation as if it were a favourite poem: "*The War Regulations Act is one that can supersede existing legislation, and that a despotic government is necessary in a national emergency*."

Alexander snorted as he thought back to the beginning of the War, when the Act was rushed through Parliament with those opposing it accused of being German-supporting traitors. "Hun supporters, the worst defamation, with the exception of being an Oscar Wilde," he thought.

"Very dramatic," said Denton. "It's a question of the law, of sedition in wartime." He looked from Alexander to Elizabeth, undecided about whom he most despised. "What does von Z mean on the blackboard? The book group contributions go to von Z. Explain that, please." Denton's eyes met Elizabeth's and she looked away. She saw him slinking out of her sister's bedroom. She heard her sister weeping.

"Professor von Zedlitz was dismissed from the University because of the Alien Teachers Act, as you very well know, that law being the work of a conservative bunch of paranoid politicians being swayed by uneducated populists ..." said Alexander.

"And why would you be fundraising for a German alien?"

"He's a naturalised New Zealander. You would know the circumstances as well as anyone, Detective. The press hounded him and the politicians followed. The entire University Senate voted to retain him. Is the entire Senate seditious?"

"You didn't answer why you're raising funds for him. And you know the law means that anyone naturalised is not exempt from being an agent of the enemy. You are therefore supporting the enemy financially, and that is grand sedition."

"Oh, grand sedition, like the Grand Inquisition, is it to be? Simple sedition wouldn't do for assisting a banished teacher? We help him and his New Zealand born wife because they're now destitute," said Alexander.

"He's one of the country's most respected academics and he's been treated appallingly," said Elizabeth, reaching past the detective without saying "excuse me" to stub out the half-smoked cigarette. She had been waiting for this situation for the two years since the book group had decided to donate their contributions to the von Zedlitz family.

"Sedition is sedition," said Denton. "I'll assess this. It raises more than an eyebrow."

"Yes, of course it would, *Crawford*," she said.

"It can't be overstated what a dangerous situation our country faces with Germans and their supporters. The informant said you're openly discussing the Russian Revolution and how that event is relevant to our country's current situation. I believe a Miss…Miss…" He pulled out a notebook and read: "*Hortensia Rutherford is an agitator, a socialist, advocating revolution in New Zealand in support of the Communists.*"

"For goodness' sake. Miss Rutherford a Communist agent? She's rich," exclaimed Alexander. "Hortensia a Rosa Luxemburg? What manifest fantasy."

"Then why is she a simple teacher? Well dressed? A woman? And an infiltrator? The notes say she's a Smart Alec, well informed about Russian affairs, detailed facts about revolution…"

"And freedom of speech?" asked Alexander "Critical analysis of a novel written in the eighteen-sixties by the greatest Russian writer?" He smiled at his revelation and saw himself as if suspended and looking down into his shop filled with books on topics anyone might like to ask for: ancient techniques of breadmaking; ritual pollution in Hinduism; Samuel Butler's theory of New Zealand being a social laboratory; the distinctions between Medieval and Renaissance painting; Māori links to Tahitian mythology. Recent customer enquiries passed through his mind in an erudite inventory; he saw the faces of the people making the requests: the delightful Mrs. Mill for the breadmaking; the eccentric Reverend Ramsbottom seeking information on ritualised phallic worship in Hinduism; the handsome student with the ginger moustache he, Alexander, had wanted to kiss, asking about egalitarianism in the new colony; the haughty Kelburn woman enquiring as to when iconography transitioned into secularism in European art; and Miss Stone-Wiggs, who always wore white, seeking information on Māori mythology and its links across the wider Pacific.

"Maronite ideology? Would that be as equally seditious in the circumstances?" Alexander asked, rising with the aid of a shell embedded Italian cane and limping to the bookshelf from which he plucked a leather-bound volume, the title of which he read: *l'Histoire du Traité du Mont Liban*. He glanced at Elizabeth, her mouth ajar in a mixture of surprise and delight, and to the detective, who looked bilious.

"This is what someone brought to me to sell. I won't say who that was because when the War is over, I will return it to her. But the authorities accused this woman of being an enemy alien because she's from a part of the Ottoman Empire. Yet she's a Maronite Christian and fled Ottoman hegemony for New Zealand because, as she said, 'It's the place furthest in the world from the Ottomans and it's Protestant and therefore democratic'. And now they're being hounded for being enemies." He thought with some regret that he may have divulged too much about his customer to whom he had given a handsome price for the collection of historical texts on Levantine history because, like von Zedlitz, her family had been ruined financially.

"Try not to sell them," she had said in her lilting French-Arabic accent. "I'll be back. All wars end, but in the meantime, we're going underground and need the money." He placed the tome on the desk as if to invite Denton to peruse it, to dig deeper into the existential questions that had just been posed. He adjusted his tie and thought: "What is it about human hatreds?"

The three of them remained silent, each in their respective thoughts: The detective on his need for alcohol and the state of his stomach, which ached with something he was sure was cancer; Elizabeth about how silly this all was and how it might end in jail, humiliation, and yet more revenge. And Alexander pondering how at one moment he could be in the arms of three virile men making love and then in the next being faced by philistine accusations of something as absurd as sedition. This in a country with more cows than humans and one 12,000 miles from Europe, where ancient cities were being bombarded. He knew the situation clearly: Belgium decimated; cathedrals burned; Paris being blasted by Big Bertha. It was just all wrong and for a moment he saw why Denton was right: Germany was viciously militaristic and everyone had to be protected from its Prussian arrogance and cruelties. He wanted to cry out for the Levantine family, the Finks, the people receiving telegrams about their dead soldiers, the whole bloody thing was ridiculous, and humans were bestial in their complex and distorted games of hatreds.

"I'm not sure I like your tone, Mr. Powderham," said Detective Denton, eventually. "While I understand this might be an elite group, there are enemies of the state, and we need to assess them in order to protect that state."

"In the same way as you assessed the six, single Kelburn teachers who held a party or two for departing officers. You arrested them on grounds of running an immoral establishment because the women bought the alcohol and some of the men stayed overnight? Are we going to see a repeat of that farce, *Crawford*?" Elizabeth said, as she imagined him touching her sister, leaning in to kiss her. "We're intellectuals, unashamedly, and so was Louisa, which is why you followed her. She had a brain and was educated, and you wanted that from us, a step up the ladder, despite the paradox of your views on women." She might have added that her sister had wanted to climb down the social escape ladder. Instead, she caught herself and saw clearly the grief she had stored inside for her beloved sibling. She had a vision of scratching Denton, slapping him, but she closed her eyes and saw Louisa laughing. She said, opening her eyes and looking at him: "I've knitted seventy-three pairs of socks for soldiers in the past three years, seven blankets, collected hundreds of items for soldiers. Doesn't that make me a supreme patriot? Or is this retaliation for Louisa?"

Alexander shook his head and said: "Elizabeth, a word outside, please." He opened the door, held it for her, closed it behind them and whispered: "Don't bring Louisa into this. This will lead to jail. I should get my lawyer."

"And you're giving away secrets about Farida Zemba. He'll tell the Australian police to get them."

"Oh, dear…"

The bravado she had just admired was wilting. In a minute he would sink. She said: "Gonads, Alex, you do have a couple, I presume. Go back in there and demand an apology."

A woman in the shop laughed, even though she would not have heard that remark. A workman banged nails into boards being put up to replace the windows. Shirley appeared at the end of the passageway looking like Jane Eyre in her too-long, grey dress frock, her prominent nose silhouetted, and in her inimitable voice, high pitched, sweet, like a choirboy's, she said: "It's very esoteric, Matilda, and I utterly advise it." Elizabeth and Alexander laughed, these two who for years had provided confession and benediction to each other.

"Actually, you're right. I abandoned the Finks," he said:

"For goodness' sake, Alex, you gave them a hundred pounds. You won't rent their building in the hope they'll return."

"So, what was this about gonads?"

She patted his arm and whispered: "It's *my* head that's rattling about with all this sedition nonsense."

Detective Denton was looking at a map in the book about Maronites when Elizabeth and Alexander entered. "This is the area where the fighting is going on in Palestine," he said, looking up. "My nephew's there. We received his letter from Palestine, remarkable stamps, he says it's a beautiful country, a lot of Bedouin. He's there with the…" But he stopped, closed the book, looked about and said: "I'll be investigating this case closely. My last question is about the books your group has read this year, which my informant gave me the list of."

Elizabeth and Alexander exchanged looks. There was no list, not one specifically compiled, and certainly not one available without the assistance of an insider. But conspiracies were secondary to this first act of survival, and they dropped their respective surprise and merely questioned each other with a raised eyebrow.

"Five books by Germans or Russians. Why would that be? Don't you like our own writers?" said Denton.

"And who would our writers be?" asked Alexander. "Can you name a New Zealand Dickens or Kafka?"

"In fact, we did read one of our own, as you say, *Crawford*," Elizabeth said, sounding, she knew, too sarcastic, but now, equally, with no care for restraint. "Katherine Mansfield *In a German Pension*. I imagine you can use that against us. Her father's Harold Beauchamp, the Governor of the Bank of New Zealand as you know, so perhaps you could also question his patriotism because his wife accompanied Katherine to Prussia. It's there that she wrote this book about Germans, of all things seditious. A whole book about them, most of it quite flattering." She looked at Alexander, who was leaning against the bookshelf with all the appearances of one who was, in fact, seditious, his black linen jacket wrapped about him, his mirthful scowl, a Heathcliff or a Raskolnikov, intelligent, arrogant, mysterious – and mad. He only needed to be wearing that luxurious red turban to be the medieval man painted by van Eyck, a print of which hung in her living room.

Facing the detective, she said: "Indeed, *Crawford*, we could have read *Mexico as I Saw It* or *A Girl's Ride Across Iceland*, both by Mrs. Ethel Alec-Tweedie, a lady's travel diarist. You know she was popular before the War, if I may mention *the War* without being thought seditious, *Crawford*." She saw this man in her home on Marjoribanks Street when Louisa was dying, he with a bunch of wilting pink carnations, his head hanging.

Denton saw the facetiousness ooze from her, as it always had. It was as Louisa had insisted: "My sister is a stuck-up pompous know-it-all, and I can't stand that about my family."

"I need all the notes, especially Miss Rutherford's," he said, standing up. "I understand you, Elizabeth, from our..." He was about to say the words, but he dropped them, just as he had those pink carnations outside her house. The ensuing silence, however, said everything they knew about him: a bitter past of wives and women and infidelities; his alcoholism. Denton could see their assessment of him: class, status, education, looks, addictions. His anger was palpable, he wanted whisky and gin, brandy, all mixed together as he looked at them: the perverted Fairy who had sexual relations with deviant Māoris; and this imperious woman who engaged in filth with other females.

"The notes," he said, angrily. He held out his hand as if she were presenting them to him, but she sniffed and looked at the ceiling.

"You'll need a court order," said Alexander. "And you'll need to make sure that you don't do to us what you did to von Zedlitz because we really are New Zealanders. And those Kelburn women teachers you humiliated for having some farewell parties and whose case against them was dismissed by the High Court for its misguided insinuations about perversions, ludicrous, Denton. Be careful."

"Gosh," said Denton, trying to be equal with the intelligentsia but knowing the subtleties in the distinctions of his class and status in this supposedly egalitarian nation were deficient. His voice, even his hat and coat, were all weapons against him. He heard Louisa say: "I don't know what I saw in you, that initial excitement has vanished."

"The State has sent a lot of politicians to prison for sedition. Booksellers, no matter how high and mighty, are not exempt," he said. He mentally slapped them. "War issues aside, that Māori you hide in your house you're so close to, there are other criminalities we investigate." He picked up his hat, squashed it down on his head, and went out.

9

Cecil Meatyard was a man not too selective by nature, a condition tied closely to opportunism. For that reason, when he had spied an opening with the New Zealand Women's Anti-German League as being potentially advantageous for his wife, and by extension, for himself, he had pushed her towards it. Sybil Meatyard, always someone to take up a cause, and who saw her country as being overrun by German militarists, Chinese goldminers, Dalmatian gum diggers, Levantine haberdashers, and the general riff-raff of migrant flotsam and jetsam, had presented well when interviewed by the august group of society women who had brought together their fears and aspirations to found the New Zealand Women's Anti-German League. Under that glorious name, as their manifesto proclaimed, the League was intent upon purifying the country and ensuring that everyone eligible went off to war to serve the interests of King and country. So, with Sybil happily ensconced in her patriotic work, and earning a good wage at it, Mr. Meatyard could go about his own business being freed, at last, from the financial constraints that had plagued him since childhood. He had, for the past three years or so, enjoyed his unpaid place on the soapbox and the daily frenzies of the spectacle all in support of his wife's campaign for righteousness, not much of which he believed in.

Upon agreeing to meet Rebecca that evening "to discuss war shirkers and religion in general," Mr. Meatyard walked through the town and then, embracing the wind with fortitude, he strolled around to Oriental Parade, that long stretch of seaboard. Plump, happy, satisfied, he made his way, swinging his arms, towards the water. Where Oriental Parade emerged at the beach, he paused, despite the wind, and looked back, westwards, across the harbour and town and up to the green Tinakori hills where he lived. His abode was on Saint Mary's

Street, just off Tinakori Road, close to the Botanic Garden, and under the hills where the houses were not grand Victorian residences but held their own as superior villas. Beyond these respectable dwellings were the mean cottages of the poor, a class he came from, but which he now saw as a distant memory to be forgotten.

Cecil Meatyard was unable to have two thoughts simultaneously; one had to leave completely before the other could squeeze in. The assignation with the tart, he thought gleefully, was his conduit to Mac, and he sniggered. That upcoming adventure was now the one thought in his head, it having returned after the self-congratulatory snippet about his superior dwelling had departed.

"The silly bugger didn't even recognise me," he said into the wind. "He'll get a shock when he does. Fancy thinking I'd want that tart." Assessing the time it would take to have a bite to eat and complete his business at the residence of the banker's wife, he sauntered along the waterfront to the Olde York Teashop, where he placed himself at the window table, scratched in his toupee and signalled for service.

"Windy again, isn't it, sir," said the woman who came to serve him. "Tea and sandwiches do?"

"With a cream cake," he said, straightening his green tweed waist coat.

"Bloody Wellington," he thought. "Whoever thought we'd end up in this windswept seaport?" The dark green, turgid water reminded him of the Tainui bush that he had spent a decade ripping out and burning. "Bloody Māoris. If it weren't for them, we'd be rich."

"A cream cake, sir," said Mrs. Mabel Stonehouse, the proprietress of the Olde York Teashop. "And a pot, I can pour if you want," she added cheerfully. She knew some men couldn't, wouldn't, pour their own tea, while some women, even ladies, wanted to. One could never tell which group of tea drinkers anyone belonged to, those who poured and those who did not, not these days anyway. Once upon a time everyone would have expected their tea poured for them. It had been enough to ask if they required milk before picking up the pot and pouring, careful not to spill, because for Mrs. Stonehouse there was nothing worse than spillage. Spillage, or avoiding such, was within one's control and she found it remarkable that people actually spilled when pouring, especially semi-professional men, notably clerks, and younger women, usually those not married, or elderly women recently widowed and in the first stages of grieving.

On other big issues she had similarly long surmised that it was a confusing world. Change, generally, was one such issue, and like the pouring of tea, which had always been the preserve of the waitress, one tried to avoid, for the constant changing of things simply meant disorder. And disorder caused by change was, in her mind, what had led to this war and the situation that she found herself in with two grandsons fighting in the trenches. Nevertheless, she endured it all and knew she had to be strong in order to deal with such issues. She therefore said, very nicely: "I know you from where I see you doing your lectures, on the street, with your lady wife, I assume that's who she is, she's a very good speaker, she gets everyone excited."

"Very kind of you," he said, satisfied that his fame was well entrenched in the capital city.

"My two grandsons are over there fighting the enemy," she said looking out the window but seeing not the lowering skies nor the waves crashing over the seawall, but her two boys in their uniforms marching down Lambton Quay some eighteen months previously when she had farewelled them off amongst another load of reinforcements. "Very proud of them. The youngest one wrote he'd bought me a silver spoon in France, although his grandad said he'd probably looted it."

Mr. Meatyard, waiting for her to finish, toyed with his cake. She could have been his sister or sister-in-law or aunty or any other woman in his family what with those big worn hands, that large-jawed face, all of which were giveaways to what she was, and what his womenfolk were. He looked up at her and thought that she might own a nice tea shop, but she didn't have class, not like the ladies he now mixed with, albeit it only in the offices of the Women's Anti-German League, where he and Sybil might, perhaps, be invited to a morning tea every now and again.

Mrs. Stonehouse said: "But he could never have actually written he'd looted anything because of the censors. Still, what with the effort they're making to get rid of the Germans, it doesn't mean to say the boys can't help themselves to a sort of a souvenir, wouldn't you say, given the sacrifices? After all, *souvenir* is a French word, isn't it? Oh, my goodness," she said, absorbing his disinterest, "I haven't got your sandwiches."

He had things to think about and looking out over the sea was one way to do that without the nonsense that women carried on about. He thought: "I'll be able to talk better with Mac. I think he's my man for this proposal. It's a funny old world all right, all that time ago and he not even recognizing me."

"The sandwiches are fresh," said Mrs. Stonehouse, placing the plate on the linen cloth. "I'm sorry about the delay but everyone's off with this flu. It's been terrible the past week."

He polished off the sandwiches and downed two cups of tea and left the money on the table as the proprietress chatted to two elderly ladies. He turned right and went towards the row of elegant, brand-new villas with gables and ornaments and fancy verandahs.

The villas were known as the Nine Sisters on account of their distinction, a developer having whacked them up and flogged them off for an enormous profit, he'd heard. He said into the wind: "Me and Sybil will live here one day, I bet." At number 188 Oriental Parade he looked up at the imposing façade high above him and he wanted to have this one, to bring Sybil in a motorcar and say: "This is what we get from our hard work. A real Kiwi dream." At the top step he thought: "Things going as they are, I'll get one of the Nine Sisters soon enough".

At the entrance with its carved pillars and coloured parlour windows, the door opened before he rang the bell. He was greeted coldly by a tall, dark featured woman who, on ushering him in, led him down the wide hallway, up carpeted stairs and into a small room. When she had closed the door, she said: "My husband suspects. I said it's just laudanum, but he knows it's not. You can't come here anymore." She looked him up and down as if inspecting meat at the butchers, and said: "Have you got some?"

"Course I have," he said, cheerfully, noting the plushness of the Persian carpets. "Money first."

She went to the teak bureau under an oil painting of a Māori village, dark hills surrounding it, smoke sifting from the *whare*, and he shivered with the memories of such dank, lugubrious places. She took a ring of keys from her pocket and unlocked the cabinet, taking from a nook a roll of notes. "Three ounces," she said. He watched her, fascinated that someone so wealthy had come to this. When he told her how much three ounces cost, she said she didn't have that sort of money and that his price had, in her words, "become utterly exorbitant".

"Take it or leave it, as they say," he said. "Plenty of others will buy it at this price, especially Chinamen."

Her hands shook, he could see the need. She held the notes in her left hand, the rings loose on her fingers. She fanned out the notes as she walked across the ornamental carpet.

"Give me the substance first, to taste," she said, holding out her hand. She looked suspiciously at the little paper package, took it, dipped in her finger, licked it.

He watched the woman whose husband was a banker and socialite, albeit one with a murky reputation. Nevertheless, he admired her strength of character. A woman demanding that she taste the substance to make sure it was genuine meant that she had a head for business. Some of his lady clients merely winced and shoved the money at him.

She smiled, her teeth in a straight row, the colour of the mother of pearl in the bureau behind her. She held the packet to her chest. "But he suspects," she said. "I don't want any more, it's not good, this is the last time. Don't come back. He'll beat me again." She wanted sympathy, someone to say something, for him to say that this was indeed the last time she'd ever need it, that it had been a passing situation, one to bolster her spirits given that her only son was in the military in Europe. But he stood with the notes in his hands watching her lips, wondering why her husband just didn't get rid of her and save his wealth from being wasted. "I'll go back to laudanum and get off this," she said.

"Laudanum," he laughed. "Is for old ladies with dizziness and dyspepsia. You need this for your nerves, or you'll never survive. Your husband will want you to have it to steady you. A lot of society ladies use it."

"If Cameron comes back, I'll stop," she said. She pointed to a framed oil portrait of a fine-looking young man in military uniform and an officer's cap, and a stiff black moustache. "Cameron," she said. "No, no this is the last time, I'll start on some treatment. Herbs, I know herbs soaked in vinegar helped me the last time."

He laughed: "You need me, you're a nervous woman. Just use it until your son comes back. The War will end soon enough, what with the Germans in retreat." He didn't believe what he said even though there were hints of such in the press. But he saw her chest heaving, her eyes looking at him with hope: "All I want is my son back, is that asking too much? It's been four years and he's got lung problems from the gas. He's hospitalised in Sussex."

It was dark when Cecil Meatyard reached Kenneth Lane, which was mean and grubby after the magnificence of Oriental Parade. The instructions were to not arrive in daylight, and when he knocked on the door it was opened immediately and he was hurried in by the woman. Sniffing at his feet was a little white dog that looked up at him with huge black eyes, whimpering, its tail between its legs. The woman – he could see she was a tart – led him down the passage and into the small room where Mac was seated in just his trousers and woollen singlet, the empty sleeve rolled up but dangling. He was barefoot and had a cigarette between his lips. He said without removing the cigarette: "Hello, mate."

She poured two beers from a flagon and handed them each a glass, then without a word she left the room, the dog scurrying behind her.

"I knew you'd like to talk about shirkers," Mac said, getting up from the sofa and coming to him. "You understood what she was getting on about in the street when she talked to you, eh mate? There's shirkers and we know where they are and…"

"Lay off it, mate," Meatyard said. "I'm not blimmin' stupid. You're a pimp looking for customers." His eyes turned shifty. "But what about that *bint*?" he said looking over his shoulder.

"Her?" said Mac. "She's available. Isn't that what you wanted? Five quid up front." Then something crept in from far, far away and then, suddenly, with a slap, everything returned. Mac peered at Meatyard's eyes, looked him up and down, sneered, and stuttered: "It's you, you bastard."

Meatyard laughed, downed half his beer, burped loudly and said: "You're finally getting it. Going back a few years too many, are we?"

The disguises and escapes, the zig-zags in Mac's life, the long years, they all fragmented and congealed in his mind. With the images rushing about, he exclaimed: "Damn! Blast!" and a smile crisscrossed his face: "Bloody Hell, Rexy Smyth. Meatyard? I never guessed, mate. You've got fat and bearded and that thing," he said, pointing to the toupee.

"Secrets mate…" Meatyard said. "How did a Jorg become a Mac?" They embraced, two men from the same class of shenanigans.

"You bloody bastard," Mac said. "I'm not a Jorg any longer either, *Rexy*. And Cecil Meatyard, what sort of name is that?"

"I knew who you were stepping in to cut me off from Sybil, your old tricks as sharp as ever, eh?" Meatyard said with a grin. His man was still his man, nothing had changed except physical appearances, and a name. They were still in the Waikato prison playing cards, swapping plans and new adventures, being mates together in their own cell, they the only *Pākehā*. "You had two arms then. What happened to it?" Meatyard said, pointing at the missing limb.

"Nah," said Mac. "Long story. What about that wife you soapbox with? What's all that about? You of all people banging on about righteousness." Alexander's bitterness about the Meatyards began tugging in Mac's mind: good and evil, push and pull; Alexander and Meatyard, the opposites in the equation.

"Same as your arm, mate, bit of a tale for later but she's all right, serves her purpose," Meatyard said. He could see his plans fitting beautifully into place as he looked into the eyes of his long-lost prison mate. "I've been thinking about you all day, how we got ourselves together, survival, wasn't it?" He moved closer to Mac and touched his one hand as if in commiseration for it being bereft of the other. "You know how it was, you never had a father. And I never had a son." His shifty eyes moved to portray kindness. As they transitioned, he said: "And here I am once again to help my boy, my little prison matey." The years hadn't tarnished Mac's memory of that time in a dirty prison with only this man, older, wiser, tougher, and how this man had helped him, led him into this sort of practice which he'd survived on since then.

"I've thought about you a lot over the years," Meatyard said. "I saw you with that Powderham Pansy the other day and I said: 'I'll find him'. But it's mysterious, isn't it? You presented yourself to me this morning on a silver platter. If I believed in the power of prayer..." He itched his toupee. "I would've thought it was due to God, but I don't see God in this. Fate's better because God wouldn't help the likes of us two. I really liked you then, Jorg, I always..." He stood back and looked about for the beer jug but the years were flooding with emotions, becoming an inundation, and he wiped tears from his eyes with his sleeve. "Like my own son," he said. "Jorg. Jorg, all that time my Jorg, and now you're Mac, but you still mean the same to me."

As he sniffled, Meatyard saw what could have been if life were different, fair; but his vision was inescapably more about unfairness and cruelty, and it smacked him. That life was unfair was what life had taught him. He was as trapped in its injustices as much as his clients were by their addictions. The image of that Oriental Bay woman weeping as she looked at the painting of her handsome son plunged at him. More thoughts charged in and tumbled over each other, becoming too dense for his capacity to curtail or sift, and in his confusion, he blurted: "I've got a good deal for you, lots of money, a partnership to get rich, my...son...my mate..."

Mac took a step back – he had to – and gulped down his drink. He said: "Okay mate." He saw Alexander reading a book in his comfortable home surrounded by art and culture. When Alexander looked up at him it was with that superior smile which said: "You can't have my life, Mac. You weren't born into it."

"Come on," said Meatyard, "Don't you remember what we did? What a couple of mates we were, what plans?"

Mac had closed his eyes. When he opened them Alexander vanished and what he saw was Meatyard smiling, a wad of money in his hands.

"No honour amongst thieves," Mac thought. The idea of which way he should turn flicked about. The echoes of what he'd said as he left the Tinakori Road house after a night of happiness returned: "I'll fix that Meatyard bloke up for you, give him a fright." He knew he was stumbling, slipping on that slope he'd been down so many times that it no longer hurt. He closed his eyes again; Alexander was reading his book, but this time he didn't look up.

"You always did have the smile of an angel and the heart of a blaggard," Meatyard said as he held out the money. "You had two arms and I had no hair. What's fair in love and war?" he said. "Can we be a team, mate?"

"What? But I don't want that sort of trouble. I killed…" said Mac.

"Three Māoris? So, what? You got off light. What's a few years in prison? A man learns from that."

"Something's telling me…" He wanted to shout: "I hadn't meant to kill them! I'm sorry." But he was no longer a drunken lad with a musket in the bush and fighting senselessly with drunken Māori mates. He said in the full realisation that it was this man who'd saved his life, stopped him from hanging himself in prison from the shame and guilt, the bloke who'd helped him survive, taught him the tricks: "All right Dad. Like it was before. Take me."

Rebecca came into the room, the little white dog behind her. "I want you both gone, it's not safe having you here." She looked at them and the dog whimpered. "Eskimo knows what she's talking about and she's afraid. Mac, it's not right. He's supposed to be religious, promoting soldiers and the war effort." She pointed to the money in Meatyard's hand, and looked him in the eyes: "I've got my own sins and hypocrisies. I've done bad things. Keep your trap shut about me, and I will about you because I think you're evil. Now get out of my house."

10

Mabel Stonehouse was polishing the tables in the Olde York Teashop. Her arms ached, her back was killing her, her head spun with how she would keep the tea shop open with two of her four staff off with the influenza. "It's everywhere," she thought as she wiped the last table and reflected on having to explain the delays to her customers. That character with the wig who evangelised in the streets, she tried to recall his name, something to do with cows, but she was too tired and she merely saw an image of him slipping out without paying in full, banging the door behind him. She bent to pick up a serviette that had missed her attention and winced. She was about to go upstairs when at the door, despite the CLOSED notice, she saw Mrs. Rachael Chatterley waving at her, her face white and distorted.

"Good Lord," Mabel Stonehouse said seeing the terror in the woman's eyes, thinking it was the influenza, which made people hysterical. Fearful, but opening the door, she said: "What can I do for you, dear? You look upset." Rachael Chatterley stumbled into the shop, into Mrs. Stonehouse's arms, and said feebly: "Help me."

"What's the matter, dear? Come here, lie down," said Mrs. Stonehouse. Under a severely framed print of George V was a green Chesterfield. She had to half pull Mrs. Chatterley to the sofa, where she lay her down, her head against a cushion. The woman was not burning, or pink, as happened with the influenza, sickening people so quickly. With her big hand on the ailing woman's pale forehead, Mrs. Stonehouse recognised fainting, not flu. The coolness of the skin and the fluttering eyelids confirmed that.

Mrs. Stonehouse trudged up the stairs and found her husband dead to the world on the bed surrounded by accounts and miscellaneous papers. She shouted: "Russel, get up, we have an emergency." Russel

Stonehouse had a dickie heart, which he attributed to a lifetime of hard work as a merchant in the vegetable and fruit industry. She had to tug at his arm and the thought that he might have popped off frightened her further. He roused somewhat and, somnolent, followed her down the stairs. When he leaned over the woman and smelled her breath, he said: "It's the opium, pure and simple. The Chinamen flake out like this when they take too much of it."

"Go up to their house, see who's there".

"No, no…" Mrs. Chatterley said, very faintly.

"No, no…what, dear?" said Mabel Stonehouse. "Is he at home, dear?"

"I…no…do not…my husband…knows…" She fluttered and went out, her head to one side, her breathing very slow, her thin body enveloped in her enormous wet fur coat.

"Blast," said Russel Stonehouse. "What a thing to happen now."

His wife agreed, but said nothing, her back and shoulders a mass of aching muscles, her head hurting from a day which had started at five in the morning.

"Turn the lights out, Russel, what with people passing. How long does this affliction last for?"

Russel Stonehouse touched her forehead. "Lot of these Chinks smoke it. That one on Rintoul Street where we deliver the veggies was away with the fairies for a whole afternoon last week. His wife just laughed and said he'd wake up in a few hours."

"But why did she come here?" said Mabel Stonehouse. She went to the kitchen and soaked a napkin in cold water and applied it to the woman's forehead and whispered: "Dear, it's all right, take small breaths, God is with you."

"I'll go up there, then," said Russel Stonehouse.

"Help her out of this wet coat first," Mabel Stonehouse said, tugging at the heavy fur sleeves.

"Good Lord," he said as they observed purple bruises across her arms.

"Just like Nellie when her brute belts her," said Mabel Stonehouse. She shook her head at the injustices she heard about daily and yet here they were, in her own shop, with the lovely Mrs. Chatterley, always polite and dignified, coming in ill with potions and beaten about.

"Give it an hour or two and if she's not coming to, I'll get the husband down here and that's that," said Russel Stonehouse, imagining cops and undertakers and the headlines in the newspapers.

Mrs. Stonehouse made tea and they sat with Mrs. Chatterley, she holding the ill woman's hand, and prayed silently for this woman, her grandsons, her ill staff, the world.

An hour later, exhausted, he said: "My dear, I can't take this. I'm going up to investigate."

"Recall what happened to Nellie when we told her brute he was wrong to bash her," she said. When the door shut, she looked at the King and pointed at him: "Get this mess sorted out. It's your lot who started it, not us." She stared at the bearded man as if seeing him for the first time, the revelation of his irrelevance and hideousness, of him in his plumes and sashes and medals and satins with the world around him in conflagration and this tiredness, this overwhelming feeling that it was all a constant battle to survive. The exhaustion. She felt it might be the influenza, but she said: "No, no, don't give in, we'll be ruined." Her eyes were closing, sleep closing in, when Mrs. Chatterley tugged her hand and said, her eyelids fluttering: "I…I…thank you…I was so frightened…"

"Oh, thank goodness," Mabel Stonehouse said, and blessed herself. "You've come to life."

"I was alone," said Mrs. Chatterley, just audible, raising her head.

Mabel Stonehouse with a glass at the ready allowed her a sip of lemon barley water and said: "You're out of danger, dear, what was the matter, what happened?"

"I have to stay alive for Cameron. I feel I can tell you, Mrs. Stonehouse. Because really, what happened was almost the last…"

"Call me Mabel. No more formalities, Rachael, not after this. Tell me everything, dear, let's get to the bottom of this nonsense."

11

It had been three days since MacPherson had left Alexander Powderham's house, saying triumphantly: "I'll fix that Meatyard bloke up for you, give him a fright." In the living room, in the comfy chair, a cushion under his gammy foot, his slippers on, wrapped in his Kaiapoi woollen dressing gown against the lingering late September winter, Alexander realised he had been conned by a handsome trickster: "Most likely an Australian," he muttered. In addition, he reflected that he had lost five quid, his new Munster and Munster coat and his beloved felt hat in the ill-fated bargain.

"At least he can't blackmail us and I'm better off without him," he mused, as he surveyed the many oil paintings of Mitre Peak. He had added to the collection over the years, building on his grandfather's and father's acquisitions, so that the entire wall was crammed with images, mostly of the mighty Mitre Peak in its various guises. A favourite was depicted in the most luxuriously lugubrious oils, Mitre Peak being struck magnificently by lightning, the scene captured by an Otago woman known simply as *Mrs. O. P. M. 1869, Dunedin*. That radiant rendition of ecstatic light hung next to another of Mitre's greatness, but one rendered slightly insipid by a Polish artist's unequal impressions of the Dominion's particular light. The artist, a certain L.S.V. Spytkowski, had been insensitive to the crepuscular wonders of the far south. In the adjacent large and gilt framed painting by the Englishman Ramsey Lorde, the sun filtered through voluminous clouds which illuminated everything so gloriously that in Alexander's mind the scene was equal to how he felt about Aroha. The light was sifting, not so much as a spiritual metaphor, a device so popular in the 1870s when it had been painted, but as a strong conveyance of beauty, natural and enigmatic, that signified joy and gratefulness, and the mysteries of nature, all at the same time.

"Ah," Alexander sighed at all the beauty. Then, with regard to the itinerant's underwear, he smiled at the fact that Aroha had had the good sense to steal the army issue underpants as proof, at least, that this Mac had taken them off in the house, supposedly willingly, should he return and threaten blackmail.

That lustful night Alexander recalled in a mixture of loss, happiness and relief. Loss because he had genuinely liked the Australian conman: his antics, his voice, his blonde hair, his glorious appendage, his *bonhomie*, and the flecks of danger that emanated from him. Alexander had, too, felt true respect for the fact that the man had suffered so greatly in Gallipoli and had been cast aside by an ungrateful military who had as yet, they had all been informed, not paid out a penny in compensation for his war wounds. Happiness, because Mac, with the most tender stroking with his one hand, had massaged Alexander's withered leg while looking up into his eyes with the deep knowledge and compassion of one who has equally suffered the loss of a limb. Only Alexander's father and Aroha had ever been so kind, so loving, so attentive as to this deep affliction. And that this charismatic man had vanished was indeed a relief, for Alexander knew he would have fallen in love with him, thus sparking drama with Aroha. While from time-to-time Aroha had his romantic liaisons with Māori his own age, there was with that arrangement, a true understanding that that was permissible, but not so, in turn, for Alexander, who was permitted no more than a quick fling, a one-night peccadillo, and always with Aroha. An attachment, an abiding love with another *Pākehā*, Aroha would not have tolerated and Alexander, musing again on Ramsey Lorde's portrait of Mitre Peak, honoured that.

"Ah, the life of a Pansy," he thought, and flicked away, discarded forever, albeit with some reluctance, that rascally scoundrel, MacPherson.

The leg brace, the thing he most hated about himself, for it was a part of him, integral, never ending, was off for the time being, in the bedroom, far from him, with the hated thing not allowed ever to be in the beautiful living room unless attached to him. He wiggled his toes on his withered foot and with the aid of his hands lifted his leg up and down and thought how much everything depended on wealth. Even now had he wanted his leg brace, unless he struggled to get it by leaning against the walls and furniture to make his way to the bedroom, he would have needed Aroha or Orton to fetch it. It was that need for the regularity of assistance, paid or not, that had prompted him since childhood to ensure there was always money. "Without money I am simply a helpless Pansy cripple," he held as a founding motivation. And with those thoughts he tried again to concentrate on the accounts for the recently established *Educational Texts Division* of his *Te Aro Books Incorporated*, which was doing very well financially given the government contracts he had acquired during the war years.

"Tedious accountancy when I could be finalising the essays on Joseph Conrad and Elizabeth Gaskell and this one on Dostoevsky," he thought, scanning the novels around him and again forgetting the figures, with, at the back of his mind, the thought that he needed to employ someone to keep his finances. Elizabeth Gaskell, Joseph Conrad, Ivan Turgenev, Leo Tolstoy, Jane Austin, Emily and Anne Bronte, Mary Shelley, Herman Melville and others were all in a high, distinguished pile on the table next to him, begging his attention. Katherine Mansfield's *In a German Pension* sat on the very top of the pile. "How on earth did I get to be a successful businessman when I hate numbers so much?" he mused as he gazed at the elegant stack of literary works. He placed the ledger on his knees and reflected that wartime business was booming. "I wonder if I'm a hypocrite given how I feel about this conflagration?" he asked himself as he looked from Mrs. Gaskell and Jane Austin to the Dunedin lady artist's Mitre Peak, she who had painted so brilliantly and was so tragically anonymous. "But if Aroha lost his lands from a *Pākehā* government's illegal land acquisitions, then what goes around comes around, and with government profits I'll buy him the fishing boat he wants so much."

The door which led to the passageway and on to the kitchen opened and out glided Orton Gnash. He came across the floorboards and Persian carpets with a tray of tea things and hot scones, fresh cream and strawberry jam, his leather soled shoes making *pat pat* noises as he approached the chair in which, ensconced, was his master.

"Musing, are we?" Orton asked, posing as he placed the tray. "Deeply musing? Good." He took the Wedgewood china cup and saucer off the tray, and then the teapot. "Don't go to the shop today, have a rest. All this flu about, keep yourself away from crowds, keep fit and healthy. I said the same to Aroha and his new friend. Muriwai, isn't it?" He looked around the room as if after his long absence with the flu he had so much to do, and as if it had just dawned on him, given the month, that it was in fact time for spring cleaning. "Oh, I forgot the tea cosy," he chirped. "Must be the effects of this flu, but they say its contagion passes away after a few days with just the dross left, so don't worry. Nurse Winifred, she's absolutely wonderful, such a big linen cap and always absolutely spotless, said I'm free of it."

Orton Gnash was a small man, bony, a former horse jockey, and he still liked to wear shiny outfits as if he were about to go off racing on horses at a club meeting, all at the ready, nimble, elegant, well prepared. On this occasion he was dressed in a red satin shirt and long blue pants, also shiny. His black leather shoes were highly polished and looked too large for the rest of his body. "That Muriwai is a nice lad, isn't he? I'm happy Aroha has another friend, it's good for him, he thrives on it," he said, peering at Alexander. "Albeit I was fond of Bunny, the one from Taranaki, when he was around. Such strong legs. And of course, we all loved Rawiri. I wonder what happened to him? Probably got married off to a woman. Still, he was so…but Muriwai, yes, adorable, the proverbial golden chalice."

"Silver chalice. And yes, he's utterly adorable," said Alexander. "And yes, again, I'm delighted they're so happy together. It's good for my Māori, too, listening to them chatter, very good for my vocabulary and aural, oral skills."

"I'm sure it's good for your oral skills," said Orton, his left eyebrow arching. "I noticed this morning when I changed the sheets, if I don't mind adding. Still, nothing ventured nothing determined, as they say, and you're only young once."

"After eighteen years in this house there's nothing you don't know, or suspect," said Alexander. "I'm just pleased you survived this flu. I read there've been multiple deaths this week."

"Who would believe anything the papers print?"

"William said the papers aren't allowed to say how many really died at the Front in the past few weeks, or from this sickness, and he's a newspaperman. The Prime Minister might say when he arrives back next week." He took a bite of the scone with Orton watching as if he were a food taster in a royal court. "Can you believe it must be literally *tens of millions* killed because of German intransigence and an assassinated Austrian? William said that *The New York Times* estimates fifteen million dead. He was about to take another bite of the scone but said: "The police took Elizabeth's journals and letters. I just wonder why they haven't been here…yet."

"They will," said Orton. "Any papers, I can take to my place. It's got to that. And the buggers have postponed the elections again."

Alexander felt cynicism and weariness weigh more heavily upon him. With one hand on his hip, Orton said: "And this flu's not at all normal." He coughed as if to confirm it, and Alexander noticed the new lines under his eyes, and how bonier he had become. "Nurse Winifred said since the first of the month, gosh, just in a week, that the flu's become stronger. Fifteen dead in Wellington, and not old folk, but people in their forties. And twenty dead in Auckland according to Nurse Winifred, who heard down the grapefruit."

"Grapevine," said Alexander.

"Indeed, it might be grapes," said Orton as he poured more tea into the Wedgewood. "And I can't understand Āpirana Ngata coming here, such a cheek. Aroha was telling me, gosh, what a lot I missed in just a week. I couldn't stand being in bed wondering how you were being looked after. You're as useless as your father. I did fret." They laughed and the war years disappeared as they imagined old Mr. Powderham in that chair, sitting under that lamp, reading, writing, snoozing.

"Oh, for some reason, that reminds me," said Alexander, "I can't locate my sister's letter. Apparently, she's coming here and I do hate

Pansy haters. What with everything, I can't remember when they're coming with their nonsense." It was absurd. There were tens of millions of people dying and there was his sister demanding again the few baubles that their mother may have left in the attic. The cynicism, mixed with anger, swilled around, for how unfair these untruths were about his beloved father. He said: "My sister deserves nothing for being so evil."

The Mitre Peak paintings always brought to meaning some emotion and he looked to them for guidance as the anger sluiced through him: the bolt of lightning was his sister's attack; the lugubrious clouds represented his mother's abandonment of him for being different and crippled. He leaned back in his chair, saw his mother yelling, heard his father rationalising, and sighed.

"When was the letter delivered?" said Orton, looking about as if now that he was back he could pluck it miraculously from somewhere, acting on every whim for this man he adored and who paid him so handsomely to be, essentially, his butler.

"And my Munster and Munster hat. And my coat. That bugger walked off with both."

"Just between you and me, Aroha did say that as much as you all liked him, he might be a cad," said Orton. "What was his name? George? Aroha said he called himself Mac and then Tony or Jorg when he was drunk. Anyway, I hear you all had a marvellous time that night, so what's a hat and a coat when you think of it that way? Cheer up. Light at the end of the channel."

"Tunnel. Where are the men, by the way?"

"Digging that long drop deeper. Deep I told them, deep. That's what you need for a decent latrine, nothing less than ten feet deep. I told them, very nicely of course. But you can't take a horse to the trough and make it drink. Gosh, he is good looking that young man, a policeman too, so striking in his uniform."

"Is loving Māori men a predilection you learned from me or did you bring it with you? I can't recall."

"Mutual, after all is said and spoken. Oh, there were so many lovely

Māori men in the racing business. If only walls had eyes and doors ears..." Orton sighed and looked around the room, peering into past race meetings and boarding houses: Auckland, Napier, Te Awamutu, Hamilton, New Plymouth, Otaki, Foxton, Christchurch, Timaru, Invercargill. Each one went rushing through his mind and all the men associated with them in a list so long he might have stood there all day smiling at the delightful images. He looked up as excited as he would have been at the theatre admiring his favourite actors on the flickering screen. However, the men he saw from those provincial towns were real: naked, jostling, laughing, smoking, sitting in satin astride horses. "Oh, you can't tell a book by its sleeve, but you can tell the size of a man's member in a pair of satin jockey trousers," he said, teary. He laughed and was off to the kitchen from where Alexander heard a crash followed by a yell and he felt happiness pushing away the weeds in his mind now that Orton was back. He shoved aside the account books and took up his papers on *Crime and Punishment*.

Alexander was now well into the construction of an essay on the most significant characters in the novel, which was one of some twenty essays that he had composed in the past two years for a collection that would be published in England, he trusted, once the War ended. "Possibly in nineteen thirty," he reflected caustically as he scratched out a sentence and asterisked another.

"*Arkady Ivanovich Svidrigailov, the lecher and sensualist; Raskolnikov's sister Dounia Romanovna, almost too perfect but with just sufficient imperfections to make her real, unlike the too-saintly prostitute, Sonia Marmeladova, who is marvelous, but ultimately a type, a literary convenience,*" Alexander read aloud from his notebook. He looked up from his notes and thought: "But why can't a prostitute be saintly, as Dostoyevsky portrays her? She isn't a type. She's real and Dostoyevsky knew that and drew her so well. A prostitute who's lovely and caring is so unusual, it's never been done before. It's like us Pansies, we never get the respect for being humans, we're just effeminates and sodomites and never..." He watched as Orton made a quiet passage across the room with his feather duster, disappearing between the velvet curtains into the sunroom. "And of course, the sophisticated detective, Porfiry Petrovitch."

The thought of the detective circling Raskolnikov so deftly, using Raskolnikov's arrogance to assist in his own undoing brought to mind Detective Denton. That pallid face and red nose jolted Alexander further, for he recalled what Mac had said as he left the house: "I'll fix that Meatyard bloke up for you, give him a fright." Raskolnikov and Mac coalesced into one dangerous misfit. "Both of them as mad as each other and…murderous," thought Alexander, fearful of what might happen given this association. The purple curtains parted and Orton crept tippy-toe under the Fiordland collection and Alexander, trying to dispel his fears about Mac murdering someone, said: "Despite it being the morning, I'd love a whisky and water, please Orton."

When Orton returned, he said as he set down the whisky in a crystal glass from a set inherited from Uncle Percy: "Aroha and I were just talking, we think you should do something to assist Elizabeth, what with her things being taken by the police. Muriwai agrees."

"A tribunal, I see. An outrage, I agree," Alexander said, delighted that his best friends were coming to Elizabeth's defence. "I've already instructed Mr. Cromwell to make a complaint. It's that bloody War Regulations Act, everyone's a spy or an agent or involved in sedition. My poor mind, I think I'm Raskolnikov one moment, sane the next. Here I am sitting in my dressing gown ruminating about Arkady Svidrigailov and Sonia Marmeladova."

"Who on earth are they?" asked Orton, sensing scandal.

"Well, Svidrigailov represents sleaze and hypocrisy and lecher and seducer and ultimately he reminds me of that appalling Cecil Meatyard."

"Oh, Cecil Meatyard, well I remember him from the race days."

"Really? Why on earth…races…?"

"Yes, of course. He loves jockeys. For goodness' sake, we used to call him Balloon, not for nothing. He'd come and hang around and puff himself up and say things. And when he got an insult, he'd deflate and then slink away. The next minute he'd be back and make insinuations about the boys' tight satin outfits and then, well, once Scott Herders, he was a lightweight jockey from Stratford, he just fairly kicked him in the pants and chased him out and everyone started chanting 'Balloon, Balloon.'"

"Good God…I mean…really…Cecil Meatyard? But you never told me this before."

"Well, I never put two and four together. But in those days that wasn't his name. Meatyard's an invention. I only learned that quite… recently…from someone…who was that?" He stood with one hand on his hip, the other up, posing like a teapot, and Alexander snapped at him to come back to the subject: "Oh, I can't recall…but I remember one of the bookies telling me that if that Reginald Smith, oh, that's not it, but if he ever said anything quite so…suggestive again, he'd call the cops." He looked up at the ceiling and exclaimed: "Rexy Smyth, that was it! Rexy Smyth. But I never…There he is preaching. I never go into town until I went, well, recently, after you told me some old biddy called you Oscar Wilde that I put two and four together and he lives around the corner in Saint Mary's Street, in a very nice villa I'll have you know, and that shrew who called you Oscar Wilde is Sybil Meatyard, so called, and well…waters run still if they aren't deep, and she's his missus, and he's as queer as a fish from way back." He rushed to the kitchen shouting "My jam!" leaving Alexander fetching from the compartments of his mind a translation of everything he'd just learned. all of which held the magnitude of a Russian novel. Orton came back and said: "Shall I boil water for you to wash now?" He was about to add that he had saved the jam and therefore an entire box of strawberries, when there was a knock on the door.

"Oh, as I said, still waters are always flooding somewhere. I'd better get that, but what do you think? Should I pop out and warn Aroha and Muriwai to lay low?"

"If it's the police, make your way out and warn the boys to clear out."

Orton came back, closing the passage door behind him. "It's a very nice-looking young woman. She says she has your hat and coat. The hat's in a hat box, even. She's called Rebecca. Says she wants to talk to you about a letter. She looks safe. I'll get you a rug to put over your knees so you look more lady-like." He returned with an embroidered blanket of rich reds with hints of mauve and indigo, the handmade dyes having never faded, another of Uncle Percy's heirlooms. Orton spread it over his master's knees and backed away and said: "Perfect."

Alexander downed his whisky and adjusted the blanket to completely cover his withered foot. He brushed back his hair, which covered his collar, a very unusual length for a man in Wellington. He tidied the occasional table, stacking the books and closing *Crime and Punishment*. The bookmark, a long piece of red linen from a shirt that he had loved, was inserted at the page where Sonia's mother, the consumptive Katerina Marmeladova, descends into madness and bangs pots and screams in the streets of Saint Petersburg.

"Damn it," he thought. "Katerina Marmeladova. How could I not have added her to my list? She's the most fascinating character of them all. There's not a soul in New Zealand like that. Never, never could we be like the Russians, never that catastrophically frenzied." At the end of that thought, perilous in its own way, for he saw that as a huge exaggeration given the likes of Sybil Meatyard, he wanted to write his thoughts down and thus add to his essay notes on the reasons why New Zealand would never have a meaningful national literature. But in walked a very attractive woman, tall, with not a trace of makeup because it was not needed and aged somewhere in her twenties. She introduced herself as Mrs. Rebecca Routledge, of Newtown.

"Tea if you wouldn't mind, Orton," said Alexander once Rebecca, she had insisted that he call her by her first name, had been seated. There had been no need to ask Orton to make tea, but they had a cue, which was that Alexander would request tea, and if he didn't, that meant that Orton would appear in ten minutes and say that he must now get ready for the doctor, who was due any minute.

"With fresh scones, sir?" asked Orton. This was Orton's favourite part and not just because it signalled that he, Orton, approved of the visitor, but that he, Orton, was now to be perceived by the visitor as a butler, not a common servant.

She was dressed in cream and grey, the colours of the Wellington day as he had glimpsed, peeking in the morning from his bedroom window. She was neither working class nor middle class nor something from that curiously manufactured space filled by the likes of a Miss Rutherford; but she was something, and he was trying to sort out that kaleidoscope of class fragments that constituted, eventually, someone. She said, providing him with hints: "From Newtown I took the tram then changed again at Courtenay Place and I was worried I wouldn't get here before…" She said with her eyes: "I'm doing this for something bigger than what you are currently imagining my reason is for being here. Wait for me to get there." She adjusted her coat, which was a deep grey, so that her dress, a deep cream, could be viewed, allowing for the beautiful contrast of colours and fabrics.

The clothes were well tailored and good quality – but she was from Newtown. He sat and waited. "And then the tram to Tinakori Road…" And here she laughed lightly and crossed her legs as a real middle class lady from Kelburn or Karori would not, her elegant legs under her delicate skirt telling him there was a story that she hadn't yet divulged in so many words but one which, he knew, a woman as ambiguous as this one would do, eventually, for a Pansy.

"Yes, I'm sure Rebecca would like that very much," said Alexander. He knew there were people you could like instantly, about whom you would not be disappointed within a few minutes and, equally, he understood, there were few people with whom he had had that immediate resonance, outside of fiction. At least, he hoped, that would be the case with this smartly dressed woman, who, paradoxically, he saw through the moment she entered the room. It was merely the parts he was putting together, many of which belonged to him, carefully placing them one by one into the jigsaw. Or was it love at first sight? A shiver went through him, for she was as gorgeous as Madame Bovary and, in her studied way, as irreverent, and he couldn't help but suspect that she was luring him, platonically of course, much like the one-armed man had done romantically under the Bank of New Zealand. But he didn't flinch as she licked her pretty lips and twittered something about the wind in Wellington and walking along Tinakori Road and being unable to raise her umbrella.

"Yes," he said, "pour for us, please, Orton."

For a moment he felt as Gustave Flaubert must have when composing his most significant character, for here she was now manifest in front of him in Wellington, not France, half a century later. She was exactly the sort of companion he needed. Certain women he adored: Sonia Marmeladova the prostitute, so delicate and subject to life's injustices; Sonia's mother the anguished and dramatic and consumptive Katerina Marmeladova; the genteel and impoverished Dounia and her sadly distracted mother Pulcheria Alexandrovna; Madame Bovary, naughty, willful, wicked. The world was filled with wonderful women and he wanted this Madame Bovary to be the one for him, a counterweight to the rational and heady Elizabeth Norris. His father, who had steeped him in worldly sentiments from this very chair, would have said that this woman was of good character, textured and sound, no matter that she might be, as he guessed, a "woman of ill repute".

"I'm aware that this is an unscheduled visit, Alexander," she said in a voice that was not Newtown. "However, it's very important for a couple of personal reasons, which I hope we can talk about, in private." She indicated with a nod to the door through which Orton had disappeared. "I love his outfit. Is he a court jester?"

"A royal one, for me, the Queen," he said, laughing. "He understands everything and protects me. He nearly died of this flu, but he's back and bowing and being butler and he's so Victorian in a truly Wellington way. But the outfit? He was a jockey for twenty years. Can't you see that?"

She stalled at the coincidence and looked around the room and stifled the urge to say that she had read the works of Oscar Wilde and that this was his style, and that *The Ballard of Reading Goal* was unbearably sad and that was what had brought her to this house. "Strangely odd because it brings me to my first point," she said. "I'm from a racing family. My brother was a jockey. My father a bookie…"

She looked at Alexander in a manner that reminded him of the scene in *Pride and Prejudice* where Miss Bennett is taken under the spell of Mr. Darcy.

She took in a deep breath and said: "My brother drowned himself in Christchurch when he was twenty-seven. I feel I must tell you this story. You see, because…"

Alexander opened his mouth but she held up her hand and was about to speak when Orton arrived and began to fuss with another Uncle Percy piece, an Oriental folding table with a bronze top. Alexander coughed and taking the cue Orton hurriedly left the room.

"Look," she said, "I've returned your hat and coat, assuming they are yours."

"They are indeed," he said. "I imagine there's a story given that it was Mac who asked you to bring them back. I'm most grateful." He felt a shiver of something, that not-quite-right-feeling in him.

"He didn't ask me," she said with evident irritation. "He left them at my house when I told him to get out, and inside the pocket I found this letter, to you, with your address." She pulled the missing letter from her purse. "I'm here on a special mission." It was then that he realised that it was he who was Miss Bennet, not Mr. Darcy, and that he had fallen for someone under false pretences, as Miss Bennet had for that perfidious English aristocrat.

"Oh bugger, bugger, pride and prejudice indeed. I'm full of both," he thought furiously, disappointment swilling through him, and that trust, so fresh and inspirational, flooded out as he saw the unfolding scene: blackmailed by a tart from Newtown. Disappointment because he had been fooled by first looks, so superficial, just like Miss Bennet had been with that supercilious cock, Darcy. "Thinking like a Pansy always gets you into trouble. You can't tell a book by its cover, as Orton will tell me in some such mixed up aphorism." He wanted to get up but of course he couldn't, his carved cane being out of reach. "Blackmailed for being a Pansy, a lost letter," he thought.

"What? Why?" he uttered. "Letter? Does? If?"

Orton, of course, had been listening by the door. On cue he emerged fully alert to his master's reaction, and said: "The doctor will be here soon. We don't have time for tea." Alexander made a motion, his index finger to his lips, silencing him. The woman looked Orton up and down, not sensing the farce given her mission and she blurted: "My brother was a Pansy and was blackmailed and he drowned himself in the Avon River six years ago. He was a very promising jockey. And a nasty man and woman blackmailed him and he wrote a letter to me saying he couldn't take it then jumped in the river and they found his body three days later." She began to sob, her hands to her face, before wiping her eyes and saying, her voice croaking: "He…he… They killed him with their evil blackmailing. I am so filled with hatred for them, for killing Joseph, and with absolute impunity. I never had justice. No revenge, nothing."

"Oh! No!" Orton gasped. "Joseph Walden. I knew him, a wonderful lad, a marvellous jockey." He rushed to her and fell to his knees and looked up as if she were the Holy Mother or Mary Magdalene and he a penitent in a Biblical painting. Alexander watched them, his immediate emotion one of immense relief at this not being blackmail. He saw it all as in a calamitous scene from Scott or Bronte or Dickens; but this particular subject matter, he understood with bitterness, was utterly forbidden in any literary publication. With that insight, he turned his eyes to the wall of paintings and wished he were being struck by lightning so pathetic was the life that he was forced to live through being silenced, pandering always to *them*. However, with everything going on around him: fear of blackmail; a sobbing prostitute; revelations of a suicided Pansy brother; the crying and exclamations, he thought: "Was I actually just thinking that New Zealanders don't have passion, and don't act like Russians? Look at these two. If I could write all of this, I'd be producing the first great New Zealand novel."

Finally, wearily, he said, "Orton, I would love a cigarette and a whisky. Get one for each of us, please." Then he focused on the distraught woman as she dried her tears with a handkerchief. He said: "I'm so sorry to hear about your late brother, but please tell me what you want."

"To help you because I read the letter. Your sister's coming this morning. I thought how dare she say these things? I didn't want any more of this blackmail for men like you and my brother. He was so lovely. One time, the police caught him in bed with another jockey in the Braemar Guesthouse in New Plymouth. He made a fuss and said why couldn't he kiss a man if he loved him? He stood up for himself, but finally it was all too much."

She had mentioned revenge and the word echoed powerfully in his head. The whole world was at war, was churning in revenge. It was what life was based on. He saw its beauty and inherent necessity. Not for the defence of an imperialist archduke shot in Sarajevo, but for men like this jockey who had drowned himself in Christchurch. He saw Mr. and Mrs. Meatyard shouting: "Oscar Wilde!" He envisaged the revenge he wanted to extract. It was pure and simple: a bullet through both Meatyards.

"Your sister and brother..." said Rebecca. "They're coming, soon."

"Today? This morning? Oh, Lord. I had completely forgotten when, what with influenza and sedition and everything, and my shop being vandalised, and the police. What a, what a...?"

Orton wheeled in the whisky tray and handed her a cloth soaked in lavender water and said: "Sniff this, dear. I did. Does a planet of good. Your brother was a gentleman. An absolute darling." He set about the duties of dispensing whisky and cigarettes in a ceremony which, while watching, Alexander thought was as meticulous and inspiring as any conducted by a geisha.

"My brother," she said. "I suspect this is where Mac fits in. I know of his double meanings, his double everything, and he and my husband Jimmy and it's all a bit mixed up, men together, but that's life, isn't it? He and Jimmy. Except for Cecil Meatyard, but that's another story."

"Meatyard!" Alexander exclaimed. "The evangelist?"

"You mean dope peddler," she said. "Yes, it's a long story, but as your sister is due soon, I thought we should lay out this plan because I need revenge for my brother and I want to help you. I thought about it all night, which is why I have bags under my eyes. But revenge, for Oscar Wilde."

"Bags under your eyes? No, you don't," jumped in Orton. "You're gorgeous. Never. Such a fine-looking woman!"

Alexander said, excitedly: "Look, before you do, I want Muriwai and Aroha in on this. I had my own ideas about how to present the jewellery but had dropped all thought of the meeting given …life. Orton, get them for me, will you."

An hour later, in his bright jockey outfit, his hair coiffured, Orton answered the door to Lydia and Pip McCartan. He ushered them into the living room where they found Rebecca seated next to Alexander in his dressing gown and Uncle Percy's embroidered Punjabi cap.

"Oh, my demanding siblings, Lydia and Pip," he said as they entered. "Right out of *Great Expectations*." He knew their retort should be: "Oh, Miss Havisham, on her throne, in her cobwebs, forever bitter." But, as they had professed in their letter, Lydia and Pip were largely uneducated and certainly didn't read good fiction and would have no idea about the decrepit, reclusive Mrs. Havisham in her cobweb filled, disintegrating mansion.

"We've come all the way by train from Featherston, so I'd rather we got to the subject at hand with no sarcasm," said his sister, surveying everything that should have been hers. She studied Rebecca and said: "And who is this, if I might ask? I wanted a private audience."

"This is my fiancée Sonia Semyonovna Marmeladova," said Alexander. His reference to the pious and humble Saint Petersburg prostitute was emitted with not a trace of the hilarity and irony that swelled inside him.

No one spoke. As Orton would say later: "You could have heard a dropping pin." Then the alias whore from Saint Petersburg said: "I read your letter. It was disgusting to infer my future husband is unnatural. He's the most natural man I've ever met. Is that right, darling?" She looked at him with love, taking the letter from his hands and fluttering it in hers: "I do not take blackmail lightly. In Russia we execute people for such evil deeds."

They might have been in deepest Fiordland, completely removed from noise, silliness and civilisation until she said: "I am not a Russian princess for nothing. You, I assume, are Pip, which is an apt name looking at you. You might like to read this for us, Pip. Orton, please pass this to Pip."

Lydia had never been to high theatre, regarding it as a waste of time and money and would only attend a musical in Featherston if it were free. She was just beginning to perceive that this was indeed high theatre, but as yet not a farce. "Never mind reading it," she said, "we know the contents and we have only half an hour, but your girl-friend, fiancé, I say this to you if you are really his fiancé… This is our house too, you know."

Alexander snatched back the letter and said, his voice steely, his eyes on Lydia's: "How can that be if it isn't in your name? Father left it to me exclusively. Your letter is wrong, but then let's hear it. Pip, please, I forget some of it and if you want anything, I need to know it point by point. Read please."

Pip was pale, strong of body, and had some of Alexander's good looks, but neither the elegance nor arrogance of privilege. Alexander was aware that it was all a trade-off for Pip was sure-footed on two normal legs and could walk. The trade-off was unfair but, paradoxically, one he would never exchange. Infant paralysis, intellect and good fortune for one son, dullness, deprivation and sure-footedness for the other. It was to Alexander a Biblical equation. As he watched his estranged brother fall into the trap, he almost felt sorrow that this had to happen. He, Alexander Powderham, humanist, intellectual, fop, was indeed a minx and a manipulator, a Svidrigailov who, opportunistically, lorded it over others just as Svidrigailov had done to servants, and his wife whom he, Svidrigailov, had murdered.

"'Dear Alexander, Me and our brother Pip have come to the conclusion that you have stolen our rightful property by cheating us out of our inheritance and since you are a criminal of the unnatural nature we intend to contest this in court,'" read Pip, assuredly, without spectacles.

"Thank you," interrupted Alexander. "Just as we thought, Orton and Sonia, don't you agree that Pip is a good reader? That he apparently has very good eyesight to be able to read such tiny handwriting without so much as the need for eyeglasses?"

"Well, I looked at that writing, all fuzzy to me without glasses, tiny little letters and all crunched up together," said Orton. "Very difficult, tiny script."

"I'm afraid I'd need my reading glasses too," said Sonia.

"Which makes me wonder why you were able to be exempted from the military based on your near blindness, as I was informed. Really, Pip? Would you like me to notify my informants in the military that you were fibbing, that you had a very elaborate excuse made up with a Doctor Ernest Maxwell? That he prescribed glasses so thick you could fool the conscription board? At my exemption meeting there was confusion over our names, that's how I discovered your duplicity, but I kept that a secret to protect you. One of the terrible things about living in New Zealand is that we have only a million people. If you ask three people something about someone, you're bound to find out what you need to. Isn't that right Lydia, about your brother?"

"What?" said Pip. "Lydia, told me to tell that to Doctor Maxwell. If I got shot, she'd be left high and dry with no income."

Alexander saw the contempt and disappointment in Lydia's face, for once again her Fairy brother had outwitted her. Again the Pansy had triumphed through the inbred and inevitable nastiness of its nature. Her lips quivered, her eyes misted. All those years since she and Pip had been bundled out of the house collapsed into a sordid memory of seconds; suitcases and boxes, objects broken, shouts and recriminations. Alexander at the top of the stairs crying his eyes out shouting: "Mother! Mother!"

"You never get over disappointments and lost things," Lydia said. "Mother never forgave you. Until her dying day she blamed you and your evil spirit for everything, for hoodwinking our father. She said you were born evil, a Powderham through and through."

"She didn't want a cripple and a Fairy, just that man who became your stepfather, a nothing with whom she absconded." He lifted the blanket. "Look at this thing. Uncle Percy told me he was here when Mother shouted at Father that it was Father's bad Powderham blood that made me a cripple."

"And a Pansy. She hated that. Who can blame her what with Father always at your rescue?"

He regretted that he had agreed with Rebecca's plan to make him appear normal. He wanted to be left with the dignity of what he was: a crippled Pansy whose father had adored him and had done everything to make sure that his life was safe and comfortable with money, status and education.

However, suddenly, he saw his need for revenge was the antithesis of what his father would have wanted or condoned in this situation. He was sitting in his late father's chair, the symbolism of which made him shudder, the old man saying: "Forgiveness, fairness, love. They are your siblings, family." Alexander felt pity blossoming, that unmistakable sentiment growing, petals, stamen, scent, and he uttered: "I'm sorry. I can make amends for you and Pip…"

"No, Alexander! *Utu* is *utu!*" Aroha shouted as he and Muriwai burst from the velvet curtains decked out in the late Mrs. Powderham's finery. Her pearl necklaces were draped around Aroha's muscled torso, still sweaty from digging a drop latrine. Muriwai was adorned in a sequined triple frilled crimson Edwardian blouse, and the faux diamond Victorian tiara that the late Mrs. Powderham had worn on her wedding.

"You don't like Māoris, do you Lydia? Expressly forbad my Māori family from being in this house which you think is yours," said Alexander, returning to form for, once again, Aroha had saved him. "Father is watching you now, he knows the content of your letter, this hatred, these prejudices. I imagine you would never want these articles having been worn by such…such…natives."

"You hideous, mad creature," shouted Lydia.

But it was all too late, all too absurd. The Russian novel had been played out on Tinakori Road, Wellington, New Zealand and the curtain came thumping down and mutual hatreds were assured their respective successes. Pulling off his pasha's cap which he associated with a deserved and righteous despotism, Alexander waved it at his siblings and shouted: "Pansies' revenge!"

12

The image of his sister retreating down the hallway to the front door, her hands up as if in self-defence and shouting that she had been humiliated by a repugnant and unjust Fairy, had stabbed Alexander during the three days since that sad and disturbing occasion. Sad and disturbing because he saw the loss of his dignity and his humanity and the essential bonds that are supposed to bind people, family and friends, as fragile, gossamer and dangerous. Despite the decades having proven that that particular love was not available to him, other than in its truest form from his late father, the loss of family stung him yet again. He was, essentially, obviously disgusting to them, a crippled Pansy, a rich and privileged one, and additionally polluted for that. Alexander, reflecting on this, noted that in *Crime and Punishment* even Raskolnikov's family had not abandoned him.

"Lucky him, loved by his mother and sister even when he was sent off to Siberia for murdering the old women," he mused as he sipped a glass of ginger wine that Orton had made from scratch. Aroha and he were dining in their kitchen, and as he took another sip of the wine he wondered if the said Russian mother and sister would have been so magnanimous with their affections if their beloved Rodion Romanov Raskolnikov had been a Fairy. "Again," he thought, "there's no one in fiction with our story, so how can we tell what's what? We have prostitutes and murderers and lepers and philistines, adulterers and adulteresses, liars and vagabonds, but not a single Pansy except for some insidious insinuations here and there. Or fantastical images in Walt Whitman's poems."

"What's going on up there now?" asked Aroha, tapping his own head. They were speaking in *te reo*, Aroha correcting Alexander when required: "Be here with me, not lost in your dark thinking."

"I had a dream last night about your childhood French priest. He was dressed in purple and yellow robes and had butterfly wings," said Alexander in a mix of *te reo* and English.

"Eat your rabbit or it'll get cold and cold rabbit isn't very nice," Aroha said. He took a draught of the ginger wine and returned to his rabbit, saying as he held the meat on his fork: "How did that priest get all the way from France to my village?"

Alexander watched his lover's eyes, deep brown and lost in thought. Aroha was indeed far removed from the present as he pondered on the apparent irony of a priest coming all the way from France to a remote coast in New Zealand to save the souls of natives when, forty years later, he himself was being requested by Māori officialdom to go to France to kill Europeans. Aroha removed his gold framed glasses, blew on them and wiped them with his linen napkin. Alexander felt an emotion, warm, teary, as he watched Aroha, slightly myopic without his glasses, his eyes with that look of surprise as if he had witnessed something startling in the distance.

"He did wear wonderful yellow and purple garments when he said Mass, and I loved them so much I wanted to be dressed up in them. And then I'd look at my own people wrapped in blankets and try and understand how we had descended to hand-me-downs," he said, his voice a mixture of nostalgia and anguish. The coals were glowing In the fireplace, the phosphorescent blue and gold shimmering. Aroha's profile against that beauty made Alexander wince with emotion.

"You know," said Aroha, "I can see the priest standing at the altar in yellow and purple, so your dream was not a dream, it was reality."

"But why the butterfly wings? Do Māori see anything deep and mystical about that? Is that strange or symbolic?"

"You might have dreamed that because your sister and brother abused you in your own home and they called you a Fairy and a Fairy has wings and your dreams are realities now and mixed up like dreams are, so it's simple. But why you dreamed about that priest I can't think. Give me time. And eat your rabbit and *puha*."

"There's too much European psychology in that answer. I was asking what Māori would say about that dream. I think you've swallowed Jung's bait."

"You came home with Jung's works and banged them into me. Jung this and Jung that and we had to look into our dreams every morning." He laughed and made a funny face at Alexander. "Don't you remember that period? It was worse than with this Russian. You spoke like a psychology book for weeks. Dreams are just dreams, Alex, just like this rabbit is just a rabbit even though it's been stuffed with herbs and breadcrumbs." He was half jesting; he knew that Jung had answered age old questions and that his people's future was wrapped up in whatever *Pākehā* dished out for the taking. He understood that history, progress, change were inevitable and that was good, if it was for a positive purpose. At that moment he wanted Āpirana Ngata in the kitchen to have a discussion about how their people were influenced by all of this and what it meant for their future. It was just sad, disappointing, that yet another result of this war was the rifts it had caused, or made deeper, amongst Māori.

"About your dream," he said. "How did we think before modern psychology? I mean it, Alex. I can't remember what my thinking was like before this stuff got into my head. I don't know what Māori would have said about dreaming about butterflies."

"You've been living with educated *Pākehā* too long."

"That's what Ngata accused me of, yet he's up there at Parliament surrounded by Europeans."

"Anyway, psychology wasn't invented by modern Europeans. They just have a new interpretation of what the ancient Romans or Greeks or Indians or Persians thought, surely, or for that matter, your people's psychology. In a hundred years people will say what we think is old fashioned and will be torn apart and re-examined."

"I wonder what rabbits think," said Aroha. "Let alone dream."

"Pavlov. Jung. Nietzsche. Freud. All this modern psychology is eating us, settling into our brains, forming our thinking and I'm not convinced for the betterment of things. Even that old rag *Truth* is full of it and trying to analyse us Pansies. 'Queer', as they now call us, when before we were left to exist with just a few moans about us now and again."

"Oscar Wilde was hounded into prison," said Aroha, eyeing the cigarettes. "*Pākehā* have always hated Pansies. Don't you read the Bible?"

"Psychology will destroy us. They'll use it against us, build up a cause, a hatred. It's already happening, it has been since Oscar got done in. A rag of a magazine can call itself *Truth* so what does that tell us about what the herd believes in *their* truth?"

"Don't get too anxious, it's not that bad."

"What about Robert Gant's photos from the eighteen eighties of men in the Wairarapa kissing and holding hands and touching each other? He wouldn't get away with that now. It's changed, changing. I can imagine the authorities doing a sort of pogrom on us, like they did to the Jews in Russia."

Neither spoke, the only sounds were the water hissing in the iron teapot on the stove and the crash of wind outside as the southerly tore up the coast. Alexander concentrated on the rabbit and the mashed pumpkin, all prepared by Orton, and thought: "I'm going to write a novel where all the characters are men who love men and the women love women and no one is normal."

"I said to stop thinking dark things."

"I'm not. I'm writing a great novel about a *Pākehā* man loving a Māori man."

"Now you really are in dangerous dreams territory. Can you imagine anyone publishing that? I can't imagine they'd even publish a love story about a *Pākehā* man and a Māori woman."

"Rebecca's story is worth writing about, her survival and how she rationalises working in the oldest profession, as she called it," said Alexander, returning to *te reo* but stumbling over the syntax, which Aroha corrected.

"And who in New Zealand would publish a novel about a war widow prostitute?" said Aroha. "Madame Bovary was French and that was published in France, never here. For goodness' sake, Alex."

"I'll write a novel called *Monsieur Powderham.*"

"*Madame Powderham,* more like it."

"Anyway, I liked Rebecca very much. She's different, well-read, sceptical, and look how happily she embraced us, and she adored Orton, and that fantastic play we put on for Lydia and Pip was good stuff."

"It's good you gave her a job. Funny that she could do accounts and yet she's a prostitute. Well, she won't be now she's going to do your accounts for you."

Alexander abandoned *te reo* in order to express the complexity of his thoughts: "She said she was selective and went only with men who treated her well and with whom she had a rapport, which is why she wouldn't sleep with Meatyard. I never thought of this either, really, but she said that she wouldn't work on accounts if she wasn't paid the same as a man, so essentially, if she was going to be exploited, she might as well do it for good money and that's why she did that sort of work."

"Strange sort of a justification," said Aroha. "She must have been very poor to sell her body to military men."

Alexander sipped his wine, the ginger, grown in their garden, was pungent, earthy. "You know, the funny thing about life is how funny it is. A one-armed Australian with an enormous appendage, an endearing prostitute, Muriwai who shows up with a Māori politician to conscript you and then becomes your lover, and there's a world war raging, and my siblings run out screaming that I'm a Fairy and that Māoris have taken over my household. And eating pumpkin, rabbit and *puha* on a wet, windy night with my Māori lover in Wellington. Surely that's a novel." They looked at each other and there was nothing else to think of but that delicious time that was theirs in those seconds when the world outside was so tormented.

"Now, I see your dream. I know why you dreamed Father Dominque had wings. Thank Father Dominque," said Aroha as he reached for Alexander's hand. "He told me when I was a boy that *Takatāpui* is Māori, that it's all right to be a Fairy. He taught me to fly," he said, mixing *te reo* and English. "He had wings too, that he accepted himself for being a French *Takatāpui*."

"Ah, and so my dream was thanking the priest for giving you the wings you wanted?"

"That'll do. The ones I needed to fly out of the village. I must have liked that old priest too much. I waited for him at the door of the priest's residence, what do you call it?"

"Presbytery."

"I was holding lilies I picked in the valley and my mother said I was a good boy to take them to the church for mass. But I had picked them for Dominique. When I stood there looking up at him, my heart beating, he told me to go and put them in the church. He shut the door on me. He was a good priest. But he loved me. And out of that I got my wings and a scholarship."

"How do I say 'fate' in Māori?"

"It's more luck than fate."

"True, look where it got you," said Alexander in *te reo*, laughing at the ambiguity of his statement. "I'm so tired. I can't think in Māori any longer."

"Tired of *te reo*?" said Aroha in *te reo*, not wanting to drop his language. "In fifty years, no one will even speak it. What about that statue in Auckland in memory of Māori because we're disappearing? And they're sending Māori off to get killed and Ngata comes here and blasts me and he's supposed to be the saviour of Māoridom."

They were well into the second bottle of Orton's potent wine and Aroha was becoming moody and morose. He shifted a rabbit bone across the plate with his fork as Alexander watched the dark cloud rumbling in with the inevitable thunder following closely. "There's no use having two storms, mine about life's stupidity and yours about Māori. Everything's a mess, and now this sickness, but we have ways of staying sane, and who we are," Alexander said, reaching for Aroha's hand. "Light us a smoke and let's get that fishing boat sorted out. We'll go to the Marlborough Sounds, escape all this for a few weeks."

Aroha saw Alexander's need for a physical escape beyond losing himself in the minds of demented fictional characters. He finished his wine, came behind his lover, kissed his head and whispered in *te reo*: "Alex, I respect you more than anything. Thank you for guiding me."

"Life is this wind blowing us all over the place."

Aroha licked Alexander's ear: "Does my husband like my ginger breath from inside your Aroha?"

Aroha was wearing a cream-coloured woollen sailor's jersey, which Alexander loved to see him in, it being tight and worn. He plucked at the sleeve where there was a large hole and touched the skin before running his finger down Aroha's arm and said, looking up at him: "I adore you and always have and when you breathe wine on me, I feel it even more." Still holding him from behind, Aroha leaned down and kissed Alexander's hair and said: "Can we go to the bedroom?"

"Only if you carry me, the way you do."

"I will always be your support." He helped Alexander out of the chair, leaned down so Alexander could climb onto his back, and carried him down the cold passageway to the bedroom.

The bedroom was at the back of the house, and the wind, whipping the huge trees in the back garden, provided the room with even more of a sense of sanctuary. It was as if the world were empty, with Wellington's rough elements at their best so that no one would ever stir in that weather. The room was large and lit by two lamps, the shades dark green so the effect was indulgently mysterious, decadent. Aroha laid Alexander on the double bed, his head against the down cushions and began to undress him.

"You're always beautiful," he told Alexander, looking down at him. Slipping out of his own garments, he lay next to him, holding this man with whom he had fallen in love in the Botanic Garden one Sunday eleven years previously.

"You are what I always wanted," Aroha had told Alexander that first night when they were in bed together, in the very same position, and adding: "You will have to learn my language."

"Which means you'll have to live with me," Alexander had replied, taking a plunge he would never have expected to with a man he'd found that day in the Botanic Garden.

On that spring Sunday afternoon, Alexander had been ensconced in a dell surrounded by white, blue and mauve hydrangea, and emerald punga fronds. He was reading a novel, but the moment he saw Aroha enter the dell and look around, he was struck. The man was tall and well-built and had dark brown skin, and his thick black hair fell to his shoulders, his small black cap was tipped to one side. The black suit was tight-fitting, his white shirt and red tie and polished dark blue shoes were well put together. Whenever he thought of that precious moment, Alexander wished that they had been photographed together in that dell, Aroha standing, he sitting, their respective hats in their hands, the photo forever a poignant sepia witness. Alexander had been barely able to articulate a greeting as Aroha had approached him with a certain deference. Casting that aside, he had seated himself next to Alexander and asked what he was reading.

"Just a novel," said Alexander, blushing.

"What about?"

"Oh, it's about a man whose leg gets bitten off by a whale."

"But your leg isn't missing and it's not a book about yourself, is it?"

"A biography?"

"Is that what a book about yourself is called?"

"If it's written by someone else. If you write it, it's an autobiography."

"Are you reading your autobiography?"

"My name isn't Moby Dick, thank goodness. And my leg is deformed, not missing."

"What would you say if I call you Moby Dick."

"Moby is a rare white whale. So that might be all right."

"A very big white whale, is it?"

"Yes, and getting bigger as we speak."

"Can I catch the whale?"

"It's a sperm whale."

"That's the sort I like, a big white sperm whale."

The day had been hot and the Botanic Garden, resplendent in its mid-Victorian design, was lush from the morning's rain so that everything had seemed to be steaming. The hydrangeas' subtle perfumes, the pungas' essence of furry mustiness, and the motionless red flax smelled earthy and coastal. Eleven years later, woozy from the mulled ginger wine, as Alexander lay in Aroha's arms thinking of that precious day, the doorbell jangled and someone pounded forcefully on the front door.

Alexander sat up, all thoughts of that first day with Aroha vanishing. The doorbell clanged and clanged and Alexander recalled the doorbell in the Jewesses' flat in *Crime and Punishment* clanging and clanging on the night Raskolnikov murdered Alyona Ivanovna and her sister Lizaveta.

"This late? Police? Don't answer it," said Alexander. They looked at each other, their unease had turned to fear. This would only be an emergency, or one about to happen. But it was the banging on the bedroom window that metastasised the fear to panic. That window – the curtains had not been drawn – faced into the back garden and they were exposed together in the bedroom which, in a court of law, was sufficient to prove immorality: a Māori and a *Pākehā* both of a known immoral disposition observed *in flagrante*, which was in effect a flagrant "admission of the abominable." The wind was rattling the windows, the draft between the sashes disturbing the curtains. The white hands rapping the panes hid the face of the one peering in. With a mad movement, his face squashed against the pane, his nose pushed at it, his bloodshot eyes those of an animal, the two stricken lovers saw that it was Cecil Meatyard drawn like a giant moth to the light at the window.

13

"Stay here, do not come out," Aroha snapped as he rushed from the bedroom and thumped down the passage, through the living room to the vestibule from where Alexander heard the door open and the wind rattle the chandeliers. The mad face had disappeared from the window and, supporting himself awkwardly with his Moroccan cane and the bed, Alexander made his way to pull the curtains. He imagined Meatyard's face still there, its ghostlike whiteness, but the voices were coming from the passageway. He pulled the curtains and limped to the doorway and heard the unmistakable yelling of the madman. Leaning on his stick, using the bed and the chair for support, he reached the bureau and, struggling, opened the bottom drawer and fished amongst his underwear.

The front door was open, the wind rushing in. Meatyard had barged into the living room, his arms outstretched, pushing Aroha ahead of him with a strength that came from deep within, from his wounds, his anger. He was wet, his wig dripping, slanted. He shouted: "You Māori, where's my Mac?"

Aroha, coming to his senses, held the demented man back. Routed, Meatyard stood flailing his arms, his eyes wide, maniacal.

"Mac? Mac?" he yelled, looking around the dimly lit room: "How could he live with a Māori and a cripple? He wants me!"

Meatyard pulled away from Aroha and leaned against the sofa. It was obvious he was broken, poisoned by the drugs Rebecca had told them about. Or ill from the sickness.

Aroha said: "You don't want to be here. You'll regret it. Go home. Mac isn't here."

Meatyard didn't hear him. He leaned against the sofa and yelled: "My wife who hated him. She wouldn't…" He put his hands in his pockets and pulled out the lining.

"Turn around and go home," Aroha said. "Go now before…"

"My money, thousands, gone…" He looked at the wall of Mitre Peaks looming in the half light and took a step back, his arms up. "She stole my cash, not my boy. I was the father. I saved him in prison."

"Mac's not here. You saw we were alone. Go before…the police…"

"Police? I saw you and the cripple. I can give evidence. Tell me where Mac is…or…" He tried to adjust his toupee as he surveyed the room but bent forward and vomited over his jacket and pants, on his shoes, smearing his hands as he wiped himself.

Seeing Alexander emerge from the passageway, Aroha motioned for him not to enter.

Meatyard took several steps backward, pointed at Aroha, and yelled: "Devil! Māori! Mac killed the Māoris, not me."

"What Māori?"

"The ones that Mac killed…Not me, don't…My boy, in jail…"

"Take your bad dreams about Māori and get out."

"Who killed whom?" Alexander asked, hobbling in. "Why are you here?"

"I'll tell you why he's here," a voice screamed. "He's a ridiculous fool and I hate him!" They turned towards the shadows of the front passage where Sybil Meatyard stood, her hair over her face, her garments soaking wet. She rushed at Aroha, her hands up, and struck him.

She was crying as she wrestled with Aroha. Seeing how fruitless that was, she turned to her husband: "Money! Adulterer! Pervert! I know what you did with him! My Life! My life!" When she saw Alexander emerge from the shadows she cried: "It's Oscar Wilde!" She turned to her husband, tore off his toupee and struck him with it. "Me the victim, time and time again. I followed you to see that one-armed pervert, but it's Oscar Wilde! You said you'd finished with that prison perversion." She pointed at Alexander as if casting a spell. "Filth! Mac! You! The lot of you. Even with Māoris."

"Enough about Māori!" yelled Aroha. "Get out!"

She turned to her husband: "Now I understand. Queers selling dope. The police told me about your peddling, a rich woman who nearly died. What kind of a man are you, hiding your stuff in my, a woman's hatbox?"

"How tiny they are, what a pantomime of their own making," thought Alexander. "There's a world war, tens of millions killed, but these two acting out a Dostoyevsky novel in my home."

"How can I face my people now? The Meatyards as purveyors of poison. This conman writing he'll kill you because you fleeced him! You're not clever enough for this." She pulled a paper from her handbag, waved it at him, and read it, shouting the words: "*I will kill you, you abused me. You are meat, mate. Meat. Be very careful. You crossed your Mac and so did that stupid woman you married.*" She grasped a chair for support. "This stupid woman is not stupid, she's loved in the streets…Enough humiliation. I'm off to get the constabulary!"

"The end is the beginning," said Alexander. The way he said it, his voice, his eyes, his arm held out with the pistol. Sybil Meatyard stood rigid and stared wide-eyed at Alexander. The scene was from the Bible where the Woman of Lot is turned to salt. In his dressing gown, the pistol raised, Alexander Powderham realised with equal terror and excitement that this was the inevitable re-enactment of Raskolnikov raising his axe to smash Alyona Ivanovna. Sybil Meatyard stiffened further, as if with premature rigor mortis, her mouth agape, her eyes disbelieving at why she, so determined by righteousness, should meet such a fate. With one perfect shot through her heart, Alexander dispatched her. She slumped and fell, no longer alive with her successes and passions and hostilities and disappointments and humiliations.

They were all rigidly still, as if that Biblical invocation had been rendered timeless and universal. Alexander had not lowered his arm, the pistol remained pointed to where the deceased Meatyard had been standing. The spell, however, was short lived and the wind took a turn and howled from the open door. Cecil Meatyard seemed to come to, the fog was lifting. He crawled to the corpse and said: "Sybil. Sybil. I implored you not to change your name from Smith to Meatyard, now look where it's taken you!" He wept, huge tears flowed out. Snivelling, he turned to Aroha, his hands out, a plaintiff, and shouted: "Why does anyone live?"

"Give me the pistol," said Aroha.

Meatyard was on his knees, bending over his wife's body, touching her face as if he had loved her. Then, looking up, he saw Aroha pointing the gun at him.

"Who killed what Māori?" Aroha asked.

Meatyard hesitated as if weighing up the options. But his will was weakened. He realised the magistrate was standing above him, decided, inflexible. "MacPherson did in nineteen hundred and six, he shot them dead in the Waikato bush. They were mates but boozed, drunk, whisky, fighting over an axe and a gun. Silly buggers fighting over nothing. I got six years…but I didn't kill them, I just, they hushed it all up to stop the Waikato Māoris from rebelling. And now he'll kill me, that letter…money…gone. Nothing changes. A tiger's spots…" He began to whimper, not so much to save himself, but with remorse for what he had lost within that long and dishonest event called life, his sloshing about in it, dirty and messy just to end up with a murdered wife and a vengeful Māori. He looked around as if saying goodbye to the world in an unfamiliar room was what he deserved. His eyes then focused, became perfectly normal. Looking up at the Mitre Peaks staring down at him, he said quietly, as he blessed himself: "Please, pull the trigger."

14

Aroha Raharuhi laid down the pistol and felt for the pulse of each Meatyard, but they were both dead. The silence signified the calamity, his as much as theirs. He closed his eyes for several seconds, standing reverentially, his hands crossed over his chest, his head bowed. Supported by his cane, Alexander stood and stared up at the framed Mitre Peaks with his attention focused on the lightning bolt breaking through the clouds and striking the great mountain's pinnacle.

On opening his eyes, Aroha went to the bookshelf, selected the *Saint James Bible*, which he opened to the *New Testament*, and turned to *John 11*. He knelt and began to read aloud from *Jesus Raises Lazarus*. In a voice that did not sound like his own, he read: "*Jesus therefore again groaning in himself cometh to the grave. It was a cave, and a stone lay upon it. Jesus said, Take ye away the stone. Martha, the sister of him that was dead, saith unto him, Lord, by this time he stinketh: for he hath been dead four days. Jesus saith unto her, Said I not unto thee, that, if thou wouldest believe, thou shouldest see the glory of God? Then they took away the stone from the place where the dead was laid. And Jesus lifted up his eyes, and said, Father, I thank thee that thou hast heard me. And I knew that thou hearest me always: but because of the people which stand by I said it, that they may believe that thou hast sent me. And when he thus had spoken, he cried with a loud voice, Lazarus, come forth. And he that was dead came forth, bound hand and foot with graveclothes: and his face was bound about with a napkin. Jesus saith unto them, 'Loose him, and let him go'.*"

Alexander Powderham, white faced and shaking, hobbled to Aroha and knelt next to him. He bowed his head knowing that Aroha reading this passage signified the end, that they would be caught, for it was the same passage Sonia the prostitute had read to Raskolnikov after he had murdered the two sisters. Raskolnikov, hearing that deeply symbolic passage about spiritual death and rebirth, had fallen under the spell of the inevitability of conviction and exile to Siberia. Alexander was aware that Raharuhi in *te reo* meant Lazarus. Weighed down by this dreadful symbolism and coincidence, all deep facets of *Crime and Punishment*, he almost succumbed to prayer to that God to whom Aroha was speaking. But he said nothing, for this was the priest in Aroha emerging, that one forever just below the surface. If this was his exorcism, then this was what Aroha would do and Alexander bowed his head along with him. Aroha began to read the same verse in the same voice that was not his own but that of someone seemingly from a distant place or another time. Alexander, on his knees, shuffled to the body of the slain female Meatyard and, with considerable revulsion, poked out his finger and closed her startled eyes, first the left, then the right, which he accomplished as Aroha finished his second reading about the rise of Lazarus. "Lazarus is reading Lazarus," he thought. "It's all mad."

"And Jesus lifted up his eyes, and said, Father, I thank thee that thou hast heard me. And I knew that thou hearest me always…" read Aroha in that foreign accent.

Alexander, still on his knees, reached out, his hand shaking, to shut Mr. Meatyard's eyes, but couldn't reach them: "So many thous and thusses and hasts and hearests and shouldests," he said as he tugged the body closer by its left leg.

"I can do a modern translation when I get my life sentence," said Aroha.

"You'll be hanged within six weeks, you won't have time," said Alexander. He reached for Cecil Meatyard's expressionless eyes and closed the lids and said: "I am now Raskolnikov Rodion Romanovich, condemned to my own Siberia. You are Lazarus, or something weird."

"You're Alexander Cambridge Powderham, and don't forget it," said Aroha who, otherwise still in the aura of the long passage about ancient tombs opening with shrouded bodies arising, understood his role in the deaths of the Meatyards. However, unlike Lazarus, who rose gloriously with God's assistance, Aroha was not interested in his own atonement, nor in having the dead couple arise, nor in their spiritual survival. "I don't know why your mate Raskolnikov wanted to kill a defenceless Jewess, but yes to self-defence. These two deserved to die, *utu* for a dope peddler and war monger and Pansy hater," he said in his normal voice, the French ventriloquist having fled upon Aroha's admission of complicity in a murder. "And I only read the Lazarus passage because it's the one they gave me to read at the priest's funeral because I was his favourite altar boy. I think the priest led me to read it now. He was here the whole time."

"Oh God," said Alexander. "That's why you're speaking with a French accent. That yellow and purple butterfly has landed on you. It, he, is sucking your liquids. At long last Father Aroha I thought, but you were just mimicking a French cleric's Catholic incantations."

"Forget that French priest. Now we have to think like a rational Frenchman, the ones you educated me about, Diderot, Voltaire, Pascal, with logic, not emotion, not spirits. Be rational or we'll crumple and give ourselves away. Don't think like a Māori warrior running about chopping this and that. Or a Fairy waving his hands. Or a *Pākehā* with a musket shooting here and there. No hysteria, no wailing, no emotion. Otherwise they'll catch us."

"I schooled you well. Don't think like a Fairy Māori. Or a *Pākehā* Pansy. You say it more brutally than I did."

"We'll be heartless and rational. And you tell me there's no ghost in this room called Dostoyevsky because I don't want any of your needless Russian drama." Aroha pulled Alexander up by his shoulders and let him flop into the sofa. "Be a good little boy for Aroha."

"You're right, no more worry about Raskolnikov and omens from the novel about us getting caught and exiled to Siberia. So, my Aroha, what do we do now? Tell me, darling."

They stared at the two bodies. The blood had flowed out of Cecil Meatyard's chest, into his clothes and onto the floorboards. Sybil Meatyard lay in her blood, a rivulet of which reached to the silk kilim, soaking it. Aroha lit two cigarettes and sat next to Alexander and said:

"The priest told me that death is a liberation, the very best journey, which is why it's saved until last, a journey so good there is no return. My elders would say that the spirits will be reunited. But all of that aside, whatever we did just now was for the good of everyone, except the Meatyards. Or not, but who cares? I just want to get them buried." He drew on the cigarette and held in the smoke, taking it as far as it would go into his lungs. On the table was a glass of whisky, he got up and brought it to Alexander and said: "We were in bed, loving… and then things were tipped upside down and we murdered, each someone, murdered…I…What about our souls?"

"Where's your rationalism? You're being emotive already," Alexander retorted. He imagined himself running barefoot across a Wairarapa beach, remote, windswept, with pebbles under his feet. He saw himself returning, running up his front steps, pushing open the door and exclaiming to Aroha: "We need to clean up and prepare for what has to be the perfect crime." He tossed back the whisky and looked about hoping to see the bottle. "My Uncle Percy prepared me. In India he said there is no room for sentiment, and there should be none here either because that's what life is about, surviving on your wits, not your passions." He felt Uncle Percy with them in his Victorian military uniform on a home visit drinking port, nodding his head in agreement, rattling his sabre, saying: "My boys, we're all queers, we'll be done in if we're not strong, so toughen up."

"I know but…" said Aroha.

"We have two dead bodies in our living room, it's midnight, what shall we do?" said Alexander. He closed his eyes and hummed a line from *The Marriage of Figaro* which he had heard many a time at Freddy's in the good old days when they all gathered to sing and pantomime to famous arias. But it was Sybil Meatyard swathed in silk and satins who pranced across the stage singing wildly, followed by Cecil waving his big rings on his fat fingers. "Mad, mad, all an opera," Alexander said. He picked up the packet of cigarettes, lit two more, handed one to Aroha and asked: "What are you thinking?"

"How this all fits together, Mac saying he would assist us with the

Meatyards, the letter she read about his threat to kill Cecil, what Denton will think, about revenge and what it's led us to."

"My heart's beating wildly, I feel sick with what will happen and prison and that con man and my Aroha in prison and all I hear is *The Marriage of Figaro* blasting in my head."

"You can't go to prison. You'll last five minutes. They'd eat you." Aroha stood up, turned his back on the bodies: "I've murdered," he said. He bent his head and tears flowed down his face, into his mouth, as they had in the village cemetery when the French priest was buried. Alexander sat on the sofa, his lover's weeping musical and exquisite. Everything that had happened in these years of war leapt at him. He thought: "I must stay sane. I cannot be Raskolnikov." But he saw that ragged, emaciated student peering at him and behind him was the murdered Jewess as if strung up, dangling. He began to shake and thought: "I am that freak from Saint Petersburg."

Aroha shook Alexander as he cowered on the sofa. "Forget the black thoughts and panic. We must get rid of these people who hated us."

"We keep telling each other that, so much repetition," said Alexander, *The Marriage of Figaro* reaching a crescendo in his head, Sybil Meatyard rushing across the stage screaming she was the Countess Almaviva.

"We're both in great shock. It's working out of us," said Aroha.

"You're right, Raskolnikov panicked after he killed Alyona and Lizaveta and that's why he got caught."

"What would your Russian say to do with the bodies?"

Alexander smiled, felt his blood flowing again, saw the Countess Almaviva fall off the stage and splatter in the orchestra pit and said: "The strangest question I've ever been asked, but Raskolnikov didn't have to get rid of any bodies, only some useless baubles and he even failed that."

"The long drop I dug would fit them both, if I stand them facing each other."

"But I don't want them on our property. Oh, God no, them there forever…"

"A meat yard?" Aroha said, and laughed. "I need to be very drunk, but we can't drink now. Firstly, think about that letter." It lay near her body having just escaped the blood. "That letter is our way out. MacPherson will be blamed for their disappearance if the police read it."

"So we need to get that letter into their house. Look in her bag and see if their address is there. I don't want to touch it," said Alexander.

Aroha threw Mrs. Meatyard's handbag at the sofa. "Open the handbag, this time you have work to do, not just me."

"But now it's got your fingerprints on it."

"I'm not keeping it. For Christ's sake Alexander, be practical. Sometimes…"

"What would the real Oscar Wilde have done in these circumstances? That woman denigrated him. And here she is, was, accusing me of being Oscar Wilde and I won't suffer in a trial. Not for *her*."

"She's dead. She's gone, thanks to you. It was a good shot. I'm proud of you."

"I killed her. When I asked you how to say fate in *te reo*, you reduced it to luck and so it is, extraordinary as it may seem, but even down to the pistol. I imagined it all, and both dead. I killed the person I hated, who abused us for being…"

"Māori."

"Pansies."

"Shirkers."

"What's their address?"

The late Sybil Meatyard's handbag was embroidered and sequined, very beautifully crafted. Still, for Alexander, it felt like a violation to be opening it. But then, and he saw the ridiculous irony, he had delivered her the ultimate violation. With his hand covered in a handkerchief he extracted an envelope and read: *Mrs. Cecil Meatyard, sixteen Saint Mary's Street, Thorndon, Wellington.*

"That's ten minutes from here. Find the keys," said Aroha.

Alexander fished in her bag, an act that made him feel nauseous with multiple emotions congealing in a swarm of images. The physical reaction was to gag, the whisky spouting onto the carpet. "We murdered two people we hated," he said as he plucked out a key ring with three keys. "Go. Put the letter somewhere obvious, and wear gloves."

"What if we take the bodies and dump them in the house?" said Aroha.

"You'd have to get our horses from the paddocks, and what if someone saw you unloading big lumps at this time of the morning? I should have bought a motor car. Oh God, what have we got ourselves in for?"

"You wouldn't even buy a telephone," said Aroha, "or a gramophone."

"For God's sake, now? About the bloody gramophone, telephones? What is it about Māori and objects, things?"

"Don't, Alex…" Aroha huffed. He stubbed out his cigarette and said: "I'll bury them out back, no one will ever suspect. Tell me, who would know that we had contact with them, have you ever? I haven't."

"MacPherson is a link," said Alexander, pondering with trepidation that no crime was perfect, and asking himself where the weak link was in this one.

Aroha saw the one-armed man bending, his firm, round white buttocks exposed, turning back to look, smiling, the smile turning into a painful grin. "I'll kill him," Aroha said. "I want more revenge."

"Enough revenge. You're not Churchill or Asquith or the Kaiser."

"I'll bring water and you do what you can to clean this mess." When he returned he said: "If I get caught, be prepared to shoot yourself or go to prison and be raped and abused or get hanged." He went to the vestibule and put on his gloves and a hooded oilskin raincoat. From where he sat on the sofa, Alexander could see the moving shadows, elongated, ghostlike. It seemed as if the world had been emptied of everything living, with just spirits and spectres remaining. The wind caught the chandelier when Aroha opened the door, the noise of the bluster accompanying the weirdness of the notion that everything was ending.

With the aid of his cane, Alexander made his way to the bedroom to put on his leg brace to make things easier given how much there was to do. He thought: "From now on we have the Meatyards living with us." The thought of the sanctity of his home being polluted with these two was the most alarming thought of all. As he hobbled back down the passage he saw that he was conflicted with various emotions about his crime but understood that the inconvenience of the bodies was greater than any remorse.

"I won't get caught like Raskolnikov. He got madder after the murders and gave himself in after four hundred pages of torment and suffering. I'm cleverer than him," he told himself. With some effort he got on his hands and knees and mopped at the blood and vomit. But the bodies were like ogres and he shivered and he had to engage again in *The Marriage of Figaro*, taking the role of Cherubino, and singing it aloud to make himself get through his macabre job. His hands were messy with the vomit and blood and he gagged. When the water in both buckets was dirty, he leaned back and said: "Acknowledge that you hated them, and they deserved death, or you too will go madder and madder." He smoked a cigarette, flicking the ash into the bucket of blood and vomit water. He said, looking at Cecil Meatyard: "There's a Biblical parable in this, a new one, about Pansies who murder in Wellington, only how does it all turn out?"

Aroha returned, his raincoat dripping, the hood up. He stood above Mrs. Meatyard and said: "I should be a burglar. It's that easy." He shook himself, the water splashing over the bodies and told Alexander to light him a cigarette. "Now we have to get these monsters into the pit latrine. There's blood on this carpet, lets wrap them in it."

"It's a silk kilim Uncle Percy brought back from Calcutta. It's utterly precious. Orton would know and ask where it went."

"It's got blood on it. How will you explain that?"

"You will not bury this precious carpet with them!" said Alexander vehemently. "This is my patrimony, my…"

"Then pull it up and wash it," said Aroha in anger. "*Pākehā* and things. What is it about *Pākehā* and objects?" He stomped up the stairs and returned with two blankets, one for the female Meatyard, whom he picked up gently and laid down with equal decorum, folding her arms across her chest, as depicted on the tombs of the wives of medieval English knights. When wrapped, he slung her over his shoulder, and with Alexander limping behind him, they went out into the slanting rain and wind.

Holding the lantern, Aroha led the way along the path that twisted around his cottage and up past the vegetable garden to the bushes, which backed onto the gully beyond which was the wilderness. At the pit latrine, Aroha laid down the bundle and peered into the hole. It was ten feet deep and three-and-a-half feet wide, the excavated dirt was piled high with the shovel stuck into its peak, like the crucifix on Calvary, he thought. He lifted the excavation ladder and slotted it into the pit, the wind nearly knocking him over.

"Stand guard," he told Alexander. "I'm going to get the husband."

Aroha laid Mr. Meatyard next to his wife then helped Alexander into the hooded oilskin, which he had brought from the house, doing up the top button, pulling the hood right down so that there would be no draught. They stood at the burial site, Alexander holding the lantern as Aroha unwrapped Mrs. Meatyard from the blanket and then the husband. Looking up at Alexander, Aroha said: "They need to be holding each other to save room." He put her over his shoulder and, balancing himself, descended the ladder. A minute later he emerged and went through the same routine with Mr. Meatyard.

Alexander stared down the pit where he imagined the two Meatyards squeezed together, face to face, in an embrace, as lovers. He said: "Dear Jesus, don't let this image be the stuff of nightmares for the rest of my life, erase it please from me after this." Aroha came wet and hooded out of the informal grave and said against the wind and rain: "Good fit, eh? Thank goodness Orton told me off for not digging it deep enough in the first place."

Aroha took from a bag the Bible from which he had read the story of Lazarus and said: "Give this your blessing in whatever way you can."

Alexander merely raised his hands limply above the old, worn book, a dispensable relic from his great-grandfather, and thought: "Lazarus and the departure of the spirit. Raskolnikov reading that passage led to his capture. Why the coincidence? Oh, God, this is all so Gothic, we'll get caught." He flicked his hands at the Bible and Aroha raised it to his lips and kissed it, a motion which made Alexander imagine that French priest up on the wild East Coast in a village getting Māori boys intoxicated with his power. "Kiss this, kiss that," he thought as Aroha dropped the Bible into the pit.

Aroha plucked from the bag the bunch of dried lavender that he had taken from the vase in the kitchen which Orton had placed to absorb the smell of roasting rabbit. He smelled it and held it to Alexander to do the same, which he did for Aroha's benefit, not for that of an omnipresent spirit or the Meatyards or sentiment, but just simply because he knew Aroha was making the effort, of enacting his world that had been inbred with the priests and worship and which surfaced in moments of crisis despite all that hullabaloo about rationalism and French *philosophes*. The lavender was dropped with reverence into the impromptu grave. Finally, in went Mrs. Meatyard's handbag, the two bloodied blankets and Mr. Meatyard's toupee, which Aroha had spied peeking possum-like from under the sofa.

"What a weird world we inhabit day after day. Fact being stranger than fiction is the greatest truth ever," thought Alexander.

"Alexander," Aroha said solemnly, "hold the lantern and say some prayers if you have any in you, while I bury the Meatyards." As Aroha looked at him demanding faith, Alexander knew that Aroha was meant to be a Catholic priest. He said: "I will find some prayers, Aroha." But he failed to add that they would be incantations for Aroha to remain sane and secular, not for the traitors of humanity now about to be buried in his back garden, sullying its peace and beauty with their presence.

By three in the morning the Meatyards were buried deep under clay and dirt. "I'll cover it up with the heavy tree trimmings to make it look like a compost," Aroha said once they were inside. By four o'clock they had finished cleaning the blood and vomit and had rubbed any surface that either of the dead couple may have touched. The blood-soaked kilim was scrubbed and hanging in the wash house, the excuse for Orton being red wine spillage. Retreating to the formal lounge which they otherwise seldom used, they drank whisky and chain smoked until seven in the morning by which time the wind had ceased and the tui and blackbirds were calling and the sky was a clear bright blue. When Aroha had carried Alexander into the bedroom and laid him on the bed and was undressing him, tipsily, Alexander said: "Your three beautiful carvings have been lying out there for months, now I know why you carved them."

"Why my husband?" said Aroha, undoing Alexander's trousers, fumbling with the fly buttons.

"Erect them, they're magnificent carvings, and we'll dedicate them as The Oscar Wilde Memorial."

15

On a sunny morning two weeks after the murder of the Meatyards, Elizabeth Norris and Helen MacPhail were breakfasting in bed.

"You see," Helen said, "we were billeted to great houses and you can't imagine the grandeur. If only we had such a garden and wandered about hand in hand smelling the blossoms." She buttered her toast and applied red currant jam: "The daffodils covered the entirety of Lansdowne. And the owners were lovely." She stroked Elizabeth's hand: "One day we'll travel there in a good ship, not a troop one full of smelly men, and I'll show you what it means to be really rich and distinguished."

Elizabeth, imagining soldiers with disfiguring wounds rather than swathes of daffodils, watched as Helen was about to bite her toast, but who added: "And gorgeous paintings in the great house and nothing was removed, even with so many soldiers billeted although Lady Lacey did tell me she had taken away her best china for safe keeping." In the forty-eight hours that they had been reunited after three years apart, Helen had never referred to death or wounds or gashes or mustard gasses or diseases, let alone the twelve months she had spent on the Front. Not one reference to the refugees she had described with agonizing detail in her letters. Nothing about the towns and cities in Palestine, or the desert battles.

"Yes, dear," Elizabeth said, plucking a cigarette from the yellow packet. "I imagine that nursing in the great houses was a relief from the Front, where you must have seen so much suffering."

"At Lansdowne we were housed so well, with a water closet and electric lights and Lady Lacey herself saw to my…our…wellbeing, the nurses…" Helen shut her eyes and leaned back against the pillows and smiled as if seeing an ideal world of daffodils and water closets and gracious English ladies. However, what marched in was a struggling array of soldiers on a muddy path in some destroyed portion of Europe. She uttered a noise, the toast slipped from her hand, the red currant jam staining the linen, and the tears started.

"And such is war, with such human cleverness as mass murder, and now shellshock," Elizabeth thought. "This could be a long process." In the papers there had been much information about shellshock, a condition associated with war fatigue and terror. She recalled the strangeness of reading about men, they never mentioned women, being struck by unimaginable repercussions such as lameness, sterility, hypochondria, speechlessness, insomnia, madness.

"And what did Lady Lansdowne say about the…?" What was one supposed to say to someone shellshocked to such an extent they could remember only ladies and daffodils and aristocrats sequestering their china? Did one mention the ramshackle hospitals at the Front and the limbless and blinded men screaming in agony with the bombing so near you could hear and imagine the terrible splintering of lives? The newspapers had suggested that the therapy for shellshock was talking about such hardships, such terrors, in order to "open up".

The new, evocative term was as redolent with modern psychology as it was with the hideousness of the events that had caused it. Elizabeth had soaked up everything to do with the War, especially as it affected the psychology of those associated with it, which in her mind was everyone. The letters to the editor had proven just where the respective ideologies lay, even with something as supposedly neutral as shellshock, with one letter that had particularly upset her for its hardness: *Send these returned servicemen out to the farms, get them into physical work cutting down the bush, fencing the farmland, clearing the pumice. No need for hospitals.* She moved from recalling the printed word to the very real world next to her and said: "Lady Lansdowne must have been well prepared to receive the nurses and the wounded. I'm sure she was very pleasant and concerned. It was generous of…"

"Of what? Lady Lacey. Not Lady Lansdowne. What are you inferring,

Elizabeth? She simply let us wander her gardens sometimes accompanying me…us."

"About bombardments…Wasn't the English coast bombarded? And weren't you in danger there?"

"The only danger was…" Helen looked around the room, scrutinizing the floral curtains, the pictures, the rumpled bed, the ottoman. She plucked the sheet where the currant jam had left a red splatter and she shuddered and looked at Elizabeth as if she were not in that comfortable room. Elizabeth saw in Helen's eyes the faraway look, the loss. They were not the same eyes as when she had left on the *HMS Taranaki* three years previously when they had been filled with the excitement, a mission.

"Elizabeth, my mind, my mind. I'm sorry. I'm so tired. Seven men died of the Spanish influenza on the way back, four of them in New Zealand waters, so close to home…my mind…my mind…I nursed them…" She pressed her hands against her temples: "The men…the men…" From the hallway the grandfather clock struck ten.

Helen had been born and bred on a farm in Southland and had toughened it out down there with miners and swag men and shearers and she was strong stuff. Elizabeth looked at this woman with whom she had lived for years and saw that the Southland farmgirl's toughness was slipping, that the mask of the hardened farmer's daughter was subject to erosion.

"No tough farmer's daughter is prepared for the mass slaughter of humans," Elizabeth thought. Holding Helen's hand she wondered if Lady Lacy had fondled it with affection amongst the roses, the hand so delicate, so accomplished in the birthing of lambs, the docking of their tails, the amputation of soldiers' limbs, and the stitching of their wounds.

The clock struck again and the two women exchanged glances and laughed. "That silly old clock is as eccentric as ever," Helen said, the new wrinkles at her eyes creasing. "I'm so pleased there's some comforting continuity."

"Am I not comforting continuity? I've tried very hard to be, my darling."

"Of course you are, but you've inherited a woman with a mind tormented by what she's seen. Is this madness or just some temporary eccentricity that will slide off, end, let me be back to normal? Or will I keep banging out of order, like that clock?"

"Wellington's eccentric. Think what it's like being at the Te Aro Bookshop everyday with the people that come in there and make a hullaballoo about nothing. Alexander's beside himself with thinking he's some mad character in an intense Russian novel. I'm having a time with him to do some decent work, he's so…so…distracted lately."

"And the police and journals and letters thing? Why would they take your journals and my letters?"

"Talk about that later," Elizabeth said, thinking again, with unease, about what Denton might find and come back with given what was written in her journals, especially about Alexander and the War and what she felt about king and country. The anger welled up, caught her by the throat, that sticky, sour mixture of red currant, tea and toast gurgling. "What we need is a good walk on Mount Victoria and across the hills to the bay. Fresh air and trees and exercise and away from all this sickness, this ghastly influenza. I won't go to work, they can cope what with the new woman there." She wanted to explain so much, so many things had happened: Rebecca the bookkeeper, who was so lovely and so good at her work; the articles in the papers, even this morning's, about the Meatyards disappearing some ten days previously, their house left as is, even the tea things set up, with food on the plates. "*Highly Suspicious*", "*Foul Play*?", "*Meatyard Mystery Deepens*", all headlines that were tantalising Wellington. Crawford Denton poking his nose into everything, even at the bookshop, interviewing every member of the book group with regards to sedition.

"I've been so lonely, so alone without you, Helen," she thought. "And so excited about your return." But she said nothing of that and, dipping the napkin in the glass of water on the breakfast tray, she attempted to wipe away the stain of redcurrant jam. Words would not come to her, only images from Helen's letters and her journals. She wanted to tear away the bedclothes, get dressed, go to the police station and scream and scream at Crawford Denton. Instead, she removed the tray with the butter and toast and jam and honey and boiled eggs, all the little delicacies she knew that Helen would not have had on the arduous trip from England on the troop ship. Days of planning, thinking about exactly what Helen would like: redcurrant jam in preference to apricot; manuka honey as opposed to clover; boiled eggs still a bit runny; the toast cut into strips and buttered cold, not while hot.

And now this: her brave and confident and astute companion weeping over raw memories of death and destruction but wrapped in some irrelevance about flowers and aristocrats. Elizabeth took Helen in her arms, held her tightly, and said as she ran her fingers through her long, blonde hair: "I love you, darling. It will all be wonderful; the sun will shine. Now, let's get ready and go out into the Wellington sun and wind and blow away these cobwebs."

Helen roused herself and jumping out of bed said with excitement: "Early Christmas present for you, or we will be waiting for next winter to enjoy it." From her suitcase under the bed she pulled a cloth bag and held it out to Elizabeth. "It was Lady Lacey's, Elizabeth. She gave it to me, but it's for you."

A flash of silk, graceful linen, a luxurious lining, a soft fur collar; it was the most beautiful coat Elizabeth had ever seen. As she slid it on over her cotton nighty, she cried, the tears welling up and flowing out. She blubbered: "I missed you so. Darling. Helen, my Helen, do come back to me as you were."

"I've changed, haven't I?"

"Tell me about the coat, how it was made."

"Oh, Lady Lacey explained that, but I paid no attention. I was thinking about it on you, not me, and on occasions I hated her voice, so self-assured, British. One day, when the new batch of men arrived, they were on stretchers, their faces bandaged, arms missing. And she said something about me and about you, and I looked at her and I saw what she wanted and what she was. And a man screamed as he was dropped by the stretcher bearers and as he wept, she asked me: 'Could you…ever?' I wanted to yell at her disdain, her privileges and her sense of entitlement, no matter how lovely she was, how sweet in the garden, taking my hand, fondling it. She was simply spoilt and had learned to be lovely, learned to be gracious, it was all so...so... removed from a farm in Southland and I felt that distinction, as if I were an exotic of some sort, like the pineapples they cultivated in their glasshouse, delicious and foreign and therefore slightly suspect. And yet ready for the eating because of that." She knelt in front of Elizabeth and ran her hands lovingly down the coat. "I told Lady Lacey: 'I have Elizabeth and I have my work as a nurse.'"

"Darling, of course. And I shall love this coat. It's a sort of offering."

"We all suffer from shellshock, of sorts. You with having been stuck here, and me tormented by my experience. If I had a few happy moments in a lovely garden with a generous and caring friend, which she was, actually. But she had such anxiety to possess me. She did, obsessively. Then she conceded one late afternoon, there were blackbirds singing and I thought of you in our garden. She said simply, 'Elizabeth wins.'" Helen took from the same bag a colourful hat of homespun wool, which Elizabeth recognised from having knitted and sent off soon after Helen's departure. "No Lady Whatshername would wear this. But I didn't take it off for the three winters when not in that horrid linen nurse's cap that always seemed to be bloodstained, much the colour of that redcurrant jam."

The grandfather clock chimed the quarter hour and on the last gong Elizabeth took Helen in her arms and said, touching her face: "I adore you, Helen."

Marjoribanks Street was steep and lined largely with solid, imposing houses. A few cottages remained, each with a tumble of rose garden and a wobbly picket fence. On a corner with a Norfolk pine, where a settlers' cottage had stood, a wealthy merchant from Liverpool had built an enormous house which Elizabeth and Helen abhorred. On their way up the street, puffed from the steepness, taking turns to carry the picnic basket, the two women were startled by the emergence from a gate, much like a Jack-in-the-Box, of a man in a black suit, white shirt, black tie and wearing a high, shiny black hat.

"Good morning," Elizabeth said to the tall, spectral man, whom she knew was an undertaker at the Wilson and Wilson Funeral Home. "I hope that…"

"Afraid not, Miss. This flu's getting worse and worse." He nodded to the brick house, indicating that up there was disease and death. "You know them, do you?"

"Of course. Mr. and Mrs. Webber and little James."

"Mr. Webber died in the early morning and Mrs. Webber's down with it, but I can't get their doctor. The ambulance is flat out." He looked towards the town and harbour. "This sickness is everywhere, it's just blown up," he said, stretching out his long arms which frightened Elizabeth into thinking of a mourning scarecrow or something from the Brothers Grimm.

"Bad, bad," he enthused, but grimly. He played his part so well, his augur so convincing, that Elizabeth shivered. She thought: "It's come to this. I never saw it, even with all those signs."

"We should go and assist," said Helen, turning to the gate.

"The papers are saying very little, everything's censored," said Elizabeth.

Her Aunt Elspeth had lived with her companion Miriam across the street. As Elizabeth looked at their villa with its crisscrossed windowpanes and finial and wall trellis covered in tea roses, she saw the two women waving their hands, warning her and Helen. She watched her loved ones with longing, with loss.

She turned and looked at the undertaker, at his plaster-like pallor. "They say it arrived on the *Niagara* with the Prime Minister. He and the Minister of Finance got off in Auckland on October the twelfth. The ship should have been quarantined. The Australians wouldn't let it in."

"So did my troop ship, which docked on the same day," said Helen looking up at the infected house. "It's everywhere in the world. Why blame him just because you don't like his politics? My ship had seven deaths. The *Niagara* was cleared, and quite rightly."

"What do you mean by that?" snapped Elizabeth. "Even the papers suggested it, and two sailors died from the flu on it soon afterwards."

"You're anti-war, all our friends are. Pacifists and shirkers. It's like that if you haven't been there to see what the Huns did."

Elizabeth looked up at Mr. Wilson's face and was scarily reminded of the Hieronymus Bosch of piles of bodies dead from contagion. In the background of her version of the painting was not a wintry Dutch garden but the shimmering green hills of Wellington.

"Fifteen deaths yesterday, but it's not affecting kiddies yet, but the Health Department hasn't said a word," said the undertaker.

"The Huns deserve revenge," said Helen. "If they'd invaded our country and raped women and children, you'd think the same. But here you're all so safe, you don't see defence as justified."

Mr. Wilson's mask-like face stiffened. His job was gathering the dead in these streets, not in the mud and gore of Flanders or Passchendaele. He looked from Elizabeth to Helen to the house and pointed with his bony finger and said: "They need help. The boy's inside, the woman's very sick. I'll be back to get the body. It's black with cyanosis. You came just in time. Good luck."

Helen pushed open the iron gate with impatience when it stuck. She stomped up the path and climbed the steps without noticing the massed daffodils and scented jonquils in the border gardens. Attired In Lady Lacey's coat, Elizabeth tried to keep up, aware the garment was too dressy for a long walk in the wilds, let alone to administer to the sick. She had an impulse to take it off, discard it, fling it into the universe. She saw how ridiculous life was: the coat; the funereal scarecrow; the lugubrious Hieronymus Bosch; Lady Lacey seducing Helen; racing up steps to find dead and blackened bodies. She looked towards the villa, saw Elspeth and Miriam wave, but this time with love not alarm. She breathed in, the scent of spring flowers bringing her back, the indigo of the bluebells and the pink of the hyacinths. "Calm down," she thought. "This coat is absolutely all right, life is precious."

At the window they saw James looking out, his big blue eyes staring wild, his little hands splayed against the panes, he too appearing as a storybook character. Helen signalled for him to come to the door and the tears started when he opened it. He said: "Miss Helen, Mummy said you were sure to visit us." He took hold of her and sobbed. From inside the house they heard screaming.

"Daddy died last night and Mummy is so sick, and I went to get the doctor and he can't come, and Mr. Wilson said he'd bring a coffin and the ambulance."

"Liz, stay here with James," Helen said. "He probably needs something nice to eat. Do you like ham sandwiches, James?" She took off up the stairs, the war nurse to her station. Following the groans, she went into a room and shut the door.

"Guide me to the dining room, James," Elizabeth said. "We'll spread out the picnic. Now, tell me again, how old are you. You look very tall these days."

"Ten," he said. "I don't want to eat, and I don't want to be an orphan. Who would look after me? Who will look after us now that Daddy has died?" He pointed to the ornate plaster ceiling. She followed his gaze and thought how this was the new war, here, on these shores. She shivered with apprehension in the sunless, over-furnished room: the dark chairs, the green wallpaper, the blue carpet, and the heavily framed paintings of European mountain villages.

"I don't have those answers," she said. "It's all too shocking, isn't it? I'm so sorry. James, I'm so sorry." She held out her arms, but he backed away and said, crossly: "Germs! Germs!"

"I don't believe I'm contagious," she said. But was she? The question flooded her. The tingling sensation she'd had when observing the funeral director retraced its steps spider-like up her spine. Who would live and who would die? She looked at the mountain villages on the wall and saw their victims piled up as in the Hieronymus Bosch.

"I'm probably going to die," said James. "Daddy turned purple and this morning he got up and ran around the room and he held me and kissed me and then he got into bed and died." The boy stood perfectly still, his arms to his sides, as if rehearsing being dead in a coffin.

They heard wailing and Helen yelled: "Elizabeth! Bring warm water and cloths. Leave them outside the door!"

In the kitchen, James said: "If Mummy dies…" But she didn't know what to say; she wasn't used to this form of drama, nor to children. She had an image of Lady Lacey in a nurse's uniform wearing a tiara and holding a syringe. She shook her head to dismiss the dream fragment, but her mind was befuddled with daffodils and English houses and aristocrats were shouting at her and bombs were detonating, and she could hear "Mummy! Mummy!" as she poured water from the coal range kettle into a bowl and looked about for towels.

"James, where are the kitchen towels, dear?"

He was standing behind the door. She thought she might have been imagining him, too, a sad and frightened schoolboy, until he emerged, but with an expression proclaiming his sudden manhood, the chrysalis of innocence discarded.

He opened a cupboard and looked about and shook his head. "Mrs. Smith is hopeless," he said, using the voice of a man. "She never gets anything right, and Mummy gets so annoyed." He pulled a chair to the cupboard and stood on it and from above them they heard more yelling. "Oh," he uttered, exasperated. "The tea towels should be here. I don't know where she could have put them, she probably stole them, that's what Daddy accused her of, stealing. She stole four apples last week and an orange before that, the only one in the bowl, and when Daddy came home from work, he asked me if I'd eaten it and I said no, and it must have been Mrs. Smith who took it because she's got four children and her husband is dead. He died in a coal mine. Didn't you know that?" He jumped down and went into the dining room and she heard drawers being opened and slammed. When he appeared with two tablecloths, he said: "You may as well cut these up. They won't be any good if Mummy goes as well."

"I imagine Mrs. Smith might be accused of stealing them, if I do. And poor Mrs. Smith seems already quite…quite…inundated…"

His hands on his hips, he said in the voice of an exasperated house-wife: "Johnny her eldest one, tried to bash me up outside Saint Peter's but I told him I didn't fight Catholics because they're too dirty. Daddy said I mustn't play with them, just Protestants. But I think Daddy said that because Johnny's the son and his mother works for us." He was on a roll, she could see it in his eyes, which had turned on her. She thought he might call her Mrs. Smith with the same derision, even though she was dressed in the absurdly overdone Lady Lacey garment, for his eyes had rounded like that of the wealthy woman arguing with an upstart housemaid.

He led led the way up the stairs, she holding the bowl of water in the same way she imagined a slave would when serving a despot. He knocked on the door and said, forcefully: "Open up!" She saw that twenty-four hours previously he would have been sweet, innocent, and would have said mirthfully to his parents: "Open Sesame!" When Helen creaked open the door and peered out they knew from her eyes that Mrs. Glenys Webber was the latest victim of the Spanish influenza.

16

Alexander Powderham was in his office discussing accounts with Rebecca Routledge when Detective Crawford Denton opened the door and entered wearing a shabby grey coat and felt hat, his face flushed, his shoulders stooped. "I've read *Crime and Punishment* and *The Metamorphosis*, the so-called masterpieces. I'm here to discuss this evidence," he said sitting down, uninvited.

"Rebecca, you might like to leave us," said Alexander.

"Interesting choice for an accounts lady," said Denton when she had left. "How much she charges would be a consideration, considering…"

"Is this what you've learned from Dostoyevsky and Kafka?"

"I see Sonia Marmeladova when I see Rebecca Routledge."

"If you have questions about sedition, come to the point."

"Why does everyone have to suffer so much in *Crime and Punishment*? This is a book to depress people and make them suffer from the anxiety of being alive. Not a healthy influence in our young democracy fighting a war. Are you trying to undermine the Kiwi psyche? Depress the people and they'll give in, feel defeated? I sail a skiff. I get out on the sea and forget my troubles, but these people just roam about tormented. Is this a suitable book for our population?"

"What's seditious about a psychological crime novel?"

"It's all in the interpretations." Denton pulled the book group's notes from his satchel and held them up. "Under the War Regulations Act these opinions are seditious. Listen to Miss Rutherford…" He flicked to the green pages: "'*Germans are stereotypes in the novel, every single German is seen as idiotic, immoral, eccentric*'. This is pure prejudice, not literature."

"I thought Germans were our enemy. Or are you saying Miss Rutherford doesn't like that negative interpretation because she supports them? Are you jumping from sedition to traitorship?" said Alexander. "If I wrote a novel in which all detectives were officious, shabby, ignorant and alcoholic, then I could be accused of prejudice. She's right, Dostoyevsky does stereotype Germans, just as he does Poles and Jews and indeed Russians. If Dostoyevsky has a flaw as a writer, it's that he stereotypes whole groups of people. Goodness knows what he'd write about Wellingtonians." He looked about for cigarettes. "Archetypes is a better term. Still, we are products of the *personae*, if you don't mind such a modern interpretation. We can thank Jung for that, can't we, Detective?"

"Jung, another German. Is everything in your repertoire Hun? But the police are not your enemy, even shabby, alcoholic ones, while Germans are. So why would you categorise police so badly?"

"This could go around and around in contradictions and dead ends and doesn't constitute solid literary analysis, Detective. The novel was written in eighteen-sixty by a conservative Russian Orthodox Christian. I don't know what you're getting at." He felt like screaming at the man, at his weak analytical abilities, this anti-intellectual pretending to be something he wasn't, a bloke envious of the intelligentsia. He stiffened in his chair, saw himself as the arrogant, overtly intellectual Raskolnikov and thought, "I'll swing for this."

"Your book group is full of sedition, and is an apology for…murder. Listen to your own ideas." He flicked to Alexander's notes. "'*Raskolnikov has the right to kill because he sees himself as an extraordinary man, a Napoleon. Murder is justified if for a good cause, one that benefits mankind. Thus, a poor student who can kill a loathsome, money grabbing pawnbroker he hates, one who exploits poor people…*'" Denton stared at Alexander as if he needed to read no further with murder, not sedition, having been proven in just a few handwritten sentences.

Alexander understood what it was to be a weed pulled from the soil, to be wilting. He had been caught, the perfect crime was unraveling. Denton had smelled murder and was progressing with it. The scenes of the inevitable flowed through his head: courts, judges, derision, the gallows.

"You've played enough games," said Denton. "You support von Zedlitz. I interviewed the Finks on Somes Island. You gave them money, more assistance to Germans, Jews even. They said that you understood what it means to be a Silesian, which is German, a Jew too. That's not so odd given you look like one, like Fagin, if I too can be literary, even me, a shabby, alcoholic man can allude to literature."

Alexander flinched: crippled, ugly, unwanted, different. He heard Sybil Meatyard shout: "Oscar Wilde!" He wanted to jump up and grab his pistol and shoot Denton as he had Sybil Meatyard. "If you understand Dostoyevsky, then you know he's all about suffering and redemption. I saw people suffering and I helped them, just as I help Māori who suffer because of…"

"Because of?"

"I don't have to elaborate about Māori. There's nothing seditious in that area."

"The Waikato Māori are rebelling against European rule and conscription. Their so-called Māori queen has ordered the police out of Waikato land. She won't permit conscription of her people. That's sedition. Your friend Aroha Raharuhi supports that thinking as I understand from the Honourable Āpirana Ngata."

"Aroha hasn't read *Crime and Punishment* or *The Metamorphosis.*"

"Perhaps not. But he speaks disrespectfully to the Right Honourable Āpirana Ngata. In fact, it was the Honourable Member who came to me to investigate further what this…this…liaison with you and the Māori is all about. Sedition yes, perversion, yes and quite possibly…"

"Perversion and sedition in equal parts? It sounds like a recipe. And what was that other ingredient?" He regretted his retort. Raskolnikov had done himself in by such slips to Detective Porfiry Petrovich. He thought: "I have to get out. Flee to Argentina tomorrow."

"I imagine you think I sound like the Meatyards, all perversion and sedition. Speaking of the missing Meatyards, I'm aware you know quite a bit about their antics. I understand they chided you in public, called you certain names."

"You speak in roundabout ways. Is this how detectives get their prey? Like cats."

"It's how the detective in *Crime and Punishment* eventually wore down Raskolnikov. I liked Porfiry Petrovitch. Clever man and I'm glad I read the novel. Educated criminals think they're above the law, these self-appointed Napoleons who live for an ideal or a theory. *Crime and Punishment* should be required reading for detectives. We could rename it, *How to Catch a Rat*."

"Are you calling me a rat?"

"If you killed the Meatyards. Yes."

"How dare you insinuate that. I'm a cripple, a…"

"A rat? From what Elizabeth writes about you in her journals, I can come to that conclusion. It's all there. I imagine you haven't read your friend's opinion of you in her private writings. About the "Fairy Boss". Fairy Fagin indeed. Rat is essentially what the Honourable Āpirana Ngata calls you, a rat for corruption and perversion against Māoris."

The door opened and Elizabeth walked in. In her formal attire, she might have been headed for the opera: a classic black dress, an ivory *pieneta* in her auburn hair. She stood above Denton and said: "You are truly repulsive. I heard what you said. Fairy Boss. You're here for some weird form of revenge because I know what you did to Louisa, and now all these years later you're coming back. You raped my sister. You led her into that despair that killed her. You are a rapist, *Crawford*."

Denton stood up. "How dare you? I have your journals. I know what filth you're engaged in, what things you all do. You think you can get away with this, but…"

"Ah, but you don't have Louisa's journals, do you? Nor her letters to your wife, and your wife's responses about you."

"Mr. Powderham, follow me, now, we will discuss this further but not here."

"Am I under arrest?"

"You will be if you don't come with me."

"Contact my lawyer, Elizabeth. Where are we going, Denton?"

"You don't need a lawyer. Under the War Regulation Act you aren't entitled to one."

"Return my journals, Denton. You have no right to hold them," Elizabeth declared.

He laughed and held up the sheaf of papers: "The whole lot of you could be locked up. But I go for the big rats. The ones that corrupt and cause confusion in people's minds. Follow me, Powderham. And as for any letters and my wife and Louisa, I'm Senior Detective and I have the police on my side, an entire division in a war situation and the War Regulations Act supporting me."

The police van was parked on Cuba Street. As Alexander moved awkwardly to get into the vehicle his eyes met Muriwai's.

Denton said as the driver started the engine: "To Tinakori Road, where we shall search to see how rats live."

The Wellington streets rumbled by grim and windblown in the mid-morning, not that Alexander could see them from the back of the van. All views were in his mind: Aroha being led in chains to the gallows; scenes of himself being tortured; the screaming headlines in *Truth Magazine* about "Queers" and "Murderous Pansies". He had read in an English newspaper that immediately after the arrest of Oscar Wilde, a multitude of men of his persuasion had fled to France where they were legal under the *Code Napoléon*. He thought with agitation: "We should have left. Why did we stay in this Biblical outpost of conformity? Buenos Aires, Paris, they were both available." He saw himself once again on that proverbial vessel sailing into exile. But, like Oscar Wilde, he had left it too late, had believed too much in his invincibility. There was no chance to run. This crop of islands in the middle of a vast ocean held no hope of an easy escape, no porous border.

"Aroha, run, now," he wanted to shout across the town to his lover. He felt a warm sensation on his hand. Fearful, he thought it was something bad, an omen, a rat. But it was Muriwai's fingers. In the dim light he saw Muriwai's eyes which smiled at him, winked, fluttered, in a beautiful bouquet of reassurance.

At the house, Denton said to Muriwai: "Help this pervert out. He can't walk properly, and he thinks he's a Russian intellectual, someone who is above the law and can do what he likes." He laughed and said to the two constables waiting at the gate: "Let's see what we can find about so many mysteries."

Aroha came to the door in his shorts and singlet, his feet bare. Behind him was Orton in his horse jockey ensemble of silk and satin.

"Why am I opening the door to a knock when this is the owner of the house?" asked Aroha.

"Because the house is being searched." He pointed to Muriwai: "You take Mr. Raharuhi, and thoroughly search the back garden."

"And what might be seditious in my back yard?" asked Alexander. "German elms perhaps?"

"You have no idea what we're looking for, or perhaps you do," said Denton, which froze Alexander's stomach. However, despite the inner torment, he maintained his composure as he imagined Aroha telling him: "Be French. Be Descartes. Be rational." Rising to his full height with the support of his Moroccan cane, on the bottom step of his own home, with the police scrutinising him, Alexander decided that he would indeed take the role of the man who could be extraordinary. Other men had gone valiantly off to war to defend their democracy and so was he, now, going to defend his, with strength. He had the right to murder in order to preserve his own identity and dignity, as had the soldiers bayonetting Huns in France. He knew his very being was strength as he looked up at his loved ones, Orton and Aroha. He would not faint and babble as had Raskolnikov under pressure. "I'm not Russian and emotive. I'm a Kiwi," he said to himself as his eyes met Aroha's and, each with a knowing look, said: "Fight this as we said we would."

"Sedition," said Denton.

"Sedition! What a perfect name for a racehorse," Orton exclaimed, standing next to Aroha on the front step. "But why are you relegating the Māoris to the back yard? They're welcome inside, like these *Pākehā* constables." Both of his eyebrows were arched, a skill he had perfected in front of the mirror as a child, which now served him well, for he made both the *Pākehā* cops laugh. "Sedition indeed," he added, chillingly. "If you own a bookshop in New Zealand, it automatically means you're an outcast with the likes of cops."

In the living room, Denton said: "I understand the Māori has his sleepout. You, Philips, go and check that out. Anything suspicious, bring it in. And you, Mr. Orton, I've heard of. In fact, Elizabeth calls you an honorary uncle to Alexander, so you have that dubious responsibility. If you wouldn't mind, lead me to Mr. Powderham's bedroom."

Orton, literally, had to bite his tongue in order not to make a witticism in response to that request. He turned on his heels as it were, and marched across the wooden floors and Persian carpets, down the passageway to the bedroom.

"Why start with the bedroom?" said Alexander, coming up behind the duo, the other constable having been ordered to look about the kitchen. "Is this the official order? Evidence of perversion? Or is it that you think you might find seditious reading material on my bedside table?"

"People tend to keep their journals in their bedrooms, they write at night, in bed," said Denton, dismissing Orton with a gesture, and looking about at the grandeur of the Victorian décor. "From experience I've learned that."

"You know so much about people's bedroom habits. Elizabeth has certainly pointed out yours," said Alexander. He leaned for support against a green moquette sofa. He felt, as he looked at the bland detective, menacing even in his dull greys and browns, that despite his resolution a few minutes previously to remain strong and vigilant, that he ought to throw it all in, as had Cecil Meatyard: "Kill me, get it over and done with." And that had been the challenge Raskolnikov had faced in his ordeal with the ethereal Detective Porfiry Petrovich. Petrovich who snooped about asking questions infused with philosophical insinuations, his esoteric approach frightening Raskolnikov with their subtlety, unlike Denton whose approach was, nevertheless, as equally disturbing to Alexander who saw him as crude, rude, as subtle as a cow cocky.

"Intellectuals keep journals because they think they're such interesting people and they write their inner thoughts hoping for eventual publication," said Denton, still surveying the room as if he were imagining what went on in there, on the bed, on the sofa.

He studied the ottoman as if it were a place for certain fetishist behaviour. The long, wide mirror he looked at as if it should be weeping with shame at what it had witnessed. "*The Collected Letters of Alexander Powderham*, or *Journals of a Pervert*," he continued, looking at Alexander. "Intellectuals like your von Zedlitz. I suppose he'll write a scathing life story when the peace settles, about his perceived mistreatment. Do you think he will?"

"He would have a lot to say, but probably not about himself given his humility. He'd be more interested in asking why a supposedly democratic country had crucified its pacifists. But you're searching in my underwear drawer at this moment, not through my memoirs."

Alexander saw that this was why he was so tired. As he watched Denton explore the drawers, the exhaustion seeped through him as a substance through vegetation. Osmosis, which he had read about in a scientific journal, was, he felt, occurring within him; the leaking in, and its opposite, plasmolysis, the leaking out, just as had the Meatyards all over his carpets. The female Meatyard in her heavy winter coat with her hair messed up from the wind, was staring at him in her last moment, the pistol pointed at her. Etched forever in his mind, that look in her eyes was one of terror, but equally one of disgust at being murdered by a pervert. Returning to that moment, he felt a surge of that power surfacing and he thought: "I will not leak out for the benefit of this Denton dullard. I killed in self-defence."

"I don't keep a journal because I don't live in a democracy where the rule of law is observed for all of its constituents, no matter what they might get up to in the privacy of their bedrooms," he said. Johnny Fletcher, an old friend of his, had been arrested on a charge of "unnatural acts" in New Plymouth some years previously. An *agent provocateur* posing as a Pansy had approached him in that town's famous Pukekura Park. That mean-spirited and duplicitous situation struck Alexander as he looked at Crawford Denton rifling through his dresser. Johnny Fletcher, tall, dignified, but never very astute when it had come to soliciting in public, had told the presiding judge: "Your Honour, what I do with my appendage is my business, and I would think that the same will apply to you given I've seen you about Pukekura Park on an evening," a statement for which Johnny Fletcher had had two years added to his prison sentence. Some of Johnny Fletcher's spirit of defiance jumped into Alexander, who used it not with a cutting remark but with a withering look, and he stored away the rest, osmosis-like, for what might eventuate.

"I wonder if you know where your one-armed friend is?" asked Denton. "Given that he was a friend of your accounts lady and has been here, so I'm informed."

"What would a one-legged man want with a one-armed man?" asked Alexander, searching his mind for the right words, but feeling suddenly queasy with this revelation. For the first time, really, Alexander understood the meaning of a word that he seldom used but enjoyed the sound of: hegemony; consent plus force. Hegemony had arrived to wear him down and he, Alexander, was eroding to it as the force searched through his underwear drawer. He saw this was how it happened. Someone inferior was, after all, superior. The delegate of the state's apparatus was here dressed in a shabby grey coat and it drank too much but it was, inevitably, more powerful, as Johnny Fletcher had found out, as indeed had Oscar Wilde. "We are all caught," thought Alexander. "I am forced to consent."

"I just ask. Nothing more than a few questions," said Denton. "Much like Raskolnikov's detective, Porfiry Petrovich, softly, softly." He turned from his roughing up the handkerchiefs and underpants to observe his victim, look in his eyes, tease him with the velvet glove. From down the hallway they heard Orton shout: "Mind that china, how *dare* you!"

"The man with one arm," said Alexander, as though he were repeating a customer's request for a title in the bookshop. "Was a Bolshevik."

"Don't twist things with your diseased mind. MacPherson doesn't have the intellect to sort through political upheavals, but he was wearing your underpants from Munster and Munster. The best quality black ones, especially imported by Munster and Munster, that German shop you frequented."

Alexander took from his pocket the cigarette case imprinted with the fez-wearing Turkish man. He opened it in an attempt to shift his eyes from Denton's, so filled with loathing. Looking up, meeting Denton's eyes, and imparting an equal amount of hostility and hatred, Alexander replied: "My underwear is my underwear. I don't see what it has to do with a policeman."

"When the policeman, as you call me, is investigating a double disappearance of two notable people and their probable murder, it's quite an appropriate question to ask why the main suspect was wearing the underpants of a well-known Wellington Pansy," said Denton, his face flushed with success as he came in with his *denouement*. "You see, Alex, nothing goes unnoticed. Porfiry snapped Raskolnikov. I'm an avid reader *and* a detective, so I was reading the novel carefully. Raskolnikov made mistakes even though he thought he was so smart. A student, a so-called extraordinary man, one above the law, one who can kill two people and think he can get away with it. But he couldn't, could he? As soon as he realised he'd made mistakes, he crumpled, wanted to confess, got all weak and started making even bigger mistakes. There's no perfect crime, we all leave clues. Now, how did MacPherson get your pair of expensive Munster and Munster underpants when Mr. Munster himself said you are the only one to have ordered that size through his catalogue?"

"This has nothing to do with sedition and is therefore not under the auspices of the so-called War Regulations Act. I need my lawyer."

"You need a lawyer to answer a question about your underpants?" laughed Denton. He turned to the drawers and opened the bottom one and rummaged around. As he plucked out the pistol as if he had known all along of its existence, he said, his laugh having turned to a sneer: "A nice little ladies' pistol. This must be the one that Elizabeth recorded in her journal and with which you shot magpies, according to her account of a picnic in the back yard. When was that? Last summer, when you showed off how good a shot you are at killing birds? Do we have a permit for this?"

"My late father bought it as a curio in Rome. It belonged to Eugénie de Montijo, the wife of Napoleon the Third, so it was the pistol of an empress, not a lady. And it was Australian parrots I shot, not magpies." Alexander, looking away, his mind flushed, caught himself in the full-length mirror and from his image he gained strength. He still wore his hat, rakishly, the duck's feather poking up; his dark green suit that had been tailored for him to match his green shirt he saw with considerable pride was right out of that packet of Parisian photos that his father had brought back from Paris decades previously. He thought: "*Le Parisien.* I am a product, as Jung said. I am a persona, one with dignity and valid for that. I made myself to be this." He returned his gaze to Denton and in his head thanked Oscar Wilde.

"Owned by an empress. Still is, isn't it? *The Empress of Tinakori.* And again, a Napoleon connection. The circle seems to be closing in, doesn't it, *Alex*?" Denton laughed, mimicking Porfiry Petrovitch, as if he, the inquisitor, were at one with the suspect; a little snigger amongst friends; enticing the suspect in with confidences and humour; one after the other the astute insinuations that would induce the culprit to snap and confess. However, Denton had not mimicked Porfiry's laugh with verisimilitude, it being more the snort from a sufferer of sinusitis. His attempt at the sardonic, the witty and the vengeful in front of someone so accomplished in those skills, simply failed.

"Do you get so angry at some point that you shoot things through the eyes, as Elizabeth records you did with birds? Could you do that to a person? Or have you contained that passion to parrots?" These were, Denton thought, psychological questions, resonant with profundity, his solicitations as penetrating as those of his Saint Petersburg colleague. He stared at Alexander, who stared back, drawing on his cigarette and exhaling in a grand simulation of that postcard Parisian dandy.

The strategy to catch someone was to get them off guard by quickly changing the subject with a barrage of questions, and Denton pulled that leaf from his detective's manual: "Now, tell me about Mac and if he buggers you, or you him? Although, not wishing to imagine it at all, I imagine it's the former." He paused, Porfiry-like, to ascertain the effect of his brilliance upon his victim, this crippled Pansy, this fixture about Wellington. But there was nothing discernible, not even a blink or a wince and the Pansy, Denton observed, merely looked at him with hatred, with venom, his big eyes wide like the black patches on the petals of the flower after which he was named. "In fact," Denton continued, pointing to the bed, "I wouldn't be surprised if your boy-friend was under there now, listening. If you are Mac, you're wanted for questioning. And since you're a convicted murderer of Māoris you are, as your letter says, responsible, well, primarily, for the murder of the Meatyards, with assistance from certain friends."

The Saint Petersburg detective, so coolly intellectual, suave, and debonair, Denton continued to emulate. He waved the pistol in his hand as Porfiry might have, and made another allusion to Napoleon and murder, but the act fell flat. The Russian detective, so imbued with positive characteristics, had never employed sarcasm, spite and male bravado. In the face of these negative characteristics, Alexander's implacable calm and arrogant demeanour increasingly infuriated the Wellington detective. In the novel, Raskolnikov had fainted under in-terrogation, wilted flower-like and blabbered. This Pansy, however, so at ease with his privileges, just stood there, evilly, as a dwarf or gnome in a children's pantomime, one ill-fitted to humankind, there on the stage, its role simply to stare out and scare the children. The scraps of that Russian detective's sophisticated methodology began to rapidly dissolve. In his shabby coat the Wellington detective reverted to type, to Denton, pure and simple. Facing what he knew was an implacable, seditious Fairy, it was Crawford Denton who caved in.

"I'll get you, Powderham," he said. "By hook or by crook." He turned and stomped down the passageway to the living room where the *Pākehā* constable was eagerly waiting to display, holding them up as a trophy, a pair of underpants.

"Found them in the Māori's cottage, sir. Army issue, with *MacPherson* on the identification label. Soiled, too, with a certain incriminating male substance in them, sir."

17

Seated behind his desk with the office door shut against everything that he felt menaced him, Detective Crawford Denton studied the newspaper headlines which shouted: *Missing Meatyards Mystery Deepens!*

"The links, the links," he uttered, as he tried to imagine the missing couple through Powderham's eyes, a task which was naturally revolting given the requirement to enter the Pansy's mind. Nevertheless, as if crawling into a moist crevice filled with body lice, Crawford Denton inched in. "Using modern psychology works to catch criminals, to think like them, become them, enter into them, as in dreams, as that German says," he thought. What he could imagine was Powderham and MacPherson in the crowd watching the Meatyards. Sitting in his office trying to employ modern psychology, Denton could see the two misfits just as they had been described to him by the military man who had reported on them as a response to the call in the newspapers for witnesses. Denton squeezed his mind to see how the links merged, what had happened. "Theirs was an obvious liaison in the making," was what the military man had stated: "I could sense it, lust and perversion all over them as they chatted outside the Bank of New Zealand. The cripple offered the one-armed man a cigarette, lured him into the evil seduction. I was watching them as I listened to the unfortunate Meatyards." The blonde military man with the clipped moustache had divulged everything, leaning forward, excited by his testimony, seated in that very chair now empty in front of Denton, but with his military presence palpable, as if he were still there, eager, brave and handsome.

The waitress at the Duchess Tea Rooms also reported to Denton and had stated excitedly: "He's a queer fish all right. He stood outside the tearooms staring in as if he was hypnotised and then he went off and stood up the street a bit and that one-armed man met up with him and they talked and I took notice, I could see it all from the front tables, because even the ladies watching out the window as he'd looked in said he was a queer fish." She was a brazen little thing, Denton had happily noted, fleshy, with big breasts, a real Wellington waitress, her skirt too tight, her hair piled up. "I can see them as clear as daylight, that one-armed man gives me the willies. The next day or so he came in with that skinny bird, ordered tea and a tart, like she is." Here she blinked and smiled at Denton and blushed. "That bird he was with, she's called Rebecca, red-haired, a real Newtown…sort, shall we call it? I knew her husband and he was quite nice, really. That's what I needed to tell you, they rushed out and started talking to Mr. Meatyard, and then the old couple disappeared, didn't they? Did they kill them?" She fluttered her eyelids. "I wonder what for?"

"They met Meatyard?" he asked, taking his eyes off her breasts and looking into her eyes, small grey, like a sparrow's. She nodded as if she had brought the solution to the inquiry. "I see a lot in the tea rooms. You'd be surprised who comes in what gets said and that tart was all over Meatyard like a coque…cocque…"

"Coquette," he said for her, smiling, his eyes returning to her breasts. "I like coquettes myself," he said. "They can be very amusing."

"I don't know what you're talking about," she said, blushing: "I can hardly say the word without getting flustered."

"Stay, tell me more."

"No, sir, if I'm late, that old bag gets so cranky. You've got no idea what it's like to work in flash tea rooms. She told me I have to improve my diction."

Thinking of her days later, Denton opened his notebook, found her address, and read it aloud as if reciting an incantation, his smile like the seducer Svidrigailov's following a female street walker in Saint Petersburg: "Nancy MacTotter, flat two, forty-four Rintoul Street, Newtown. Single. Aged twenty. I need more information from her."

Next to the newspaper lay *Crime and Punishment*, which he picked up and flicked through. The intense language and the dense philosophies stared back, teasing him with their depth and replacing the images of Powderham and MacPherson with their Russian counterparts. Razumikhin, Svidrigailov, Zamyotov, Marmeladova, the ugliness of their respective appearances and names an affront to him. Each character was now somehow similar to those in the Wellington streets he, Denton, had just surveyed in his imagination for clues to the Meatyards' disappearance. He looked up, felt his head being squeezed; somewhere, somehow, in the novel's stifling chapters he knew there was an answer to the mystery of the missing Meatyards.

It seemed as if the book were taunting him for his inabilities as a modern detective to solve the crime. Disgust rose in him as a reaction to his deficiencies. How he now loathed that novel, its despicable characters, its endless repetition, its posing as a great work when, really, what it symbolised was the pretentiousness of the pseudo-intelligentsia of the Wellington book club members. Raskolnikov was an over-educated snob and fop and Dostoyevsky had imposed poverty upon him merely to propagandise the necessity of communism. The novel was nothing but a seditious stimulant to puff up and torment intellectuals into revolution. He threw down the offensive book by that ignoble Dostoyevsky as the words from Elizabeth's journal leapt up: "Alex is obsessive about Raskolnikov and the justification of murder for the better good..."

"The dirty Fairy did it, but how?" he uttered as he sat with his eyes closed and his hands on his head, Elizabeth's words burning him as he attempted to dig further into the strata of his thinking. But the stratum in which he was scratching was shallow, the profundity of his mining too superficial to breathe life into the cause and effect of suffering and how one step led to another because of it. He had read the novel; suffering, the main theme, however, had escaped him. For Denton, there was nothing beyond the ridiculous story and the dense narratives. He could not venture past communism as a possible motive, and Powderham was too rich for that to be his reason for murder. He pushed the novel off his desk because he knew that this was another case of his own insufficiencies. It had always been like this; stymied at some point that someone better would find easy access to. Louisa had told him to his face: "You can't purchase or seduce depth, Crawford. You just don't have it." He stood, agitated and disgusted, and pushed away his chair. He wanted to be out on the rough sea in his skiff, the waves slapping the boat, the wind brisk and scuttling him along, but all he saw was Louisa and Powderham and his own wife, and they were all laughing at him. The bottle of whisky was locked away in the bottom drawer and he hadn't had a drink for two hours so his throat burned with need.

Crawford Denton sweated in his office with his fingers on his keys in his left trouser pocket. His hand was grasping the keys, his mind exploding with the smell of whisky, the taste burning the lining of his mouth and nostrils. He swore loudly enough for Mr. Wallace and the two people waiting in the outside office to hear him as he took the keys and flung them across the room, where they smacked the wall and fell to the ground behind the potted aspidistra.

"Think like a man," he said as he sat down and picked up his fountain pen and sketched the circles of his thinking: "The book club. Powderham. MacPherson's note. The underpants. Raskolnikov. Elizabeth's incriminating journal." There was that rat smelling somewhere, but he couldn't find it. Why had MacPherson attended that book club meeting when the police informer had been there? Why were MacPherson's underpants in the Māori's sleepout? And Powderham's exclusive underpants found in the boarding house room in Newtown, which the police had raided on a tip off from the landlady? Denton opened his desk drawer, withdrew the letter that MacPherson had written and read it aloud, his voice husky: "*I will kill you, you abused me. You are meat, mate. Meat. Be very careful. You crossed your Mac and so did that stupid woman you married.*" He got up and walked back and forth across his spacious office. Twenty-seven years in the police force, fifteen as a detective, and there was always that moment when he thought he might never solve a case. Outside, the clouds gathered over the Tinakori hills and came roiling down, covering them as he watched from the window. It was at that moment that his secretary, Mr. Wallace, a ginger and bespectacled septuagenarian in a green tweed suit, knocked, swung open the door, came in and closed it and said in a rasping voice, his vocal chords having been compromised from five decades of smoking: "You have people here to talk about the Meatyard newspaper article today, sir."

"Who?"

"Mrs. Rachael Chatterley. Gives her address as Oriental Parade, so she's wealthy, a banker's wife."

"I know her husband. He could do with keeping his head down with regards to a few things." He saw the banker's snide face, overlooking him as he surveyed the members at The Professional Men's Club.

"Funny coincidence that she should have arrived at exactly the same time as the Reverend Ramsbottom from Thorndon Church of England. Says he has some information about sightings."

"Coincidences, indeed," Denton said. Coincidence was another thing he disliked about *Crime and Punishment*. There were too many coincidences, which was the hallmark, he thought, of a lazy writer. He went to the mantelpiece and took up his pipe, sniffing it before stuffing it with tobacco, as Wallace stood watching, waiting for instructions from his irascible superior. "This wealthy Svidrigailov fellow, for instance, is a sensualist, rapist, a lover of young girls, and yet rents a sleazy room next to an impoverished prostitute despite his being from the upper classes," Denton said, as he lit his match. "Is that improbable coincidence or a lazy literary device? Such a luxury as a writer to allow for that in solving the puzzles."

"Perhaps he just wanted to be near the prostitute, sir," said Wallace, amused by the detective's accusation that someone other than he, Denton, was a known seducer and sensualist. "Should I ask in Mrs. Chatterley first?"

"Coincidences exist in normal life. Why not in a detective novel? Who is teasing whom here, Dostoyevsky or Denton?"

"I'm not sure I catch your drift, sir. But the lady or the man first?"

"How could a one-armed man kill two people and dispose of their bodies? Could two cripples do this? And why would they? The underpants are my link."

"The Reverend or Mrs. Chatterley?" asked Wallace, wishing it were five o'clock so he could get out of there.

"Her," he said, blowing out the acrid smoke and picking the novel off the floor and dropping it on his desk with distaste, as if it too were diseased with body lice.

Mrs. Rachael Chatterley was wearing the same dark green dress as she had that day Cecil Meatyard had supplied her with the contaminated concoction of opiates. Over that dress, embroidered with strands of black sequins, she wore against the late spring chill a deep navy-blue woollen coat. Her hat, wide brimmed and elegant, was of the same dark hues, as if she had selected them to reflect the wintry harbour that she watched for hours from her handsome Oriental Bay villa. Her beauty, he noted as he looked at her enter the room, was exotic. She was the sort of woman bought by the likes of wealthy bankers and kept and coddled and spoilt. As she stood there, he still seated, he wondered if she had ever fucked anyone other than her rotund and ruddy husband.

"Have I inconvenienced you?" she asked.

"Why would that be?" he said, seeing her naked on his bed, her legs parted.

"Given that you haven't stood to greet me, I rather thought that might be the case."

He pushed himself up, flushed and disconcerted by her arrogance. "Good afternoon, Detective Crawford Denton, and you are Mrs. Chatterley with information about the disappearance of the Meatyards."

"I thought a detective would ask, rather than answer, questions," she said, sitting down without being invited, seeing the greed in him.

"My…my…apologies," he stuttered. "Rather a lot going on what with the War and the Spanish influenza."

"And what do the police do about the influenza?" she said. "Wouldn't that be the Health Department?"

"There isn't one, hardly, all the men off at the War."

"Oh, a novel. What is it? I'm a great reader too," she said, trying to rearrange the awkwardness. He slid the book across the desk and she picked it up and scanned it, and then, as if she had summed it all up, she said: "I always wanted to go to Russia. Where did you buy this?"

"Te Aro Bookshop. It's about two old Jewesses who get murdered by an intellectual and we know all along he was the murderer, but it's for the detective to figure it out."

"Two Jewesses in Russia," she said more to herself than to him, and stared at the book's intriguing cover, seemingly oblivious to him. He was a detective and, as such, he took note of her hands, which seemed to be gripping the book. When she looked up, he saw the pain in her face, a look she had not had when she entered the room.

"Yes, the murderer hates Jews, apparently," he said, getting the story wrong. "Or says he has the right to kill an old pawnbroker because, of course, being a Jewess she was one. Are you a member of the Te Aro Book Group?" She was so much like the members he wondered how he had missed her: that haughty smile and the outfit; the self-confidence; the intelligence. It was everything he had chased Louisa for all those years ago, and why, paradoxically, he had lost her. And here was another one with her elegance and refined elocution and uppity manners.

"Good Lord, no," she said. "Why? The last thing I'd do is join a club to discuss books when reading is such a private affair."

He studied her further; the cheekbones touched with a light powder rather than rouge, the hair naturally dark, the eyes betraying something he could not ascertain. He thought of portraits immortalising the English aristocracy, for she had that look about her. He said: "You wanted to tell me about…?" It was then that he realised she was not the book club set. Not at all. She was above that. She was too classy, too rich; her sophistication was calculated exclusively on those social attributes.

Her dark hair was gently pulled back and a few silky strands of it seemed to float at the sides where her hat sat just above her little bejewelled ears. She said, looking him in the eyes, direct, as if she had never feared anyone: "The paper today mentioned Mr. Meatyard again. The owner of the Olde York Teashop may have told you about me. I asked him not to just as I asked him not to go to Mr. Meatyard, which he did, being a man, and no doubt you will find out the connection between me and that Meatyard and I want to pre-empt anything nasty." The room, she felt, was suddenly oppressive and the pipe smoke revolting. She saw he had stripped her, that she was naked, his eyes devouring her. "Meatyard came to my house, you will find out, and I want you to say nothing to my husband about my coming here or about Meatyard. I was simply buying what I thought was medicine for migraines."

"And why would I tell your husband, whom of course I know?"

"Everyone does, which is why I don't want my situation disclosed. It has nothing to do with my husband, who knows nothing about my having bought the medicine." Denton had been meaning to go to her to ask about the dope peddling, but he knew she was merely a customer. The Chinese clients whom he had spoken to already were similarly innocent.

"Why shouldn't your husband know you were buying dope in his house?"

"His house?" she said, incredulous, but at the same time not. "I inherited the money for that house. It's in my name, not his." She saw he had been handsome, but she could tell from his ruddiness all that glory had dissipated early on account of drink. "It's my right to privacy," she said.

"Just as your husband has a right to be private about his secrets," he said, spitefully. "But yours," he added, "are equally unlawful, so why are we looking at an equation with both parties hiding behind screens, as it were?"

The comment about her husband's infidelities was just water off a duck's back. However, she sat silently staring at the photo of the Prime Minister in a wooden frame behind the detective, who puffed on his pipe and blew smoke through his nostrils. Her mother and grandmother were equally with her, their sudden presence both a reassurance and an agitation.

"Jewesses," she thought, miming his words in her head. "Yes, the murderer hates Jews, apparently." She could see so much hatred in this man, most of it for himself, but what she heard was her mother saying: "Rachael, as a Jewess you will always be hated." Even in death her mother's Russian accent was still strong, just as it had been on the day she had died after twenty years in New Zealand. On her death bed, holding the hand of her only surviving child, she had beseeched her, this solitary daughter, in that deeply guttural and plaintive voice: "Save me, Rachael, save me."

He wanted to say: "Cat got your tongue?" but he waited because he was good at this part of the game, he thought, and he watched as she metamorphosed from confident to agitated. From what she was doing with the ring on her gloveless left hand, twisting and turning it, he could tell that her mind was now tormented by his disclosure about her deceiving husband.

"Marry a Jew," Rachael Chatterley heard her mother saying. "Pass it through the generations."

She tugged the glove off her right hand and then pulled on each of its floppy fingers as she saw her husband on his knee in front of her proposing marriage: "I'm not a Jew but I'm a banker and I can get you out of Christchurch." She crushed her other glove in her hand as she stared at the Prime Minister, whom she barely saw. What she did see were those women in her life, long deceased, buried so far from Minsk, which they had fled with her as a child.

"Two murdered Jewesses," said Rachael Chatterley looking back to Denton. "And who killed them?"

"A Russian intellectual. There was a sort of revolution," he said, getting mixed up again with the events and story.

"Pogrom," she said, looking back at the photo behind him. Her mother and grandmother had disappeared. Only that bulky old man with white hair and bushy beard looked at her and she felt alone and cold and remorseful.

"Who?" he said.

"Mr. Pogrom," she said, despising him even more. "Tell me, who is my husband with?"

"The niece of the Mayor of Gisborne. A Miss Andrea McCleod. She inherited a sheep station."

"Ah, another heiress. But he hates the provinces, so she must be very, very rich."

"I won't tell him anything about Meatyard," said Denton, his empathy unexpectedly seeping out. She was still holding the novel, its deep blue and gold cover with the woodcut of a man's gaunt face staring at him. The title encapsulated all he did with his life: crime and punishment in its many forms haunting him, both in his profession and his private life. And this enigmatic woman in the chair sat staring out like the woodcut of the gaunt man as if she were visioning some event from which she had no escape. Something from the past moved in him, too. He felt sunshine and heard the sound of waves against pebbles. He was a child walking along a beach with a woman in a blue dress who held up a pink parasol and he saw with sudden sadness that the woman was his mother. She said as she leaned down and touched his hair: "Try and catch the seagulls, my darling."

"Take the novel," he said. "Read it, it's about suffering."

"Suffering," she said, warming to him, for his eyes had finally betrayed something: a vulnerability; a lost love; a moment of self-hatred. She wasn't sure which, but he had that look that said: "Help me, I'm trapped." Folding her gloves and smoothing them gave her a moment to avoid his eyes. She said: "Suffering is what we all endure. Strength through struggle, it's an old Russian saying." She smiled for the first time and said: "Eventually we get our rewards. My son arrived back two days ago, completely unexpectedly after four years, three of them in the trenches. I simply can't bear to be away from him a moment longer. His lungs are poor, he was gassed, they let him go." She stood up and popped the book into her bag.

The Reverend Ramsbottom from the Thorndon Church of England entered and shook hands and said he preferred to stand on account of his hemorrhoids. For a moment it appeared as if he had forgotten his mission and he looked about before he leaned back his head and snorted. "My third born son is over there," he said, pointing at the window, indicating that over there, across the oceans, was a junior Ramsbottom in the trenches: "Mrs. Ramsbottom and I are hoping this conflagration is soon over." He looked at his watch – the gold leaf was spotted – attached to his waistcoat as if to check for that illusive conclusion. "Speaking of time, it was at exactly eleven o'clock on the twenty-third that I saw Mr. Meatyard going very quickly down Tinakori Road. Should I carry on?"

Denton had been wondering how this man could be taken seriously by his Kiwi parishioners, even that stuck-up, educated, well-off sort who lived in the vicinity of the University College where this nincompoop preached. How was it possible that the word of God could be emitted from such a receptacle? Then the revelation that he, this Englishman speaking in a voice that had all the hallmarks of something between an eccentric parson and a headstrong headmistress, had seen Meatyard: "Yes, yes, please," Denton said.

"I did see him. I know the man. Silly as a two-bob watch, mind you. All that carry-on outside the Bank of New Zealand and never an intelligent word, just a lot of haranguing. I don't think all Germans deserve to be hounded about like that. A good number are second or third generation and, for goodness' sake, the Windsors are Germans. Nevertheless, the War's going on and we must support king and country. And it was exactly at eleven because I always leave the house at exactly eleven because Mrs. Ramsbottom retires at five to eleven and by the time I'm outside with Misty and Peeves it's eleven, and he was running quite agitatedly. Is agitatedly an adverb, a genuine one? One can't tell with language these days. The War has had such an effect on language. I'll have to check. Agitated at least, quite a fast pace, and Misty barked at him, but Peeves was doing his business."

There was nobody like this character in all of *Crime and Punishment*, Denton reflected. The breach of cultures between Imperial England and Imperial Russia was too great, despite the ancestral links at the respective imperial levels. This man was quintessentially English and he had transplanted himself as such to Wellington, lock, stock and barrel. Denton sat down and studied this vicar dressed in a funny outfit and a funny hat and who wore a look of bewilderment as if he knew that here at the bottom of the world he was far removed from a population who would think him normal. He thought: "Why am I comparing or registering everyone against the characters in *Crime and Punishment*? Who am I, for example?"

"Quite simply, eleven. My watch is infallible."

"Do you know Powderham's house? Was Meatyard near there?"

"Oh, yes, quite. He turned in there, I was nearby myself, the dogs always rush about, you know, especially in the wind. Powderham's a strange creature, is he not? Sort of rather Oscar Wilde. Very Oscar Wilde in fact."

"And did you see Mrs. Meatyard?"

"A decent woman wouldn't be out at that time of night."

"What?" asked Denton.

"Well, it's not right is it? Simply not. She'd have been at home, as expected."

"But Mr. Meatyard did go into Powderham's?"

"Well, not quite that accurate, are you? To what I said. Unfortunately," the Reverend Ramsbottom replied. "I said not. Not necessarily. But near."

"Thank you so much, sir," Denton said as he stood and flicked his hand. The need for a drink had begun to boil through his body and his mind seethed with the images of Mrs. Chatterley and the dolly waitress and the Meatyards and Powderham. "Get out," he implored the images. But that now-detested novel flung itself at him and all of its characters fell out and were crawling about midget size on the floor at his feet. They looked up begging for his attention: the evil sensualist Svidrigailov, that mad Raskolnikov, the crazed Marmeladova woman, the suave Saint Petersburg detective who would have solved this Meatyard puzzle in a flash. "My God," he said. "Madness is real." He went to the aspidistra and found his keys. With leaden legs he trod to his desk and said in answer to his own question about whom he might be in *Crime and Punishment*: "Svidrigailov, definitely. And look what nastiness happened to him."

18

Several days later at nine in the morning, Alexander Powderham was snuggled up in bed and thankful that he was alone at home and able to read Franz Kafka's *The Metamorphosis* without interruption. Orton's elderly Aunt Hyacinth was ill with the influenza and he had rushed off to her high, narrow villa over in Mount Victoria to care for her. Aroha, his canvas bag slung over his shoulder, dressed in the torn sailor's jersey, old shorts and a pair of army boots he had found in the Botanic Garden, had come in with a cup of tea. Alexander had looked up from the novel just as Gregor the main protagonist, a cockroach, had scurried under the sofa, his insect whiskers twitching as he listened to his family say how much they hated him.

"I love you, Alex. My only real friend," said Aroha.

"And Muriwai?"

"No, he's my brother, different."

"Gregor in *The Metamorphosis* is *my* brother now," said Alexander. "He's a cockroach like me. I adore him, I so see myself."

"What about that Raskolnikov fellow you've been in love with for weeks?"

"Raskolnikov is dead to me. That affaire ended up with two dead bodies in the garden and my realisation that I'm not at all tormented by being a murderer. I'm just a bit nauseated by having them out there, that's all."

"I'll do something about that," said Aroha. He looked towards the window, the curtains drawn across them, but he too felt the depth of disgust that they were rotting in the garden. "I don't care that they're dead, only that they're out there. I'll never feel bad about what we did. I made that promise to myself."

"I'm the same. I'm surprised I have no regrets or penitence. Nor did

Raskolnikov, *whoops*, him again. But I don't want to be called names any longer. Cripple, Pansy. No more names, never."

"I need to get out of Wellington for a day or so. I'm going to Mākara to swim and walk the cliffs and I'll bring back crayfish."

"Find lemons in an orchard. Everyone's hunting them down what with this bloody influenza. There's not a pill or medication in the shops. It's bad. We should go bush or sail away."

"Māori are really getting it badly. I should go, help in the *marae*."

"I don't want you to. I can't lose you, Aroha."

"Just to Otaki with medicines and food, not stay. I could get the train and then horses and be back in three days. I will. I should."

"Send supplies through the rail, but don't go and get sick." Alexander heard himself as smug, safe, uncaring. "Go bush for a couple of days and think about what we can do. But I cannot lose you."

"I'm scared of dying. Muriwai said young men and Māori get it the worst."

"Getting rid of the bodies is what we must do. That's our pestilence. But go to Mākara and breathe fresh air and swim in salt water. It's all that mustard gas and the diseases from the trenches and now innocent people here must die because of the Europeans fighting."

"You talk like a Māori. At least one that knows what's happened and cares about it." He extracted two cigarettes from a packet, lit them, and handed one to Alexander.

"I'm not brave. I haven't lost a country. I was part of the problem," said Alexander examining the cigarette, not feeling like one, but smoking it in order not to offend Aroha. "The irony is that we're all fighting because Belgium was invaded. The injustice about that, the English shout. But what about Māori? Has anybody ever seen that injustice?" Agitation replaced fear. "Really. Āpirana Ngata is a traitor to his people. I…we… He looked after Māori welfare but now sends them off to die in Europe."

"You make up for it." Aroha looked towards the window and shivered as he saw himself lowering the bodies into the pit, the dead Meatyards holding each other, face to face, rotting, he above them with the cross stuck in the mound of mud and dirt. He dropped his bag and pushed back his long hair and started crying, his hands cupping his face.

Alexander stubbed out the cigarette and, leaning up, took Aroha into his arms. "Go to the coast and swim and see this all as we have for the past four years. We're not in Europe, but it's war nevertheless, and you and I are part of it. We killed to protect ourselves as this country is supposedly doing to protect itself from its enemies. We're not murderers, we're normal soldiers fighting for *our* cause, *our* rights."

"You're right. I know. It's the visions I get. They frighten me," said Aroha wiping his tears. With that shy little boy smile that Alexander loved, Aroha said goodbye and left, his cigarette still burning in the ashtray. When he heard the front door shut and the house was silent, Alexander relaxed into the pillows, drank the cold tea from the Wedgewood cup, and whispered: "Families." He saw his siblings accusing him in the living room and that scene replayed as a comic opera but turned tragic as it came to its climax. For a few upsetting moments he regretted it and wished he had a family that wasn't tormented, or one that he could now crawl back to and from whom he could seek forgiveness. But those thoughts shrivelled as he heard his sister shrieking and he dismissed her with a flick of his hand and thought: "To hell with you, really, why did I waste my thoughts on familial penance?" He picked up *The Metamorphosis* and opened it and smiled, for here was the truth about what families did to people like him and Aroha, to Pansies, and he jumped back into the pages.

It was all glorious reading and, approaching the novel's tumultuous conclusion, Alexander saw with utter clarity that Gregor was a Pansy and that the cockroach – dispensable, dirty, despicable, deviant – was the metaphor for that hated condition of the Oscar Wilde type. By the end of the book the cockroach was dead from violent abuse, hatred and neglect at the hands of his own family. Breathing in deeply, much affected, Alexander snapped shut the book, kissed it, and said: "Pansies unite, we have nothing to lose but our chains."

For months the newspapers had been showcasing the Russian

Revolution in grainy black and white images of people swarming through the streets with flags and banners. Alexander closed his eyes and imagined those anonymous people were he and Aroha and Muriwai and Orton, Elizabeth and Helen and Edwina, Freddy, the one-armed man, and that Syrian coal merchant who every now and again came by for some manly entertainment. A whole city of them rising up. Thousands of Fairies were swarming through the streets in rebellion against the likes of the two dead antagonists in his garden. Denton, his nasty siblings, everyone who despised Pansies and forced them into cockroaches would be eradicated.

"The Russian revolutionaries have a red flag, we should have one," he mused. "But what colours?" He thought he heard a door open or shut, a noise from somewhere, and he opened his eyes, but there were no further sounds and he took his pen and notepaper from the side table intending to write his notes about the novel for the next book group meeting.

"Extraordinary interpretation, the cockroach as me," he thought. "But how am I going to provide this analysis that Gregor's family loves him until they discover he's a sexual deviant at which point he becomes, in their eyes, no better than a cockroach whom they eventually eliminate?" He laughed and saw the book group's consternation. He took up his cup, saw it was empty, and wished he could be with Franz Kafka, who was obviously a sodomite. Only a sodomite could have written this story about him, them, us, these people running through the streets flying a flag that honoured deviants just as the red flag was being hoisted by those who were eliminating their respective chains of injustice and oppression in Russia. He was poised to put pen to paper when he saw a movement and his heart pounded, his blood instantly freezing. Raskolnikov with an axe, Denton with handcuffs, the ghostly Meatyards decaying and revengeful; his mind leapt with all of the grisly imagery available to a Gothic novelist. At the doorway, leaning against the frame with an unlit cigarette in his mouth, his cap pulled down his forehead, was Mac, who said as his eyes met those of his startled lover: "Miss me?"

In a rapid transition Alexander's heart twisted from pulsing with fright to beating with desire. Pushing himself up, extending his right arm, he said, his voice deep with emotion: "Come to me."

"Will you want me smelling like this?" Mac said, approaching the bed, taking Alexander's outstretched hand, kissing it: "I've been living rough."

The cockroach appeared in Alexander's mind, its little head peeping from beneath the sofa where it had been hiding from hateful humans, its whiskers, the antennae, constantly adjusting to sentiments, dangerous or not, under which it, the outcast, operated. The insect's eyes, Alexander saw, were his own, Alexander Powderham's. The insect's antennae, sensing the reprieve of the wonderful, flicked this way and that. Alexander, flinging aside the blankets, gazed up at Mac: "Only a cockroach could love something as equally dirty."

Mac was leaner, his hair roughly shorn, his body smelled of sweat, moss and soiled linen. For time that did not have gongs and ticking and hour hands to measure it, they did what they needed in order to prove they were human and not despised insects, the lowliest, most hated of all creatures, the cockroach.

"I love your body," said Alexander.

"I love yours equally."

"I love the way you hold me with one arm. No one with two arms ever held me so comfortably."

"I saw you that day in the street when the Meatyards were shouting and I knew you'd be really good in bed, or anywhere for that matter. I could tell you were naughty. Where did you learn these tricks?"

Alexander laughed with happiness. Raskolnikov, Gregor Samsa, Denton, the endless war, the influenza, the Meatyards, they had all sailed off into the sunset. Sailing in, this man, tall, masculine, toughened, one smelling of hardship and hunger, whom, it felt to Alexander, was the friend he had always wanted. In as many words, he said that to MacPherson.

"Aroha?"

"He's family, you're fantasy."

"Aroha's the man for you. He's wonderful in all senses of the word. And he loves you. I can't have you because you have him, I know that."

"Aroha was never a fantasy."

"That's not very fair on Aroha. And fantasies don't last."

"I never knew I could love someone like you. I mean that you could love me. The tough boy at school. That I would be accepted."

"I wanted to be you when I was growing up. Safety, security, a nice house and a real dad and a mother who loved me. Books. Education. Did you want the opposite of what you had here, poverty and hardship?"

"But you're educated. It's obvious. Why the mask?"

"I couldn't read or write until I was ten when my mother's sister pulled me out of the Waikato bush where my father kept me like an animal, like he was. If Aunty hadn't taken me away, I'd be even more feral than I am. In Auckland she pampered me. She urged me to be a lawyer. Me? At nineteen I ran away to find my father, and that's when it all went bad again."

Alexander, sensing that knowing too much spoils the fantasy, kissed Mac and said: "There's cheese and onions and bread on the kitchen counter."

Leaning on Mac for support, they went naked to the kitchen where they made tea and ate and looked at each other as if this were the final chapter, the end as the beginning. Alexander said, "When I was licking you clean, I thought I'd never again think about the War, the influenza, the Meatyards…"

"Where did you bury them?"

"Out the back."

"You are me. You just don't realise it. You don't know how beautiful you are and you don't know how bad you are, how evil. As am I. Beautiful and evil. But you have class to hide behind, I don't."

"Did you really go to Gallipoli?"

"Egypt and Palestine, then Gallipoli. I fought for my country, I lost my arm, shot off by a Turk who I killed as my arm dangled, bleeding me to death. But a mate saved me. At the beach he got hit by a bullet and died. I saw it happening, his blood all over me. His name was Robert Baird. Robert Baird. Robert. A true mate. I got taken to Crete and from there eventually back to this bloody sheep farm of a place. Robert was buried in fuckin' Gallipoli. There's no fuckin' justice. And I don't think I have much more time, what with one thing and another. I don't know. Bugger me, not even a cross on his grave, a bloke like that. Just a mound of dirt." He looked up at the ceiling as if inspecting the fly shit. He saw, however, Robert Baird smiling at him, in the background eroded cliffs and gun emplacements, and he shivered. He reached out both arms, but one was falling off, bleeding him to death, and Robert was crying. Looking back at Alexander, he tasted that warm, sticky blood and felt himself shouting, but silently, no words being possible as he watched his friend dying. "To survive Gallipoli to get buggered by this disease. It's men in their forties who are dying the most. What's your idea about that, mate, eh? Justice? You know about things, about death. Murder. Is there justice in this smug little country I fought for?"

The tears that Alexander had wanted to release ever since he had murdered the Meatyards and buried them in his sacred garden rushed out. Through them, bitter and salty in his mouth, he uttered: "I have had no regrets. Not once. I never thought: 'I'm wicked. I killed two people, I murdered. What does that mean?'"

"It means you're a cold-blooded murderer, but one who knows what he must do to survive in a situation. What's the difference between what you faced and what I did at Gallipoli? I shot a Turk in the face."

"In *Crime and Punishment*, the murderer believes he has the right to shed blood in accordance with his conscience. The Russian detective says that's a most terrible philosophy. Is it? Could it be worse than any official, legal sanctions, as with this war?"

"And self-defence? What did the detective say about that?"

"Raskolnikov didn't kill in self-defence. I did."

"Then why are you thinking in darkness, mate? You killed two people who were abusing you, you told me about that Oscar Wilde stuff and they have no right. They were shouting at men to go off to the War to get butchered. I saw that war with my own eyes and it was a lie. Gallipoli was a farce, a terrible, needless slaughter. Turks died like rats; we died the same. At least the Turks were defending their own land. We weren't. The Meatyards were executioners."

"I read the book five times. I remember the detective saying that whoever has a conscience will no doubt suffer, if he realises his mistake. That's his punishment, on top of penal servitude. But I haven't suffered. Does that mean I was right? Or just callous?"

"But mate, you are suffering. What were all those tears about? This stuff you're talking about. You've suffered, and now enough."

"But Raskolnikov, Dostoyevsky didn't…"

"Fuck books. Free your mind. Of course, you think about the killings. I still do about the three men I killed in self-defence when drunk in the Waikato bush."

"Do you see the face of the Turk you shot?"

"I see Robert Baird's face. And, yes, I do see the Turk looking at me with a rifle pointed at my head, and if I hadn't swung back as I did, I'd be dead. He wanted me dead. Just as the Meatyards wanted you dead or in prison, or Sybil did anyway. Cecil was simply a fool who deserved what he got."

"He wanted to be dead. Aroha killed him. I shot her through the heart with a single bullet. All that aiming at Australian parrots in my garden paid off. It was a single, perfect shot." Alexander met Mac's eyes and laughed. "I did. I never did it so accurately at the circus with those silly arrows we fired at pirates, no matter how many times I tried."

"A single bullet. You'd have got a medal if you done it in Gallipoli. Self-defence is never a mistake. I killed the three Māori because if I hadn't, I would have been murdered. We were all drunk, Meatyard was being stupid and said something and they had my throat with a knife and Meatyard wounded one badly to free me and then the fight really began, and the two Dalmatians got killed too, by the Māori." He was speaking breathlessly, rushing through the events as if they had just happened. "But no one ever knew about the Dagoes who we buried in the bush. Life's like that. Look at this giant, terrible war. We're all dying. Aroha was right when he said it's *utu* we're all involved in." He lifted the cheese knife to his jugular and laughed. "A Turk or me? I take me. I lost my arm to those bastards."

MacPherson, Mac, the soldier, the conman, the lost child, the male lover; at that moment he was in every way so beautiful and so right that Alexander said: "I will no longer be a cockroach."

"Fair enough, mate," Mac said. "I have to think about what to do to escape. The cops are after me. They even have your underpants."

"How did you get away from the boarding house?"

"That bloody landlady turned me in, but I had gone down the back steps to the dunny and the silly buggers didn't look in there. They just assumed good old Mac had slipped away once again, the escape artist. But I was just having a shit and I could see them through the slats in the dunny door, the three cops and that idiot Denton. I was wiping my bum as they left."

"Denton suspects but he can't find the links and for some reason he's too afraid to arrest me. I think because of Louisa's letters and journals. I don't know, but he's slowly hanging me. He'll find you. Lets' flee to Argentina."

"Nah, mate. I'll take the rap. I'm the suspect because of the letter they no doubt found. It was dumb, dumb, I should never have written it. Why do people leave written trails? Notes and letters, we're all obsessed with the written word, and look where it gets us. But dumb. I'm the only suspect. That dope money. Jesus. Mate, Denton's merely teasing you to get me."

"Who stole what from whom?"

"Mate if I'd had any money, I wouldn't have gone to a dirty doss house in Newtown. I'm a loser. I lose everything, and I've lost you because I can't have you in the first place. So, I guess I haven't lost you. Just never had you…." He took Alexander's hand. "When you gave me your flash hat and coat and five quid, I knew you wanted me. I'll never forget that kindness, mate. I loved wearing your underpants. And mate, I'll never turn you in about the Meatyards…" He nodded to the garden and smiled. Alexander saw it was the same grin as the one he'd fallen for outside the Bank of New Zealand and he thought: "Look where that led me." He took a deep breath, contemplated taking a half-smoked, dead cigarette from the ashtray, and said: "Mac. Don't lie to me."

"Look me in the eyes. I told you everything. I went to the War and I got shot up and that's the biggest thing that ever happened to me and..." As if he had read Alexander's mind, he took the cigarette, gave it to Alexander, told him to light it, and said: "Come on mate. We can't waste time talking, let's fuck some more."

19

The Te Aro Book Group discussions had begun on the dot at seven in the booklined meeting room. The early November weather, although chilly, was much improved from that of the previous meeting when the wind had howled as if it had descended from Russia to the base of the Pacific, just to accompany the trial of *Crime and Punishment* by the Wellington intelligentsia. On this occasion the windows were open to blow away the influenza germs that everyone was so alert to and fearful of.

"Edwina isn't able to attend," said Elizabeth Norris, "On account of both her parents having passed away within the last week, and she herself is unwell. And I'd like to welcome back William Wigram who has been very busy with war reporting but has nevertheless, like a good boy, prepared his notes on *The Metamorphosis*." William was seated next to Hortensia Rutherford, and he smiled, looking around him. When he looked at Hortensia, his face lit up and he blushed, the crimson highlighting his ginger hair and moustache.

"We perhaps shouldn't have come either," said Gerald Hoskins, the beekeeper, his scarf wound around his neck to ward off infection. He had not removed his cap to ensure that the virus couldn't enter through his scalp, a common belief of how the illness sought out its victims. "I've never seen such a catastrophe. Even the bank was closed today."

They were all expecting that he would relate how his bees were faring given the influenza and what effect it might be having on his swarms. But he merely muttered something about the relation of illness to bad air as a common thread in seventeenth century poetry, his literary specialty. Then he literally shut his mouth because he believed that his nostril hairs were effective guards against inhaling illnesses in the same way as bees' hairy legs were efficacious in ensuring the distribution of pollen.

"If we could cough into our handkerchiefs," said Elizabeth, who had been drilled by Helen on how to approach the epidemic. "If you should need to sneeze, try to do so outside, please. But we do have to keep on living and communicating." She wasn't as convinced as she sounded given her next-door neighbour was seriously ill and Helen, who had volunteered at Newtown Hospital, reported that people were lining up for treatment and that bed space was running out. "Simply not enough doctors and nurses, they're all at the War or sick," she'd said as she went cheerfully off to work: "In fact, the book group shouldn't be meeting."

"*The Metamorphosis,* by Franz Kafka, is not a work written as German propaganda, so if any *agent provocateur* is here, you may as well depart now," said Elizabeth.

There were a few timid laughs. Mr. Oliver Tricklebank, tall and wiry and wearing an impeccable suit with an elegant red woollen tie, said in a voice that revealed his high level of education, including at Oxford: "We should be very cautious about what we say with regards to the police given how despicable and overriding they have become." As a former senior banker in various financial establishments, including in London, he was much respected. However, he had succumbed to a bitterness driven by his belief that gross capitalism had catapulted the world into this hideous conflagration.

"That Denton fellow came to see me and actually asked if Miss Rutherford were a subversive. Of course I informed Miss Rutherford the next day, did I not, Miss Rutherford?" he said, addressing her. "Not by telephone or telegram, however, of course, on account of the current sensibilities, if not hostilities. But now I'm incensed for I learned from Miss Rutherford that's she's being punished by her school board for what she said about Dostoyevsky's literary accomplishments." The twelve club members looked from one to the other, their eyes telling different stories, none of which had anything to do with *The Metamorphosis* but everything to do with the situation Oliver Tricklebank had just detailed.

Miss Rutherford, in the same becoming outfit as she had worn at the previous meeting, stood and said, her voice deeper than usual: "I condemn the actions of the authorities for denying me my freedom of speech. This is New Zealand, not Germany, not Russia. This war is not making us democratic, quite the contrary. When are we going to have elections? They are long overdue." She looked about the room. "And all my school colleagues, all women of course, supported me against these outrageous allegations, and the headmistress abused the school board, all men of course, for their recklessness in admonishing me on account of Denton's false allegations."

"It was Denton who arrested the Kelburn women teachers for holding farewell parties for officers. Houses of ill repute was the accusation. He never arrested the officers who went to the parties. We need to get him," said Mrs. Mabel Hewitt, who had returned to the group after some absence. "Look at the suffering those Kelburn school teachers went through, all because of his false allegations of moral misconduct. How can we allow men to be like this, and the police?"

"Indeed," said William Wigram, standing. "We of the press feel the same thing with all the censorship imposed upon us. Miss Rutherford being censored for saying what she should be able to in a democracy is wrong! This willy-nilly, ad hoc, arbitrary censorship we're forced to endure as if we're somehow vassals of…repressed in some despotic state." He looked around. "No. it's blanket, deliberate, systematic censorship. It continues with the government telling us not to publish the numbers of influenza deaths. I say enough."

"My list of questions about the novel," said Elizabeth. She saw Alexander's sardonic eyes, a drone's, self-satisfied, superior, useless, staring at her. Suddenly, she didn't like him. She said angrily: "Should we not postpone this meeting until after the Spanish influenza, until we collectively feel well again? This flu, this flu…"

"It's not a Spanish influenza at all," said William. "Spain reported it first because they don't have war restrictions on what they say, being sensibly neutral, and they've been lumped with it forever, no doubt."

"Most interesting," said Elizabeth. "There they are Germany's neighbours and not in the War, and here we are at the bottom of the world and sending everyone we can to it."

"But what about Denton?" asked Miss Rutherford. "He can't be allowed infallibility."

"Goodness gracious," said Mabel Hewitt, who had been a Catholic nun called Sister Chrysogonus but had renounced her vows and married a widower with eleven children. "Denton came to my house. He'd read my notes and he asked me what I meant by saying that Dostoyevsky was a prophet and that his commitment to change was the sign of hope for the human race." She stood up. "I admire Dostoyevsky because he knows redemption is progress. What does that have to do with the disappearance of the Meatyards? He was trying to make links with them and our supposed sedition. Denton asked me about them. What was he implying? I told him, 'How dare you talk to me about the Meatyards' disappearance?' I chucked him out. You all know I was a nun for twelve years in the Fiji Islands. This would never have happened there. Fijians understand redemption just as Dostoyevsky does. I was very close to a powerful Fijian chief, and that's where I became undone, but that's another story." She raised her arm as if to bless herself. "And as for that cockroach fellow I…"

Alexander struggled to his feet. "Thank you for your honesty Mrs. Hewitt. Speaking of cockroaches, Denton has confused sedition with the Meatyards." He took a deep breath. "But about the novel. I think the cockroach was a sexual deviant, a psychological case of defiance which meant that he could no longer support being persecuted. In some countries he would not have had to change from human to insect. In countries with a *Code Napoléon* he would have had no reason to be so self-hating. Men of that persuasion are freer. Here they are cockroaches."

Miss Rutherford smiled at him. Gerald Hoskins nodded as if saying: 'Drones do it.' Alexander spread his arms, theatrically, absorbing the group's anticipation and continued: "My metamorphosis must be reversed. We should have the *Code Napoléon* in New Zealand. It's a tragedy the French didn't colonise these islands instead of the British."

As the book group absorbed the news, and as if to deliberately fill the ensuing vacuum of human sounds, Gladys Finch, the dithery, rheumy-eyed tea lady, screamed as she spilled boiling water on her little finger. Everyone looked towards the kitchen as if from there came the nation's popular reaction to Alexander's extraordinary revelation.

Elizabeth Norris looked at her old friend who only a few minutes ago she had decided she no longer liked on account of his sardonic eyes, his superior attitude, his veneer of impregnability, his sneer and wealth and mixed reputation of dandy and altruist. Now she wanted to hug him, call him a fool for this public confession and tell him simultaneously that she adored him even more for his honesty and bravery in a place as philistine as Wellington, where everyone knew about him but pretended they did not.

Professor Karr stood and said: "Hear, hear, good chap! Fine association!" Then, segueing with a reference to Denton, he stated that New Zealand was being throttled by extremism and that fanaticism needed to be turned on its head and that he, Doctor Karr, felt that there was something personal about the Denton situation. "Why did he come to my house and ask me what I know about you, Elizabeth, and what you might have written in your personal journals?"

"What!" exclaimed Elizabeth? "My journals? To you?" She tossed her notes on the table. "Explain what you mean by 'personal', Professor," she said before realising he might do that given the evening's revelations.

"Perhaps in private because he, Denton, did say…"

"My sister?" said Elizabeth standing.

"I…yes…"

Elizabeth stood and said: "If our friend can divulge her past as a nun in Fiji and Alex why he thinks he's a cockroach, then I can clarify that my late sister Louisa was stalked by Denton. When she rejected him, he raped her. After that she was trapped in a sinister web from which she couldn't escape until…" The sinister web felt attached to her face. "That's why he wanted my journals, because he knows I have an account of what happened, why she killed herself. He didn't find her journals or letters because they were…" She wiped her face with her fingers, detaching what she felt there, and looked around the room: Elspeth, Miriam, Helen, Edwina, Louisa; all the women she loved were standing, clapping. "I seek justice for Louisa," she declared.

"I think you mean revenge," said Alexander.

"My goodness," said Hortensia Rutherford, standing, as by then were most of the club members. "When he came to my house he was very forward. I asked him to leave but he didn't, and I was frightened…I'm so terribly sorry, Elizabeth. I see what must have happened." She closed her eyes. When she opened them she smiled and added, her voice as clear as if she were detailing the logic of French grammar to her students: "We must have the bravery to respond, as have the Russian people against their oppressors."

Alexander recalled Miss Rutherford in the street outside the Duchess Tea Rooms when he had felt the poignancy of his lack of manhood and his desire to have such a wife. It seemed an age had passed since then. With his public confession he realised that the end of that era had arrived, as had the beginning of a new one. As he looked at the members of the book group, at their moving mouths, their story-telling eyes, their agitation, he felt himself flying about in a cosmic draft where things floated around and which could only be reassembled on his command as something other than this thing so subject to hegemony, that unequal and unfair equation of consent plus force that pushed him into physical, ethical and moral powerlessness. "I think, therefore I am, and what I am is a writer," he thought.

All of the things floating about in Alexander in that cosmic orbit now made sense to him. His body and his mind would be integrated as one, as Descartes had insisted. He saw what he needed to do with that stunning realisation of what it meant to be cohesive. It was to write about realities like his. The New Zealand novel had no such depth or substance, nothing about the diversity of life in these far-flung islands. There had never been a Dostoyevsky or a Kafka, let alone a Walt Whitman or an Oscar Wilde. It would be he who would do it. Freedom leapt in with the clarity of why he was alive. Life as stymied, as a cockroach, must end.

"This is all anti-democratic," said Professor Karr. "Profoundly authoritarian. He can try and punish us…that's what it is. I decided when he was preaching to me in my own home about sedition and the War Regulations Act, that he was salacious, lecherous. He looked at my maid when she brought in tea as if he were about to pounce on her. And Miss Rutherford, and Elizabeth, her late sister…"

"We should go to the Police Commissioner, the Prime Minister. All these books about injustice we read, yet we do nothing. This man who accuses us of sedition…" cried Elizabeth. "Professor, use your contacts, we'll go as a group." She saw that Alexander had entered a swoon, his smile meandering between serene and crazy. She thought: "Goodness, Heathcliff is going downhill." She edged towards him, skirting the old tea trolley with which Gladys Finch was fussing.

Alexander watched Elizabeth approaching and half curtsied as if she were Descartes' mistress arriving with more news about the famous Frenchman's personal desires in the bedchamber. Like a courtier imparting the intrigues of court into the mistress's willing ear, he whispered into Elizabeth's: "Secrets are for operas, my dear, and eventually they burst out in an agitated aria. Be very aware of how the opera can render life so very dangerous."

"Oh, very Alexandrian. But resulting in wailing as with Gladys screaming at that extraordinary moment of your cockroach revelation," she whispered. "Especially dramatic with the *prima donna* delivering her confession. Well done, darling!" She laughed and understood that laughter was the only way out of this ridiculous situation, of dealing with this life. "What other secrets do you have?" she asked, feeling she was being mother, confidant, spy, detective. "You're more like Raskolnikov than a cockroach. Or isn't there a difference?"

"Am I? Is that what you wrote in your journals and what Denton now knows, surmises, given you've told him in your wide ranging and injudicious writing? You see what your liberty to write has achieved?"

"I've known all along you did it, Raskolnikov," she whispered. "It's just a question of how and where and that's what Denton is about to find out, isn't it?"

He saw her trap, but he was no longer Raskolnikov, and he was not going to confess on bended knee to the Wellington proxy of that Saint Petersburg prostitute Sonia Marmeladova who had coerced Raskolnikov into telling her everything. He would neither consent to that nor be forced to. He closed his eyes and raised his eyebrows and pursed his lips to demonstrate he had no intention of being the rat between her fangs, with contrition and penitence in Siberia the pathetic conclusion of his story. He shivered as he breathed in, she so close: he had always thought her perfume *Violets Delight* magnificent but now it made him nauseous. The tea trolley creaked behind him, its wheels squeaking: the noise of banging gavels, of gallows, of swinging ropes. He said In the softest voice: "To hell with your hegemony. You have no idea what it is to be a zig-zag of lightning over a Fiordland mountain."

20

For three days Rachael Chatterley had immersed herself in *Crime and Punishment*, her mind thick with a panoply of Slavic images, sometimes nightmarish. The accompanying thoughts leapt and tumbled over each other as she rushed from page to page, from scene to scene, burrowing down into the heartache of what it was to be a woman and a Jewess in Saint Petersburg in the 1860s. As she read, breathlessly, she understood her mother's warnings of what it was to be a despised Jewess hunted down by haters, evil with disfigured thinking, as it was with that vile character Raskolnikov. By chapter four, when Raskolnikov's tormented mother Pulcheria Alexandrovna is wringing her hands in despair at the vagaries of life and the situation in which she finds her son, Rachael saw everything as if she were there with the agitated woman.

"The pogroms," she whispered to herself in the intimacy of her private living room in her Oriental Bay villa. "Mother was right. This was our history. This Dostoyevsky has recorded the infamy for me to…to…" Rachael Chatterley looked about her room: the security and luxury; the beautiful things. A chilly damp wind, however, descended from a mountain, its rolling mist saturating her as it came closer and closer; a door being banged upon, then kicked in, screams and shouts, whistles, hysteria.

"Why do you think we came to the bottom of the world?" her mother was saying. Rachael, a mixture of emotions, felt both the freedom of having been released from that Russian oppression and, at the same time, the responsibility of being true to herself, finally, for here the primary oppression for being a Jew was within herself. "And," she whispered, "the oppression of my jealous, greedy, hated husband."

By the end of the third day of reading, and when the sad fate of

Pulcheria Alexandrovna had been disclosed in the epilogue, Rachael understood that she would no longer permit her own soul and body to be eroded as had been the case with Raskolnikov's unfortunate mother, who had quite simply died from the misery of her life unravelling. "Dostoyevsky is right, strength through struggle, as my own mother said. Very Russian. It's what I must embrace to preserve my sanity rather than kill myself with poisons and potions." She stood at the living room window looking out at Oriental Bay, the sea a steely grey with the subdued sun glinting upon it. She had just finished the novel which she held in her hand, the wretched and horrid Raskolnikov having been banished to Siberia, where he suffered the anguish he so deserved.

Rachael watched a ship slide across harbour, its trail of smoke hanging above the windless silver surface and envisaged her family on its decks: her mother, Rosa Shapiro Izrailevich, was looking anxiously at the dark mountains of this new country; her father, Iosif Izrailevich Abramovich, already ill and with three years to live, was gripping the rails; her grandmother, Riva Zetzky Shapiro, wearing an embroidered woollen cap over her grey hair, was holding the hand of Efim, her eight year old grandson; and she, Rachael Shapiro Abramovich, was a baby in her mother's arms. Everything was so clear she might have been on that sleek vessel forty-two years previously, only then, she surmised, it would have had sails, not smokestacks. She was wrapped in the green blanket which she still possessed as an heirloom, woven by her mother's sister in Minsk as a farewell memento for the family whom, the aunt knew, she would never see again given how far away they were going.

Rachael knew little about her past. The grandmother had lost herself in a maze of silent memories. Her widowed mother was too busy with wealth creation as her businesses flourished in Christchurch to bother to impart much about their history. Rachael understood that her mother had rejected a good deal of the past that had rejected her. The aunt who had woven the blanket was never heard from again, the rest of the family had fled to America and vanished.

"How much is Jewish, how much isn't?" Rachael asked herself as she looked across to the ship, which might have been leaving or arriving, or was simply stranded. "Stuck like I have been for so many years," she thought. Her eyes misted and the images of Dostoyevsky's Russians merged along with those of her long departed family, their respective personae metamorphosing one into the other. Efim was laid out on a slab of marble in the undertaker's room in Christchurch in 1880, his face bloodied from the horse kick that had killed him at age eleven. Efim became the spectral, handsome Razumikhin. Her mother was a combination of Sonia, Katerina, Dounia, Pulcheria. Her grandmother was unequivocally Alyona Ivanovna the pawnbroker with the thin, grey hair and the startled look of one about to be murdered. Rachael saw that three days submerged in *Crime and Punishment* had reshaped her thinking. The atavism was palpable. She had made a pact with herself which had denied her the spirit in which she had been born: "I will cut off my past and what I was in order to avoid what they faced in Minsk." She smiled with the tragic irony of one who has renounced something only to return to it with the full knowledge of what loss, what damage, had been incurred in the meantime.

"A Faustian pact," she said. "I am Faust."

A funeral procession passed slowly along Oriental Parade: the black cab, the black hearse, the flower laden coffin pulled by four stalwart black horses with plumes of black feathers around their necks. Earlier that morning a procession had filed by with two scraggly horses, not even black, pulling an open cart with two children's coffins, upon which lay the offerings of randomly picked flowers: wild arum lilies, common white daisies, sprigs of lilac. The half-dozen mourners were dressed in the best outfits of the poor, what they would have worn to a musical or a parade or to church.

This procession of more august mourners, Rachael noted, all wore black hats, the men black suits, the women long black dresses. They meandered rather than walked, apparently disoriented by grief. An elderly woman swathed in an early Edwardian mourning outfit paused and looked up at the two-storey villa, right up to the living room window from which Rachael stood gazing down.

For both women there was instant recognition: mother for daughter; sister for sister; two long-ago separated friends. The mourning woman looked away, the knowledge too intense, and surveyed her surroundings: left, right, behind her, as if for confirmation that she was alive and in her daughter's funeral procession and not in a moment separated from time or one pulsing with nightmares. She looked back at the window where the woman still stood looking down. Rachael wanted to wave, to beckon her up, to embrace her, to say "mother". She stood motionless, thinking how separated she was from everything she had abandoned: her race, her religion, her family, everyone she had lied to for decades. She dropped *Crime and Punishment* and knelt and prayed in Yiddish, which she had not thought in or spoken for years.

Over the previous week, the increasing clutches of the epidemic had driven Rachael Chatterley to quarantine in her home. But for having rushed to see Denton four days previously, she had not gone out. The delivery boy had been instructed to leave the groceries at the door. The florist was told not to bother with the weekly delivery and the house maid had been given two months' wages and to return when called for. Only her son Cameron had been in and out despite her pleas for him to stay inside. He had looked at her as Raskolnikov had into the eyes of Pulcheria Alexandrovna, a son lost to his mother through some strange affliction. She had winced when she looked at his eyes, those of his long-deceased grandfather, dark, beautiful, as equally haunted, as they had searched her eyes as if pleading: "What is your secret, Mother? Is it as huge as mine?"

On her knees, Rachael Chatterley thought: "I should have told you I know your secret and about your cursed letters, about my lost years, what you lost in return." She rose and looked at everything she materially possessed, all of which she would have abandoned to annul the Faustian pact she had made with the Devil. "What is there for grieving mothers to learn?" she asked, making her way down the stairs to prepare soup for Cameron should he come home for lunch.

She poured boiling water into the teapot, which she covered with the tea cosy. As she lifted it to pour, she heard the kitchen door open and saw her husband, his face blotched and red, his hair tousled.

"Oh," she exclaimed. "I wasn't expecting you. Gisborne, wasn't it?"

Owen Chatterley was dressed in an expensive woollen suit, which he had added to her account at Munster and Munster. His tie was askew, the top shirt button undone, his face flushed with what she knew was the effect of whisky. He looked away to avoid her contempt and said, slurring his words: "Gisborne, first place in the world to see the sun rise in the morning. Makes a man feel wanted, seeing the morning sun so early."

"Would you expect to see the sun rising in the evening? There's no need to be redundant."

"Why do I deserve such spite? Couldn't you just for once be…nice? Can't I even have a kiss after a week in bloody Gisborne?"

"Weren't there sufficient kisses in Gisborne?" she asked, taking a teacup from the cupboard. He sneezed several times. She looked up, fearful. She said, backing away from him: "If you have the influenza, go into the bedroom. Go back to Gisborne, let her look after you."

"Where is our son?" He wiped his face with his handkerchief and shook his head as if trying to dispel a nightmare.

"Walking."

"Of course he is. Fairies do that to find victims."

She poured tea and added sugar but had no desire to drink it.

"What about my tea? In my own house. You didn't pour me tea, and I haven't seen you for a week." He came to within a few paces of her. She smelled alcohol and something musty, wretched.

My own house. It was a refrain with which he would taunt her. He took a step towards her but she moved back.

"Have a divorce. Marry the woman and take her inheritance. But you will never get mine. What is she, a sheep farmer? A mayor's niece or daughter? Now get out of my house, my life, you don't deserve the likes of me or your son."

"A Jew and a Pansy." He laughed, but as if just hearing her words, he shouted: "What do you mean, sheep farmer, mayor? How? Who?"

188

"The whole town knows you're a philanderer and I'm informed the mayor of Gisborne wants you out of his sight, away from his niece."

"He's like you, that son of mine. Du…du…duplicitous…a Jew, like you. I've been done in by you both. I'll throw those letters in his face, tell him to get out of my house. Where are the letters?"

"He's been hurt by war. You know nothing of suffering. You just inflict it, year after year." She heard another voice: "Christians hate us. They'll get us, you wait, you will see this."

The kitchen was painted a dark green and the late afternoon light had faded. She wanted to turn on the electric lights but he was in the way of the switches.

"Pogrom, Jewesses," she heard a woman shout.

"I inflict it?" he said, taking a step away from her as if she were the one who might be contaminated by influenza.

"Give me my freedom, a divorce, and be free of us if we are so vile."

"But no settlement? I get nothing?"

There were knives on the table and she saw the danger. As she looked from the knives to him they read each other's thoughts. She saw the murdered Saint Petersburg Jewesses lying in their blood on the floor.

"Why would someone who has given nothing expect something in return?" she asked. The characters in *Crime and Punishment* screamed with laughter at her haughty statement, their hysterical voices tumbling throughout her darkening kitchen. She picked up the teacup for something to do with her hands, but he rushed at her and pushed her back, the teacup against her face, the hot water scalding her, the tea in her eyes. He slapped her face with his open hand as she heard the chorus of screams from Sonia, Katerina, Pulcheria, Dounia, Marfa, Natasha, Polenka, all the Russian women who had suffered at the hands of their menfolk and whose emotions and feelings had saturated her.

"You…You…" he shouted, pushing her against the cupboard. "I'm your husband and you will divorce me with my share. I'm the man. Jewess to the core. My one son deformed."

He pushed her down and kicked her chest and held her to the floor with his boot. "I've had those disgusting letters in my mind since I read them. You coddled him, made him queer."

She was praying in Yiddish as she tried to coil up, but he released his foot and backed away, screaming. She looked up and saw blood flowing from his nose, then from his mouth. He leaned against the table, the blood running down his face to his chest, to the floor. She got up and backed away to avoid him as much as the blood for she knew this was the sign of imminent death. He rushed out of the kitchen. The prayer was screaming in her head, a discordant chorus. She followed the trail of blood up the stairs. At the living room door, she saw him fling himself about the room, blood still spurting from his mouth and nose as he pulled things off the furniture and threw them at the walls. His eyes were crazed. He yelled: "I will kill him!"

She stood fixated yet knowing she should run down the stairs and out of the house.

"Letters, male. Indecent…my son, Cameron…"

She waited for her moment. As he tried to open her writing desk, kicking it, punching the delicate walnut façade, she slammed shut the door and locked it.

21

She peeped through the keyhole and saw her husband on the sofa panting. Her relief was that he was no longer throwing things and ranting. He was violent, but he had never been destructive. She knew from the newspapers that the delirium could turn people vicious and suicidal, with victims jumping from windows. There were stories of infected soldiers leaping into the ocean from their troop carriers. Her body was bruised and she thought he might have broken her ribs. When she touched her face, she felt blood and, nauseous and fearful, she dabbed at it with her dress, but she didn't move, her body rooted to that spot outside the door, vigilant to so many things: her past, her future, her tormented and likely dying husband. She saw herself in Christchurch in that dark blue room with the thick mauve curtains and the portrait of her father looking down at his womenfolk, his eyes quizzical and benevolent and she looking up at him as a child.

She begged in Yiddish for some understanding as she stared at the patterns of the rimu woodgrain on the door, how they merged and tangled together and said aloud: "Why are our people forced into suffering?"

In a voice that seemed to be coming through the centuries, her grandmother whispered: "You'd be dead in Minsk if we hadn't fled, but being two things is difficult, so merge them into one."

Her grandmother's statement was so simple it was revelatory. To come to a country that didn't burn Jews, and which wasn't ruled by a Tsar with the oppression of an autocratic theocracy was something for which she knew she should be thanking her family. Her grandmother's message was as clear as the merging grain in the rimu woodwork. "I'm a Jewish Kiwi," she thought. "What else could I be? But I married that rotter and I caused my suffering."

Her husband screamed "Fairy! Jewess!"

"Fairy? Jewess?" she heard behind her and she jumped in fright. Cameron Chatterley stood at the top of the stairs in his military uniform, his cap tucked under his arm. "I don't understand. Is that Father?"

"Cameron. Listen, he loves you. He's ill, that's all."

"Pansy! Queer! I want his letters!"

"He's broken," she said, her hands against her ribs. She saw her son might never return to her. "Your father wants to destroy both of us."

"What?" said Cameron. "How...?"

"My son a Pansy! I will not have that!"

Her son's eyes told her what to do next. She went to the room where she had taken Mr. Meatyard. As she turned the key in the desk drawer, she heard Dostoyevsky's words about self-preservation. She realised the two Jewesses hadn't even screamed as Raskolnikov had raised the axe and killed them. They were Jews who had not resisted. From the drawer she took the bundle of six letters she had tied with a red ribbon foraged from a hat because she understood they were of the utmost importance to her son's happiness. Next to them was the container filled with the contaminated opium, one spoonful of which had nearly killed her.

"These arrived a week before you did and he opened and read them. I did not," she said.

Cameron Chatterley took the bundle with shaking hands. He looked at her and then at the living room door.

"He told me what was in them. I know only what he shouted at me."

"Me a Pansy?" he said, holding the letters to his chest. "From a drunk like him?"

"He's dying."

"So did real men in trenches who were sacrificed, unlike him, a failure. What is this about Jewesses?"

"My maiden name is Rachael Shapiro Abramovich. Your maternal grandparents were Russian Jews from Minsk and spoke Yiddish when they arrived here in eighteen seventy-three. Which means you are Jewish, as the line is passed through the mother." In her forty-three years she had never before felt so free. She saw her son's eyes turn from hatred to frost to warmth to love.

He laughed before falling to his knees and wrapping himself around her. "I damn knew all my life I was this…this…not his," he said. "The letters. Abraham Bellow is my friend from New York, a Jew."

"Your grandmother would have been able to explain how these things happen. I've felt her with me all day." She looked into his eyes as he looked up at her, but he was somewhere she could not fathom.

"I was literally stuck in ordure and mud and I killed more men than I can say and I was gassed. But I lived. I am as you know, a man who cannot love women. There are names for it. Homosexual, ironically or not, coined by a German."

She ran her hands through his hair.

"You're a Jew and I'm a Jewess and I just told him I want a divorce, and he has the influenza, which I hope will kill him."

"We should kill him. One more won't matter to me. Mother, give me the key."

When Cameron entered the room, his father was on the floor, on his back.

"I have the medicine to help you," Rachael said.

"Which one would you prefer to assist you?" asked Cameron. "The Jewess or the Pansy?"

As depleted as Owen Chatterley was, he tried to reach her but he was too weak, or too resigned to what he knew was coming.

"Open your mouth, Owen. This is the medicine that will release you." She held out the glass of water with its fatal potion.

Cameron lifted his father and tipped back his head, his mouth open, gasping for water which he gulped down. Within two minutes he was dead.

"Twenty-five years of my life passed with you, Owen Chatterley, and now that pogrom is over," she said. After washing her hands, she went to the telephone.

"It is indeed an emergency," she said. She knew from the papers that the telephone exchange was not functioning to capacity due to the number of operators affected by the epidemic and that only emergency calls would be passed through. She was advised to call the undertaker. When she spoke to Mr. Wilson, he said he could be there by ten o'clock in the evening.

"That's too long," she said. "Come now and bring a death certificate and have a doctor sign it and I'll quadruple your fees. There will be no funeral, just a burial at the Karori Cemetery, which you can arrange."

Rachael Chatterley and her son had scrubbed out the kitchen by the time the funeral director arrived with two assistants. At the front door as Mr. Wilson was departing, she said: "Thank you for coming as quickly as you could, I'm in deep grief, as is my son, Cameron." She handed him the money.

"Sixteen removals so far today, Mrs. Chatterley," said Mr. Wilson. "Are you sure there will be no funeral service? I'll let you know the site of the grave. As busy as they are, the cemetery people are very careful about the usual requirements."

"I thought there were mass graves. I heard they're burying people with no indication as to who they are...were..." she said.

"I didn't like to say, to worry you. But the very poor and the ones we don't know about are being buried together. A lot of people in the boarding houses and itinerants who die with no family. We don't even know names. It's like a war."

"No, it's not," said Cameron from the hallway. "War is immeasurably different."

"Yes, sir. Apologies, sir," said Mr. Wilson, noting the man's officer status. "Thank you for informing me, thank you for the service you have given our country. I do understand my mistake, sir."

"My son was three years in the trenches. He saw a lot. He did a lot of things that most normal people..." She looked at the two men. Their respective stories loomed at her and she saw that all she had ever done was cherish her privacy, read books and suffer an unhappy marriage. She was cocooned and privileged and that struck her as a wretched anomaly when everyone else had been suffering and sacrificing. "This novel has unravelled my complacency," she thought.

"My apologies," Cameron said. "I didn't mean to be rude. It's this… this…"

"I understand," said Mr. Wilson. "My cousin Jock got back two weeks ago. He'll never be the same again, but then he lost a leg. He said Flanders nearly killed him mentally, not physically. Still, he's been out in his garden planting vegetables. I think he'll come right. He's got his old mother and a wife and two kids, so he has to, doesn't he? He couldn't just leave the War any more than he can leave his responsibilities here, can he?"

The images jumbled in Cameron's head: the dead, shouts, bombs. He said in a matter-of-fact voice: "I was ordered to shoot a deserter in France. No formal inquiry. My fellow officers picked him up. A chap from Hamilton, apparently, a shoemaker, and twenty minutes later he was stood in front of a wall and then my Commander told me and three fellow officers to shoot him. One of us had a blank."

Rachael Chatterley, her head cluttered with the deed of murder, the images, this new story being just one more in a jigsaw of horrors, said in an equally composed voice: "Well, Mr. Wilson. You are very busy. Thank you for coming as you did."

The undertaker, tall, gaunt, dressed in black, fixed his grey eyes on the handsome, stalwart man in military uniform who had just confessed to slaughtering a soldier, a working man. Then he fixed his gaze on her, the distinguished looking woman who was so composed she appeared false. "How people die is always cruel, whether an innocent man from Hamilton, or a rich Wellington banker," he said, his voice bitter. "And what they die of. And in this case of what seeps out of their mouth after death. Your husband had the influenza. I might tell the doctor just that, and nothing additional. He won't even look into the coffin or notice the effects of poison. Of murder." He stood at the top of the steps in his tall black hat, his long face spectral, the colour and texture of old lilies. His eyes narrowed. With precision he spat at their feet. He turned, and went down the steps until all they saw was a hat that disappeared as he went left into Oriental Parade.

"He just spat at us. Will he tell…?" she said.

"You coldly killed your husband, and now you're worried about an undertaker you paid off? No, Mother, this is the last of it."

She saw in a new light this cherished son whom she had lost at fifteen when he had abandoned himself to introspection. As he leaned against the kitchen cupboard, she realised he had many of Raskolnikov's characteristics, his dark feelings being the most significant. Where Raskolnikov had lain on his filthy sofa for days, Cameron had lounged, moody and sullen. Suddenly unafraid of the intimate nature of her enquiry given they had just participated jointly in such a heinous action, she asked: "Was it this homosexual business that made you so glum and silent when you rejected us?"

"Of course it was. I was unhappy, defeated. I could see I was different…" He asked himself if it really was appropriate to say these things to his mother, with whom he had never discussed anything of depth or import. But the paradox of why he had never spoken out allowed him to continue. "I wanted to be normal. If I lay about and sulked despite everything you gave me, love, things, then… I was a pervert who thought he shouldn't live. I hated that I'd been born like this, that you'd given me this…this…disease. I'd read in *Truth Magazine* that it was from the mother." He stared at his outstretched hands as if there, symbolically, he was able to assess the wasted years and the suffering. However, what came to mind was the image of the very kind face of someone filled with compassion. "And you know what saved me? One day I went to the Te Aro Bookshop where I found a book about Ancient Greece. As I was looking at it, Alexander Powderham started talking to me and then…"

"No, not Powderham!" she cried. "Did…? He's a real Pansy…"

"What do you mean?" he said. "He assisted me, helped…Was so very…He saved me from suicide."

"Be calm," she said. "You've had time to think about this situation of what you are. I've had but a few hours. Powderham is a Pansy and looks like one and you do not, so where is the difference? Explain to me. I'm a woman who knows nothing of this except that you are all I have. I've lived my life through you and for you and if you are thinking of running off to New York or killing yourself because of your mental and physical wounds, at least explain to me beforehand what it is that you like about men."

"I never chose this path any more than I did the one that sent me to France to be mentally dismembered. Just as you never chose to be a Jewess." He paused, then said, laughing: "Which makes me a Jew too, does it not? I'm a Jew? God help me, you did say that. I never…I mean…That's what you said upstairs, isn't it? I'm Jewish? My God, I'm a Jew."

Watching him laugh softened her and in unison they said: "We are both Jews." They embraced, holding each other so tightly that she thought of Pulcheria Alexandrovna who, in the whole novel, had never held her son Raskolnikov.

"Mother, how strange life is, how glorious. I'm holding the only person I ever loved. As I was saying, it's the people we find at special moments who get us through the worst of it. That day Powderham gently talked to me as I was self-consciously buying the book about Greek love. We talked, he was a gentleman, and I was saved because he explained how I was feeling as a boy of fifteen who thought about men and suicide. I'd see you and know I had sinned even for thinking about such. I knew Father was looking at me because he would have known being the sort of man he was, so violent so…so…masculine. Oh God, he probably thought I was different because I was a Jew. He may not have thought I was a homosexual, or perhaps he thought I was a Fairy because I was a Jew…a Fairy Jew. Oh God, so many new thoughts."

She clasped his shoulders and looked at him and thought: "This is like being with him when I was breastfeeding, or when I bought him that toy clown and he kissed me every time he picked it up and said: 'Thank you Mummy, thank you for being my Mummy, Mummy.'"

"Do you know what it feels like to be Jewish?" he asked.

"Yes, until mother died and I was all alone, then I decided I didn't want to be one. It was inconvenient, just as if I'd said: 'I no longer like those shoes and that hat'. When she died, I wanted all of that to die with her, the oppression of it all, her memories and moods and the differences she brought. In Christchurch I'd wanted to be friends with normal girls, and she…It never left me, of course, but I was raised in New Zealand, I had that strong association."

"A rejection as simple and cold-hearted as that, shoes, a hat?"

They were both startled when the doorbell rang.

"Deny everything," he said.

Rachael went to the door and on opening it was relieved to see Mr. and Mrs. Stonehouse from the Old Yorke Teashop.

"Dear Mrs. Chatterley. We just heard and I said we must come and give our condolences." Mrs. Stonehouse was so genuine, her eyes so full of sympathy, that Rachael started to cry.

"How proud you must be of such a strapping young man and his services overseas," Mr. Stonehouse told Rachael as he shook Cameron's hand.

"So proud," echoed Mrs. Stonehouse, holding a plate of currant scones covered in a linen cloth.

"I've just made a pot of tea," said Rachael, unexpectedly pleased to have these cheerful visitors despite her fears of contagion.

"Oh, we can't stop," said Mrs. Stonehouse. "You may have noticed we've turned the teahouse into an alleviation centre, if you please. Just for the duration of this…this…evil illness."

"I didn't," said Rachael. "You must be flat out."

"Indeed. It's a trial getting help. People are ill or attending to loved ones or terrified. Cook got sick yesterday and I've been at it since early… really…" She wiped her eyes with her sleeve, having handed the scones to Rachael, and said: "So many deaths…If you'd like to help…"

"I will," said Rachael, thinking of what she needed to do to flush away the ugliness of what had happened. "I can make soup. I'd be happy to contribute financially."

Mrs. Stonehouse started to cry.

"She was always a great soup maker. I dreamed of it in the trenches," said Cameron. "What would you need me for? Any activity will do."

Mrs. Stonehouse sobbed. Two weeks previously her oldest grandson had been killed somewhere she couldn't pronounce and this handsome man in uniform only sharpened her sorrow.

22

The day after six representatives of the Te Aro Book Group had met with the Prime Minister, the Right Honourable William Massey, to declare their consternation and unhappiness with the prevailing anti-democratic situation in the Dominion and their displeasure at being hounded by a lecherous and misinformed detective, John Donovan, the New Zealand Commissioner of Police, called Detective Crawford Denton to his office.

It was a bleak day, which reflected the mood of the influenza-afflicted populace. On the wall behind the Commissioner of Police hung a gilt-framed, coloured portrait of George V. Hanging next to this plumed royal personage was a weather-stained photo of the Prime Minister. The two eminent personages, both of whom had their eyes averted from the peoples they governed, wore with ease their respective distinctions and privileges. The Police Commissioner was a handsome, wiry man who, despite his years and responsibilities, maintained a head of wavy black hair. Above his brown eyes were bushy black eyebrows which, when raised, gave the impression of a morepork. In his uniform and reviewing the notes from the Office of the Prime Minister, he looked up, owl-like, when Detective Denton was ushered in.

"You have a black eye," he said, greeting the detective with a cold smile. "What, if I may ask, and I may, happened for a senior detective to have such?" He stood and extended his hand. The one he grasped felt clammy and he decided, what with the influenza being so prevalent, that he would issue a directive that handshaking during police work was to be avoided. "Sit," he said. "Whoever accosted you should be charged."

"I walked into a wall," said Denton, looking away, firstly at George Frederick Ernest Albert and then at the Prime Minister.

"Drunkenly, Denton?"

"No, sir, Commissioner. I simply…I'm very overworked what with the lack of manpower."

"Senior detectives don't walk into walls, Denton. And if they do, they probably need to be stood down or sent to an asylum." Donovan was a Catholic and had been educated by nuns under the strictest of regimes, firstly as a child in Ireland. From his arrival in Hokitika at the age of seven the local Brides of Christ, who were committed to instilling virtue in children as a result of the heightened moral requirements imposed by living within the lasciviousness of a rough-and-tumble gold-mining town, completed the task of his spiritual and moral education. As a result, and as his wife reminded him, he knew he could be as severe, fastidious, cold and direct as a nun when he sensed corruption.

"I was walking quickly. It was very dark…" Denton realised he sounded ridiculous and that he should have pleaded illness to avoid this appointment. His mind went from one thought to another, each one rushing over the last, and he heard Nancy MacTotter scream as he tried to kiss her in her Newtown flat, which he had visited on the pretext of gathering more evidence.

"As I said, Denton, I have business from the highest office to talk about," the Commissioner said, and he turned and pointed to the Prime Minister. "From the highest I add, again, so it's a good thing you are not appearing as an employee of the New Zealand Police Force in front of *him* with a dubious explanation as to why you look like a thug." The room was darkened by shadows, even at mid-morning. Deep down in him the Commissioner felt that everything was wrong on this planet: his brother Andrew was in the Hokitika Hospital with this influenza, the telegram informing him having arrived early that morning, the knock on the front door of his Kelburn house alarming everyone given that his son was at the Front.

"The PM asks me to tell you that you need to desist from the sedition inquiry on the members of the Te Aro Book Group, with whom he met at his offices. They went to protest that you were inflicting unnecessary charges and insinuations that could not be justified under the War Regulations Act. I might add, Denton, this is a very august group of people, well-educated and, as the PM said to me, a very well-connected bunch and articulate and very much of the opinion that you are hounding them for more personal reasons. Can you explain?"

MacTotter was screaming at him, her eyes wide, angry, and as he pushed her down and laughed, he looked up and saw a man's fist swing at his face.

"Are you here, Denton, or elsewhere?" asked the Commissioner.

"They are somehow linked to the disappearance of the Meatyards, sir. That's all in my report of last week, which I was anticipating you would have read or been informed of by Chief Inspector Griffin."

"Who has been in hospital for the past few days, as you will well remember, Denton. Half the force is down with this flu and you look as if you might be too. What about the Meatyards? You've found nothing on them, but we know that MacPherson did it and he's vanished, naturally enough." He coughed and said: "Look, it's hard for everyone. This flu, the War, the lack of men still with us. Everything's a bit harsh. But look at you sitting there all bunched up and worn down and positively elderly, if not done for. I do wonder Denton. And then there's this issue with your attitude towards the fairer sex. This should never have come to my attention, let alone to that of the Prime Minister. But Miss Rutherford…" He squinted at the paper in front of him on account of his not having put on his reading glasses: "And Miss Norris, both of whom claim you have made insinuations and overtures." He squinted more closely, his eyes going down the page, his head from side to side. "What's this about your taking their personal papers and not returning them? Miss Norris is the niece of my wife's dear friend in Dunedin, for goodness' sake."

"We can under the War Regulations Act, sir. There's evidence about all of them, including the pervert owner of the Te Aro Book Shop. I just have to find MacPherson to see how they all fit together."

"The PM's alarmed we might be getting into the same situation as we did with the Kelburn lady teachers' scandal. They were teachers for goodness' sake, merely mixing with some officers. Don't you like lady teachers, Denton? Middle-class women? Something against that class, have you?" He looked around as if the women were there, the very sort with whom his wife fraternised. "Under your direction the police accused them of keeping a house of ill repute and you know what happened then, every suffragette type in the country came to their defence, including Lady Stout and Lady Liverpool, even the Lady Mayoress. Even my wife. Teachers, librarians. They were simply having farewell parties for officers and what did you, yes you, do? Charged them! Even *Truth Magazine* defended them. I should have got rid of you then. And what are we doing here?" He waved the papers. "A book group, a schoolteacher. Miss Rutherford is the step-daughter of the Chairman of the Reserve Bank and his wife is Lady Stout's daughter. Oh dear! Oh dear! Professor Karr. Powderham himself. This can't be another swipe at the educated elite. Get the one-armed man, charge him with the disappearances. It was about a dope deal gone wrong. There is nobody else, and I repeat, *nobody else*, involved in the Meatyards' case." He stood up happy with his decisiveness and went to the window, where he wondered if his brother and son were still alive. But the sunless sky darkened and chimney pots desultorily emitted smoke and he felt the rain spots dribbling down the windowpane were dribbling into him.

"Who punched you? Who gave you a black eye?" he said, turning.

"I was walking home in the dark. On the corner of Ghuznee Street a man accosted me, he was sick with the influenza, he just came up and punched me, sir. He was delirious."

"And why did you not state that directly instead of this wall business?"

"I…it…it's been a difficult week what with the influenza and the additional work, sir."

"The Health Department's under-equipped, the hospitals not coping. It's the people who're saving the situation, not the Government. Ladies' groups doing the work, even the teashop on Oriental Parade is now a soup kitchen while we all look ineffective. The PM's furious.

Absolutely furious!" He heard someone saying the same thing. "Absolutely furious!" reverberated in his mind. He met Denton's gaze: "Get this one-armed fellow and quick. Forget about Pansies. We've got a tired and demoralised population and pursuing sedition charges against a high-level bunch is politically dangerous, and quite ridiculous given the current situation with doctors and nurses dying, our population being decimated."

The Commissioner had been in the police force for thirty-three years and he understood how absurd people were and what bizarre things could occur given the human condition. A one-armed man and a bunch of Fairies sharing intimacies was, in fact, a strong possibility. He thought of the case where the old spinster had murdered her neighbour with poisoned fruitcake because he, the neighbour, had told her that her dog barked too loudly so she, the spinster, had sneaked into his house and laced his cake with poison. But the police had charged the neighbour's wife who had at that time been in Auckland. What a case that was. *Truth Magazine* had gone wild with it, even insinuating that it was a case of the spinster's frustrated love for the neighbour.

Doubt, deep and dark, crept into the Commissioner's mind. Maybe Denton had reason to be so relentless. What would happen if there were sedition and a German uprising occurred in Wellington? Whose head would then be lopped off? He saw himself the potential victim, as if he were the executioner and the executed. Prevarication was anathema to him but taking blame and punishment was a fear far greater. Indecision and equivocation, the ugly twins, were poking him as he looked up at the Prime Minister and the King.

"What link is there to the book group or Powderham to the one-armed man, this MacPherson, who left a note saying he'd kill Meatyard who was himself a criminal from all the considerable evidence?"

"They were wearing each other's underpants, sir. In some hideous and perverted distortion of normality. They were each other's admirers, in that sort of unspeakable way."

"Oh my God," he said, imagining the scenario of the two men

exchanging underwear. "Wearing each other's underpants? Was that a sort of pact? A Pansy cult sort of thing?"

"Apparently, sir, they love underpants, admire them," said Denton, appreciating the thaw, seeing equivocation crawling in. "Dirty, perverted things these Fairies get up to."

"But…but…underpants. I know this Powderham, a badly crippled fellow. His father founded the Society for the Relief of Indigent Gentlewomen. But a cripple and a one-armed man murdering two normal people? How would they dispose of the bodies? Tell me that!"

"I went to Powderham's house to search. We need to do another and this time more rigorously because I have new information that Meatyard was seen near Powderham's the night of his disappearance. I also found out that Meatyard had met with MacPherson and the woman who had just started at Powderham's shop as a bookkeeper, and until then she was a prostitute. Her neighbours reported to me that MacPherson went regularly to her immoral dwelling, and that Meatyard had been there on the same night as MacPherson. I can put the puzzle together, sir, really."

"But if he's a Fairy, why would he be visiting a prostitute who has a good job? Why have you not followed up? It's a jumble of suppositions, Denton and I…" That terrible feeling of being unable to make decisions without thinking he had made the wrong one pulled at the Commissioner. Equivocation was a sin, he knew that. Deep in his mind the words of warning from so long ago reassembled. As if from an echo chamber he heard Sister Agnes saying them, the words being emitted, she so long-ago deceased, her mouth moving, her habit so tightly tucked around her face she was permanently pink. He recalled her smell of decayed lilies as he heard the incantation: "Listen, children, indecision is the first step to moral decay. Decay leads to sin and sin to your decline and fall and Hell and eternal damnation. It's the Devil's work."

"With all due respect, sir, the Powderhams of the world will be making their case of innocence when they are guilty. I found a pistol in the Pansy's bedroom. And MacPherson's underpants, soiled, if

I may say so, with illicit male substances. I will go again and search his garden more thoroughly."

"Pistol? Soiled? Why in his garden?" Again someone yelled: "Absolutely furious! Absolutely furious!" in his head. The voice was effeminate, high and squeaky. The Commissioner winced and, fleetingly, saw a face which might have been weeping.

"Powderham and MacPherson are familiar, intimately. Meatyard had to have been murdered there. And buried."

"Crippled Fairies can't kill people, can they? It's a distortion of imagination, Denton." Donovan paused and thought of the spinster sneaking into her neighbour's house. That lovely old lady with the sweetest smile might have been his granny and yet she, unsuspected for so long, had been a callous murderer. *Truth Magazine* had uncovered the whole story, the headlines had been very damaging for the police. The Commissioner felt he was being led into another trap by the sinners, the deviants, the nuns had warned him about as a child in that dark, cold classroom way down there in Hokitika. What if a crippled pervert could be as equally evil as the spinster? "Search the garden again? Who with?" he asked.

"I've had one of the special Māori recruits, what's his name? Muriwai Munu. He looked in the garden but found nothing. But I'm suspicious. We need to dig there."

"Buried in Powderham's garden?"

"Well, their house backs onto the bush. And Powderham lives with a Māori."

"Pansies and intellectual ladies, and now Māoris. Ngata had us employ Māori constables to assist with all things Māori, as well you know. Use this Muriwai to infiltrate the Powderham household then. See what he can find, Māori to Māori. I suppose Powderham's Māori is also a Pansy. What a world we live in."

"Am I clear Sir, to continue the investigation as is? Follow leads?"

The Commissioner looked at Denton, at the black eye, at the slouching shoulders. "Not you. No. The Māori constable will. Āpirana will be pleased I'm delegating authority to his boys and I've got to take seriously these accusations of your abuse against respectable women, Rutherford and Norris. I can't have you sniffing around them given what they've brought against you. In fact, Elizabeth Norris, her sister I believe, and I understand it's all written in the woman's journal, you apparently raped her. Indeed, why are we even having this conversation? I should have simply told you to get out the moment you came in. If only the Chief Inspector wasn't dying of influenza. I should have had you arrested. I'll leave the accusation of rape for a week. But be prepared to sink or swim according to the evidence."

He sat down beneath the King and ran his hands through his hair, and that voice shouted "Absolutely furious! Absolutely furious!" Then, remembering his image as the Commissioner should be one of iron and steel in front of his men, he stood and shouted at Denton: "You've been an utter disgrace. Look at you, a seducer, we all knew that, and a drinker and still in the police force. You will not be much longer. Appoint that constable Muriwai to find out if Powderham and his Māori associate have anything to do with MacPherson and the Meatyards and he has a week to do it and then we drop the case until later or simply call it 'missing persons'. You leave the book group alone. I will call you in next week, and what I tell you about your future won't be felicitous."

When Denton had left, the Commissioner sat down, his head hurting from the way the world spun around on its pivot of stupidity and cruelty. "Absolutely furious!" clanged in his mind and he closed his eyes and listened to the voice. As the voice began to fade, he had a sense of foreboding. When the refrain ceased he saw with horror that it had been his brother Andrew shouting it in his head. His brother who had refused all efforts for him to marry. Andrew, who had long ago confessed to being a Fairy and proud of it, living with that Scotsman Jock in a house like husband and wife. And he, the Commissioner, knew equally at that moment that the refrain went out that it was his beloved brother Andrew who had just died of the influenza down there on the West Coast, in Hokitika.

23

On the day after the Commissioner of Police had reprimanded Detective Crawford Denton for ineptitude, moral impropriety and mismanagement, six members of the Te Aro Book Group, along with Aroha and Rebecca, met at the bookshop to further their plans to assist with the response to the epidemic which, by that first week of November, had increased its ferocity. Edwina Castle had died the previous week and had been buried, with most of the book group members in attendance at her funeral on a very grey day.

"It was so sad, our dear friend Edwina," Elizabeth said, but changing tack so she wouldn't weep. "Epidemic or pandemic? William, you work for the press. Is the Government telling the truth about the numbers or do they simply not know? We've been hoodwinked about the number of war dead." She had smoked two *De Reszke* consecutively, having been informed by her doctor that smoking warded off the influenza: "All that heat and smoke in your mouth and lungs is good for you in these circumstances. You can smoke up to thirty a day. I'm saying that to all my lady patients. Men may smoke forty." Lady Lacey's gorgeous coat was wrapped about her and she wore the very *de mode* hat of matching colours, which Helen had fashioned from velvet and satin since returning from Europe, painstakingly stitching it together evening after evening as Elizabeth read aloud Edith Wharton's *The Custom of the Country*.

"That's the question we should have asked the Prime Minister," she added, "but either an epidemic or a pandemic wouldn't look good in the papers given they blame him for bringing back the influenza in his ship four weeks ago." It was an argument still transfixing the country, the hysteria of the infection distorting people's memories. Alexander wanted to remind her that she had stood outside the shop a month ago listening to the telegram man informing them about the increase in flu cases at that time, two weeks *before* the arrival of the *Niagara*. However, filled with ennui, and not wishing to risk her temper, he desisted.

Attired in a louche, crumpled, black linen suit, a soft cotton shirt adorned with a satin bow tie, Alexander slumped further in his chair feeling as if he were being suffocated. "If only there were an escape from this Meatyards horror," he thought with a turgid mishmash of accompanying images. The books around him looked down, the tomes on poetry and theatre and philosophy and literature to his right, to his left the erudition on science, engineering and architecture. "All of this and I end up obsessed with two hateful warmongers buried in my beautiful garden."

An afternoon with Mac would change that mournful thinking. He smiled wanly at the thought of kissing the one proffered hand. The sheer eroticism of being on his knees, naked, taking that now revered, rough limb with its short blonde hairs and thick fingers, and licking it. With considerable determination to push out the dangerous thought, but it persisting nevertheless, he had to confess that he was in love with the enigmatic, one-armed ex-serviceman, prostitute and murderer: "I need lust. I want adventure," he thought, sensing Mac, his touch, his aroma.

The pain of thinking about this man, who was everything a fantasy could conjure, was that lightning bolt striking his favourite mountain, and throughout his body his desires zig-zagged equally. "I'll turn Muriwai and Aroha to finding him, if anyone can, they will. Oh, God, the life of Pansies," he thought. Then, coming to and realising the importance of the meeting, and that he was being a spoiler for sitting there so lugubrious, so moody, he sat up. Like an unwilling hostess, he smiled at everyone and began to pay attention to something other than himself and his delicious fantasies of being on his knees administering to a salacious, masculine conman.

"It wasn't the *Niagara* that brought in the flu," said Helen. "Auckland was full of flu. This country is obsessed with how the flu arrived, but not with how to care for it."

"My doctor said it was a lesser strain before the *Niagara*," said Elizabeth, fiddling with her lighter, trying hard not to snap at Helen. "People were dying before he arrived back, but not in that gruesome way we see now when they turn black and spurt blood. Oh, I should just smoke and smoke all day."

Hortensia Rutherford, clutching a yellow daisy she had picked on her way to the meeting, rose to the occasion: "I'm sure he used his privileged position to eschew quarantine. The ship was stopped from going on to Sydney. Why is it the Australians are so much more civilised than we are? They even had a referendum on conscription, and it didn't get voted in and we were just bullied into it. They quarantined everything, too. That's called sanitisation. Edwina would have known about that, dear, poor Edwina. No wonder she aways wore black, she *foresaw* this catastrophe!"

"Hortensia, *dear*. Do you really think Australians are humanitarians? They have their own nervousness with anything different. Have women and the natives the vote?" said William, who sat proudly next to her. Everyone looked at William, then at Hortensia, then back to him, his use of the endearment the giveaway. He smiled and laughed, took Hortensia's hand and held it up. Elizabeth exclaimed, noticing the engagement ring: "Oh, my goodness. Is it true? When?"

"Indeed, she has accepted," said William.

"It looks like love!" cried Rebecca. "At last some beauty! Congratulations. Oh, how gorgeous, look at the diamonds, and rubies."

Politics and disease rushed from the room as William kissed Hortensia's hand as would a paramour in a French novel. Hortensia leaned upon his shoulder with that intimacy permitted in society on such an occasion.

"Gladys," called Alexander. "Gladys." Mrs. Gladys Finch, long widowed, popped her head through the butler's pantry, as in a pantomime, her wrinkled face rouged and powdered. "There's champagne in the cooling cupboard, please, with seven glasses," said Alexander waving both his hands. The happiness at such an occasion lifted him from his sultry, love-filled moment and, catching Aroha's eye, he flushed with the exciting idea that this kind of love, that between men, was anarchic, and that within anarchy was freedom. "The Life of Pansies," he thought. "That's the title for my novel."

"My sincerest congratulations. Amidst such horrors, life goes on," said Oliver Tricklebank. "I wish I were in such a felicitous position."

"Well, with all the widows and the deaths of tens of thousands of good men," said Helen, with bitterness, "that ought not to be a problem. Think what women now must endure because of men's wars and the miseries men create for women. Women as the victims, yet again."

"Helen! We're celebrating!" said Elizabeth, not caring for the dark cynicism in this moment of reprieve, and not for the first time wondering how much shellshock could someone have before it was an excuse for bad manners and belligerence.

"We *can* celebrate," said Helen moodily. "But must women's distorted lives be the result of men's stupidities? Are we things, items?" With the deaths of some eighteen-thousand New Zealand soldiers, the figure having been reported in the press that week for the first time, she knew things had changed irrevocably for women and that there would be an entire generation of them condemned to spinsterhood with all of the associations of being unmarried, unloved, wretched, poor, despised, dried up – witches.

With caution, sensing danger, her friends looked at Helen as if Edwina Castle had returned from the dead, her suffragette sentiments warming up, charging towards full throttle. William and Hortensia caught each other's eye, showing both trepidation and resignation, under the terror of Helen's advance as she stomped into another of her monologues.

"There we were in front of that buffoon of a Prime Minister and he chirping about the great sacrifices of our nation as if we were Africans sacrificing chickens on a voodoo altar, when I've seen first-hand the piles of bodies of our men. Think of the losses. Who will farm the land? Who is there to marry?"

No one spoke as they followed her timidly down a slippery passageway, greasy with blood and gore. They knew what Helen had blurted was correct and that her conscience and its logic were pure; only how she had said it was not. The tedium of being so piously reminded was an affront, as if those who had stayed in New Zealand had no idea, not even just a little bit, about what suffering and deprivation might entail. It was all as if she, the purist, could alone know the truths. Mr. Tricklebank coughed politely. Aroha studied the ceiling. Elizabeth, cringing, looked at her companion and thought with angst and regret: "Indeed, only an ideologue."

Alexander, indicating to Gladys to hurry up as she wheeled in the trolley, and trying to soothe things, said: "The damage of the War is incalculable to us all. How everyone has suffered." Aroha put his hands to his face, and from between his splayed fingers he grimaced at Alexander and waited for Helen's grenade to explode.

"Rubbish. What poppycock. What have *you* suffered, Alexander?" cried Helen. "You've gained from the War, war profiteering on obtaining the government contracts for schoolbook distribution. Everything has gone the way of the petty bourgeoisie and the farmers. Who has assisted women? What about widows? What about the women who so-called *gained* by being able to do the men's work? Do they get men's wages?" Very pale, shaking, she stood up and said: "Drink your champagne and enjoy yourselves because I will not." She glanced at Hortensia and William: "I congratulate you, but I cannot swallow my anger at having come back to this pompous, smug, self-contented city when…when…" She flicked her hand at the images that slapped her. She smelled the acrid smoke of towns on fire and the stench of refugees straggling the dirt roads across Belgium.

"Darling," Elizabeth said as she went to Helen, who stood with eyes wide open. "There, there. We're your very best friends who have waited for you these years while you made the sacrifices." Wrapped in Elizabeth's arms, so close to Lady Lacey's garment, Helen shuddered. She looked around, bewildered.

"Let's toast to the downfall of the thugs who make wars," Elizabeth said. She put her arm around Helen, kissed her hair, led her to her chair and sat down next to her, holding her hand.

211

"Actually, Helen, my darling friend, I think you're absolutely right," said Hortensia. "Every word, my dear sister." She stood, pulling up William with her, and saluted Helen with her champagne glass, which Gladys had served to everyone throughout the drama.

"To Helen, for truth and what she says and for our need to act, and to Alexander and Aroha for offering the premises and funds for this venture to provide for the afflicted. And to Elizabeth and Helen ..." Hortensia stumbled and wondered if it were appropriate to recognise Elizabeth's unspoken relationship with Helen, the intimacy and truth of it. Elizabeth saved her and stood and raised her glass: "Here's to Helen and me, who were engaged and married long before you even met the lovely William. Here's to all of us. Aroha and Alex, William and Hortensia, Liz and Helen, and our dear departed Edwina, and all we need to do is find Oliver a wife."

"I'm available," said Gladys Finch, whose husband had dropped dead at forty. She, in maroon and pink, blue and grey, shaky, in her seventies, her champagne glass at the ready, curtsied. With that denouement the group reassembled their respective thoughts and spontaneously broke into long suppressed laughter.

Three hours later, at eleven o'clock in the morning, and after much discussion and laughing, and having finished four more bottles of champagne, the Te Aro book group had assigned positions for each other in the establishment of a make-shift hospital catering to women and girls in Alexander's expansive premises next door. Helen was elected as overall nursing and staff manager, Rebecca for finances, Aroha for the procurement and distribution of food and Elizabeth to coordinate the whole enterprise with William and Hortensia and Oliver visiting the neighbourhood to see who required assistance.

"I'm very honoured," said Helen, rising. "As you see, I'm also very fragile and need, really need, something to keep me going. I so want to do something. It's exciting and we can, all of us..."

Elizabeth saw that this woman whom she adored and respected, and who had been damaged by war, might heal and again be embedded in her Wellington life. She closed her eyes to thwart her tears and saw her much-loved Aunt Elspeth and Miriam waving from their cottage window. Everything so topsy-turvy, chaotic, war, disease, idiocy, rushed about in her head, but the two women at the window were waving, signalling not to give in. "Thank you," Elizabeth thought. "Your love is inspirational, this love down the generations of women." She caught Aroha's eye as he winked at her, saw his beauty, what it meant to have such friends, winked back at him, and reached for her cigarettes.

"I asked the Defence Department for beds, furniture and kitchen things and they'll deliver them tomorrow. Everything will be set up in twenty-four hours with their help and we'll work and work," said Helen.

Rebecca, who was taking notes on the proceedings, said: "The women of the Voluntary Aid Detachment are only too keen to help. Six lady volunteers, all retired nurses, are available for shifts. They even supply the uniforms. And three Red Cross cooks are signed up. I haven't seen such community spirited people, ever."

"It's a good thing all these organisations were set up over the past few years," said Hortensia. "Imagine if we had to start from scratch to address this pandemic. Something good did came out of the War."

"We start our work tomorrow morning at six," said Rebecca. "Good on the so-called intelligentsia of Wellington!"

24

Later in the afternoon on the same day that the Te Aro Book Group had made plans to assist in the amelioration of the influenza epidemic, Detective Crawford Denton was seated in his office waiting for Constable Muriwai Munu. When Norman Wallace the wheezing, ginger-haired secretary knocked on the door, Denton assumed it was the constable who would be ushered in. It was, however, the Reverend Ramsbottom, who was announced. He was dressed in several different weaves and shades of tweed. His dark blue cap would have accompanied him from the Old Country, given its jaunty *fin-de-siècle* style of the previous century. The suit was brown and black in a houndstooth pattern and was cut to highlight the form of his admirable physique, of which, to judge from the way the Reverend held himself when standing, he was very proud. His dark green waistcoat of a much rougher tweed was hand spun cloth from the Isle of Muck. Tucked marsupial-like into a leather lined pocket was his fob.

"It's Sherlock Holmes," thought Denton on seeing the eclectically attired reverend. Getting up from behind his desk to shake the man's hand, he said: "This is a surprise, Reverend. People are staying at home these days."

"Well, I did telephone, but the little miss wouldn't put me through. She said not unless it's an emergency, and I said your name and the little miss, when I told her it was information I needed to impart, decided, if you please, that that wasn't sufficient cause as declared by the Government, and so she wouldn't connect me. Well, I never. As I said last time, the War has aggrieved us all. What was that about? Oh yes, the use of adverbs and adverbial phrases. But I haven't come here to discuss grammar. I was actually going to have a blast at the zinc-sulphur inhalator at the Town Hall, which apparently cures one of the germs if one has them in the throat. But not in the nose, necessarily. Well, so I was told by one of the parishioners whose name in this case is not important."

Denton had barely slept since having been so admonished by the Commissioner of Police, and so rankled by that severe reprimand and knock to his already battered dignity, that he had gone straight to his house and opened a bottle of whisky and downed it. By early the following morning, another had followed down the hatch, neat. As such, he had missed a day of work. Forty-eight hours later his hands still shook and he looked at Ramsbottom and wanted dearly to go back to the bottle and fully accept that reality, the one he knew he could not reject. Also echoing in his head was the Commissioner's pledge: "Denton dismissed! Denton dismissed!"

"Yes, the zinc-sulphur inhalator should save lives, one hopes," said Ramsbottom as he waited for the detective to return, for it was clear he was far away, the cause of which, the Reverend knew, being a problem with the bottle.

"We all need to have a blast from the zinc-sulphur inhalator," said Denton, half-heartedly, thinking he needed whisky, not some medicinal concoction sprayed in his face while surrounded by hundreds of people all clamouring for the same and spreading their germs in the meantime. "And today's business would be, Reverend?"

"I was chatting to old Mrs. Watson, Eleanor as I have now come to call her, we being quite friendly after all of the years she's been living near my house on Tinakori Road, right on the corner of Saint Mary's Street, in fact. You might know her red cottage, because it's almost on the footpath, in fact just two front steps off, and she complains of the noise of horses and drunkards. Just opposite the Chinaman's fruit shop, if you know the one."

"I do. Yang Chen."

"No, it's Chen Yang," said the Reverend. "You see, Chinamen have their surnames back to front. But then again, if I get increasingly mixed up these days with my English adverbials, why not with this form of Sino nomenclature?" He laughed loudly at his erudition,

215

which he had masked as a joke, and as he did, his head back, his teeth exposed, Denton imagined him in a damp field in Surry shouting: "Foxes!" Or some such thing because the images came at him swift and fast and were all mixed up like those black and white stills in the moving pictures. Composed haphazardly, in fragments, in his mind were cold and misty English fields and thatched cottages and men in red breeches on horseback charging after little animals, that sort of scene he'd gleaned of England from seeing them on crockery, most notably that dinner set from his childhood, which still gave him the willies when he thought of it as he did then with the Reverend barking at him in that horsey English accent. The shaking of his hands and the knowledge that if he didn't drink, he would simply go mad made him want to biff the ludicrous preacher who went on and on as a toy doll does with its perpetual bleating if turned on its head. He reached for his pipe and sucked it and the sour taste alleviated for a second that other addiction, but only for a second, before he stood and said aggressively: "Yang Chen."

"No, it's not, I can assure you, because they aren't like us and Chen would be a surname. But it's backwards, and on the sign on the fruit shop they have it forwards, if you like, not backwards, so its Chen Yang. I buy my greens there and that's what Mrs. Watson, Eleanor of course because we are quite familiar now what with her living on the corner of Saint Mary's Street, I may have told you that already, that's what she said, because she knows that Māori fellow who lives at Powderham's place and Mrs. Watson, Eleanor, said she saw him, this Māori fellow, going past her house that night and he went up and turned into Saint Mary's Street and you know what's there, don't you?" He was talking as if he were telling bedtime fairy tales to children, his voice a combination of faux excitement and condescension: "Dear little kiddies, and what did the Big Bad Wolf do *then*?"

Just at that point, the secretary entered the room without knocking or excusing himself and said: "Constable Munu is here for his appointment, sir." He might have thought he was doing Denton a favour in that this was a ploy to send Ramsbottom packing. But suddenly

Denton's demeanour and attitude changed. A sinister look appeared in his eyes, one mixed with opportunism, that eye-slanting, devious glance associated with criminal activity in the silent pictures. And his smile was that of a petty criminal in an Arthur Conan Doyle novel when arrested for the theft of mock pearls when, really, no one knew it was he who had also nicked the diamonds. Denton said: "He can wait. Don't disturb me."

Revenge leapt in him. The Big Bad Wolf he had just been thinking of came with his big yellow fangs and jeered at everyone as it decided who to eat first: Powderham or the Māori or the one-armed man, any of whom he, Denton, was reassured would lead to the solution of the Meatyard murders. Everything was suddenly in his grasp, there, handed to him on a silver platter thanks to this absurd Ramsbottom, who only a minute ago he, Denton, would have eagerly fed to the Big Bad Wolf itself.

"Please, sir, sit down and continue your most interesting conversation about Mrs. Eleanor Watson and what she told you," he said, the need for drink easing, the taste in his mouth not so sour.

Reverend Ramsbottom, for his part in this sudden change of heart, one he only subliminally registered, had been unable to fathom why New Zealanders never took the time to listen to him and fidgeted this way and that and always found an excuse to rush off uttering something akin to: "Gosh, is that the time?" or "Right, the early bird catches the worm, Reverend." He had put it down to the colony's relative godlessness. Spending time with a man of the cloth, he'd reasoned, meant less time for clearing the bush and establishing a material base for a nation which was, recognisably, much more secular than the one he had fled in his thirties to avoid the aversion he had felt there although, similarly, he had never quite ascertained the nature of what *that* equivocation towards him had entailed either. He was, therefore, gratified to be offered a seat and time for discourse, and as he seated himself, despite his piles, he uttered, conspiratorially: "She's a very nice old lady, lives off dahlias and daisies in the summer and twigs and pinecones in the winter. Chen Yang has been very good to her, which just goes to show that we are all God's children, and the Chinaman can be as good as anybody else."

"I'm slightly lost there," said Denton, for a moment forgetting that echo of the Commissioner's voice, ceaselessly repeating in his ear: "Denton dismissed! Denton dismissed! Will not be felicitous."

"About what, Detective? The zinc?"

"Daisies and twigs."

"Oh, clearly that's the case. She's very poor. Mrs. Ramsbottom often goes down with a bottle of jam or pickles or such. Bread even, if she's baked enough."

"And she lives off twigs and daisies?"

"She grows the daisies and dahlias in summer and pops across the road to Chen Yang and he sells them for her, and I believe takes only a fraction of the money. Which is very Christian even if he isn't, and I don't like to ask what he is. Buddhist perhaps, which is in itself, I understand, a very noble institution. Or belief? Perhaps it might be a path, but not a religion because they don't actually have a god like we do. It's a godless path, I imagine. No, it's a path with no god, that's it. I suppose it has the moral authority of Stoicism, don't you think? And she collects cones and twigs in the Tinakori hills in winter, although she says that's hard now at eighty-seven and with the arthritis." He ventured forth on how the old age pension functioned and how he had assisted her to get one and that New Zealand was the first country in the world to have such, or was it Prussia? Denton had long abandoned the meander. Only when the question was repeated twice, did he focus on this man dressed up like a mad country squire blinded to colour and its coordination.

"Germany put in a pension in the eighteen-eighties, after unification with Prussia, as a bulwark to socialism. There, an encyclopaedic memory, have I not?" said Denton, trying hard to enter into the spirit of things as he sluiced through the Reverend's jetsam for information. "Tell me why the Māori was going up the road, what Mrs. Watson said."

"Well, you could ask her in person because she doesn't turn in until well after midnight, on occasions at two o'clock in the morning I'm

informed, for she reads a lot. That's interesting about some poor people, they make great readers. Or it might be that because she's old she
can't sleep, so she reads. That may be, but she's used to my coming by
at eleven, which is why I know her so well, as I take Misty and Peeve
out at five to eleven when Mrs. Rams…"

"You told me the routine last time you visited," said Denton, struggling. And then he realised his mistake of showing aggression, something the Russian detective never did, he being far too sophisticated
and psychologically attuned. Denton, momentarily distracted by
Porfiry Petrovitch, thought: "I must improve my techniques in order to think like a Russian and to be more psychological." There were
so many ways he should improve, and the Commissioner's words
leapt at him about dismissal, for he saw why he was in such trouble:
he deserved it. Going to Nancy MacTotter's and forcing her to kiss
him had ended in a black eye and possible dismissal. The echo of
the Commissioner's voice droned even more loudly and his sharp
face and his stern mind congealed within Denton's as he faced that
of Ramsbottom, whose face in turn was ruddy and patchy with gold
hairs and suited exactly one of the fox hunters on his Aunt Lucy's
English village scene dinner set, the serving dish of which he, Denton,
had broken in a fit of rage when he was eleven and staying at her
house in Te Awamutu.

"You are a spoilt little boy, in fact *spoiled* is more appropriate," his
Aunt Lucy had yelled at him as he stood with the Brussels sprouts
and pumpkin and shards at his feet.

"I'm deeply saturated by both conditions," Denton said.

"What?" said Reverend Ramsbottom.

"Spoiled, spoilt."

"Oh, grammar, we won't talk about grammar, notwithstanding,"
said the vicar.

"I…" said Denton, his mouth aflame with the need for alcohol, his
Aunt Lucy fifty years later still staring angrily at him, floral apron,
hands on hips.

"Are you quite well? Detective?" enquired Ramsbottom. "There's a lot of sickness about. You could accompany me to the zinc-sulphur inhalator if you wanted. It's very good, I'm informed by Mr. Parsonage, my parishioner. Crowds going in to suck on it, I believe."

"Not today, and I'm quite well, just overworked what with the lack of manpower." He wanted to add: "They even promote Māoris they're so short staffed. And they chuck me out because of an attempted kiss and a sapphist's missing journal." Another flush of injustice went rushing through him, acid-like, but he now knew the solution for its deleterious effects: Ramsbottom's declarations were cold, hard evidence and he saw the plot ending in triumph. With excitement he said: "Did she see Mrs. Meatyard that night?"

"Oh goodness yes, as I told you."

"No, you didn't."

"Yes, I did, just now. Eleanor said she, that is Mrs. Meatyard, whom she knows, went running down the street not long after her husband had and it was at the end of the street that I saw him, her husband, but not her. I wonder why not? Perhaps that was when Peeves took off after a rabbit and I went running after him, the dog that is, not the rabbit."

"Mrs. Watson knows Mrs. Meatyard?"

"Oh, apparently, and so I'm told by Eleanor, that Mrs. Meatyard was very generous with her time and charity and quite helped the old people in the street with bits and pieces, food, money. Everyone loved her. Her public appearances, all that yelling, was really ridiculous, but as a woman she was quite Christian. You never found them. They could be down there, rotting."

"Down where?" said Denton, alert.

"At Powderham's. That's where he went, isn't it? Or it makes sense he did, given the Māori who lives with Powderham went to the Meatyards' house after both of them had rushed out and ran down Tinakori Road as I told you. Mr. Meatyard went towards Powderham's house, there's only the two houses about there, Miss Knight's house and his, and Miss Knight's is quite far from his and she's half dead and Meatyard wouldn't be going to see Miss Knight at midnight, would he? Unless…? No…No…not that. I say, haven't you thought all of this, yourself? And then his Māori came running back ten minutes later and Eleanor knows him because he gives her vegetables from his garden. Apparently, he's a very nice boy like that. Rhubarb's his specialty, she said. His rhubarb's never salty, as it can be when grown in acidic soil, so his soil must be…"

"Who said?" snapped Denton.

"Eleanor, of course. I think she said the Māori's name is Aroha, yes, she did. It means love in their language, so I'm told. Simple. Aroha. Love. No surnames with Māoris, none of that Chen Yang mix-up there, is there? Yes, she knows him, swears by seeing him that night. But she didn't know anything about them being missing until I spoke with her the other night when I was looking for Misty, who took off. And she never reads the newspaper, Eleanor that is. She's not all there in many respects, quite old, not really listening anymore and she confuses dahlias and daisies of late, but she was very interested when I told her about the Meatyards being in the paper and missing and she filled in all the facts."

"And she never saw either or both of them returning?"

"Apparently not, and furthermore, what's interesting is that she has a row of dahlias outside her cottage, prize dahlias if the truth be known, you may know them. That narrow strip of flowers, but of course only in summer. And the wind and rain were very bad. So she went outside to check their stakes which she keeps in even when the blooms are not blooming, are out of season rather, just stumps, but the stakes remain in the soil. That was at just after eleven and she said to Mrs. Meatyard, who was running past, and I quote her: 'Dear, what a night to be out.' That's what Eleanor told me, and Mrs. Meatyard had quite a look on her, quite frenzied according to my informant. And in a wet fur coat, like a bear." He looked at his pocket watch and exclaimed, "Oh I must be off, the zinc-sulphur inhalator closes at six and I mustn't miss out."

He rose on his long, thin legs and shook hands and looked at Denton, and for a moment he appeared quite normal despite everything. It was

221

suddenly, as if deep down in his being, there was someone normal there who could have a conversation without all the Chen Yang, Yang Chen and twigs and daisies business. For a few more seconds he looked into Denton's eyes and the person trapped deep down in there screamed in a shrill wail filled with pathos, it seemed, for help to get out. And then he said, reverting right back to the persona of twigs and daisies: "My, my, my…zinc," and he turned and rushed out.

Several minutes later, Constable Muriwai Munu was admitted to the office and was left standing as Denton sat and looked up at him. For a full twenty seconds Denton said not a word but studied the young constable as if here were someone who didn't exist except in his, Denton's, imagination. The echo droned "Dismissed! Dismissed!" Accompanied by that haunting and foreboding refrain were the images that streamed into his brain, infecting him: the Prime Minister was shouting at the Commissioner: "Dismiss Denton!" Denton could see the Te Aro Book Group members standing in the Prime Minister's office – those perverse women who performed intimate relations with each other in the same bed; and those Pansy men, all posing as normal citizens.

Muriwai remained standing without a movement, not even a finger twitched, his gaze focused above the detective, whose madness was so apparent. In the secretary's office where he had waited for twenty minutes before being admitted, Muriwai had felt excitement about what was to happen. In this interview, he had been informed by Āpirana Ngata, he would be placed to lead the Meatyard investigation. That news, astonishing on so many accounts, had flooded his mind and his excitement was palpable.

"Be respectful when you talk with Denton," Āpirana Ngata had advised him. "He's alcoholic and abusive. I'm telling you this because as a young Māori you need to toughen up in a *Pākehā* way." And then there was the fact that he had shared such intimacies with MacPherson and Powderham and Aroha in the same bed, that magic of being there, with them, being so free. Aroha and he had trekked together three times to the Mākara coast since then and every time, deep in the bush, they had said things to each other that the constable now thought of in front of this soulless *Pākehā*.

The one-armed man, Denton knew, held the secret and that secret involved his being at Powderham's residence. In his drawer he had MacPherson's letter to Meatyard threatening him with death. Denton for the moment, forgetting the constable, tried to imagine the one-armed man killing two people and getting rid of them, his mind bewitched by the case, the need to resolve it, not later, but at this moment. What would Detective Porfiry Petrovitch have done in these circumstances? he wondered. In the novel, Detective Petrovitch had told Raskolnikov in so many words: "If you intend to kill yourself or run off to America, just leave a note, write a letter, just a sentence or two to say you killed the Jewesses, that would be very helpful. That's all I need, written evidence of collusion, guilt." A written confession was exactly what he, Denton, wanted. He took from his desk a clean piece of paper and wrote in a mad catharsis what he wanted to find in an envelope addressed to him: "*I killed the Meatyards and disposed of their bodies at sea. I am much more devious and murderous than you ever imagined. Hahahaha. Yours sincerely, C. Denton.*" He added his own initials as if in some perverse way he could channel the soul of the killer as Detective Petrovitch had Raskolnikov's by absorbing the mantle of the killer's psychology, by *being* him, seeing how he thought and acted. With psychology one could reel in the killer, hook him, as one would a fish mesmerised by the bait dangling in front of it.

"Yes," he said softly, reading the note he had just written and facetiously, teasingly signed, "this is exactly what I want from MacPherson." Motive was another issue, he realised, with some concern for his note-writing catharsis. What would MacPherson's have been? Money? He almost jumped for joy. Of course, it was a paid killing, the one-armed man was Powderham's agent. Powderham, the wealthy and evil Oscar Wilde would have paid the destitute MacPherson. It was so simple. He snatched up his pen and in a moment of triumph he added to the note: "*P.S: I did it for perverse reasons, because I am perverse. Catch me if you can! C. D.*"

He looked up at the immobile Māori imagining he was waving MacPherson's version of the note in front of his superiors and vindicating himself, the astonishment and congratulations in their respective faces, and their look of remorse for having been so unrelentingly cruel to him as soon as they had received it, MacPherson's written confession. "This is what I need, confession, confession," he said, and scrunched up his letter and dropped it on his desktop where it unfolded with the allusion of a primitive, living sea creature.

Denton got up, crossed the room and looked out the window, and then looked back at the constable, who hadn't moved and had his back to him. The rat was in the room, he smelled it. The rat was this Māori in his uniform playing at being a *Pākehā* when where he belonged was on the mat. There was this feeling about him, something, this feeling emanating from him, the young man and the rat were the same creature and he, Denton, the Porfiry Petrovitch of Wellington as he now saw himself, would soon know everything. Just as that Russian master detective had worn down Raskolnikov to obtain his confession, so would he now grab the criminals. He said from behind Muriwai, who did not turn: "Why did Aroha have the one-armed man's dirty underpants in his room? You were talking to him. I saw you laughing together in the back garden, which you were supposed to be searching."

The clock made its ticking sounds and from the office came Norman Wallace's deathly cough rattle. Muriwai did not answer. His grandfather had been a village councillor, a man with no formal education, not the *Pākehā* sort, and who had the deep knowledge of the lore of the Tainui-Waikato.

"I asked you a question."

"And I gave you my answer."

Denton smiled as he watched the constable stand rigid, immobile. It was just as it was in *Crime and Punishment* with the Russian detective's psychological approach when, by using his intuition, he finally gets a confession. The Commissioner's echo suddenly stopped, the ensuing silence was exquisite. He watched the Māori, saw his perfidy, his people's insouciance.

In the weeks that Muriwai and Aroha had been together, Muriwai had learned there was a thing called political philosophy. On their treks to Mākara through the burnt landscape and what remained of the bush, Aroha had told him things about life that were not dissimilar to what his grandfather had imparted when he, Muriwai, was a boy learning about what was, essentially, Māori political philosophy. The man behind him, teasing him as a cat might a mouse, the paw trying to scratch and intimidate, treating him, a Tainui-Waikato, with such disrespect, had something to do with this thing Aroha talked about, this *Pākehā* version of how Māori conducted their lives.

"I have walked to Mākara and watched the coast, and the water. Have you watched water, Detective?" asked Muriwai.

"What?" said Denton. "About water. What has that got to do with underpants?"

"Waters' end."

"Don't speak in Māori riddles, with me," said Denton. "I've had quite enough of sedition. When Cullen was the Commissioner of Police, he himself went into the bush and rooted out the rebellious Māoris. Don't you remember the Uruwera campaign in nineteen-sixteen? Sedition was sedition. That's the kind of Commissioner we need now, but what happened to men like Cullen?"

"The Government's doing the same now in the Waikato. They killed four of us for refusing conscription and have threatened Queen Te Puea Herangi."

"Your queen was reduced to a minor princess when your people signed at Waitangi, constable," said Denton getting his history of the Treaty and the establishment of Kīngitanga mixed up. The rain hit the windows with a fierce northerly blast accompanying the darkening hour. The sting of whisky ached in him. With a sudden sharp feeling in his head, the echoes started again, but this time it was a taunting chant in women's voices. He continued, his voice matter-of-fact, as if he were reciting from a shopping list, not on the advantages of eliminating a people: "If this were Russia, we could just go in and..." But even he stopped short of saying what he might have ordered had he held such power. "I asked you about underpants and if you know this one-armed man, this deserter."

"He's not a deserter. He lost his arm at Gallipoli and was sent back. He was a fighter, a real man. He actually volunteered for his country."

"Ah, interesting that you should know that when I don't. Who informed you? Who do you know that has this knowledge?" That he had not lost his tricks, that he was as canny and as catlike as Detective Porfiry Petrovitch made him smile. He imagined himself on a barstool in a public house in an hour ordering a double whisky, his vindication being rewarded with alcohol.

Muriwai realised with anger that he had divulged too much. The dog now had its bone and would tear at it.

"I asked who informed you?"

"I investigated at the War Office. I'm a constable and I knew where to ask questions about the main suspect when no one else had. I went yesterday when I was informed that I would be leading on this case."

"You're not on this case. You came only once when we were short-staffed. But you seem to know a lot...inside stuff." A *Pākehā* would have turned and faced him. With such a display of cowardice, Denton knew he could come in for the kill, that this was the link he had needed. "Intuition," he thought, "is as good as patience." Thunder rumbled and four seconds later – Denton counted them – the lightning struck. "Who did you speak to at the War Office? Tell me. I'm a detective and I will check your story."

Muriwai's grandfather had said to him as they stood above the vast stretch of black sand beach on the West Coast, their destination after five days of walking from the Waikato: "This beach is Muriwai. You are twelve years old, my *moku,* and this is your name. I wanted you to see what your name sounds and looks like at this water's end of Aotearoa. Look at the current, at the power of our waters, and hear them crashing and returning on our home. The water goes out and the water comes in and it's always an end from whichever direction. You are named for that strength."

"Why are you a part of that Pansy circle?" asked Denton, knowing he was in grasp of his goal and that by this time tomorrow he would be exonerated. With an attempt at mirth he added: "You don't seem to want to answer my question." But the high-pitched chanting in his mind increased in volume with the unmistakable voice of that waitress MacTotter cursing him.

"Because my grandfather is telling me I shouldn't, and because you should be informing me that the Prime Minister thinks you have abused women and that you are an alcoholic and because the Commissioner of Police told you to appoint me the lead investigator in the Meatyard disappearance and to forget chasing good people about sedition. I know because Āpirana Ngata told me. The Commissioner told him and he was informed by the Prime Minister himself, so who wins here will be decided by warriors and you are not one." Keeping his back to Denton, Constable Muriwai Munu walked out.

It was sleeting by seven o'clock on that same evening, the freezing rain coming in from the Wairarapa and bringing with it the pungent, primal scents of the Island's central forests. At the police barracks, Muriwai changed out of his uniform. Black was his favourite colour and he admired himself in the mirror in his highly polished black boots, well fitted, black serge trousers, dark grey shirt and a darker grey tie with a black woollen jacket, one he had found with a fiver and a silver lighter in it on a seat in the Supreme Court. Still admiring himself, he slipped on a hooded oilskin raincoat, a police issue meant for officer class and above. He added a rakish bowler hat with a narrow brim around the base of which was a dark grey band.

"You look smart, you Māori. All black." He laughed at his image, referenced his grandfather with a nod of his head, and left the room.

He ran up Parliament Street intent on his urgent purpose, turned left, and continued to the top of the steep hill from where a riderless black stallion galloped full speed in the direction of the Prime Minister's official residence. On reaching the row of workingmen's houses that veered off into bramble and pine, he heard a woman scream from behind a window that fronted the footpath, but he didn't stop. At the bottom of the asphalt zig-zag he paused for breath and was confronted by the smell of the wild, wind-thrashed fennel, its sweet and sickly smell which he associated with bad omens and illness. At the top of the zig-zag he climbed over the wooden fence half rotten with age to the bullock track on which he entered the sanctity of the bush.

He knew the route well because he had never used the streets to Aroha's for fear of being seen. At the top of the first rise he turned off his police issue flashlight and, in the distance, he saw Mount Victoria studded with lights and below them the lights on the town flat. The rain began in earnest and it felt beautiful to be running in it, washing from him the nastiness of what he had endured during the day. He thought: "The Meatyards deserved *utu*, so does Denton." The stench of Denton's pipe smoke and the intolerable atmosphere of his office had finished Muriwai's workday and set a new direction for him as a policeman. Under the cleansing comfort of the rain, he thought: "I want to work for people, not against them." He laughed at himself, in the rain, the happiness in him as he saw the future with Denton gone, his new family protected, and he a detective for the New Zealand Police Force.

When he reached the back of the imposing house and peered through the bushes at Aroha's cottage, he said: "This is now my life." He climbed over the fence and went down the garden path and looked in the kitchen window where he saw Aroha and Alex and, to his surprise, Mac. He didn't knock, there was no need to, he was going to his *whanau*.

"Bugger me," Mac said. "You're a good-lookin' fella when you're wet."

"I thought you'd be far from here," Muriwai replied. "Denton knows. He's coming."

"Knows what?" asked Alexander.

"That you're all mixed up in the Meatyards." He related the events of his meeting with Denton and Aroha poured him a whisky and told him to drink it down to steady himself. "But it's true, I heard that vicar geezer Ramsbottom. The secretary kept the door ajar to listen. The vicar said some old lady on Tinakori Road saw Aroha running up and down there the night the Meatyards disappeared."

Only then did Alexander remember that Muriwai didn't know that he and Aroha had killed the couple and that the bodies were buried in the backyard. Aroha, Mac and Alexander looked at each other, their dilemma in their hesitation.

Muriwai looked at Mac: "Did you kill them? The letter you wrote Meatyard saying you'd kill him. Did…? You did. Of course, you did. That's why I'm here. Denton will come tonight or tomorrow."

Mac laughed and finished off his whisky, looked at Alexander and Aroha and said: "I killed them. You're right. I confess to the policeman. Just as you can confess that you fucked me and I fucked you and we all fucked each other, which will leave you as a contaminated witness, is that the legal term? Compromised? Anyway, mate, now you know I did it. I'm off tomorrow for the wop-wops, getting out before you catch me."

"Where are they buried?" asked Muriwai.

"What does Denton know?" Aroha said in *te reo* and looking at the kitchen door expecting to see police burst in.

"Denton asked me today why I like your underpants and he knows I'm mixed up in this. He's almost worked out everything. It's you, all of us, I mean, you boys, all together, me. If the bodies are out there, we need to dig them up and get rid of them."

"I killed Mrs. Meatyard," said Alexander.

"I killed Mr. Meatyard," said Aroha. "Alex and I buried them out there."

"I didn't kill them, but I wish I hadn't killed the three Māori in Waikato and I ask again for forgiveness," said Mac.

"I forgive you. But think about now, not then," said Muriwai. He bent and rubbed his face across Mac's stubbly hair: "We'll dig them up, get them out. I know what to do with them."

"This is a ghoulish communion," said Alexander. "Aroha, get my leg brace."

"We need to do what our Muriwai says," Mac said.

"There goes the perfect crime," said Alexander seeing the end of the evening's happy denouement and by extrapolation the gallows.

"Denton just knows," said Muriwai. "He pulled it all together as I stood in his office and he wrote a confession letter about the murders, I don't get why he would confess like that when he didn't murder them…"

"That Denton committed the murders?" said Alexander.

"Yes, a note saying about everything. I watched him, he added about throwing their bodies off a skiff, like he was seeing it all, everything happening. He read it. Why write that if he didn't do it? But he knows you did it."

"Psychology, psychology," said Alexander. "Somehow he's channelling his ghosts, I wonder if he's read Pavlov?"

"He won't come tonight in this weather," said Aroha.

"He might. He's angry because the Commissioner was told to sack him and make me the detective."

"You?" said Alexander. "This plot's more complicated than *Crime and Punishment*. Ouch, my brace. You're hurting me, Aroha."

"We can kill Denton tonight if he comes alone. But what if he's with some others?" said Mac.

"We'll all go to the hangman," said Aroha. "Stop moving your bloody leg, Alex. You're drunk. I can see us all swinging."

"Karori Cemetery's just over these ridges," said Muriwai. "I was there. They don't even have enough bags for the dead. They say they register everyone, but if there's no family, they dump them in a trench behind where the Hindus and Chinamen get buried. We can dump them in the trench for the unknown."

"Good thing we've had a few drinks, mates, because they're gonna look and smell like Hell," Mac said. "At least they won't weigh anything." He got up and took hold of Alexander and told Muriwai and Aroha to join him in a sort of scrum.

25

It was the intuitive and confident Saint Petersburg Detective Porfiry Petrovitch who walked out of the Wellington Central Police Headquarters later the same evening as the respective visits from the Reverend Ramsbottom and Constable Muriwai Munu. It was the depraved sensualist Arkady Ivanovich Svidrigailov, the true villain of *Crime and Punishment*, who arrived at Rebecca Routledge's cottage two hours later.

As he had closed the door to his office, his secretary had thrown him a sour look and had pointedly not replied when Denton wished him a good evening. At the top of the wooden stairs, a colleague had been similarly dismissive. At the bottom of the stairs, a senior sergeant with whom Denton had always had a friendly acquaintance merely nodded his head when Denton said something about the rain and wished him goodnight. But Detective Porfiry Petrovitch did not notice. In his mind was the triumph he would receive in the days following his round-up of the conspirators in the disappearance of the Meatyards. All talk of his ignominy and dismissal would have been erased, any thought of impropriety with women forgotten and he, Denton, would be free of this worry and the echoes that haunted him. As he walked down the steps of the Police Headquarters, relieved, high-spirited, and into the rain, Denton recognised that the echoes had stopped, that his mind was free of that cacophony.

The wind had come up and the rain was slanted. At the corner of Panama Street and Lambton Quay, a violent gust caught his umbrella and flipped it inside out. As he struggled with the umbrella, the wind, seemingly in recognition of his plight, took his hat and blew it into the dark. Nobody was about, their fear of influenza and the ferocity of the weather had the population cowering for shelter. There was not a motorcar or horse and cart or motor ambulance. The rain too teased him as he looked about for his hat, with rivulets of cold water running down his back, soaking him. He could not locate the hat. He cursed as he looked along the ill lit street. He peered about: in an unkempt doorway; behind a cluster of wooden posts; in a shopfront around which loose newspaper circled; along the water-swollen gutter. Slowly, what emerged in his vision was not his hat but his secretary's sour face and that of his equally dismissive colleague at the top of the stairs and then that of the senior sergeant at the bottom of the steps. It was then that he pictured himself in the gutter searching for a hat, and the anxiety sluiced though him as icily as the rain through his coat.

"I wish the hell I had never read that book," he thought, the feeling of unease creeping further into him, as he imagined Svidrigailov slinking about these very streets with the eyes of the lecher who, finally, in the last pages of *Crime and Punishment*, could find no other solution but suicide to atone for his depravity. At the tram stop he had to share the wooden shelter with a woman in a coat from the 1890s. Her hat with wet feathers poking from a felt base appeared as something long dead and stuffed by a taxidermist. She carried a bunch of flowers wrapped up in cloth that was also dripping wet. Across Lambton Quay, a constable made his way under the shop verandahs, his flashlight flickering.

"No lights," said the woman. "It's a strange sort of affair isn't it? And this sickness. I'm so frightened I didn't want to come out. They say the War caused it, with all that gas and the Prime Minister's ship." The mention of the Prime Minister aroused the echoes in his head. He had an impulse to put up his hands and block the noise as if it were entering from an external source and not from deep within the cavities of his psyche.

"Are the trams running?" he asked.

"Oh, I expect so, it's only just after seven, but it's a very strange how-do-you-do, isn't it? I must get to my sister's, her youngest passed away. She hasn't got anything in the house, not even a halfpenny." They both heard a motor approaching and at the same time they peered down Lambton Quay hoping for the tram, but it was an ambulance thudding along, the muddy street churned up by its tyres as it passed. "Not a halfpenny and the cost of living just going up and up. Her husband's a drunkard, she's a lazy little minx, and it's always me who has to come to the rescue, but that poor wee thing, she passed away." The woman, her head moving as if shaking off flies, had stopped addressing Denton and was talking to herself. Within him, the spectre of *Crime and Punishment* slunk about as a presence, an omen, not unlike this woman in the antiquated outfit with her bunch of dying flowers.

"It's psychological, everything," he said to the wind and rain, but she cocked her head and answered as if, finally, someone understood her.

"That's what *Truth Magazine* says. I read it the moment it comes out. Psychology, you just need to think something and it eventuates."

"Does it?" he asked, perking up at this further omen supporting his attempt at channelling the murderer by writing the letter of confession.

"My sister's a great one for psychology, she brings the spirits to her, talks to them and gets advice as if she's just, just, well, you know, with them, bringing things forth."

"Why do you say that?" he asked. "Can you see things? Does she tell the future?"

"Oh, she does, for a shilling, a lot, but it's worth knowing what'll happen, psychologically speaking. Mind you, she didn't see the demise of her little one from this disease, did she?"

The thought of hot mint tea and cinnamon smelling incense jumped into his thoughts, and for a moment he was comforted as he stood buffeted by the wind. The woman, psychology now abandoned, was pursuing a distracted monologue on farming. Accompanying the mint tea and incense were the images of the spiritualists in his living room, that gaggle of Wellington ladies, his wife amongst them, at their get-togethers to conjure the dead with their hands above the Ouija board.

"Oh spirits, abide by the feeling, the wonder within, do what you must to meet the one you seek," his wife was saying, the candles fluttering in the high silver candelabra, her lady friends around her, their eyes closed, their heads held back as they imagined the departed, seeking them from the afterlife.

"What am I doing, a man, one of my age and profession? I've sunk into this women's nonsense. What did I do by writing that note confessing like a lady spiritualist, trying to bring MacPherson forth? That's my wife's sort of nonsense," the wet and bedraggled detective thought.

"Should have stayed on the farm, chickens, a cow, leeks, potatoes; the wee lass would have lived. But no, Wellington, easier to get drink, and with all that fresh air, but no, she didn't see the future, did she, surrounded by disease," said his companion, her hat moving up and down as she spoke. In a moment of panic, he realised he was suffering from equal delusions, all of them tumbling about, the result of the War and the influenza. Mad, everyone. And that Māori had simply stood there silent as if transcending this…this…He could not find the word, but he heard the constable say something about water's end. That was an omen, a new one, ominous and filled with foreboding and not unlike this feeling of fear about madness manifested in his writing of a note that would bring forth a man with one arm to confess to a double murder.

He slipped out of the shelter and into the rain and, head bent, hurried down Lambton Quay and turned left into an alleyway sided by the streaked and poorly painted facades of wooden shops and houses. At one, on his left, he heard a woman scream and that was followed by a man shouting. The detective in him forced him to stop and listen, but the Svidrigailov lurking in the same cavities urged him to move on and find what he really needed, a way out of this unhappy and ludicrous situation of the echoes and voices and faces. He remained standing in the rain, and through a gap in the curtain peered into the room. A woman in a flimsy outfit, a chemise of some kind, was vomiting blood, which a man was trying to catch in a china potty. The rain had soaked him, even his feet, his shoes filled with water. As he watched the goings on he felt as if he were being tossed from his skiff into the freezing harbour, submerged, drowning.

234

"I ought…" he said. "I should…" But he didn't move and the voices in his ears increased in volume. The bleeding woman turned and flung herself onto a sofa as another woman, much older, came running in with a blanket and behind her an old man in a dressing gown and amongst the three of them they lifted the ill woman and carried her out of the room.

"My God," uttered Denton. "The world is going mad, everywhere the Black Death." He made his way in the dark down the alleyway and where it made a crooked turning into another, even narrower lane, he reached up and pulled the bell at the side of a cracked and unpainted door. There was no answer and he saw in front of him the faces his colleagues who had shunned him.

"Everyone knows what's going to happen to me, even the clerks," he thought, staring at the chipped door. He was about to turn and retrace his steps and go up the hill to Tinakori Road, to Powderham's house. He thought: "Go, search the garden, find the bodies, I know that's where they are." Fury broke in him, replacing the ennui and paranoia. Instead of his colleagues' faces, he envisaged Powderham's: decadent, angular, smug, Pansy-looking. And the two Māoris, the features of whom, to Denton, were indistinguishable. MacPherson's face, which Denton had never seen, made its appearance as one as Pansy-like as Powderham's: self-satisfied, ironic, nasty, a true Pansy countenance. The door opened a crack and the gaunt face of a skinny man appeared.

"Got a bottle, Jack?" said Denton trying to smile, thinking that the face was not unlike those from that horrible novel by that horrible Russian anarchist. "It's a bit wet, need a bit of lubrication, mate."

"The price of a bottle's gone up, exponentially, Detective," said Jack, looking up and down the alleyway to make sure there were no cops on the beat as Denton shivered in the porchway. "Exponentially, as my wife says." He cackled and ran a finger across his toothless gums and looked into Denton's face and said: "You don't look right, mate. You need a drink right now, here, come inside and have a snifter, that'll warm you up."

He led Denton down the narrow passage that hadn't been swept, the dust and detritus, the rubbish, everything filthy. In the little room a bright fire lit up the walls and flicked shadows about as if, Denton thought, the house was on fire, the flames orange and blue, and there was a strong smell of smoke and coal and kerosene and rubbish. He took off his coat and looking around for somewhere to hang it, a woman said from behind him: "Give it here, love, I'll take it," which she did without his even turning. "You haven't got the sickness have you, dear?" the voice said. "Oh, look here's my Jack with a warm whisky." He heard the door shut as she went out. The glass was warm in his hand and as he slumped down, wet and bedraggled on a hardbacked chair, he felt the first release of pain. He lifted the glass, sipped it, and then, in one greedy gulp, he tossed it back. The effect of the triple dose swilled throughout him within a second. In the voice of a dying man demanding morphine, he said: "Get me more, get me more."

An hour later, with a bottle of cheap plonk in his coat pocket, Denton retraced his steps, only with less precision, down the alleyway and out to Lambton Quay, where the last tram of the evening had stopped to pick up three passengers.

"Newtown," he said, handing over the fare before lurching down the aisle where he sat by himself and burped up whisky.

"I should've," he said as he imagined Powderham's back garden, a big hole in the vegetable patch in which the bodies were buried. "Should've, should've."

"We all should've dear," said the same woman who had called her spiritualist sister a minx. She leaned over the seat and whispered: "You a bit drunk now, aren't ya? Could do with a snifter myself."

"What?" he said, smelling her rouge and powder, and the half-decayed flowers.

"You left me at the tram shelter just when we were getting to know each other. I was talking away and then you'd just disappeared and I thought, 'I scared him off with my prattle.'" She laughed and looked around, but no one took any notice, the four or five passengers sitting pensively as if ready to chase away anyone with symptoms of the illness.

"I would've walked all the way but it's too far in the rain and I just sat there, me and my flowers," she continued. "Just waiting, but nothing arrived and now…" The tram clanged to a stop and the driver shouted, "Courtenay Place", but no one got on or off and it clanged back into action and jolted on its rails and made its staccato way up Kent Terrace. Marjoribanks Street was on their left and Denton recalled trudging up the steep hill and entering Elizabeth Norris' house and searching and finally finding the journal and the book group notes. "I should've burned them," he thought. "Or…" What he should have done with them he couldn't decide, the whisky leaving him, the desire to get out the bottle for a swig, the need for nicotine.

"Sapphist," he thought.

The woman leaned in and said: "I'm going to my sister's place to pay my respects, but I could be persuaded otherwise."

Denton reached into his upper pocket, took out his notebook, unwrapped it from the water protection cloth, and pulled out his police identification and showed her without looking back.

"You can't scare me," she said. "I was just being friendly. You ask anyone on this tram if I wasn't being just friendly." But she sat back and held her flowers and her tongue and thought about what it would take to get out of the disease filled town and back to the country and her chickens.

"Newtown, Rintoul Street," the driver shouted as the tram clanked and shuddered and stopped, its currents dying. Denton got up, he was feeling more stable, his feet steadier. At the corner of Kenneth Row, he took a swig from his bottle and lit a cigarette, the rain having stopped. Nearby was Nancy MacTotter's house where he had received a black eye and bruise to his confidence. As he drew on the cigarette, he thought: "Why am I doing this again?" But the thought disappeared with the rapidity of the match he dropped in the flooded gutter and he stumbled on.

"She's a prostitute, I have to charge her, legitimately, part of the Powderham circle and all that," he thought as he reached Rebecca Routledge's gate, unlatched it, and knocked on her door. A dog barked, and through the opaque glass panels he saw a light and then a figure approaching, and the door opened.

"What do you want at my house, Denton?"

"I want to ask you questions."

"About? Now? At this time of night?"

"Where's MacPherson?"

"What?"

"Your illegal activities, a house of ill repute. Under the War Regulations Act any single woman doing what you do is in violation of…" The dog was at his trouser leg, pulling the cloth. "You little bastard," he said. He was more drunk than he might have thought, and he toppled, the dog pulling at his trousers.

"And what do you propose to do now that you're on the porch floor with a dog biting your leg?" asked Rebecca. She saw the light flick on in the front room in the house opposite. "Look, your informants are watching you. A drunk being done in by a tiny dog." She laughed, and as he tried to get up she bent and picked up Eskimo and carried her into the house, shutting the door in his face. But she hadn't locked the door, or the lock had failed, and he opened it. He knew he should go back, but he rushed up the passageway, tormented by so much. As he entered the living room, she swore at him and raised both fists. The first punch hit his left eye, the second his right, and he cried out and backed against the door.

"You think that after being brought up on racecourses I don't know how men act?"

He lurched at her and he fell. When he looked up, he was merely an old man, prematurely aged from his various ailments.

"Get out!" she yelled. "You are so hated. Even the Prime Minister said you're a rapist. You're revolting, a mad man."

"But…prostitute. Under the War Regulations Act…"

"Get up, get out, you fool."

"You were seen with MacPherson. Tell me where he is and I'll get you off any charges."

She laughed as he struggled against the sofa to push himself up.

"Mac's in San Francisco. You're so slow, stupid. Everyone but you knows Mac left. They're all laughing at you, even your wife, the poor creature. And you're about to be dismissed for raping Elizabeth's sister."

She pushed him towards the door and down the passageway, the dog yapping at his ankles. As she pushed him out she said something before slamming the door, a snippet of which he caught: "old, humiliated, vermin".

He stood in her porch. The heavy rain had returned with thunder, and between each clap the lightening was just ominous seconds apart. The street was utterly dark, even the neighbour's light had been turned out. To his right was a wicker basket filled with firewood and a big bundle of twigs tied with a rope which he saw in the flash of lightening. Svidrigailov moved in him. The passages in the novel, which he had read and reread about Svidrigailov's suicide in the dirty, flooded street in Saint Petersburg, he felt marching into his head. His wife, her small eyes filled with hatred, stared at him and within them there was nothing that said she would contact him after his death. He pulled the rope from the bundle of twigs with one swift yank. He looked around. Above him, right across the porch, was a supporting beam. He thought about having a swig of whisky and a cigarette, but he said: "Why bother?"

26

It was sudden, swift and shocking how Aroha Raharuhi succumbed to the epidemic. On returning home from viewing old fishing boats for sale at Seatoun, he entered the front door drenched in sweat, bent over in agony, and had time only to utter hoarsely: "I'm as buggered as those boats. Alex, be with me forever."

Seated in his reading chair with a cup of tea in his left hand, a copy of *Rhodes' History of the African Expeditions* in the other, Alexander was thinking not of the Dark Continent but of the ramifications of Denton's extraordinary suicide two days earlier. He watched pop-eyed as his lover staggered through the living room and disappeared down the passageway. Without the aid of either his cane or leg brace Alexander lurched from the chair, the teacup breaking on the floor as he flung himself towards the sofa from where he pushed himself across to the wall of Mitre Peaks.

With his hand up for support he made his way hopping and stumbling after Aroha, yelling: "Orton! Orton!" Sprawled across their grand double bed on his back, he found Aroha unconscious, his jaw locked, his neck stretched as if he had died with the rigor mortis already setting him as solid as a statue.

"I did this to you, my Aroha," sobbed Alexander, clutching his lover's legs. "Is this divine punishment? It had to happen; I knew it would." The piles of rubbish in his mind, so superficially camouflaged by rationalism, hope and self-acknowledged denial, flew about as would the real detritus of civilisation in a violent tempest: sheets of corrugated iron; the railings of ornate balustrades; oil paintings; his book collection; railway lines; linen outfits and floppy hats; the wires that carried electricity from pole to pole despoiling the streets with their ugliness: they all crashed and whirled as the thoughts of everything that had happened since the murders coagulated into why this beautiful man was sprawled on their bed and dying.

"We have to be quick, no need for this nonsense," said Orton, pulling Alexander up and pushing him into the bedside chair and turning to the prostrate Aroha. "Good God, you've got it bad all right, like my Aunty, but even at eighty she survived. Alexander, go and telephone a doctor. Get Helen. Don't be morbid at this moment."

"My brace."

"Bugger the brace. Take your crutches for once." Orton was a very dexterous man, and nimble, as if circus-trained. He jumped over a leather ottoman and from behind the kauri cupboard he grabbed the hated crutches, jumped back into place and handing them to Alexander, said: "Get going. You're hopeless in a drama. I'll look after this situation."

Alexander Powderham had had to endure crutches for many years in his childhood. Tormented that when using them he looked like some devilish Dickensian character, they remained his enemy and were hidden away waiting for an emergency such as a night-time fire or earthquake. But, with unaccustomed agility, for they provided greater freedom of movement, and with his mind focused on survival, he found himself on Tinakori Road. With a few dozen flying leaps, his coat tails flapping, he was at the Beauchamps' grand villa and was rapping the iron claw knocker frantically. It being eight in the morning Mr. Harold Beauchamp, the Chairman of the Bank of New Zealand, was still there, his flash car parked in the driveway. When the maid answered the door she yelled in alarm.

"It will be the influenza," said Harold Beauchamp pulling on his navy-blue coat as he came down the grand staircase, at the bottom of which Alexander stood, white-faced and rigid. "Who's got it?" he asked as if enquiring about a bank matter.

"Aroha, help, please, Harold."

"Ah, I saw him from the window earlier and noticed he was limping. It's unbelievable what's happening." They recognised in each other's eyes the intensity of their respective losses and suffering. Despite their differences in the way their lives were conducted, they held a similarly jaundiced idea of how things happened which, they would have ultimately admitted, was what had made them both successful businessmen and, therefore, respectful of each other.

"I refused to have a telephone or motor, what thinking was that?" said Alexander, distracted by his need to be requesting assistance for the use of one now and ashamed of his eccentric aversions: no car, no telephone, no gramophone, when Aroha had badgered him for years to join modernity.

"Last night I heard there are but six doctors still functioning in this entire city with only a handful still attached to the hospitals," said Harold Beauchamp before turning, his impressive hat in one hand, his gloves in the other. He beckoned the maid and told her to gather from the upstairs bureau everything he had readied in anticipation for an affliction in his household: the ammoniac quinine, digitalis and aspirin and morphia.

"I don't have any of that in the house," said Alexander in a voice filled with contrition, if not confession, and feeling even more incompetent and infantile in the shadow of Mr. Beauchamp, who stood tall on two good legs. "It's worse than the War," he said, fumbling for conversation while they waited for the maid.

"No, it isn't, Alex, with all due respect. The War was man-made, this is an act of God, or nature, if you prefer, but losing my son Leslie was the War, and therefore fundamentally intentional."

"The things, sir," the maid gasped as she came down the stairs with a portmanteau.

"Don't you want to take Aroha to your own hospital?" Harold Beauchamp asked as they pulled up outside Alexander's residence. "I commend you for opening it. I should have done something equal. But I'm so selfishly preoccupied with my own grief. Yes, indulgently, I'm told, given the general sacrifice." Mr. Beauchamp looked at Alexander, his eyes moistening at the mention of his only son blown to bits by his own ordinance while in military training in England.

"You lost Leslie and there is nothing general about that. And Aroha will stay in his own home, but please ask your driver to go to my little hospital and tell Elizabeth and Helen to come urgently. I'll be forever grateful."

"When I was in London recently my daughter Katherine, you well know the story, everyone does, she even changed her name to Mansfield she's so disgusted with my bourgeois carry-on, as she says. She said…" The thought of his daughter marrying a man in London she had known for forty-eight hours and dressing entirely in black for the civil ceremony taunted him as he sat in his finery in his American motorcar. At the same time, the front door of the house opened and Orton stood as both judge and jury as he witnessed the two men in conversation while Aroha lay dying. He shouted and waved his arms as Harold Beauchamp said: "Katherine said she deeply respects you for holding on to what you believe and not fleeing like the rest of the disgruntled intelligentsia does to London or Sydney. With all due respect given your circumstances, I understand why you might have."

"But not equally why I haven't?" asked Alexander.

"Your extraordinary butler needs you," said Mr. Beauchamp as Alexander dithered with his crutches. "I always did wonder about him, her, if you know what I mean?"

"No, Harold, I don't at all understand what you mean. Orton is the most dependable person I've ever known, my father being the only exception." He struggled with the door handle and crutches and portmanteau as the driver came to his rescue. "However, Harold, thank you for the medicines, which of course Orton will know how to administer. I am truly grateful to you."

Once in the bedroom, feeling as if he had been absent for years, abstracted with anxiety, Alexander asked Orton: "Will my Aroha live or die?"

"I'm not God," Orton said, dipping a sponge in a basin. "But he's got it very bad, even worse than Aunty."

Alexander dropped his crutches and sank to his knees and uttered: "I'm sorry for what I did, what we did, I know what caused this." He begged that god he had avoided and scolded all his life for forgiveness, and to let Aroha live. "It was a sin, a mistake, we shouldn't have," he said.

"Is it buggery or fellatio you're worried about, Alexander? You'd think it was murder, you know, a good old-fashioned crime," said Orton. Taking the morphia from the portmanteau, he said: "Perfect. This knocks them out, lets them into a place where they have no concerns, just the body fights, not the mind. It's the same with horses."

Alexander's eyes met Orton's and he said over a dry tongue: "Murder? Why do you ask that?"

Aroha stirred as if he were miraculously coming alive and Alexander shuddered at the image of Lazarus rising from the dead. The symbolism of Aroha reading the Lazarus story over the dead Meatyards was so real in so many respects. Aroha, Love, Raharuhi, Lazarus; Aroha was rising.

"I'm cursed by Dostoyevsky," Alexander thought. "I will always be Raskolnikov. It's crime and punishment forever. Love Aroha. Love Lazarus. My Siberia."

"Who murdered whom?" said Orton, unscrewing the lid on the bottle of morphine. "Is that what you would have asked Denton as he was swinging on Rebecca's porch? Was it really that ridiculous detective who killed the Meatyards? Highly improbable, I'd venture. There was no motive." He looked at Alexander, his eyebrows arched: "Or did someone else? Or maybe two people murdered the detestable Meatyards."

Aroha stirred and murmured and tried to raise his head.

Orton was holding the syringe. "Alexander," he said, "answer my question, which might help with Aroha's recovery, certainly yours." He deftly administered the drug into Aroha's arm and looked back at Alexander.

Alexander was still kneeling, his mind churning with Orton's words and the terror of Dostoyevsky's curse. Within that clutter was a very clear vision of a noose and a hangman and of people jeering and yelling: "Murderer! Oscar Wilde!"

"Get up. Come here. Sponge him with this, it's vinegar and formalin and hot water. And don't fret. Fretting will kill him and you. And if murdering the Meatyards is in the equation, you'd better not say a word to anyone but me, because once the cat is out of the bag it can't get back in, or is that a genie? I get confused between cats and genies, just as you are about who killed whom. But the Meatyards are now killing you. Exorcism is your only way out."

Alexander pulled himself up using the ottoman for support. Standing above him, Orton added: "Was it Jesus who drank vinegar and urine at the Crucifixion? Or was it you who took the poisoned chalice and did things which you think have caused Aroha's illness and for which you want forgiveness? Although from whom is the question? I get confused with Biblical stories, let alone what Alexander Powderham gets up to at night with his companions, not that I'm one to judge."

Alexander held aloft the sponge, which Aroha had found on the beach, and which had all the attributes of an old body organ: beige and rough and oozy. Everything seemed like that: the city, the country, the world. Looking at Aroha, seeing his eyelids flutter, his dry lips parted, the life force struggling, he thought: "I am this sponge, I am this diseased organ."

"Milk is spilt, Alexander. Even if in some quarters people might think Denton did kill the Meatyards, it's a porous affair, isn't it?" said Orton, his arms crossed against his red satin top over which he wore what was essentially a woman's mauve cardigan. "We all have deep secrets, and you should tell your Orton, spill it, get it out. Confess and get well. Exorcism, Alex. Your father would have recommended it, but to me, before the police get it, and I can find a solution. You know I always can. Denton almost got you. The police will, eventually."

"I don't know what you're implying."

"I have a secret," said Orton. "Several men, mostly itinerant jockeys, know about it, and most of them are dead, but that's all milk under the bridge with them, but a secret you don't know about and would never know about had it not come to this. Your father knew, and in so many, many ways, some delightful. Let me confess it and then you can yours, and then we'll be equal because I love you and Aroha and this will extract the poison. Your father would have wanted it, and I belonged to him."

Alexander held his lover's hand which was even more limp since Orton had administered the morphine. "When will this ever end?" he thought. "How could Orton have belonged to…?" His father seemed to be there castigating him, he, Alexander, still a boy, never a man, forever infantilised.

"My secret for yours," said Orton in a curiously feminine voice. "Break the wound, open it, release the toxins."

"He sounds like a witch," thought Alexander: the voice, the demeanour; everything about Orton was changing, even this curious wisdom about wounds and poisons was oddly unfamiliar. Alexander held up the dripping sponge: "What secret could you have that is as great as mine?" he asked.

Orton, always elegant in his special way, stood proudly, his back straight, his shoulders squared. He took three steps back and unbuttoned his silky pants and let them slip to his ankles. "Get ready. And inspect. You will have five seconds to witness what I am. And then you will tell me your secret and it's a pact until death, and beyond." His underwear of sheer, almost transparent silk, women's underwear in fact, he slipped down by wiggling his hips and a deft flick of his fingers at the waistband. With his legs spread, his face defiant, he exposed his genitals to Alexander.

"I was born as female, but never wanted to be one," he said. "A man born in a woman's body is a god inflicted deception."

Alexander dropped the sponge onto Aroha's chest. He looked up at Orton's face and then back at the genitals. "I killed Sybil and Aroha killed Cecil, out there in the living room," he said.

"And you buried them in the toilet pit I told Aroha to dig but which got covered up without him asking my permission, and then sometime later you disinterred them. Am I right?"

"Yes, yes, we did, with Mac."

"And Muriwai?"

246

"Yes, Muriwai."

Orton bent, pulled his pants up, fastened them, came to Alexander and kissed his forehead and then bent and kissed Aroha and said: "You never ever realised I was your new mother. I love you both more than ever. Now, never a word to anyone about any of this, and you need to go to your sister's and brother's and say you're sorry and ask forgiveness for being so ghastly. Let me bring my darling boy back to health. Do as I say and don't begrudge me anything for this intrusion, but we both want what's best for us and Aroha and your staying will handicap that. Now go, do much penance and try and get into the good graces of divine forces. I'll make something up for Elizabeth and Helen when they arrive. He may live, he may not, but leave it to Lady Orton."

27

His lover dying of the Spanish influenza, chucked out by his own servant as being a handicap after exhibiting his…her…genitalia and then
admitting to being his father's mistress, a mother, all seemed too much
for Alexander Powderham to bear. Halting in the street, momentarily
with his eyes closed and his fists clenched, Alexander assessed that
litany of humiliations as a sign that he was being further punished,
Dostoyevsky style. And Franz Kafka, the inventor of the human cockroach, was poking him with his pitchfork just as he had his protagonist
Gregor Samsa, the unfortunate Pansy from Prague.

"I told myself that I'd risen above European novelists, and Pavlov and
his salivating dogs, and psychologists twisting our minds," Alexander
thought as he continued on his crutches down the hill towards the
Wellington Railway Station. A magnificent gust of wind came rushing up the gully from the harbour, nearly blowing Alexander off his
crutches. The ferns and flaxes along the path flicked and slithered.
The sweet and stinky odour of the wild fennel mixed with the smell
of sea salt and the pungent heaviness of the Tinakori hills.

"Why didn't my father, he, and she, her, oh pronouns, pronouns, it,
me, she, her, him, they, their, just tell me she was a she, a her, a he?"
Seeing Orton exposing himself …herself…in order to glean a confession to murder rattled Alexander further. "What is it about sex
and identity that makes people so, so…idiotic in their thinking?"
But, coming to, he said: "I'll put Orton's duplicity to one side. Aroha's
wellbeing and my atonement are my priority." He listened to the wind,
and breathed in deeply. "In Featherston I'll hand Lydia a cheque for
a thousand pounds, no, two thousand pounds, with a pledge of an
annual stipend and the return of any memorabilia she wants. Pip
won't want anything, he's too stupid." However, realising his nastiness,

his spiritual parsimoniousness, or lack of magnanimity towards his brother and how that might play negatively against Aroha's recovery, he paused on the bridge over the old cemetery. Looking down at the graves of the early settlers, his grandfather's amongst them, he begged God to forgive him and to let Aroha live.

"Aroha made me human, or tried, but what humanity I still have as a cockroach, I say, I'm…" he muttered.

Suddenly, church bells clanged and chimed: all at once every bell in the town burst into a chorus, a cacophony. From the port the ship whistles blew high and tinny or in baritone. An elderly man approached in a grey coat with a grey hat pulled down so that his ears were bent in half at the brim. Alexander recognised him as the swagman who drank and slept amongst the graves below them.

"Bloody lot of use that war was," the man said, gruffly, in anger, and trudged on.

"What?" said Alexander, pausing, his legs on the pathway as the bells pealed. "War over?"

Seagulls cawed above him, the wind howled, the bells were interminable. He shook his head as if to release himself from everything, the noise and the news of the end of the War were all an abstraction. But he hurried forward on his hated crutches and addressing God, he said: "Like Pascal, I'm willing to make the wager. If you exist, I'm lucky. If not, I'm unluckier to have wasted my time in believing in you. But God, please, I'll sign cheques and be nice to Lydia and Pip and give the Finks the house free for five years, and keep the soup kitchen open for the poor, and buy Aroha a fishing boat if you let him live, my great love."

By the time he reached the bottom of Parliament Street the philosophical and ethical hypocrisy of adopting Pascal's Wager was manifest in his mind as being needy and irrational. He said to the wind: "This is what seeing Orton's genitalia has done, my lover is dying, the War…the War…Dostoyevsky's curse….I've returned to theology."

Thus tormented, he reached the railway station, where everyone, even ladies, were tossing their hats into the air. A woman with a hat the size and shape of an afternoon tea cake threw it as high as she could and jumped up to catch it and shouted: "The Huns are done, long live the King!"

But Alexander Powderham could take no part in this joy, his desperation, cynicism and ennui being too entrenched. As he lurched on his crutches, the woman who had just caught her hat shouted at her child: "Look out for the crippled man."

"Armistice," a man shouted "Arm…" before he was cut off with a shout about the King. What remained in Alexander's mind from that truncated utterance was the trigger to thinking about Mac.

"I need you now, one amputee and one cripple together, as one, to take stock of everything," he thought as he paused and squinted up at the train timetable and noticed with astonishment that the Featherston train would leave in two minutes. Exhausted, he reached the ticket counter and blurted: "Featherston?"

The ticket seller, a young woman with a handkerchief tied over her lower face, replied: "Better make a run of it, platform six. Here's your ticket, but take off now because it's leaving."

"Run for it," he said, mimicking her. As he turned, his coat caught in his crutches and he fell on his face, his arms outstretched. The train whistled. Looking up, he shouted: "For God's sake, help a bloody cripple get to the train!"

"The Featherston train has been delayed, sir," said a policeman helping Alexander to his feet. "On account of the Armistice. Seems the train driver snuck off for a celebration."

"If you wouldn't mind just retrieving my hat," said Alexander, as he leaned against the policeman, shaken, while the young ticket seller, who had rushed from behind her counter, handed him his crutches: "There you go, sir," she said, sweetly. "If you get the policeman to help you to the train, sir. I'm so sorry to have told you to make a run for it. I didn't realise your disposition. Please forgive me, sir," she said.

"Oh, no, thank *you*," he said, his need for contrition for being alive, for murdering, for ensuring Aroha's survival being so great.

The policeman, hirsute, good looking, had retrieved the hat and was trying to place it on Alexander's head: "Nice hat, sir, very fashionable," he said. "Munster and Munster, what's more, very nice." He tried to position the crutches under Alexander's arms. Alexander, however, felt as if everything was floppy, as if he were just a dilapidated scarecrow wearing Fagin's outfit, a bent top hat, a swirling overcoat. The situation was so odd: the broad and busy Wellington Railway Station, people shouting the joyous news of Armistice, people staring at him as he fussed with his crutches, the policeman trying to assist him. He had an image of someone shouting: "Oscar Wilde is a murderer!"

"I'm trying to help, sir, you're a bit shaky," said the policeman.

Alexander looked up at the policeman who had a bristly, black moustache that covered his upper lip – which Alexander concentrated on as he asked him: "Did you know Detective Crawford Denton? I just wondered. You know, you being a policeman." He added, looking with faux humility into the policeman's eyes: "You know, the one who hanged himself?"

"Talk of the town, still is. Odd sort of a thing, but there you have it. He went mad with shame and fear, and so he should have for killing those Meatyards. Even left a confession note saying he'd thrown their bodies into the sea, they say he had a skiff. Odd sort of a to-do, all right."

At the train, Alexander said: "He killed the Meatyards. I suppose that's quite officially the word."

"I believe so. It's said he was blackmailing them, or was it them him, about money for selling dope? Anyway, there's irrefutable evidence with a note, that's what the Police Commissioner said to my mate who's taken charge of the case. He says it's cut and dried that Denton did it, but what the motive was is not entirely clear. Madness, it's assumed, with a lot of help from the bottle." He lifted Alexander up and into the carriage. "They were blaming a soldier who fought in Gallipoli and lost his arm in service. Fancy blaming a bloke who sacrificed everything. And how could he do it with one arm and get rid of the bodies? It was Denton who covered up his own story by blaming an innocent serviceman, according to the constable who's taken charge. A Māori bloke too, very smart sort of fellow."

"Jolly good," said Alexander as the policeman assisted him into his seat.

"A pleasure to help a gentleman as yourself, sir," he said. "Especially with this sudden armistice, quite an occasion." He looked into Alexander's eyes and smiled and wetted his lips, the pink tip of his tongue poking through the black moustache: "Now I'm off to make sure the populace keeps this celebration orderly. Shouldn't be having one given the influenza, all the germs, but that's what's happening in town, thousands flocking down to celebrate. You're best out of it up in Featherston." He smiled, turned, and left the carriage and walked down the station platform as Alexander watched him, mollified by the news about Denton and strengthened by the kindnesses afforded him in the station. He let the idea of niceness, peace and the fact that he was comfortably seated in a train taking him away from Wellington absorb his mind. He sank into his seat, sighed and told that nebulous God that Aroha must live because he, Alexander, was so obviously doing his penance through physical and mental humiliation.

Two hours later, at the Featherston station, which was a two-roomed wooden affair with a red corrugated iron roof, dozens of people had gathered to celebrate Armistice. As Alexander struggled through the crowd, he heard the words and phrases of peace and thanksgiving as if it were the beginnings of a brave new world. He shuddered at the intensity of such hope but felt that even he was excited, despite his fears about Aroha dying and what that would mean for a life without him.

"Pavlov, Pascal, Descartes, Dostoyevsky, Jung, Denton, Powderham, what a list of confusions," he thought as he heard above the hubbub a woman shout: "God save the King. Long live our menfolk who fought! Down with those war shirkers! Imprison them!"

"I'll give Lydia two thousand pounds. In her hands. You watch, Pascal, two thousand for my wager with God. And an annual stipend paid through her solicitor. This is my mission, I'll even say I'm sorry," he thought as he struggled through the throng on his crutches.

"Peace! But who didn't help us? That's the question!" the woman shouted above a chorus of hurrahs.

Hemmed in as he was amongst the crowd, Alexander felt a growing sense of foreboding. That voice, it was so reminiscent of that of the woman he'd murdered, and he had a terrible premonition that it signified his lover's death. That particular voice rising above the noise of the crowd. A mouth rounding, pouting, stained teeth, pale lips, and he heard the voice shouting at him, and he shuddered at the vision that accompanied it.

"That's right!" shouted a man, and the chorus rose and everyone was clapping and cheering. "She's right! King and country! Shirkers to prison! God save the King!"

Alexander, trapped amongst the people, most of whom were men, tried to see the woman but he couldn't. He poked a man in front of him and said: "Who's that speaking?"

"She's a right one. Got a good voice, been around here a long time. I'm their neighbour, just down the street from them. Here, mate, you need a hand?" The man, he would have been in his late fifties and was wearing a suit of dull grey gabardine and a battered hat, took Alexander by the shoulder and shouted: "Move away, lame cripple coming through." The people parted and a woman in a green hat with crochet yellow flowers, said kindly: "There you go, dear, go to the front. Have a good look."

The helpful man said: "She's been doing this a few weeks. Never a peep out of her in all these years and now she's got the town caught up in her fire. My wife said she's got a bee in her bonnet. Brother tried, but he's weak whisky compared to her, a bit simple."

Alexander and the helpful man were squeezed out of the crowd and found themselves immediately in front of the platform. Looking up, Alexander said: "This is my Siberia."

Those flying objects, the books and oil paintings, his linen outfits, the telephone and electricity poles, gramophones and wires, the detritus of civilisation, flew about in his mind the whole way back to Wellington on the very train he had arrived on, he having been pushed up into it at the last moment by the helpful man as the final whistle blew and the conductor shouted: "Oi! Oi! Bit late for scrambling on like that!"

At the station in Wellington, his mind was filled up with so much that he thought of his crutches as wings on which he was flying up to Tinakori Road, for there wasn't a taxi motor anywhere. At the corner of Parliament Street, where he nearly bumped into some drunken soldiers, he saw his sister as if she were standing at the corner on a soapbox dressed as she had been in red, white and blue, the colours of the Dominion's flag, and shouting at him: "Vermin! Vermin!" Then he fled across the bridge and up the fennel smelling zig-zag.

"Aroha," he said as he pushed open his front gate, exhausted, his arms aching with the trial of having been on crutches for hours and hours, from his mind having been flung in so many directions. He grasped the doorknob and rested his head against the door to his sanctuary, ill with anticipation. But he knew from his excursion, from having made a pact with himself on the return home, that there was no god, no Pascal, no Raskolnikov-like contrition or repentance or confessions required, no Dostoyevsky curse, for what he and Aroha had done was justified.

The door opened and he fell into Elizabeth's arms. She pulled him up, firmly grasped his shoulders, and kissed his forehead: "It's been a long day. It's a pretty stiff case of meningitis, but he's alive and re-covering. How was Featherston, did you accomplish what you needed to up there?"

He was gasping on the doorstep, the lightening striking him as he stood on the mountain peak, the jagged bolt deflecting.

"Yes, I did," he said, in a mixture of tears and laughter.

The End

www.ingramcontent.com/pod-product-compliance
Lightning Source LLC
Chambersburg PA
CBHW071555110726
47908CB00007B/2107